ODD JOHN
&
SIRIUS

TWO SCIENCE-FICTION NOVELS BY

OLAF STAPLEDON

DOVER PUBLICATIONS, INC.
NEW YORK

International Standard Book Number: 0-486-21133-9
Library of Congress Catalog Card Number: 72-77999

Manufactured in the United States of America
Dover Publications, Inc.
31 East 2nd Street, Mineola, N.Y. 11501

Contents

ODD JOHN

A STORY BETWEEN JEST AND EARNEST

BY

OLAF STAPLEDON

DOVER PUBLICATIONS, INC.
NEW YORK

Contents

CHAPTER I

JOHN AND THE AUTHOR

WHEN I told John that I intended to write his biography, he laughed. "My dear *man!*" he said, "But of course it was inevitable." The word "man" on John's lips was often equivalent to "fool." "Well," I protested, "a cat may look at a king." He replied, "Yes, but can it really *see* the king? Can you, puss, really see me?"

This from a queer child to a full-grown man.

John was right. Though I had known him since he was a baby, and was in a sense intimate with him, I knew almost nothing of the inner, the real John. To this day I know little but the amazing facts of his career. I know that he never walked till he was six, that before he was ten he committed several burglaries and killed a policeman, that at eighteen, when he still looked a young boy, he founded his preposterous colony in the South Seas, and that at twenty-three, in appearance but little altered, he outwitted the six warships that six Great Powers had sent to seize him. I know also how John and all his followers died.

Such facts I know; and even at the risk of destruction by one or other of the six Great Powers, I shall tell the world all that I can remember.

Something else I know, which will be very difficult to explain. In a confused way I know why he founded his colony. I know too that although he gave his whole energy to this task, he never seriously expected to succeed. He was convinced that sooner or later the world would find him out and destroy his work. "Our chance," he once said, "is not as much as one in a million." And then he laughed.

John's laugh was strangely disturbing. It was a low, rapid, crisp chuckle. It reminded me of that whispered crackling prelude which sometimes precedes a really great crash of thunder. But no thunder followed it, only a moment's silence; and for his hearers an odd tingling of the scalp.

I believe that this inhuman, this ruthless but never malicious laugh of John's contained the key to all that baffles me in his character. Again and again I asked myself *why* he laughed just then, what precisely was he laughing *at,* what did his laughter really mean, was that strange noise really laughter at all, or some emotional reaction incomprehensible to my kind? Why, for instance, did the infant John laugh through his tears when he had upset a kettle and was badly scalded? I was not present at his death,

5

but I feel sure that, when his end came, his last breath spent itself in zestful laughter. Why?

In failing to answer these questions, I fail to understand the essential John. His laughter, I am convinced, sprang from some aspect of his experience entirely beyond my vision. I am therefore, of course, as John affirmed, a very incompetent biographer. But if I keep silence, the facts of his unique career will be lost for ever. In spite of my incompetence, I must record all that I can, in the hope that, if these pages fall into the hands of some being of John's own stature, he may imaginatively see through them to the strange but glorious spirit of John himself.

That others of his kind, or approximately of his kind, are now alive, and that yet others will appear, is at least probable. But as John himself discovered, the great majority of these very rare supernormals, whom John sometimes called "wide-awakes," are either so delicate physically or so unbalanced mentally that they leave no considerable mark on the world. How pathetically one-sided the supernormal development may be is revealed in Mr. J. D. Beresford's account of the unhappy Victor Stott. I hope that the following brief record will at least suggest a mind at once more strikingly "superhuman" and more broadly human.

That the reader may look for something more than an intellectual prodigy I will here at the outset try to give an impression of John's appearance in his twenty-third and last summer.

He was indeed far more like a boy than a man, though in some moods his youthful face would assume a curiously experienced and even patriarchal expression. Slender, long limbed, and with that unfinished coltish look characteristic of puberty, he had also a curiously finished grace all his own. Indeed to those who had come to know him he seemed a creature of ever-novel beauty. But strangers were often revolted by his uncouth proportions. They called him spiderish. His body, they complained, was so insignificant, his legs and arms so long and lithe, his head all eye and brow.

Now that I have set down these characters I cannot conceive how they might make for beauty. But in John they did, at least for those of us who could look at him without preconceptions derived from Greek gods, or film stars. With characteristic lack of false modesty, John once said to me, "My looks are a rough test of people. If they don't begin to see me beautiful when they have had a chance to learn, I know they're dead inside, and dangerous."

But let me complete the description. Like his fellow-colonists, John mostly went naked. His maleness, thus revealed, was immature in spite of his twenty-three years. His skin, burnt by the Polynesian sun, was of a grey, almost a green, brown, warming to a ruddier tint in the cheeks. His hands were extremely large and sinewy. Somehow they seemed more mature than the rest of his body. "Spiderish" seemed appropriate in this connexion also. His head was certainly large but not out of proportion to his long limbs.

Evidently the unique development of his brain depended more on manifold convolutions than on sheer bulk. All the same his was a much larger head than it looked, for its visible bulk was scarcely at all occupied by the hair, which was but a close skull-cap, a mere superficies of negroid but almost white wool. His nose was small but broad, rather Mongolian perhaps. His lips, large but definite, were always active. They expressed a kind of running commentary on his thoughts and feelings. Yet many a time I have seen those lips harden into granitic stubbornness. John's eyes were indeed, according to ordinary standards, much too big for his face, which acquired thus a strangely cat-like or falcon-like expression. This was emphasized by the low and level eyebrows, but often completely abolished by a thoroughly boyish and even mischievous smile. The whites of John's eyes were almost invisible. The pupils were immense. The oddly green irises were as a rule mere filaments. But in tropical sunshine the pupils narrowed to mere pinpricks. Altogether, his eyes were the most obviously "queer" part of him. His glance, however, had none of that weirdly compelling power recorded in the case of Victor Stott. Or rather, to feel their magic, one needed to have already learnt something of the formidable spirit that used them.

CHAPTER II

THE FIRST PHASE

JOHN'S father, Thomas Wainwright, had reason to believe that Spaniards and Moroccans had long ago contributed to his making. There was indeed something of the Latin, even perhaps of the Arab, in his nature. Every one admitted that he had a certain brilliance; but he was odd, and was generally regarded as a failure. A medical practice in a North-country suburb gave little scope for his powers, and many opportunities of rubbing people up the wrong way. Several remarkable cures stood to his credit; but he had no bedside manner, and his patients never accorded him the trust which is so necessary for a doctor's success.

His wife was no less a mongrel than her husband, but one of a very different kind. She was of Swedish extraction. Finns and Lapps were also among her ancestors. Scandinavian in appearance, she was a great sluggish blonde, who even as a matron dazzled the young male eye. It was originally through her attraction that I became the youthful friend of her husband, and later the slave of her more than brilliant son. Some said she was "just a magnificent female animal," and so dull as to be subnormal. Certainly conversation with her was sometimes almost as one-sided as conversation with a cow. Yet she was no fool. Her house was always in good order, though she seemed to spend no thought upon it. With the same absent-minded skill she managed her rather difficult husband. He called her "Pax." "So peaceful," he would explain. Curiously her children also adopted this name for her. Their father they called invariably "Doc." The two elder, girl and boy, affected to smile at their mother's ignorance of the world; but they counted on her advice. John, the youngest by four years, once said something which suggested that we had all misjudged her. Some one had remarked on her extraordinary dumbness. Out flashed John's disconcerting laugh, and then, "No one notices the things that interest Pax, and so she just doesn't talk."

John's birth had put the great maternal animal to a severe strain. She carried her burden for eleven months, till the doctors decided that at all costs she must be relieved. Yet when the baby was at last brought to light, it had the grotesque appearance of a seven-months fetus. Only with great difficulty was it kept alive in an incubator. Not till a year after the forced birth was this artificial womb deemed no longer necessary.

I saw John frequently during his first year, for between me and the father, though he was many years my senior, there had by now grown up a curious intimacy based on common intellectual interests, and perhaps partly on a common admiration for Pax.

I can remember my shock of disgust when I first saw the thing they had called John. It seemed impossible that such an inert and pulpy bit of flesh could ever develop into a human being. It was like some obscene fruit, more vegetable than animal, save for an occasional incongruous spasm of activity.

When John was a year old, however, he looked almost like a normal new-born infant, save that his eyes were shut. At eighteen months he opened them; and it was as though a sleeping city had suddenly leapt into life. Formidable eyes they were for a baby, eyes seen under a magnifying glass, each great pupil like the mouth of a cave, the iris a mere rim, an edging of bright emerald. Strange how two black holes can gleam with life! It was shortly after his eyes had opened that Pax began to call her strange son "Odd John." She gave the words a particular and subtle intonation which, though it scarcely varied, seemed to express sometimes merely affectionate apology for the creature's oddity, but sometimes defiance, and sometimes triumph, and occasionally awe. The adjective stuck to John throughout his life.

Henceforth John was definitely a person and a very wide-awake person, too. Week by week he became more and more active and more and more interested. He was for ever busy with eyes and ears and limbs.

During the next two years John's body developed precariously, but without disaster. There were always difficulties over feeding, but when he had reached the age of three he was a tolerably healthy child, though odd, and in appearance extremely backward. This backwardness distressed

Thomas. Pax, however, insisted that most babies grew too fast. "They don't give their minds a chance to knit themselves properly," she declared. The unhappy father shook his head.

When John was in his fifth year I used to see him nearly every morning as I passed the Wainwrights' house on my way to the railway station. He would be in his pram in the garden rioting with limbs and voice. The din, I thought, had an odd quality. It differed indescribably from the vocalization of any ordinary baby, as the call of one kind of monkey differs from that of another species. It was a rich and subtle shindy, full of quaint modulations and variations. One could scarcely believe that this was a backward child of four. Both behaviour and appearance suggested an extremely bright six-months infant. He was too wide awake to be backward, too backward to be four. It was not only that those prodigious eyes were so alert and penetrating. Even his clumsy efforts to manipulate his toys seemed purposeful beyond his years. Though he could not manage his fingers at all well, his mind seemed to be already setting them very definite and intelligent tasks. Their failure distressed him.

John was certainly intelligent. We were all now agreed on that point. Yet he showed no sign of crawling, and no sign of talking. Then suddenly, long before he had attempted to move about in his world, he became articulate. On a certain Tuesday he was merely babbling as usual. On Wednesday he was exceptionally quiet, and seemed for the first time to understand something of his mother's baby-talk. On Thursday morning he startled the family by remarking very slowly but very correctly, "I—want—milk." That afternoon he said to a visitor who no longer interested him, "Go—away. I—do—not—like—you—much."

These linguistic achievements were obviously of quite a different type from the first remarks of ordinary children.

Friday and Saturday John spent in careful conversation with his delighted relatives. By the following Tuesday, a week after his first attempt, he was a better linguist than his seven-year-old brother, and speech had already begun to lose its novelty for him. It had ceased to be a new art, and had become merely a useful means of communication, to be extended and refined only as new spheres of experience came within his ken and demanded expression.

Now that John could talk, his parents learned one or two surprising facts about him. For instance, he could remember his birth. And immediately after that painful crisis, when he had been severed from his mother, he actually had to *learn* to breathe. Before any breathing reflex awoke, he had been kept alive by artificial respiration, and from this experience he had discovered how to control his lungs. With a prolonged and desperate effort of will he had, so to speak, cranked the engine, until at last it "fired" and acted spontaneously. His heart also, it appeared, was largely under voluntary control. Certain early "cardiac troubles," very alarming to his parents, had in fact been voluntary interferences of a too daring nature. His emotional reflexes also were far more under control than in the rest of us. Thus if, in some anger-provoking situation, he did not *wish* to feel angry, he could easily inhibit the anger reflexes. And if anger seemed desirable he could produce it. He was indeed "Odd John."

About nine months after John had learnt to speak, some one gave him a child's abacus. For the rest of that day there was no talking, no hilarity; and meals were dismissed with impatience. John had suddenly discovered the intricate delights of number. Hour after hour he performed all manner of operations on the new toy. Then suddenly he flung it away and lay back staring at the ceiling.

His mother thought he was tired. She spoke to him. He took no notice. She gently shook his arm. No response. "John!" she cried in some alarm, and shook more violently. "Shut up, Pax," he said, "I'm busy with numbers."

Then, after a pause, "Pax, what do you call the numbers after twelve?" She counted up to twenty, then up to thirty. "You're as stupid as that toy, Pax." When she asked why, he found he had not words to explain himself; but after he had indicated various operations on the abacus, and she had told him the names of them, he said slowly and triumphantly, "You're stupid, Pax, dear, because you (and the toy there) 'count' in tens and not in twelves. And that's stupid because twelves have 'fourths' and 'threeths', I mean 'thirds', and tens have not." When she explained that all men counted in tens because when counting began, they used their five fingers, he looked fixedly at her, then laughed his crackling, crowing laugh. Presently he said, "Then all men are stupid."

This, I think, was John's first realization of the stupidity of *Homo sapiens,* but not the last.

Thomas was jubilant over John's mathematical shrewdness, and wanted to report his case to the British Psychological Society. But Pax showed an unexpected determination to "keep it all dark for the present." "He shall not be experimented on," she insisted. "They'd probably hurt him. And anyhow they'd make a silly fuss." Thomas and I laughed at her fears, but she won the battle.

John was now nearly five, but still in appearance a mere baby. He could not walk. He could not, or would not, crawl. His legs were still those of an infant. Moreover, his walking was probably seriously delayed by mathematics, for during the next few months he could not be persuaded to give his attention to anything but numbers and the properties of space. He would lie in his pram in the garden by the hour doing "mental arithmetic" and "mental geometry," never moving a muscle, never making a sound. This was most unhealthy for a growing child, and he began to ail. Yet nothing would induce him to live a more normal and active life.

Visitors often refused to believe that he was mentally active out there for all those hours. He looked pale and "absent." They privately thought he was in a state of coma, and developing as an imbecile. But occasionally he would volunteer a few words which would confound them.

John's attack upon geometry began with an interest in his brother's box of bricks and in a diaper wallpaper. Then came a phase of cutting up cheese and soap into slabs, cubes, cones, and even into spheres and ovoids. At first John was extremely clumsy with a knife, cutting his fingers and greatly distressing his mother. But in a few days he had become amazingly dextrous. As usual, though he was backward in taking up a new activity, once he had set his mind to it, his progress was fantastically rapid. His next stage was to make use of his sister's school-set of geometrical instruments. For a week he was enraptured, covering innumerable sheets.

Then suddenly he refused to take any further interest in visual geometry. He preferred to lie back and meditate. One morning he was troubled by some question which he could not formulate. Pax could make nothing of his efforts, but later his father helped him to extend his vocabulary enough to ask, "Why are there only three dimensions? When I grow up shall I find more?"

Some weeks later came a much more startling question. "If you went in a straight line, on and on and on, how far would you have to go to get right back here?"

We laughed, and Pax exclaimed, "*Odd* John!" This was early in 1915. Then Thomas remembered some talk about a "theory of relativity" that was upsetting all the old ideas of geometry. In time he became so impressed by this odd question of John's, and others like it, that he insisted on bringing a mathematician from the university to talk to the child.

Pax protested, but not even she guessed that the result would be disastrous.

The visitor was at first patronizing, then enthusiastic, then bewildered; then, with obvious relief, patronizing again; then badly flustered. When Pax tactfully persuaded him to go (for the child's sake, of course), he asked if he might come again, with a colleague.

A few days later the two of them turned up and remained in conference with the baby for hours. Thomas was unfortunately going the round of his patients. Pax sat beside John's high chair, silently knitting, and occasionally trying to help her child to express himself. But the conversation was far beyond her depth. During a pause for a cup of tea, one of the visitors said, "It's the child's imaginative power that is so amazing. He knows none of the jargon and none of the history, but he has *seen* it all already for himself. It's incredible. He seems to visualize what can't be visualized."

Later in the afternoon, so Pax reported, the visitors began to grow rather agitated, and even angry; and John's irritatingly quiet laugh seemed to make matters worse. When at last she insisted on putting a stop to the discussion, as it was John's bedtime, she noticed that both the guests were definitely "out of control." "There was a wild look about them both," she said, "and when I shooed them out of the garden they were still wrangling; and they never said good-bye."

But it was a shock to learn, a few days later, that two mathematicians on the university staff had been found sitting under a street lamp together at 2 a.m. drawing diagrams on the pavement and disputing about "the curvature of space."

Thomas regarded his youngest child simply as an exceptionally striking case of the "infant prodigy." His favourite comment was, "Of course, it will all fizzle out when he gets older." But Pax would say, "I wonder."

John worried mathematics for another month, then suddenly put it all behind him. When his father asked him why he had given it up, he said, "There's not much in number really. Of course, it's marvellously pretty, but when you've done it all—well, that's that. I've *finished* number. I know all there is in that game. I want another. You can't suck the same piece of sugar for ever."

During the next twelve months John gave his parents no further surprises. It is true he learned to read and write, and took no more than a week to outstrip his brother and sister. But after his mathematical triumphs this was only a modest achievement. The surprising thing was that the will to read should have developed so late. Pax often read aloud to him out of books belonging to the elder children, and apparently he did not see why she should be relieved of this duty.

But there came a time when Anne, his sister, was ill, and his mother was too occupied to read to him. One day he clamoured for her to start a new book, but she would not. "Well, show *me* how to read before you go," he demanded. She smiled, and said, "It's a long job. When Anne's better I'll show you."

In a few days she began the task, in the orthodox manner. But John had no patience with the orthdox manner. He invented a method of his own. He made Pax read aloud to him and pass her finger along the line as she read, so that he could follow, word by word. Pax could not help laughing at the barbarousness of this method, but with John it worked. He simply remembered the "look" of every "noise" that she made, for his power of retention seemed to be infallible. Presently, without stopping her, he began analysing out the sounds of the different letters, and was soon cursing the illogicality of English spelling. By the end of the lesson John could read, though of course his vocabulary was limited. During the following week he devoured all the children's books in the house, and even a few "grown-up" books. These, of course, meant almost nothing to him, even though the words were mostly familiar. He soon gave them up in disgust. One day he picked up his sister's school geometry, but tossed it aside in five minutes with the remark, "Baby book!"

Henceforth John was able to read anything that interested him; but he showed no sign of becoming a book-worm. Reading was an occupation fit only for times of inaction, when his over-taxed hands demanded repose. For he had now entered a phase of almost passionate manual constructiveness, and was making all manner of ingenious models out of cardboard, wire, wood, plasticine, and any other material that came to hand. Drawing, also, occupied much of his time.

CHAPTER III

ENFANT TERRIBLE

AT last, at the age of six, John turned his attention to locomotion. In this art he had hitherto been even more backward than the appearance of his body seemed to warrant. Intellectual and constructive interests had led to the neglect of all else.

But now at last he discovered the need of independent travel, and also the fascination of conquering the new art. As usual, his method of learning was original and his progress rapid. He never crawled. He began by standing upright with his hands on a chair, balancing alternately on each foot. An hour of this exhausted him, and for the first time in his life he seemed utterly disheartened. He who had treated mathematicians as dull-witted children now conceived a new and wistful respect for his ten-year-old brother, the most active member of the family. For a week he persistently and reverently watched Tommy walking, running, "ragging" with his sister. Every moment was noted by the anxious John. He also assiduously practised balancing, and even took a few steps, holding his mother's hand.

By the end of the week, however, he had a sort of nervous breakdown, and for days afterwards he never set foot to ground. With an evident sense of defeat, he reverted to reading, even to mathematics.

When he was sufficiently recovered to take the floor again, he walked unaided right across the room, and burst into hysterical tears of joy—a most un-John-like proceeding. The art was now conquered. It was only necessary to strengthen his muscles by exercise.

But John was not content with mere walking. He had conceived a new aim in life; and with characteristic resolution he set himself to achieve it.

At first he was greatly hampered by his undeveloped body. His legs were still almost fetal, so short and curved they were. But under the influence of constant use, and (seemingly) of his indomitable will, they soon began to grow straight and long and strong. At seven he could run like a rabbit and climb like a cat. In general build he now looked about four; but something wiry and muscular about him suggested an urchin of eight or nine. And though his face was infantile in shape, its expression was sometimes almost that of a man of forty. But the huge eyes and close white wool gave him an ageless, almost an inhuman look.

He had now achieved a very striking control of his muscles. There was no more learning of skilled movements. His limbs, nay the individual muscles themselves, did precisely as he willed. This was shown unmistakably when, in the second month after his first attempt to walk, he learned to swim. He stood in the water for a while watching his sister's well-practised strokes, then lifted his feet from the bottom and did likewise.

For many months John's whole energy was given to emulating the other children in various kinds of physical prowess; and in imposing his will upon them. They were at first delighted with his efforts. All except Tommy, who already realized that he was being outclassed by his kid brother. The older children of the street were more generous, because they were at first less affected by John's successes. But increasingly John put them all in the shade.

It was of course John, looking no more than a rather lanky four-year-old, who, when a precious ball had lodged in one of the roof-gutters, climbed a drain-pipe, crawled along the gutter, threw down the ball; and then for sheer joy clambered up a channel between two slopes of tiles, and sat astraddle on the crest of the roof. Pax was in town, shopping. The neighbours were of course terrified for the child's life. Then John, foreseeing amusement, simulated panic and inability to move. Apparently he had quite lost his head. He clung trembling to the tiles. He whimpered abjectly. Tears trickled down his cheeks. A local building contractor was hurriedly called up on the phone. He sent men and ladders. When the rescuer appeared on the roof, John "pulled snooks" at him, and scuttled for his drain-pipe, down which he descended like a monkey, before the eyes of an amazed and outraged crowd.

When Thomas learned of this escapade, he was both horrified and delighted. "The prodigy," he said, "has advanced from mathematics to acrobatics." But Pax said only, "I do wish he wouldn't draw attention to himself."

John's devouring passion was now personal prowess and dominance. The unfortunate Tommy, formerly a masterful little devil, was eclipsed and sick at heart. But his sister Anne adored the brilliant John, and was his slave. Hers was an arduous life. I can sympathize with her very keenly, for at a much later stage I was to occupy her post.

John was now either the hero or the loathed enemy of every child in the neighbourhood. At first he had no intuition of the effect his acts would have on others, and was regarded by most as a "beastly cocky little freak." The trouble was simply that he always *knew* when others did not, and nearly always *could* when others could not. Strangely he showed no sign of arrogance; but also he made no effort to assume false modesty.

One example, which marked the turning-point in his policy towards his fellows, will show his initial weakness in this respect, and his incredible suppleness of mind.

The big schoolboy neighbour, Stephen, was in the next garden struggling with a dismembered and rather complicated lawn-mower. John climbed the fence, and watched for a few minutes in silence. Presently he laughed. Stephen took no notice. Then John bent down, snatched a cog-wheel from the lad's hands, put it in place, assembled the other parts, turned a nut here and a grub-screw there, and the job was finished. Stephen meanwhile stood in sheepish confusion. John moved toward the fence saying, "Sorry you're no good at that sort of thing, but I'll always help when I'm free." To his immense surprise, the other flew at him, knocked him down twice, then pitched him over the fence. John, seated on the grass rubbing various parts of his body, must surely have felt at least a spasm of anger, but curiosity triumphed over rage, and he inquired almost amiably, "*Why* did you want to do that?" But Stephen left the garden without answering.

John sat meditating. Then he heard his father's voice indoors, and rushed to find him. "Hi! Doc!" he cried, "if there was a patient you couldn't cure, and one day some one else came and cured him, what would you do?" Thomas, busy with other matters, replied carelessly, "Dunno! Probably knock him down for interfering." John gasped, "Now just *why?* Surely that would be very stupid." His father, still preoccupied, answered, "I suppose so, but one isn't always sensible. It depends how the other fellow behaved. If he made me feel a fool, I'm sure I'd *want* to knock him down." John gazed at his father for some time, then said, "I see!"

"Doc!" he suddenly began again, "I must get strong, as strong as Stephen. If I read all those books" (glancing at the medical tomes), "shall I learn how to get frightfully strong?" The father laughed. "I'm afraid not," he said.

Two ambitions now dominated John's behaviour for six months, namely to become an invincible fighter, and to understand his fellow human-beings.

The latter was for John the easier task. He set about studying our conduct and our motives, partly by questioning us, partly by observation. He soon discovered two important facts, first that we were often surprisingly ignorant of our own motives, and second that in many respects he differed from the rest of us. In later years he himself told me that this was the time when he first began to realize his uniqueness.

Need I say that within a fortnight, John was apparently a changed character? He had assumed with perfect accuracy that veneer of modesty and generosity which is so characteristic of the English.

In spite of his youth and his even more youthful appearance John now became the unwilling and unassuming leader in many an escapade. The cry was always, "John will know what to do," or "Fetch that little devil John, he's a marvel at this kind of job." In the desultory warfare which was carried on with the children of the Council School (they passed the end of the street four times a day), it was John who planned ambushes; and John who could turn defeat into victory by the miraculous fury of an unexpected onslaught. He was indeed an infant Jove, equipped with thunder-bolts instead of fists.

These battles were partly a repercussion of a greater war in Europe, but also, I believe, they were deliberately fostered by John for his own ends. They gave him opportunities both for physical prowess and for a kind of unacknowledged leadership.

No wonder the children of the neighbourhood told one another, "John's a great little sport now," while their mothers, impressed more by his manners than his military genius, said to one another, "John's a dear these days. He's lost all his horrid freakishness and conceit."

Even Stephen was praiseful. He told his mother, "That kid's all right really. The hiding did him good. He has apologized about the mower, and hoped he hadn't jiggered it up."

But fate had a surprise in store for Stephen.

In spite of his father's discouragement, John had been spending odd moments among the medical and physiological books. The anatomical drawings interested him greatly, and to understand them properly, he had to read. His vocabulary was of course very inadequate, so he proceeded in the manner of Victor Stott, and read through from cover to cover, first a large English dictionary, then a dictionary of physiological terms. Very soon he became so fluent that he had only to run his eye rapidly down the middle of a printed page to be able to understand it and retain it indefinitely.

But John was not content with theory. One day, to Pax's horror, he was found cutting up a dead rat on the dining-room floor, having thoughtfully spread a newspaper to protect the carpet. Henceforth his anatomical studies, both practical and theoretical, were supervised by Doc. For a few months John was enthralled. He showed great skill in dissection and microscopy. He catechized his father at every opportunity, and often exposed the confusion of his answers; till at last Pax, remembering the mathematicians, insisted that the tired doctor must have respite. Henceforth John studied unaided.

Then suddenly he dropped biology as he had dropped mathematics. Pax asked, "Have you finished with 'life' as you finished with 'number?'" "No," replied John, "but life doesn't hang together like number. It won't make a pattern. There's something wrong with all those books. Of course,

I often see they're stupid, but there must be something deeper wrong too, which I can't see."

About this time, by the way, John was actually sent to school, but his career lasted only three weeks. "His influence is too disturbing," said the head mistress, "and he is quite unteachable. I fear the child, though apt in some limited directions, is really subnormal, and needs special treatment." Henceforth, to satisfy the law, Pax herself pretended to teach him. To please her, he glanced at the school books, and could repeat them at will. As for understanding them, those that interested him he understood as well as the authors; those that bored him he ignored. Over these he could show the stupidity of a moron.

When he had finished with biology, John gave up all intellectual pursuits and concentrated on his body. That autumn he read nothing but adventure stories and several works on jiu-jitsu. Much of his time he spent in practising this art, and in gymnastic exercises of his own invention. Also he dieted himself extremely carefully upon principles of his own. John's digestive organs had been his one weak spot. They seemed to remain infantile longer even than the rest of his body. Up to his sixth year they were unable to cope with anything but specially prepared milk, and fruit juice. The food-shortage caused by the war had added to the difficulty of nourishing John, and he was always liable to minor digestive troubles. But now he took matters into his own hands, and worked out an intricate but very scanty diet, consisting of fruit, cheese, malted milk, and whole-meal bread, carefully spaced with rest and exercise. We laughed at him; all but Pax, who saw to it that his demands should be fulfilled.

Whether through diet, or gymnastics, or sheer strength of will, he certainly became exceptionally strong for his weight and age. One by one the boys of the neighbourhood found themselves drawn into a quarrel with John. One by one they were defeated. Of course it was not strength but agility and cunning that made him fit to cope with opponents much bigger than himself. "If that kid once gets hold of you the way he wants, you're done," it used to be said, "and you can't hit him, he's too quick."

The strange thing was that in every quarrel it seemed to the public that not John but the other was the aggressor.

The climax was the case of Stephen, now captain of his school's First Fifteen, and a thoroughly good friend to John.

One day when I was talking to Thomas in his study we heard an unusual scuffling in the garden. Looking out, we saw Stephen rushing vainly at the elusive John; who, as he leapt side, landed his baby fist time after time with dire effect on Stephen's face. It was a face almost unrecognizable with rage and perplexity, shockingly unlike the kindly Stephen. Both combatants were plastered with blood, apparently from Stephen's nose.

John too was a changed being. His lips were drawn back in an inhuman blend of snarl and smile. One eye was half closed from Stephen's only successful blow, the other cavernous like the eye of a mask. For when John was enraged, the iris drew almost entirely out of sight. The conflict was so unprecedented and so fantastic that for some moments Thomas and I were paralysed. At last Stephen managed to seize the diabolic child; or was allowed to seize him. We dashed downstairs to the rescue. But when we reached the garden, Stephen was lying on his stomach writhing and gasping, with his arms pinned behind him in the grip of John's tarantula hands.

The appearance of John at that moment gave me a startling impression of something fiendish. Crouched and clutching, he seemed indeed a spider preparing to suck the life out of the tortured boy beneath him. The sight, I remember, actually made me feel sick.

We stood bewildered by this unexpected turn of events. John looked around, and his eye met mine. Never have I seen so arrogant, so hideous an expression of the lust of power as on that childish face.

For some seconds we gazed at one another. Evidently my look expressed the horror that I felt, for his mood rapidly changed. Rage visibly faded out and gave place first to curiosity then to abstraction. Suddenly John laughed that enigmatic laugh of his. There was no ring of triumph in it, rather a note of self-mockery, and perhaps of awe.

He released his victim, rose and said, "Get up, Stephen, old man. I'm sorry I made you lose your hair."

But Stephen had fainted.

We never discovered what it was all about. When we questioned John, he said, "It's all over. Let's forget about it. Poor old Stephen! But no, *I* won't forget."

When we questioned Stephen a few days later, he said, "I can't bear to think of it. It was my fault, really. I see that now. Somehow I went mad, when he was intending to be specially decent, too. But to be licked by a kid like that! But he's not a kid, he's lightning."

Now I do not pretend to be able to understand John, but I cannot help having one or two theories about him. In the present case my theory is this. He was at this time plainly going through a phase of concentrated self-assertion. I do not believe, however, that he had been nursing a spirit of revenge ever since the affair of the mower. I believe he had determined in cold blood to try his strength, or rather his skill, against the most formidable of his acquaintances; and that with this end in view he had deliberately and subtly goaded the wretched Stephen into fury. John's own rage, I suspect, was entirely artificial. He could fight better in a sort of cold fury, so he produced one. As I see it, the great test had to be no friendly bout, but a real wild-beast, desperate encounter. Well, John got what he wanted. And having got it, he saw, in a flash and once for all, right through it and beyond it. So at least I believe.

CHAPTER IV

JOHN AND HIS ELDERS

THOUGH the fight with Stephen was, I believe one of the chief land-
marks in John's life, outwardly things went on much as before; save that
he gave up fighting, and spent a good deal more time by himself.
Between him and Stephen, friendship was restored, but it was henceforth an uncomfortable friendship. Each seemed anxious to be amicable,
but neither felt at ease with the other. Stephen's nerve, I think, had been
seriously shaken. It was not that he feared another licking, but that his
self-respect had suffered. I took an opportunity to suggest that his defeat
had been no disgrace, since John was clearly no ordinary child. Stephen
jumped at this consolation. With a hysterical jerk in his voice he said, "I
felt—I can't say what I felt—like a dog biting its master and being punished. I felt—sort of guilty, wicked."

John, I think, was now beginning to realize more clearly the gulf that
separated him from the rest of us. At the same time, he was probably feeling a keen need for companionship, but companionship of a calibre beyond
that of normal human beings. He continued to play with his old companions, and was indeed still the moving spirit in most of their activities;
but always he played with a certain aloofness, as it were with his tongue
in his cheek. Though in appearance he was by far the smallest and most
infantile of the whole gang, he reminded me sometimes of a little old man
with snowy hair condescending to play with young gorillas. Often he
would break away in the middle of some wild game and drift into the
garden to lie dreaming on the lawn. Or he would hang around his mother
and discuss life with her, while she did her house-work, tidied the garden,
or (a common occupation with Pax) just waited for the next thing to
happen.

In some ways John with his mother suggested a human foundling
with a wolf foster-mother; or, better, a cow foster-mother. He obviously
gave her complete trust and affection, and even a deep though perplexed
reverence; but he was troubled when she could not follow his thought or
understand his innumerable questions about the universe.

The foster-mother image is not perfect. In one respect, indeed, it is
entirely false. For though intellectually Pax was by far his inferior, there
was evidently another field in which she was at this time his equal, perhaps even his superior. Both mother and son had a peculiar knack of ap-
preciating experience, a peculiar relish which was at bottom, I believe,
simply a very special and subtle sense of humour. Often have I seen a

covert glance of understanding and amusement pass between them when
the rest of us found nothing to tickle us. I guessed that this veiled merri-
ment was in some way connected with John's awakening interest in persons
and his rapidly developing insight into his own motives. But what it was
in our behaviour that these two found so piquant, I could never discover.
With his father John's relation was very different. He made good use
of the doctor's active mind, but between them there was no spontaneous
sympathy, and little community of taste save intellectual interest. I have
often seen on John's face while he was listening to his father a fleeting
contortion of ridicule, even disgust. This happened especially at times when
Thomas believed himself to be giving the boy some profound comment
on human nature or the universe. Needless to say it was not only Thomas,
but myself also and many another that roused in John this ridicule or revulsion. But Thomas was the chief offender, perhaps because he was the
most brilliant, and the most impressive example of the mental limitations
of his species. I suspect that John often deliberately incited his father to
betray himself in this manner. It was as though the boy had said to himself,
"I have somehow to understand these fantastic beings who occupy the
planet. Here is a fine specimen. I must experiment on him."

At this point I had better say that I myself was becoming increasingly
intrigued by the fantastic being, John. I was also unwittingly coming
under his influence. Looking back on this period, I can see that he had
already marked me down for future use, and was undertaking the first
steps of my capture. His chief method was the cool assumption that though
I was a middle-aged man, I was his slave; that however much I might
laugh at him and scold him, I secretly recognized him as a superior being,
and was at heart his faithful hound. For the present I might amuse myself playing at an independent life (I was at this time a rather half-hearted
free-lance journalist), but sooner or later I must come to heel.

When John was nearly eight and a half in actual years, he was as a
rule taken for a very peculiar child of five or six. He still played childish
games, and was accepted by other children as a child, though a bit of a
freak. Yet he could take part in any adult conversation. Of course, he was
always either far too brilliant or far too ignorant of life to play his part in
anything like a normal manner; but he was never simply inferior. Even
his most naive remarks were apt to have a startling significance.

But John's naivety was rapidly disappearing. He was now reading an
immense amount at an incredible rate. No book, on any subject which did
not lie outside his experience, took him more than a couple of hours to
master, however tough its matter. Most he could assimilate thoroughly in
a quarter of an hour. But the majority of books he glanced at only for a
few moments, then flung aside as worthless.

Now and then, in the course of his reading, he would demand to be
taken (by his father or mother or myself) to watch some process of manu-

facture, or to go down a mine, or see over a ship, or visit some place of historic interest, or to observe experiments in some laboratory. Great efforts were made to fulfil these demands, but in many cases we had not the necessary influence. Many projected trips, moreover, were prevented by Pax's dread of unnecessary publicity for the boy. Whenever we did undertake an expedition, we had to pretend to the authorities that John's presence was accidental, and his interest childish and unintelligent.

John was by no means dependent on his elders for seeing the world. He had developed a habit of entering into conversation with all kinds of persons, "to find out what they were doing and what they thought about things." Any one who was tactfully accosted in street or train or country road by this small boy with huge eyes, hair like lamb's wool, and adult speech was likely to find himself led on to say much more than he intended. By such novel research John learned, I am convinced, more about human nature and our modern social problems in a month or two than most of us learn in a lifetime.

I was privileged to witness one of these interviews. On this occasion the subject was the proprietor of a big general store in the neighbouring industrial city. Mr. Magnate (it is safer not to reveal his name) was to be accosted while he was travelling to business by the 9:30 train. John consented to my presence, but only on condition that I should pretend to be a stranger.

We let the quarry pass through the turnstile and settle himself in his first-class compartment. Then we went to the booking office, where I rather self-consciously demanded "a *first* single and a half." Independently we strayed into Mr. Magnate's carriage. When I arrived, John was already settled in the corner opposite to the great man, who occasionally glanced from his paper at the queer child with a cliff for brow and caves for eyes. Soon after I had taken my post, in the corner diagonally opposite to John, two other business men entered, and settled themselves to read their papers.

John was apparently deep in *Comic Cuts,* or some such periodical. Though this had been bought merely to serve as stage property, I believe he was quite capable of enjoying it; for at this time, in spite of his wonderful gifts, he was still at heart "the little vulgar boy". In the conversation which followed he was obviously to some extent playing up to the business man's idea of a precocious yet naive child. But also he *was* a naive child, backward as well as diabolically intelligent. I myself, though I knew him well, could not decide how much of his talk on this occasion was sincere, and how much mere acting.

When the train had started, John began to watch his prey so intently that Mr. Magnate took cover behind a wall of newspaper. Presently John's curiously precise treble gathered all eyes upon him. "Mr. Magnate," he said, "may I talk to you?" The newspaper was lowered, and its owner endeavoured to look neither awkward nor condescending.

"Certainly, boy, go ahead. What's your name?"

"Oh, my name's John. I'm a queer child, but that doesn't matter. It's you we're going to talk about."

We all laughed. Mr. Magnate shifted in his seat, but continued to look his part.

"Well," he said, "you certainly are a queer child." He glanced at his adult fellow travellers for confirmation. We duly smiled.

"Yes," replied John, "but you see from my point of view you are a queer man." Mr. Magnate hung for a moment between amusement and annoyance; but since we had all laughed, except John, he chose to be tickled and benevolent.

"Surely," he said, "there's nothing remarkable about me. I'm just a business man. Why do you think I'm queer?"

"Well," said John, "*I'm* thought queer because I have more brains than most children. Some say I have more brains than I *ought* to have. *You're* queer because you have more *money* than most people; and (some say) more than you ought to have."

Once more we laughed, rather anxiously.

John continued: "I haven't found out yet what to do with my brains, and I'm wondering if you have found out what to do with your money."

"My dear boy, you may not believe me, but the fact is I have no real choice. Needs of all sorts keep cropping up, and I have to fork out."

"I see," said John; "but then you can't fork out for *all* the possible needs. You must have some sort of big plan or aim to help you to choose."

"Well now, how shall I put it? I'm James Magnate, with a wife and family and a rather complicated business and a whole lot of obligations rising out of all that. All the money I control, or nearly all, goes in keeping all those balls rolling, so to speak."

"I see," said John again. " 'My station and its duties,' as Hegel said, and no need to worry about the sense of it all."

Like a dog encountering an unfamiliar and rather formidable smell, Mr. Magnate sniffed this remark, bristled, and vaguely growled.

"Worry!" he snorted. "There's plenty of that; but it's practical day-to-day worry about how to get goods cheap enough to sell them at a profit instead of a loss. If I started worrying about 'the sense of it all' the business would soon go to pieces. No time for that. I find myself with a pretty big job that the country needs doing, and I just do it."

There was a pause, then John remarked, "How splendid it must be to have a pretty big job that needs doing, and to do it well! *Do* you do it well, sir? And does it *really* need doing? But of course you do, and it must; else the country wouldn't pay you for it."

Mr. Magnate looked anxiously at all his fellow travellers in turn, wondering whether his leg was being pulled. He was reassured, however, by John's innocent and respectful gaze. The boy's next remark was rather disconcerting. "It must be so *snug* to feel both safe and important."

"Well, I don't know about that," the great man replied. "But I give the public what it wants, and as cheaply as I can, and I get enough out of it to keep my family in reasonable comfort."

"Is that what you make money for, to keep your family in comfort?"

"That and other things. I get rid of my money in all sorts of ways. If you must know, quite a lot goes to the political party that I think can govern the country best. Some goes to hospitals and other charities in our great city. But most goes into the business itself to make it bigger and better."

"Wait a minute," said John. "You've raised a lot of interesting points. I mustn't lose any of them. First, about comfort. You live in that big half-timbered house on the hill, don't you?"

"Yes. It's a copy of an Elizabethan mansion. I could have done without it, but my wife had set her heart on it. And putting it up was a great thing for the local building trade."

"And you have a Rolls, and a Wolseley?"

"Yes," said the Magnate, adding with magnanimity. "Come up the hill on Saturday and I'll give you a run in the Rolls. When she's doing eighty it feels like thirty."

John's eyelids sank and rose again, a movement which I knew as an expression of amused contempt. But why was he contemptuous? He was a bit of a speed-hog himself. Never, for instance, was he satisfied with *my* cautious driving. Was it that he saw in this remark a cowardly attempt to side-track the conversation? After the interview I learned that he had *already* made several trips in the Magnate car, having suborned the chauffeur. He had even learned to drive it, with cushions behind him, so as to help his short legs to reach the pedals.

"Oh, thank you, I should love to go in your Rolls," he said, looking gratefully into the benevolent grey eyes of the rich man. "Of course, you couldn't work properly unless you had reasonable comfort. And that means a big house and two cars, and furs and jewels for your wife, and first-class railway fares, and swank schools for your children." He paused, while Mr. Magnate looked suspiciously at him. Then he added, "But you won't be *really* comfortable till you've got that knighthood. Why doesn't it come? You've paid enough already, haven't you?"

One of our fellow passengers sniggered. Mr. Magnate coloured, gasped, muttered, "Offensive little brat!" and retired behind his paper.

"Oh, sir, I'm *sorry*," said John, "I thought it was all quite respectable. Surely it's just like Poppy Day. Pay your money, and you get your badge, and everyone knows you have done your bit. And that's true comfort, to know that everyone knows you're all right."

The paper dropped again, and its owner said, with mild firmness,

"Look here, young man! You mustn't believe everything you're told, specially when it's libellous. I know you don't mean harm yourself, but— be more critical of what you hear."

"I'm frightfully sorry," said John, looking pained and abashed. "It's so hard to know what one may say and what not."

"Yes, of course," said Magnate amiably. "Perhaps I had better explain things a bit. Any one who finds himself in a position like mine, if he's worth his salt, has to make the best possible use of his opportunities for serving the Empire. Now he can do this partly by running his business well, partly by personal influence. And if he is to have influence he must not only be, but also appear, a man of weight. He must spend a good deal on keeping up a certain style in his way of life. The public does attend more to a man who lives a bit expensively than to a man who doesn't. Often it would be more comfortable not to live expensively. Just as it would be more comfortable for a judge in court on a hot day to do without his robe and wig. But he mustn't. He must sacrifice comfort to dignity. At Christmas I bought my wife a rather good diamond necklace (South African—the money stayed in the Empire). Whenever we go to an important function, say a dinner at the Town Hall, she's got to wear it. She doesn't always want to. Says it's heavy or hard, or something. But I say, 'My dear, it's a sign that you count. It's a badge of office. Better wear it.' And about the knighthood. If anyone says I want to buy one, it's just a mean lie. I give what I can to my party because I know quite well, with my experience, that it's the party of common sense and loyalty. No other party cares seriously for British prosperity and power. No other cares about our great Empire and its mission to lead the world. Well, clearly I *must* support that party in any way open to me. If they saw fit to give me a knighthood, I'd be proud. I'm not one of those prigs who turn up their noses at it. I'd be glad, partly because it would mean that the people who really count were sure I was really serving the Empire, partly because the knighthood would give me more weight to go on serving the Empire with."

Mr. Magnate glanced at his fellow passengers. We all nodded approval. "Thank you, sir," said John, with solemn, respectful eyes. "And it all depends on money, doesn't it? If *I'm* going to do anything big, I must get money, somehow. I have a friend who keeps saying, 'Money's power.' He has a wife who's always tired and cross, and five children, ugly dull things. He's out of a job. Had to sell his push-bike the other day. He says it's not fair that *he* should be where he is and—*you* where you are. But it's all his own fault really. If he had been as wide awake as you, he'd be as rich as you. Your being rich doesn't make anyone else poor, does it? If all the slum people were as wide awake as you, they'd all have big houses and Rollses and diamonds. They'd all be some use to the Empire, instead of being just a nuisance."

The man opposite me tittered. Mr. Magnate looked at him with the sidelong glance of a shy horse, then pulled himself together and laughed. "My lad," he said, "you're too young to understand these things. I don't think we shall do much good by talking any more about them." "I'm sorry," John replied, seemingly crushed. "I thought I did understand." Then after a pause he continued: "Do you mind if we go on just a *little* bit longer? I want to ask you something else."

"Oh, very well, what is it?"

"What do you think about?"

"What do I think about? Good heavens, boy! All sorts of things. My business, my home, my wife and children, and—about the state of the country."

"The state of the country? What about it?"

"Well," said Mr. Magnate, "that's much too long a story. I think about how England is to recover her foreign trade—so that more money may come into the country, and people may live happier, fuller lives. I think about how we can strengthen the hands of the Government against the foolish people who want to stir up trouble, and those who talk wildly against the Empire. I think——"

Here John interrupted. "What makes life full and happy?"

"You *are* a box of questions! I should say that for happiness people need plenty of work to keep them out of mischief, and some amusement to keep them fresh."

"And, of course," John interposed, "enough money to *buy* their amusements with."

"Yes," said Mr. Magnate. "But not too much. Most of them would only waste it or damage themselves with it. And if they had a lot, they wouldn't work to get more."

"But you have a lot, and you work."

"Yes, but I don't work for money exactly. I work because my business is a fascinating game, and because it is necessary to the country. I regard myself as a sort of public servant."

"But," said John, "aren't *they* public servants too? Isn't their work necessary too?"

"Yes, boy. But they don't as a rule look at it that way. They won't work unless they're driven."

"Oh, I see!" John said. "They're a different sort from you. It must be wonderful to be you. I wonder whether I shall turn out like you or like them."

"Oh, I'm not really different," said Mr. Magnate generously. "Or if I am, it's just circumstances that have made me so. As for you, young man, I expect you'll go a long way."

"I want to, terribly," said John. "But I don't know *which* way yet.

Evidently whatever I do I must have money. But tell me, why do you *bother* about the country, and about other people?"

"I suppose," said Mr. Magnate, laughing, "I bother about other people because when I see them unhappy I feel unhappy myself. And also," he added more solemnly, "because the Bible tells us to love our neighbours. And I suppose I bother about the country partly because I must have something big to be interested in, something bigger than myself."

"But you *are* big, yourself," said John, with hero-worship in his eyes, and not a twinkle.

Mr. Magnate said hastily, "No, no, only a humble instrument in the service of a very big thing."

"What thing do you mean?" asked John.

"Our great Empire, of course, boy."

We were arriving at our destination. Mr. Magnate rose and took his hat from the rack. "Well, young man," he said, "we have had an interesting talk. Come along on Saturday afternoon about 2.30, and we'll get the chauffeur to give you a quarter of an hour's spin in the Rolls."

"Thank you, sir!" said John. "And may I see Mrs. Magnate's necklace? I love jewels."

"Certainly you shall," Mr. Magnate answered.

When I had met John again outside the station, his only comment on the journey was his characteristic laugh.

CHAPTER V

THOUGHT AND ACTION

DURING the six months which followed this incident, John became increasingly independent of his elders. The parents knew that he was well able to look after himself, so they left him almost entirely to his own devices. They seldom questioned him about his doings, for anything like prying was repugnant to them both; and there seemed to be no mystery about John's movements. He was continuing his study of man and man's world. Sometimes he would volunteer an account of some incident in his day's adventure; sometimes he would draw upon his store of data to illustrate a point in discussion.

Though his tastes remained in some respects puerile, it was clear from his conversation that in other respects he was very rapidly developing. He would still spend days at a stretch in making mechanical toys, such as electric boats. His electric railway system spread its ramifications all over the garden in a maze of lines, tunnels, viaducts, glass-roofed stations. He won many a competition in flying home-made model aeroplanes. In all these activities he seemed at heart a typical schoolboy, though abnormally skilful and original. But the actual time spent in this way was really not great. The only boyish occupation which seemed to fill a large proportion of his time was sailing. He had made himself a minute but seaworthy canoe, fitted both with sail and an old motor-bicycle engine. In this he spent many hours exploring the estuary and the sea-coast, and studying the sea-birds, for which he had a surprising passion. This interest, which at times seemed almost obsessive, he explained apologetically by saying, "They do their simple jobs with so much more *style* than man shows in his complicated job. Watch a gannet in flight, or a curlew probing the mud for food. Man, I suppose, is about as clever along his own line as the earliest birds were at flight. He's a sort of archiopteryx of the spirit."

Even the most childish activities which sometimes gripped John were apt to be illuminated in this manner by the more mature side of his nature. His delight in *Comic Cuts,* for instance, was half spontaneous, half a relish of his own silliness in liking the stuff.

At no time of his life did John outgrow his childhood interests. Even in his last phase he was always capable of sheer schoolboy mischief and make-believe. But already this side of his nature was being subordinated to the mature side. We knew, for instance, that he was already forming opinions about the proper aims of the individual, about social policy, about international affairs. We knew also that he was reading a great deal of physics, biology, psychology, astronomy; and that philosophical problems were now seriously occupying him. His reaction to philosophy was curiously unlike that of the normal philosophically minded adult human being. When one of the great classical philosophical puzzles attracted his attention for the first time, he plunged into the literature of the subject, read solidly for a week, and then gave up philosophy entirely till the next puzzle occurred to him.

After several of these raids upon the territory of philosophy he undertook a serious campaign. For nearly three months philosophy appeared to be his main intellectual interest. It was summer-time, and he liked to study out of doors. Every morning he would set off on his push-bike with a box of books and food strapped on the carrier. Leaving his bicycle at the top of the clay cliffs which formed the coastline of the estuary, he would climb down to the shore, and settle himself for the day. Having undressed and put on his scanty "bathers," he would lie in the full sunshine reading, or thinking. Sometimes he broke off to bathe or wander about the mud flats watching the birds. Shelter from rain was provided by two rusty pieces of corrugated iron sheeting laid across two low walls, which he built of stones from a ruined lime-kiln near at hand. Sometimes, when the tide was up, he went by the sea route in his canoe. On calm days he might be seen a mile or two from the coast, drifting and reading.

I once asked John how his philosophical researches were progressing. His answer is worth recording. "Philosophy," he said, "is really very helpful to the growing mind, but it's terribly disappointing too. At first I thought I'd found the mature human intelligence at work at last. Reading Plato, and Spinoza, and Kant, and some of the modern realists too, I almost felt I had come across people of my own kind. I walked in step with them. I played their game with a sense that it called out powers that I had never exercised before. Sometimes I couldn't follow them. I seemed to miss some vital move. The exhilaration of puzzling over these critical points, and feeling one had met a real master mind at last! But as I went on from philosopher to philosopher and browsed around all over the place, I began to realize the shocking truth that these critical points were not what I thought they were, but just outrageous howlers. It had seemed incredible that these obviously well-developed minds could make simple mistakes; and so I had respectfully dismissed the possibility, and looked for some profound truth. But oh my God, I was wrong! Howler after howler! Sometimes a philosopher's opponents spot his howlers, and are frightfully set up with their own cleverness. But most of them never get spotted at all, so far as I can discover. Philosophy is an amazing tissue of really fine thinking and incredible, puerile mistakes. It's like one of those rubber 'bones' they give dogs to chew, damned good for the mind's teeth, but as food—no bloody good at all."

I ventured to suggest that perhaps he was not really in a position to judge the philosophers. "After all," I said, "you're ridiculously young to tackle philosophy. There are spheres of experience that you have not touched yet."

"Of course there are," he said. "But—well, for instance, I have little sexual experience, yet. But even now I can see that a man is blathering if he says that sex (properly defined) is the real motive behind all agricultural activities. Take another case. I have no religious experience, yet. Maybe I *shall* have it, some day. Maybe there's really no such thing. But I can see quite well that religious experience (properly defined) is no evidence that the sun goes round the earth, and no evidence that the universe has a purpose, such as the fulfilment of personality. The howlers of philosophers are mostly less obvious than these, but of the same kind."

At the time of which I am speaking, when John was nearly nine, I had no idea that he was leading a double life, and that the hidden part of it was melodramatic. On one single occasion my suspicion was roused for a few moments, but the possibility that flashed upon me was too fantastic and horrible to be seriously entertained.

One morning I happened to go round to the Wainwrights to borrow one of Thomas's medical books. It must have been about 11.30. John, who had recently developed the habit of reading late at night and rising late in the morning, was being turned out of bed by his indignant mother. "Come and get your breakfast before you dress," she said. "I'll keep it no longer." Pax offered me "morning tea," so we both sat down at the breakfast-table. Presently a blinking and scowling John appeared, wearing a dressing-gown over his pyjamas. Pax and I talked about one thing and another. In the course of conversation she said, "Matilda has come with a really lurid story to-day." (Matilda was the washerwoman.) "She's as pleased as Punch about it. She says a policeman was found murdered in Mr. Magnate's garden this morning, stabbed, she says." John said nothing, and went on with his breakfast. We continued talking for a while, and then the thing happened that startled me. John reached across the table for the butter, exposing part of his arm beyond the end of the dressing-gown sleeve. On the inner side of the wrist was a rather nasty-looking scrape with a certain amount of dirt still in it. I felt pretty sure that there had been no scrape there when I saw him on the previous evening. Nothing very remarkable in that, but what disturbed me was this: John himself saw that scrape, and then glanced quickly at me. For a fraction of a second his eyes held mine; then he took up the butter-dish. In that moment I seemed to see John, in the middle of the night, scraping his arm as he climbed up the drain-pipe to his bedroom. And it seemed to me that he was returning from Mr. Magnate's. I pulled myself together at once, reminding myself that what I had seen was a very ordinary abrasion, that John was far too deeply engrossed in his intellectual adventures to indulge in noctural pranks, and anyhow far too sensible to risk a murder charge. But that sudden look?

The murder gave the suburb matter for gossip for many weeks. There had recently been a number of extremely clever burglaries in the neighbourhood, and the police were making vigorous efforts to discover the culprit. The murdered man had been found lying on his back in a flower-bed with a neat knife-wound in his chest. He must have died "instantaneously," for his heart was pierced. A diamond necklace and other valuable pieces of jewellery had disappeared from the house. Slight marks on a window-sill and a drain-pipe suggested that the burglar had climbed in and out by an upper storey. If so, he must have ascended the drain-pipe and then accomplished an almost impossible hand-traverse, or rather finger-tip-traverse, up and along one of the ornamental timbers of the pseudo-Elizabethan house.

Sundry arrests were made, but the perpetrator of the crime was never detected. The epidemic of burglaries, however, ceased, and in time the whole matter was forgotten.

At this point it seems well to draw upon information given me by John himself at a much later stage, in fact during the last year of his life, when the colony had been successfully founded, and had not yet been discovered by the "civilized" world. I was already contemplating writing his biography, and had formed a habit of jotting down notes of any striking incident or conversation as soon as possible after the event. I can, therefore, give the account of the murder approximately in John's own words.

"I was in a bad mess, mentally, in those days," said John. "I knew I was different from all other human beings whom I had ever met, but I didn't realize *how* different. I didn't know what I was going to do with my life, but I knew I should soon find something pretty big and desperate to do, and that I must make myself ready for it. Also, remember, I was a child; and I had a child's taste for the melodramatic, combined with an adult's cunning and resolution.

"I can't possibly make you really understand the horrible muddle I was in, because after all your mind doesn't work along the same lines as mine. But think of it this way, if you like. I found myself in a thoroughly bewildering world. The people in it had built up a huge system of thought and knowledge, and I could see quite well that it was shot through and through with error. From my point of view, although so far as it went it was sound enough for practical purposes, as a description of the world it was simply crazy. But what the right description was I could not discover. I was too young. I had insufficient data. Huge fields of experience were still beyond me. So there I was, like some one in the dark in a strange room, just feeling about among unknown objects. And all the while I had a frantic itch to be getting on with my work, if only I could find out what it was.

"Add to all this that as I grew older I grew more and more lonely, because fewer and fewer people were able to meet me half-way. There was Pax. She really could help, bless her, because she really did see things from my angle—sometimes. And even when she didn't she had the sense to guess I was seeing something actual, and not merely fantasies. But at bottom she definitely belonged with the rest of you, not with me. Then there was you, much blinder than Pax, but more sympathetic with the active side of me."

Here I interposed half seriously, half mischievously, "At least a trusty hound." John laughed, and I added, "And sometimes rising to an understanding beyond my canine capacity, through sheer devotion." He looked at me and smiled, but did not, as I had hoped he would, assent.

"Well," he continued, "I was most damnably lonely. I was living in a world of phantoms, or animated masks. No one seemed really alive. I had a queer notion that if I pricked any of you, there would be no bleeding, but only a gush of wind. And I couldn't make out *why* you were like that, what it was that I missed in you. The trouble really was that I didn't clearly knew what it was in *myself* that made me different from you.

"Two clear points emerged from my perplexity. First and simplest, I must make myself independent, I must acquire power. In the crazy world in which I found myself, this meant getting hold of much money. Second I must make haste to sample all sorts of experience, and I must accurately experience my own reactions to all sorts of experience.

"It seemed to me, in my childishness, that I should at any rate *begin* to fulfil both these needs by bringing off a few burglaries. I should get money, and I should get experience, and I should watch my reactions very carefully. Conscience did not prick me at all. I felt that Mr. Magnate and his like were fair game.

"I first set about studying the technique, partly by reading, partly by discussing the subject with my friend the policeman whom I was afterwards forced to kill. I also undertook a number of experimental and innocuous burglaries on our neighbours. House after house I entered by night, and after locating but not removing the small treasures which they contained, I retired home to bed, well satisfied with my progress.

"At last I felt ready for serious work. In my first house I took only some old-fashioned jewellery, which, I surmised, would not be missed for some time. Then I began taking modern jewellery, cash, silver plate. I found extraordinarily little difficulty in acquiring the stuff. Getting rid of it was much more ticklish work. I managed to make an arrangement with the purser of a foreign-going vessel. He turned up at his home in our suburb every few weeks and bought my swag. I have no doubt that when he parted with it, in foreign ports he got ten times what he gave me for it. Looking back, I realize how lucky I was that the export side of my venture never brought me to disaster. My purser might so easily have been spotted by the police. Of course, I was still far too ignorant of society to realize the danger. Bright as I was, I had not the data.

"Well, things were swimmingly for some months. I entered dozens of houses and collected several hundred pounds from my purser. But naturally the suburb had got thoroughly excited by this epidemic of housebreaking. Indeed, I had been forced to extend my operations to other districts so as to dissipate the attention of the police. It was clear that if I went on indefinitely I should be caught. But I had been badly bitten by the game. It gave me a sense of independence and power, especially independence, independence of your crazy world.

"I promised myself three more ventures. The first, and the only one to be accomplished, was the Magnate burglary. I went over the ground pretty carefully, and I ascertained the movements of the police pretty thoroughly too. On the actual night all went according to plan until, with my pockets bulging with Mrs. Magnate's pearls and diamonds (in her full regalia she must have looked like Queen Elizabeth), I started back along that finger-traverse. Suddenly a torch flashed on me from below, and a quiet cheery voice said, 'Got you this time, my lad.' I said nothing, for I recognized the voice, and did not wish mine to be recognized in turn. The constable was my own particular pal, Smithson, who had unwittingly taught me so much.

"I hung motionless by my finger-tips, thinking hard, and keeping my face to the wall. But it was useless to conceal my identity, for he said,

'Buck up, John, boy, come along down or you'll drop and break your leg. You're a sport, but you're beat this time.'

"I must have hung motionless for three seconds at most, but in that time I saw myself and my world as never before. An idea toward which I had been long but doubtfully groping suddenly displayed itself to me with complete clarity and certainty. I had already, some time before, come to think of myself as definitely of a different biological species from *Homo sapiens,* the species of that amiable bloodhound behind the torch. But at last I realized for the first time that this difference carried with it what I should now describe as a far-reaching spiritual difference, that my purpose in life, and my attitude to life, were to be different from anything which the normal species could conceive, that I stood, as it were, on the threshold of a world far beyond the reach of those sixteen hundred million crude animals that at present ruled the planet. The discovery made me feel, almost for the first time in my life, fear, dread. I saw, too, that this burglary game was not worth the candle, that I had been behaving very much like a creature of the inferior species, risking my future and much more than *my* personal success for a cheap kind of self-expression. If that amiable bloodhound got me, I should lose my independence. I should be henceforth known, marked, and in the grip of the law. That simply must not be. All these childish escapades had been a blind, fumbling preparation for a life-work which at last stood out more or less clearly before me. It was my task, unique being that I was, to 'advance the spirit' on this planet. That was the phrase which flashed into my mind. And though at that early stage I had only a very dim idea about 'spirit' and its 'advance,' I saw quite clearly that I must set about the more practical side of my task either by taking charge of the common species and teaching it to bring out the best in itself, or, if that proved impossible, by founding a finer human type of my own.

"Such were the thoughts that flashed on me in the first couple of seconds as I hung by my finger-tips in the blaze of poor Smithson's torch. If ever you do write that threatened biography, you'll find it quite impossible to persuade your readers that I, a child of nine, could have had such thoughts in such circumstances. Also, of course, you won't be able to give anything of the actual character of my new attitude, because it involved a kind of experience beyond your grasp.

"During the next two seconds or so I was desperately considering if there was any way to avoid killing the faithful creature. My fingers were giving out. With their last strength I reached the drain-pipe, and began to descend. Half-way I stopped, 'How's Mrs. Smithson?' I said. 'Bad,' he answered. 'Look sharp, I want to get home.' That made matters worse. How *could* I do it? Well, it just *had* to be done, there was no way out of it. I thought of killing myself, and getting out of the whole mess that way. But I couldn't do that. It would be sheer betrayal of the thing I must live for. I thought of just accepting Smithson and the law; but no, that, I knew, was betrayal also. The killing just had to be. It was my own childishness that had got me into this scrape, but now—the killing just had to be. All the same, I hated the job. I had not yet reached the stage of liking *whatever* had to be done. I felt over again, and far more distressingly, the violent repulsion which had surprised me years earlier, when I had to kill a mouse. It was that one I had tamed, you remember, and the maids wouldn't stand it running about the house.

"Well, Smithson had to die. He was standing at the foot of the pipe. I pretended to slip, and fell on him, overbalancing him by kicking off from the wall. We both went down with a crash. With my left hand I seized the torch, and with my right I whipped out my little scout's knife. The position of the human heart was not unknown to me. I plunged the knife home, leaning on it with all my weight. Smithson flung me off with one frantic spasm, then lay still.

"The scrimmage had made a considerable noise, and I heard a bed creak in the house. For a moment I looked at Smithson's open eyes and open mouth. I pulled out the knife, and then there was a spurt of blood."

John's account of this strange incident showed me how little I had known of his real character at that time.

"You must have felt pretty bad on the way home," I said.

"As a matter of fact," he answered, "I didn't. The bad feeling ended when I made my decision. And I didn't go straight home. I went to Smithson's house, intending to kill his wife. I knew she was down with cancer and in for a lot of pain, and would be broken-hearted over her husband's death; so I decided to take one more risk and put her out of her misery. But when I got there, by secret ways of my own, I found the house lit up and awake. She was evidently having a bad night. So I had to leave her, poor wretch. Even that didn't really upset me. You may say I was saved by the insensitivity of childhood. Perhaps to some extent; though I had a pretty vivid notion of what Pax would suffer if she lost her husband. What really saved me was a kind of fatalism. What must be, must be. I felt no remorse for my own past folly. The 'I' that had committed that folly was incapable of realizing how foolish it was being. The new 'I,' that had suddenly awakened, realized very clearly, and was anxious to make amends so far as possible; but of remorse or shame it felt nothing."

To this confession I could make only one reply, "Odd John!"

I then asked John if he was preyed on by the dread of being caught. "No," he said. "I had done all I could. If they caught me, they caught me. But I had done the job as efficiently as it is ever done. I had worn rubber gloves, and left a few false fingerprints, made by an ingenious little instrument of my own. My only serious anxiety was over my purser. I sold him the swag in small instalments over a period of several months."

CHAPTER VI

MANY INVENTIONS

ALTHOUGH I did not at the time know that John was responsible for the murder, I noticed that a change came over him. He became less communicative, in a way more aloof from his friends, both juvenile and adult, and at the same time more considerate and even gentle. I say "in a way" more aloof, because, though less ready to talk about himself, and more prone to solitariness, he had also his sociable times. He could indeed be a most sympathetic companion, the sort in whom one was tempted to confide all manner of secret hopes and fears that were scarcely admitted by oneself. One day, for instance, I found myself discovering, under the influence of John's presence and my own effort to explain myself, that I had already become very strongly attracted to a certain Pax-like young woman, and further that I had been kept from recognizing this feeling through an obscure sense of loyalty to John. The discovery of the strength of my feeling for John was more of a shock than the discovery of my feeling for the girl. I knew that I was deeply interested in John, but till that day I had no idea how subtle and far-reaching were the tentacles with which the strange child had penetrated me.

My reaction was a violent and rather panicky rebellion. I flaunted before John the new-found normal sexual attraction which he himself had pointed out to me, and I ridiculed the notion that I was psychologically his captive. He replied, "Well, be careful. Don't spoil your life for me." It was strange to be talking like this to a child of less than ten years old. It was distressing to feel that he knew more about me than I knew about myself. For in spite of my denial, I knew that he was right.

Looking back, I recognize that John's interest in my case was partly due to curiosity about a relationship which he himself could not yet experience, partly to straightforward affection for a well-known companion, partly to the need to understand as fully as possible one whom he intended to use for his own ends. For it is clear that he did intend to use me, that he did not for a moment intend me to free myself. He wanted my affair with the Pax-like girl to go forward and complete itself not only because, as my friend, he espoused my need, but also because, if I were to give it up for his sake, I should become a vindictive rather than a willing slave. He preferred, I imagine, to be served by a free and roving hound rather than by a chained and hungry wolf.

His feeling for individuals of the species which, as a species, he heartily despised, was a strange blend of contempt and respect, detachment and affection. He despised us for our stupidity and fecklessness; he respected us for our occasional efforts to surmount our natural disabilities. Though he used us for his own ends with calm aloofness, he could also, when fate or our own folly brought us into trouble, serve us with surprising humility and devotion.

His growing capacity for personal relationships with members of the inferior species was shown most quaintly in his extraordinary friendship with a little girl of six. Judy's home was close to John's, and she had come to regard John as her private property. He played uproarious games with her, helped her to climb trees, and taught her to swim and roller-skate. He told her wildly imaginative stories. He patiently explained to her the sorry jokes of *Comic Cuts*. He drew pictures of battle and murder, shipwreck and volcanic eruption for Judy's sole delight. He mended her toys. He chaffed her for her stupidity or praised her for her intelligence as occasion demanded. If any one was less than kind to her, John rushed to her defence. In all communal games it was taken for granted that John and Judy must be on the same side. In return for this devotion she mauled him, laughed at him, scolded him, called him "stoopid Don," showed no respect at all for his marvellous powers, and presented him with all the most cherished results of her enterprise in the "hand-work" class at school.

I once challenged John, "Why are you so fond of Judy?" He answered promptly, imitating her unusually backward baby speech, "Doody *made* for be'n' fon' of. Can't not be fon' of Doody." Then after a pause he said, "I'm fond of Judy as I'm fond of sea-birds. She does only simple things, but she does them all with style. She be's Judy as thoroughly and perfectly as a gannet be's a gannet. If she could grow up to do the grown-up things as well as she does the baby things, she'd be glorious. But she won't. When it comes to doing the more difficult things, I suppose she'll mess up her style like—like the rest of you. It's a pity. But meanwhile she's—Judy."

"What about yourself?" I said. "Do you expect to grow up without losing your style?"

"I've not *found* my style yet," he answered. "I'm groping. I've messed things pretty badly already. But when I *do* find it—well, we shall see. Of course," he added surprisingly, "God may find grown-ups as delightful to watch as I find Judy; because, I suppose, he doesn't want them to have a finer style than they actually have. Sometimes I can feel that way about them myself. I can feel their bad style is part of what they are, and strangely fascinating to watch. But I have an idea God expects something different from me. Or, leaving out the God myth, *I* expect something different from me."

A few weeks after the murder, John developed a surprising interest in a very homely sphere, namely the management of a house. He would spend an hour at a time in following Martha the maid about the house on her morning's work, or in watching the culinary operations. For her entertainment he kept up a stream of small talk compounded of scandal, broad humour, and chaff about her "gentlemen friends." The same minute observation, but a very different kind of talk was devoted to Pax when she was in the pantry or the larder, or when she was "tidying" a room or mending clothes. Sometimes he would break off his tittle-tattle to say, "Why not do it this way?" Martha's response to such suggestions varied from haughty contempt to grudging acceptance, according to her mood. Pax invariably gave serious attention to the new idea, though sometimes she would begin by protesting, "But my way works well enough; why bother?" In the end, however, she nearly always adopted John's improvement, with an odd little smile which might equally well have meant maternal pride or indulgence.

Little by little John introduced a number of small labour-saving devices into the house, shifting a hook or a shelf to suit the natural reach of the adult arm, altering the balance of the coal-scuttle, reorganizing the larder and the bathroom. He tried to introduce his methods into the surgery, suggesting new ways of cleaning test-tubes, sterilizing instruments and storing drugs; but after a few attempts he gave up this line of activity, since, as he put it, "Doc likes to muddle along in his own way."

After two or three weeks John's interest in household economy seemed to fade, save for occasional revivals in relation to some particular problem. He now spent most of his time away from home, ostensibly reading on the shore. But as the autumn advanced, and we began to inquire how he managed to keep himself warm, he apparently developed a passion for long walks by himself. He also spent much time in excursions into the neighbouring city. "I'm going to town for the day to see some fellows I'm interested in," he would tell us; and in the evening he would return tired and absorbed.

It was toward the end of the winter that John, now about ten and a half, took me into his confidence with regard to the amazing commercial operations which had been occupying him during the previous six months. One filthy Sunday morning, when the windows were plastered with sleet, he suggested a walk. I indignantly refused. "Come on," he insisted. "It's going to be amusing for you. I want to show you my workshop." He slowly winked first one huge eye and then the other.

By the time we had reached the shore my inadequate mackintosh was letting water through on my shoulders, and I was cursing John, and myself too. We tramped along the soaked sands till we reached a spot where the steep clay cliffs gave place to a slope, scarcely less steep, but covered with thorn bushes. John went down on his knees and led the way, crawling on all-fours up a track between the bushes. I was expected to follow. I found it almost impossible to force my larger bulk where John had passed with ease. When I had gone a few yards I was jammed, thorns impaling me on every side. Laughing at my predicament and my curses, John turned and cut me adrift with his knife, the same, doubtless, as had killed the constable. After another ten yards the track brought us into a small clearing on the steep slope. Standing erect at last, I grumbled, "Is *this* what you call your workshop?" John laughed, and said, "Lift that." He was pointing to a rusty sheet of corrugated iron, which lay derelict on the hillside. One end of it was buried under a mass of rubbish. The exposed part was about three feet square. I tugged its free end up a couple of inches, cut my fingers on the rusty jagged edge, and let go with a curse. "Can't be bothered," I said. "Do your own dirty work, if you can." "Of course you can't be bothered," he replied, "nor would anyone else who found it." He then worked his hand under the free corners of the sheet, and disentangled some rusty wire. The sheet was now easily lifted, and opened like a trap door in the hillside. It revealed a black hole between three big stones. John crawled inside, and bade me follow; but before I could wedge my way through he had to move one of the stones. I found myself in a low cave, illuminated by John's flash-light. So *this* was the workshop! It had evidently been cut out of the clay slope and lined with cement. The ceiling was covered with rough planks, and shored up here and there with wooden posts.

John now lit an acetylene lamp, which was let into the outer wall. Shutting its glass face, he remarked, "Its air comes in by a pipe from outside, and its fumes go out by another. There's an independent ventilation system for the room." Pointing to a dozen round holes in the wall, "Drainpipes," he said. Such pipes were a common sight on the coast, for they were used for draining the fields; and the ever-crumbling cliff often exposed them.

For a few minutes I crouched in silence, surveying the little den. John watched me, with a grin of boyish satisfaction. There was a bench, a small lathe, a blow-lamp, and quantities of tools. On the back wall was a tier of shelves covered with a jumble of articles. John took one of these and handed it to me, saying, "This is one of my earlier gadgets, the world's perfect wool-winder. No curates need henceforth apply. The Church's undoing! Put the skein on those prongs, and an end of wool in that slot, then waggle the lever, so, and you get a ball of wool as sleek as the curate's head. All made of aluminum sheeting, and a few aluminum knitting needles."

"Damned ingenious," I said, "but what good is it to you?"

"Why, you fool! I'm going to patent it and sell the patent."

Producing a deep leather pouch, he said, "This is a detachable and untearable trouser-pocket for boys; and men, if they'll have the sense to use it. The pocket itself clips on to this L-shaped strip, so; and *all* your trousers have strips like this, firmly sewn into the lining. You have *one* pair of pockets for *all* your trousers, so there's no bother about emptying pockets when you change your clothes. And no more holes for Mummy to mend. And no more losing your treasures. Your pocket clips tight shut, so."

Even my interest in John's amazing enterprise (so childish and so brilliant, I told myself) could not prevent me from feeling wet and chilled. Taking off my dripping mackintosh, I said, "Don't you get horribly cold working in this hole in the winter?"

"I heat the place with this," he said, turning to a little oil-stove with a flue leading round the room and through the wall. He proceeded to light it, and put a kettle on the top, saying, "Let's have some coffee."

He then gave me a "gadget for sweeping out corners." On the end of a long tubular handle was a brush like a big blunt cork-screw. This could be made to rotate by merely pressing it into the awkward corner. The rotatory motion was obtained by a device reminiscent of a "propelling" pencil, for the actual shaft of the brush was keyed into a spiral groove within the hollow handle.

"It's possible the thing I'm on now will bring more money than anything else, but it's damned hard to make even an inch or two of it by hand." The article which John now showed me was destined to become one of the most popular and serviceable of modern devices connected with clothing. Throughout Europe and America it has spawned its myriads of offspring. Nearly all the most ingenious and lucrative of John's inventions have had such outstanding success that almost every reader must be familiar with every one of them. I could mention a score of them; but for private reasons, connected with John's family, I must refrain from doing so. I will only say that, save for one universally adopted improvement in road-traffic appliances, he worked entirely in the field of household and personal labour-saving devices. The outstanding fact about John's career as an inventor was his knack of producing not merely occasional successes but a steady flow of "best sellers." Consequently to describe only a few minor achievements and interesting failures must give a very false impression of his genius. The reader must supplement this meagre report by means of his own imagination. Let him, in the act of using any of the more cunning and efficient little instruments of modern comfort, remind himself that this may well be one of the many "gadgets" which were conceived by the urchin-superman in his subterranean lair.

For some time John continued to show me his inventions. I may mention a parsley cutter, a potato-peeler, a number of devices for using old razor-blades as penknife, scissors, and so on. Others, to repeat, were destined never to be taken up, or never to become popular. Of these perhaps the most noteworthy was a startlingly efficient dodge for saving time and trouble in the watercloset. John himself had doubts about some, including the detachable pocket. "The trouble is," he said, "that however good my inventions are, *Homo sapiens* may be too prejudiced to use them. I expect he'll stick to his bloody pockets."

The kettle was boiling, so he made the coffee and produced a noble cake, made by Pax.

While we were drinking and munching I asked him how he got all his plant. "It's all paid for," he said. "I came in for a bit of money. I'll tell you about that some day. But I want *much* more money, and I'll get it too."

"You were lucky to find this cave," I said. He laughed. "Find it, you chump! I made it. Dug it out with pick and spade and my own lily-white hands." (At this point he reached out a grubby and sinewy bunch of tentacles for a biscuit.) "It was the hell of a grind, but it hardened my muscles."

"And how did you transport the stuff, that lathe, for instance?" "By sea, of course." "Not in the canoe!" I protested. "Had it all sent to X," he said, naming a little port on the other side of the estuary. "There's a bloke over there who acts as my agent in little matters like that. He's safe, because I know things about him that he doesn't want the police to know. Well, he dumped the cases of parts on the shore over there one night while I pinched one of the Sailing Club's cutters and took her over to fetch the stuff. It had to be done at spring tide, and of course the weather was all wrong. When I got the stuff over I nearly died lugging it up here from the shore, though it was all in small pieces. And I only just managed to get the cutter back to her moorings before dawn. Thank God that's all over. Have another cup, won't you?"

Toasting ourselves over the oil-stove, we now discussed the part which John intended me to play in his preposterous adventure. I was at first inclined to scoff at the whole project, but what with his diabolical persuasiveness and the fact that he had already achieved so much, I found myself agreeing to carry out my share of the plan. "You see," he said, "all this stuff must be patented and the patents sold to manufacturers. It's quite useless for a kid like me to interview patents agents and business men. That's where you come in. You're going to launch all these things, sometimes under your own name, sometimes under sham names. I don't want people to know they all come from one little brain."

"But, John," I said, "I should get stung every time. I know nothing about the job."

"That's all right," he answered. "I'll tell you exactly what to do in each case. And if you do make a few mistakes, it doesn't matter."

One odd feature of the relationship which he had planned for us was that, though we expected to deal with large sums of money, there was not to be any regularized business arrangement between us, no formal agreement about profit-sharing and liabilities. I suggested a written contract, but he dismissed the idea with contempt. "My dear man," he said, "how could I enforce a contract against you without coming out of hiding, which I must not do on any account? Besides, I know perfectly well that so long as you keep in physical and mental health you're entirely reliable. And you ought to know the same of me. This is to be a friendly show. You can take as much as you like of the dibs, when they begin to come in. I'll bet my boots you won't want to take half as much as your services are worth. Of course, if you start taking that girl of yours to the Riviera by air every week-end, we'll have to begin regularizing things. But you won't."

I asked him about a banking account. "Oh," he said, "I've had one running for some time at a London branch of the ——— Bank. But the payments will have to be made to you at your bank mostly, so as to keep me dark. These gadgets are to go out as yours, not mine, and as the inventions of lots of imaginary people. You're their agent."

"But," I protested, "don't you see you're giving me absolute power to swindle you out of the whole proceeds? Suppose I just use you? Suppose the taste of power goes to my head, and I collar everything? I'm only *Homo sapiens,* not *Homo superior."* And for once I privately felt that John was perhaps not so superior after all.

John laughed delightedly at the title, but said, "My *dear* thing, you just won't. No, no, I refuse to have any business arrangements. That would be too 'sapient' altogether. We should never be able to trust one another. Probably I'd cheat you all round, just for fun."

"Oh, well," I sighed, "you'll keep accounts and see how the money goes."

"Keep accounts, man! What in hell do I want with accounts? I keep 'em in my head, but never look at 'em."

CHAPTER VII

FINANCIAL VENTURES

HENCEFORTH my own work was seriously interfered with by my increasing duties in connexion with John's commercial enterprise. I spent a great deal of my time travelling about the country, visiting patent agents and manufacturers. Quite often John accompanied me. He had always to be introduced as "a young friend of mine who would so like to see the inside of a factory." In this way he picked up a lot of knowledge of the powers and limitations of different kinds of machines, and was thus helped to produce easily manufacturable designs.

It was on these expeditions that I first came to realize that even John had his disability, his one blind spot, I called it. I approached these industrial gentlemen with painful consciousness that they could do what they liked with me. Generally I was kept from disaster by the advice of the patent agents, who, being primarily scientists, were on our side not only professionally but by sympathy. But quite often the manufacturer managed to get at me direct. On several of these occasions I was pretty badly stung. Nevertheless, I learned in time to be more able to hold my own with the commercial mind. John, on the other hand, seemed incapable of believing that these people were actually less interested in producing ingenious articles than in getting the better of us, and of every one else. Of course, he knew intellectually that it was so. He was as contemptuous of the morality as of the intelligence of *Homo sapiens*. But he could not "feel it in his bones" that men could really "be such *fools* as to care so much about sheer money-making as a game of skill." Like any other boy, he could well appreciate the thrill of beating a rival in personal combat, and the thrill of triumph in practical invention. But the battle of industrial competition made no appeal whatever to him, and it took him many months of bitter experience to realize how much it meant to most men. Though he was himself in the thick of a great commercial adventure, he never felt the fascination of business undertakings as such. Though he could enter zestfully into most of man's instinctive and primitive passions, the more artificial manifestations of those passions, and in particular the lust of economic individualism, found no spontaneous echo in him. In time, of course, he learned to expect men to manifest such passions, and he acquired the technique of dealing with them. But he regarded the whole commercial world with a contempt which suggested now the child, and now the philosopher. He was at once below it and above it.

Thus it was that in the first phase of John's commercial life it fell to me to play the part of hard-headed business man. Unfortunately, as was said, I myself was extremely ill-equipped for the task, and at the outset we parted with several good inventions for a price which we subsequently discovered to be ludicrously inadequate.

But in spite of early disasters we were in the long run amazingly successful. We launched scores of ingenious contrivances which have since become universally recognized as necessary adjuncts of modern life. The public remarked on the spate of minor inventions which (it was said) showed the resilience of human capacity a few years after the war.

Meanwhile our bank balance increased by leaps and bounds, while our expenses remained minute. When I suggested setting up a decent workshop in my name in a convenient place, John would not hear of it. He produced a number of poor arguments against the plan, and I concluded that he was determined to cling to his lair for no reason but boyish love of sensationalism. But presently he divulged his real reason, and it horrified me. "No," he said, "we mustn't spend yet. We must speculate. That bank balance must be multiplied by a hundred, and then by a thousand."

I protested that I knew nothing about finance, and that we might easily lose all we had. He assured me that he had been studying finance, and that he already had a few neat little plans in mind. "John," I said, "you simply mustn't do it. That's the sort of field where sheer intelligence is not enough. You want half a lifetime's special knowledge of the stock market. And anyhow it's nearly all luck."

It was no use talking. After all, he had good reason to trust his own judgment rather than mine. And he gave evidence that he had gone into the subject thoroughly, both by reading the financial journals and by ingratiating himself with local stockbrokers on the morning and evening trains to town. He had by now passed far beyond the naive child that had interviewed Mr. Magnate, and he was, as ever, an adept at making people talk about their own work.

"It's now or never," he said. "We're entering a boom, inevitable after the war; but in a few years we shall be in the midst of such a slump that people will wonder if civilization is going smash. You'll see."

I laughed at his assurance, and was treated to a lecture on economics and the state of Western society, the sort of thing that in eight or ten years was to be generally accepted among the more advanced students of social problems. At the end of this discourse John said, "We'll put half our capital into British light industry—motors, electricity and so on, because that sort of thing is bound to go ahead, comparatively. The rest we'll use for speculation."

"We'll lose the whole lot, I expect," I grumbled. Then I tried a new line of attack. "Anyhow isn't all this money-making a bit too trivial for *Homo superior?* I believe you're bitten by the speculation bug after all. I mean, what is the object of it all?"

"It's all right, Fido, old thing," he answered. (It was about this time that he began to use this nickname for me. When I protested, he assured me that it was meant to be Φαίδω, which name, he said, was connected with the Greek for "brilliant.") "It's all right. I'm quite sane still. I don't care a damn about finance for its own sake, but in the world of *Hom. sap.* it's the quickest way to get power, which means money. And I must have money, big money. Now don't snort! We've made a good little start, but it's *only* a start."

"What about 'advancing the spirit,' as you called it?"

"That's the goal, all right; but you seem to forget I'm only a child, and very backward too, in all that really matters. I must do the things I *can* do before the things I can't *yet* do. And what I can do is to prepare— by getting (*a*) experience, (*b*) independence. See?"

Evidently the thing had to be. But it was with grave misgiving that I agreed to act as John's financial agent; and when he insisted on indulging in various wild speculations against my advice, I began to tell myself that I had been a fool to treat him as anything but a brilliant child.

John's financial operations did not spontaneously hold his attention as his practical inventions had done. And by now both kinds of activity were being subordinated increasingly to the study of human society and the absorbing personal contacts which came to him with adolescence. There was a certain absent-mindedness and dilatoriness about his buying and selling of stock, very exasperating to me, his agent. For though most of our common fortune was in my name, I could never bring myself to act without his consent.

During the first six months of our speculative ventures we lost far more than we gained. John at last woke up to the fact that if we went on this way we should lose everything. After hearing of a particularly devastating disaster he indulged in a memorable outburst. "Blast!" he said. "It means I must take this damned dull game much more seriously. And there's so much else to be done just now, far more important in the long run. I see it may be as difficult for me to beat *Hom. sap.* at this game as it is for *Hom. sap.* to beat apes at acrobatics. The human body is not equipped for the jungle, and my mind may not be equipped for the jungle of individualistic finance. But I'll get round it somehow, just as *Hom. sap.* got round acrobatics."

It was characteristic of John that when he had made a serious mistake through lack of experience he never tried to conceal the fact. On this occasion he recounted with complete detachment, neither blaming nor excusing himself, how he, the intellectual superior of all men, had been tricked by a common swindler. One of his financial acquaintances had evidently guessed that the boy's interest in speculation had ulterior sources, in fact that some adult with money to invest was using him as a spy. This individual proceeded to treat John extremely well, and to "prattle to him about his ventures," anxiously pledging him to secrecy. In this way *Homo superior* was completely diddled by *Homo sapiens*. John insisted that I should put large sums of money into concerns which his friend had advocated. At first I refused; but John was blandly confident in his alleged "inside information that it's an absolute scoop," and finally I consented. I need not recount the history of these disastrous speculations. Suffice it that we lost everything that we had risked, and that John's friend disappeared.

For some time after this disaster we refrained from speculation. John spent a good deal of his time away from home and away from his workshop also. When I asked what he had been up to, he usually said, "studying finance," but refused any further information. During this period his health began to deteriorate. His digestion, always his weakest spot, gave him some trouble, and he complained of headaches. Evidently he was leading a rather unwholesome life.

He began to spend many of his nights away from home. His father had relatives in London, and increasingly often John was allowed to visit them. But the relatives did not for long tolerate his independence. (He disappeared every morning and returned late at night or not till the next day, and refused to give an account of his actions.) Consequently these visits had to cease. But John, meanwhile, had learnt that, in summer, he could live the life of a stray cat in the Metropolis, in spite of the police. To his parents he said that he knew "a man who had a flat who would let him sleep there any night." Actually, as I learned much later, he used to sleep in parks and under bridges.

I learned also how he had occupied himself. By a series of tricks of the "gate-crashing" type he had managed to make contacts with several big financiers in London, and had set about captivating and amusing them, and unobtrusively picking their brains, before they sent him by car with a covering note to his indignant relatives, or paid his railway fare home to the North, and sent the letter by post.

Here is a specimen, one of many such documents which caused much perturbation to Doc and Pax.

DEAR SIR,

Your small son's bicycle tour came to an untimely end yesterday evening owing to a collision with my car near Guildford. He fully admits that the fault was his own. He is unhurt, but the bicycle is past repair. As it was late, I took him to my home for the night. I congratulate you on having a very remarkable boy whose precocious passion for finance was extremely entertaining to my party. My chauffeur will put him on the 10.26 at Euston this morning. I am telegraphing you to that effect.

Yours faithfully,
(*Signed by a personage whose name I
had better not divulge.*)

John's parents, and I also, knew that he was on a bicycling tour, but we supposed him to have gone into North Wales. The fact that he had been so soon encountered in Surrey proved that he must have taken his bicycle by train. Needless to say, John did not turn up by the 10.26 from Euston. He gave the chauffeur the slip, poor man, by jumping out of the car in a traffic jam. That night he spent as the guest of another financier. If I remember rightly, he arrived in the late afternoon at the front door with a story that he and his mother were staying somewhere near, and that he had lost his way and forgotten the address. As police inquiries failed to discover his mother in the neighbourhood, he was kept for the night, and then for the following night, in fact for the Saturday and Sunday. I have no doubt that he made good use of the time. On Monday morning, when the great man had gone to business, he disappeared.

After some months spent partly on such adventures, partly on close study of the literature of finance and political economy and social changes, John felt himself ready to take action once more. He knew that I was likely to be sceptical of his plans, so he operated with money standing in his own name, and told me nothing until, six months later, he was able to show me the results in the shape of a considerable sum standing to his credit.

As time passed it became clear that he had mastered financial speculation as effectively as he had mastered mathematics. I have no knowledge of the principles on which he went to work, for henceforth I played no part in his business deals, save occasionally as his agent when a personal interview was to be undertaken. I remember his saying once when we were reviewing our position, "After all there's not much in this speculation game, once you know your facts and get the hang of the way money trickles about the world. Of course there's a frightful lot of mere flukiness about it. You can never be *quite* sure which way the cat will jump. But if you know your cat well (*Hom. sap.* I mean), and if you know the ground well, you can't go far wrong in the long run."

By the use of his new technique John gradually, throughout the earlier part of his adolescence, amassed a very imposing fortune, much of which was legally owned by me. It may seem strange that he never told his parents about his wealth until the time came for him to use it on a lavish scale. "I don't want to upset their lives sooner than I need," he said, "and I don't want to give them the worry of trying not to blab." On the other hand he allowed them to know that *I* had come in for a lot of money (supposed to be entirely due to luck on the Stock Exchange), and he was glad that I should help his parents in a number of ways, such as paying for the education of his brother and sister, and taking them all (John included) on foreign holidays. The parental gratitude, I may say, was extremely embarrassing. John made it more so by joining unctuously in the chorus, and dubbing me "The Benefactor," which title he soon shortened aggravatingly to "The Benny," and subsequently changed to "The Bean."

CHAPTER VIII

SCANDALOUS ADOLESCENCE

ALTHOUGH during a large part of his fourteenth year finance constituted John's main occupation, his attention was never wholly absorbed by it; and after his period of intensive study and speculation he was able to continue the business of gaining monetary power while giving the best of his energies to very different matters. He was increasingly intrigued by the new experiences consequent on adolescence. At the same time he was very seriously engaged on the study of the potentialities and limitations of *Homo sapiens* as manifested in contemporary world-problems. And as his opinion of the normal species became more and more unflattering, he began to turn his attention to the search for other individuals of his own calibre. Though all these activities were pursued together, it will be convenient to deal with them separately.

The onset of John's adolescence was very late compared with that of the normal human being, and its duration was extremely prolonged. At fourteen he was physically comparable with a normal child of ten. When he died, at twenty-three, he was still in appearance a lad of seventeen. Yet, though physically he was always far behind his years, mentally, and not merely in intelligence but also in temperament and sensibility, he often seemed to be incredibly advanced beyond his actual age. This mental precocity, I should say, was entirely due to imaginative power. Whereas the normal child clings to the old interests and attitudes long after more developed capacities have actually begun to awaken in him, John seemed to seize upon every budding novelty in his own nature and "force" it into early bloom by the sheer intensity and heat of his imagination.

This was obvious, for instance, in the case of his sexual experience. It should be said that his parents were for their time exceptional in their attitude to sex in their children. All three grew up unusually free from the common shames and obsessions. Doc took a frankly physiological view of sexual development; and Pax treated the sexual curiosity and experimentation of her children in a perfectly open and humorous way.

Thus John may be said to have had an exceptionally good start. But the use which he made of it was very different from that which satisfied his brother and sister. They were exceptional only in being permitted to develop naturally, and in thus escaping the normal distortions. They did all that most children were solemnly forbidden to do, and they were not condemned. I have no doubt that they practised whatever "vices" they happened to think of, and then passed light-heartedly to other interests. In the home circle they would prattle about sex and conception in a shameless manner; but not in public, "because people don't understand yet that it doesn't matter." Later they obviously had their romantic attachments. And later still they both married, and are seemingly well content.

The case of John was strikingly different. Like them, he passed in infancy through a phase of intense interest in his own body. Like them he found peculiar gratification in certain parts of his body. But whereas with them sexual interest began long before consciousness of personality had become at all precise, with John self-consciousness and other-consciousness were already vivid and detailed long before the onset of adolescence. Consequently, when that great change first began to affect him, and his imagination seized upon its earliest mental symptoms, he plunged headlong into kinds of behaviour that might have been deemed far beyond his years.

For instance, when John was ten, but physiologically much younger, he went through a phase of sexual interest more or less equivalent to the infantile sexuality of the normal type, but enlivened by his precocious intelligence and imagination. For some weeks he amused himself and outraged the neighbours by decorating walls and gate-posts with "naughty" drawings in which particular adults whom he disliked were caricatured in the act of committing various "wicked" practices. He also enticed his friends into his evil ways, and caused such a storm among the local parents that his father had to intervene. This phase, I take it, was due largely to a sense of impotence and consequent inferiority. He was trying to be sexually mature before his body was ready. After a week or two he apparently worked through this interest, as he had worked through the interest in personal combat.

But as the months advanced into years, he obviously felt an increasing delight in his own body, and this came in time to change his whole attitude to life. At fourteen he was generally taken for a strange child of ten, though it was not unusual for an observer sensitive to facial expression to suppose him some kind of "genius" of eighteen with arrested physique. His general proportions were those of a ten-year-old; but over a childlike skeleton he bore a lean and knotted musculature about which his father used to say that it was not quite human, and that there ought to be a long prehensile tail to complete the picture. How far this muscular development was due to nature, and how far to his deliberate physical culture, I do not know.

His face was already changing from the infantile to the boyish in underlying structure; but the ceaseless expressive movements of mouth and nostrils and brows were already stamping it with an adult, alien, and almost inhuman character. Thinking of him at this period, I recall a creature which appeared as urchin but also as sage, as imp but also as infant deity. In summer his usual dress was a coloured shirt, shorts and sandshoes, all of them fairly grubby. His large head and close platinum wool, and his immense green-rimmed, falcon eyes, gave one a sense that these commonplace clothes had been assumed as a disguise.

Such was his general appearance when he began to discover a vast attractiveness in his own person, and a startling power of seducing others to delight in him no less luxuriously than he did himself. His will to conquest was probably much exaggerated by the knowledge that from the point of view of the normal species there was something grotesque and repellent about him. His narcissism was also, I imagine, aggravated and prolonged by the fact that, from his own point of view, there was no other to meet him on an equal footing, none fit for him to regard with that blend of selfishness and devotion which is romantic love.

I must make it clear that in reporting John's behaviour at this time I do not seek to defend it. Much of it seems to me outrageous. Had it been perpetrated by anyone other than John, I should have unhesitatingly condemned it as the expression of a self-centred and shockingly perverted mind. But in spite of the most reprehensible incidents in his career, I am convinced that John was far superior to the rest of us in moral sensibility, as in intelligence. Therefore, even in respect of the seemingly disgraceful conduct which I have now to describe, I feel that the right course is not to condemn but to suspend judgement and try to understand. I tell myself that, if John was indeed a superior being, much of his conduct would certainly outrage us, simply because we, with our grosser sensibility, would never be able to apprehend its true nature. In fact, had his behaviour been simply an idealization of normal human behaviour, I should have been *less* disposed to regard him as of an essentially different and superior type. On the other hand it should be remembered that, though superior in capacity, he was also juvenile, and may well have suffered in his own way from the inexperience and crudity of the juvenile mind. Finally, his circumstances were such as to warp him, for he found himself alone in a world of beings whom he regarded as only half human.

It was in his fourteenth year that John's new consciousness of himself first appeared, and shortly after his fourteenth birthday that it expressed itself in what I can only call an orgy of ruthless vamping. I myself was one of the few persons within his circle at whom he never "set his cap," and I was exempt only because he could not regard me as fair game. I was his slave, his hound, toward whom he felt a certain responsibility. One other who escaped was Judy; for there again he felt no need to enforce his attractiveness, and there again he felt responsibility and affection.

So far as I know, his first serious affair was with the unfortunate Stephen, now a consciously grown-up young man who went to business every day. Stephen had a girl friend whom he took out on Saturdays on his motor-bike. One Saturday, when John and I were returning from a business trip in my car (we had visited a rubber factory), we stopped for tea at a popular roadside café. We found Stephen and his girl inside, almost ready to leave. John persuaded them to "stay and talk to us for a bit". The girl was obviously reluctant, having perhaps already had reason to dislike John's behaviour toward her man; but Stephen delayed departure. Then began a most distressing scene. John behaved toward Stephen in a manner calculated to eclipse the young woman at his side. He prattled. He sparkled with just the right standard of wit to fascinate Stephen and pass over the head of his simple companion. He kept the whole conversation well beyond her powers, occasionally appealing to her in a manner likely to trap her into making herself ridiculous. He faced Stephen now with the shy hauteur of a deer, now with seductiveness. He found excuses to move about the room and display his curiously feline, though also coltish, grace. Stephen was obviously captivated against his will, and, I feel sure, not for the first time. Toward the girl his gallantry grew laboured and false. She, poor outclassed little creature, could not conceal her distress, but Stephen never noticed it, for he was hypnotized. At last she looked at her watch and tremulously snapped, "It's frightfully late. Please take me home." But even as they were leaving the room John enticed Stephen back for a final sally.

When the couple had gone I told John very emphatically what I thought of his behaviour. He looked at me with the offensive complacency of a cat, then drawled, *"Homo sapiens!"* Whether he was referring to me or to Stephen was not clear. But presently he said, "Tickle him the right way, and you've got him."

A week later people were talking about the change in Stephen. They said "he ought to be ashamed to carry on that way with the boy," and that John would be ruined. When I saw the two of them together, I felt that Stephen was struggling heroically against an obsession. He shunned all physical contact with John, but when contact came, either by accident or through John's contrivance, he was electrified, and could not help prolonging it under a pretence of ragging. John himself appeared to be suffering from a conflict of luxury and disgust. It was clear that he was gratified by his conquest, but at the same time he was repelled. Often he would terminate an amatory brawl with harshness, venting his repulsion by some unexpected piece of brutality, pushing his thumb fiercely into Stephen's eye, or tearing at his ear. As on an earlier occasion, my disgust and indignation at this kind of behaviour seemed to lead John to self-criticism. He was not above learning from his inferiors. His attitude to Stephen changed back to "man to man" comradeship, tempered by an almost humble gentleness. Stephen, too, slowly woke from his infatuation, but he woke with lasting scars.

For some weeks John refrained, so far as I know, from activities of this kind. But his behaviour toward his elders had become definitely more self-conscious and more body-conscious. He was evidently discovering in his own person an interest which had hitherto escaped him. He studied the art of displaying the bizarre attractiveness of his young body to the best advantage in the eyes of the inferior species. Of course he was far too intelligent to indulge in those excesses of adornment which so often render the adolescent ludicrous. Indeed, I doubt whether any but the most intimate and persevering observer would have guessed that the artistry of his behaviour was at all conscious. That it actually was so I inferred from the fact that it varied according to the standards of his audience, now expressing the crudest sort of self-delight and shameless seductiveness, now attaining to that unadorned and steely grace which was to characterize the later John.

During the eighteen months before he reached the age of sixteen John indulged in occasional and abortive love-affairs with older boys and young men. He was still sexually undeveloped, but imagination forestalled his physique, and made him capable of amatory sensitiveness beyond his years. Throughout this phase, however, he seemed indifferent to the fact that most girls showed some degree of physical repulsion in his presence.

But when he was sixteen, and in appearance a queer sort of twelve-year-old, he turned his attention to woman. For some weeks the girls with whom he came in contact had shown a more positive, often a positively vindictive, attitude to him. This suggests at least that they were being forced to take note of him with new eyes, and that he had already begun to study a new technique of behaviour, directed toward the opposite sex.

Having perfected his technique, he proceeded to use it with cold deliberation upon one of the acknowledged stars of local society. This haughty young woman, who bore the surprising name of Europa, was the daughter of a wealthy shipowner. She was fair, large, athletic. Her normal expression was a rather contemptuous pout, tempered by a certain cow-like wistfulness about the eyes. She had been engaged twice, but rumour affirmed that her experience of the opposite sex had been far more intimate than was justified by mere betrothal.

One afternoon down at the bathing place accident (seemingly) brought John to the notice of Europa. She was lying in the sun, attended by her admirers. Unwitting, she had settled herself close to John's towel. Her elbow was on the corner of it. John, needing to dry himself after a swim, approached her from behind, mildly tugged at the towel and murmured, "Excuse me." She turned, found a grotesque young face close to her own, gave a start of repulsion, hastily released the towel, and recovered her composure by remarking to her audience, "Heavens! What an imp!" John must have heard.

Later, when Europa executed one of her admirable dives from the top board, John evidently managed to get entangled with her under water, for they came up together in close contact. John laughed, and broke away. Europa was left gasping for a moment, then she, too, laughed, and returned to the diving platform. John, looking like a gargoyle, was already squatting on one of the boards. As she stretched her arms for the dive, she remarked with kindly contempt, "You won't catch me this time, little monkey." John dropped like a stone, and entered the water half a second behind her. After a considerable time they appeared together again. Europa was seen to smack his face, break from his clinging arm, and make for shore. There, she sunned and preened herself.

John now disported himself in her view, diving and swimming. He had invented a stroke of his own, very different from the "trudgeon" which was still at this time almost unchallenged in the remote northern provinces. Lying on his stomach in the water and flicking his feet alternately, while his arms behaved in the ordinary "trudgeon" manner, he was able to outstrip many experts older than himself. Some said that if he would only learn a decent stroke he would develop into a really fine swimmer. No one in the little provincial suburb realized that John's eccentric stroke, or something very like it, a product of Polynesia, was even then ousting the "trudgeon" from the more advanced swimming circles of Europe and America, and even England.

With this eccentric stroke John displayed his prowess before the reluctantly attentive eyes of Europa. Presently he came out of the water and played ball with his companions, running, leaping, twisting, with that queer grace which few could detect, but by which those few were strangely enthralled. Europa, talking to her swains, watched and was evidently intrigued.

In the course of the game John threw the ball, seemingly by accident, so that it knocked her cigarette from her hand. He leapt to her, sank on one knee, took the outraged fingers and kissed them, with mock gallantry and a suggestion of real tenderness. Every one laughed. Still holding Europa's hand, he brought his great eyes to bear upon her face, inquiringly. The proud Europa laughed, unaccountably blushed, withdrew her hand.

This was the beginning. There is no need to follow the stages by which the urchin captured the princess. It is enough to dwell for a moment on their relations when the affair was at its height. Little knowing what was in store for her, Europa encouraged the juvenile philanderer, not only at the swimming pool, where they gambolled together, but also by taking him out in her car. John, I should say, was much too wise, and much too occupied with other matters, to make his society cheap. Their meetings were not very frequent; but they were frequent enough to secure his prey.

The metaphor is perhaps unjust. I do not pretend to be able to analyse John's motives adequately, even the comparatively simple motives of his adolescence. Though I feel fairly sure that the origin of his attack upon Europa was his new craving to be admired by a woman in her prime, I can well believe that, as the relationship developed, he came to regard her in a much more complex manner. He sometimes watched her with an expression in which aloofness struggled not only with contempt but with genuine admiration. His delight in her caresses was doubtless in part due to dawning sexual appreciation. But though he could imaginatively judge her and enjoy her from the point of view of the male of her species, he was, I think, always conscious of her biological and spiritual inferiority to himself. The delight of conquest and the luxury of physical contact with a full-blooded and responsive woman were always for him poisoned by the sense that this contact was with a brute, with something which could never satisfy his deeper needs, and might debase him.

On Europa the relationship had striking effects. The swains found themselves spurned. Bitter taunts were flung. It was said that she had "fallen for a kid, and a freak kid, too." She herself was obviously torn between the need to preserve her dignity and the half-sexual, half-maternal hunger which John had inspired. Horror at her plight and revulsion from the strangeness of the thing that had enthralled her made matters worse. She once said something to me which revealed the nerve of her feeling for John. It was at a tennis party. She and I were alone for a few minutes. Examining her racquet, she suddenly asked, "Do *you* blame me, about John?" While I was trying to reply, she added, "I expect *you* know what a power he has. He's like—a god pretending to be a monkey. When you've been noticed by him, you can't bother about ordinary people."

The climax of this strange affair must have happened very shortly after that incident. I heard the story from John himself several years later. He had laughingly threatened to invade Europa's bedroom one night by way of the window. It seemed to her an impossible feat, and she dared him to do it. In the small hours of the following morning she woke to a soft touch on her neck. She was being kissed. Before she had time to scream a well-known boyish voice made known that the invader was John. What with astonishment, amusement, defiance and sexual-maternal craving, Europa seems to have made but a half-hearted resistance to the boy's advances. I can imagine that in the grip of his still childish arms she found an intoxicating blend of the innocent and the virile. After some protest and sweet struggle she threw prudence to the winds and responded with passion. But when she began to cling to him, revulsion and horror invaded him. The spell was broken.

The caressing fingers, which at first had seemed to open up for him a new world of mutual intimacy, affection, trust, in relation with a spirit of his own stature, became increasingly sub-human, "as though a dog were smelling round me, or a monkey." The impression became so strong that he finally sprang from the bed and disappeared through the window, leaving his shirt and shorts behind him. So hasty was his retreat that he actually bungled the descent in a most un-John-like manner, fell heavily into a flower-bed, and limped home in the darkness with a sprained ankle.

For some weeks John was painfully torn between attraction and repulsion, but never again did he climb into Europa's window. She, for her part, was evidently horrified at her own behaviour, for she deliberately avoided her boy-lover, and when she encountered him in public she acted the part of the remote though kindly adult. Presently, however, she realized that John's attitude to her had changed, that his ardour had apparently cooled and given place to a gentle and disconcerting protectiveness.

When John took me into his confidence about his relations with Europa, he said, if I remember rightly, something like this. "That one night gave me my first real shaking. Before, I had been sure of myself; suddenly I found myself swept this way and that by currents that I could neither stem nor understand. I had done something that night which I knew deeply I was *meant* to do, but it was somehow all *wrong*. Time after time, during the next few weeks, I went to Europa intending to make love to her, but when I found her I just didn't. Before I reached her I'd be all full of the recollection of that night, and her vital responsiveness, and her so-called beauty; but when I saw her—well, I felt as Titania felt when she woke to see that Bottom was an ass. Dear Europa seemed just a nice old donkey, a fine one of course, but rather ridiculous and pitiable because of her soullessness. I felt no resentment against her, just kindness and responsibility. Once, for the sake of experiment, I started being amorous, and she, poor thing, rejoiced like an encouraged dog. But it wouldn't do. Something fierce in me rose up and stopped me, and filled me with an alarming desire to get my knife into her breasts and smash up her face. Then something else woke in me that looked down on the whole matter from a great height and felt a sort of passion of contemptuous affection for us both; but gave me a mighty scolding."

At this point, I remember, there was a long silence. At last John told me something which it is better not to report. I did, indeed, write a careful account of this most disturbing incident in his career; and I confess that at the time I was so deeply under the spell of his personality that I could not feel his behaviour to have been vile. I recognized, of course, that it was flagrantly unconventional. But I had so deep an affection and respect for both the persons concerned that I gladly saw the affair as John wished me to see it. Years later, when I innocently showed my manuscript to others of my species, they pointed out that to publish such matter would be to shock many sensitive readers, and to incur the charge of sheer licentiousness.

I am a respectable member of the English middle class, and wish to remain so. All I will say, then, is that the *motive* of the behaviour which John confessed seems to have been double. First, he neeeded soothing after the disastrous incident with Europa, and, therefore, he sought delicate and intimate contact with a being whose sensibility and insight were not wholly incomparable with his own; with a being, moreover, who was beloved, who also loved him deeply, and would gladly go to any lengths for his sake. Second, he needed to assert his moral independence of *Homo sapiens,* to free himself of all deep unconscious acquiescence in the conventions of the species that had nurtured him. He needed, therefore, to break what was one of the most cherished of all the taboos of that species.

CHAPTER IX

METHODS OF A YOUNG ANTHROPOLOGIST

JOHN had been engaged in studying his world ever since he was born; but from fourteen to seventeen this study became much more earnest and methodical than it had been, and took the form of a far-reaching examination of the normal species in respect of its nature, achievement and present plight.

This vast enterprise had to be carried on in secret. John was determined not to attract attention to himself. He had to behave as a naturalist who studies the habits of some dangerous brute by stalking it with field-glass and camera, and by actually insinuating himself among the herd under a stolen skin, and an assumed odour.

Unfortunately, I cannot give at all a full account of this phase of John's career, for I played but a minor part in it. His disguise was always the precocious but naive "schoolboy" character which had served him so well in making contact with financiers; and his approach was very often a development of the "gate-crashing" tactics which he had used in the same connexion. This technique was combined with his diabolically skilled vamping. Always his methods were nicely adjusted to the mentality of the particular quarry. I will mention only a few examples, to give the reader some idea of the procedure, and then I will pass on to record some of the ruthless judgements which his researches enabled him to make.

He effected contact with a Cabinet minister by being taken ill outside the great man's private residence at the moment when the minister's wife was entering the house. It will be remembered that John had remarkable control over his organic reflexes, and could influence his glandular secretions, his temperature, his digestive processes, the rate of his heart-beat, the distribution of blood in his body, and so on. By careful manipulation of these controls he was able to produce a disorder the symptoms of which were sufficiently alarming though its after-effects were not serious. A pale pathetic wreck, he was laid on a couch and mothered by the minister's wife while the minister himself phoned for the family doctor. Before the physician arrived, John was already an intriguing little convalescent, and was busy attaching the minister to himself with subtle bonds of compassion and interest. The medical pundit did his best to conceal his bewilderment, and recommended that the boy should rest where he was till his parents were found. But John wailed that his parents were away for the day, and the house would be shut till the evening. Might he stay until their return, and then go home in a taxi? By the time he left the house he had already gained some insight into the mind of his host, and had secured an invitation to come again.

The artificial illness had proved so successful that it became one of his favourite methods. He used it, for instance, to make contact with a Communist leader, supplementing it with an account of his shocking home-conditions since his father "got the sack for organizing a strike." Variants of the same method of artificial illness, with appropriate religious trimmings, were used also upon a bishop, a Catholic priest, and several other clerical gentlemen. It also proved effective with a woman M.P.

As an example of a different approach I may mention that John bagged an eminent astronomer-physicist by writing him a schoolboyish letter of the naive-brilliant kind, begging to be shown over an observatory. The request was granted, and John turned up at the appointed *rendezvous* equipped with schoolcap and a pocket telescope. This meeting led to other connexions among physicists, biologists, physiologists.

The epistolary method was also used upon a well-known Cambridge philosopher and social writer. This time the handwriting was disguised; and, when finally John called on his man, he turned up with dyed hair, dark glasses and a Cockney accent. He intended to assume a very different character from that which had served with the astronomer; and he was anxious to avoid all possibility that the philosopher might identify him as the lad whom the astronomer had encountered.

The letter by which he effected this contact was nicely adapted to its purpose. It combined crude handwriting, bad spelling, dislike of religion, scraps of striking though crude philosophical analysis, and enthusiasm for the philosopher's books. I quote a characteristic passage:

My father beet me for saying if god made the world he made a mess. I said you said it was silly to beet children, so he beet me again for knowing you said it. I said being abel to beet a fellow didn't proove he was wrong. He said I was evil to answer back on my father. I said wots good and evil anyhow but just wot I like and dont like. He said it was blastphemy. *Please* let me call and ask you some questiuns about how a mind works and wot it is.

John had already made several visits to the philosopher's rooms in Cambridge, when he received a note from the astronomer. I should have explained that a young schoolmaster in a London suburb was allowing John to use his flat as a postal address. The astronomer asked John to come and meet "another very wide-awake boy," who lived in Cambridge and was a friend of the philosopher. The ingenuity and relish which John displayed in defeating the repeated efforts of both men to bring about this meeting afforded me an amusing sidelight on his character, but I have not space to describe it.

The epistolary approach was used with equal effect upon a well-known modern poet. In this case the style of the letter and the *persona* which John assumed in the subsequent interviews were very different from those which had served for the astronomer and the philosopher. They were adjusted, moreover, not precisely to the conscious mentality of the poet as he was then known to the public and to himself, but to a mood or attitude in him which was *subsequently* to dominate his work. I quote the most striking passage from John's letter:

In all my hideous frustration of spirit, at home, at school, and in my confused attempts to come to terms with the modern world, the greatest comfort and source of strength is your poetry. How is it, I wonder, that, although you seem simply to describe a tortured and degenerate civilization, the very describing lends it dignity and significance, as though revealing it to be, after all, not *mere* frustration, but the necessary darkness before some glorious enlightenment.

John's efforts were not directed solely upon the intelligentsia and the leaders of political and social movements. Using appropriate methods, he made friends with engineers, artisans, clerks, dock-labourers. He acquired first-hand information about the mental differences between South Wales and Durham coal-miners. He was smuggled into Trade Union meetings. He had his soul saved in Baptist chapels. He received messages from a mythical dead sister in spiritualists' *séances*. He spent some weeks attached to a gipsy caravan, touring the southern counties. This post he apparently gained by showing his proficiency at petty theft and at repairing pots and pans.

One activity he repeated again and again, spending on it a length of time which seemed to me disproportionate to its significance. He became very friendly with the owner of a fishing smack near home, and would often spend days or nights with this man and his mate on the estuary or the open sea. When I asked John why he gave so much attention to the fishing community and these two men in particular, he said, "Well, they're damned fine stuff, these fishermen, and Abe and Mark are two of the best. You see, when *Homo sapiens* is up against the sort of job and the sort of life that's not really beyond him, he's all right. It's only when civilization gives him a job that's too much for his intelligence or too much for his imagination that he fails. And then the failure poisons him through and through." It was not till long afterwards that I realized his ulterior purpose in giving so much attention to the sea. At one time he became very friendly with the skipper of a coasting schooner, and made several voyages with him up and down the narrow seas. I ought to have realized that one motive of these adventures was the desire to learn how to handle a ship.

One other matter should be mentioned here. John's study of *Homo sapiens* now extended to the European Continent. In my capacity of family benefactor I was charged with the task of persuading Doc and Pax to join me on excursions to France, Germany, Italy, Scandinavia. John always accompanied us, with or without his brother and sister. Since Doc could not leave his practice frequently or for long at a time, these occasional family holidays had to be supplemented by trips in which the parents did not participate. I would announce that I had to "run over to Paris to a journalists' conference," or to Berlin to see a newspaper proprietor, or to Prague to report on a conference of philosophers, or to Moscow to see what they were doing about education. Then I would ask the parents to let me take John. Consent was certain, and our plans were often laid in detail before it was given. In this way John was enabled to carry on abroad the researches that he was already pursuing in the British Isles.

Foreign travel in John's company was apt to be a humiliating experience. Not only did he learn to speak a new language in an incredibly short time and in a manner indistinguishable from that of the native; he was also amazingly quick at learning foreign customs and intuiting foreign attitudes of mind. Consequently, even in countries with which I was familiar I found myself outclassed by my companion within a few days after his arrival.

When it was a case of learning a language entirely new to him, John simply read through a grammar and a dictionary, took concentrated courses of pronunciation from one or two natives or from gramophone records, and proceeded to the country. At this stage he would be regarded by natives as a native child who had been in foreign parts for some time and had lost touch somewhat with his own speech. At the end of a week or so, in the case of most European languages, no one would suspect that he had ever been out of the country. Later in his career, when his travels took him farther afield, he reckoned that even an Eastern language, such as Japanese, could be thoroughly mastered in a fortnight from his landing in the country.

Travelling with John on the European Continent I often asked myself why I allowed this strange being to hold me perpetually as his slave. I had much time for thought, for John was as often as not away hunting some writer or scientist or priest, some politician or popular agitator. Or else he was getting in touch with the workers by travelling in third or fourth class railway carriages, or talking to navvies. While he was thus engaged he often preferred to be without me. Every now and then, however, I was needed to act the part of guardian or travelling tutor. Sometimes, when John was particularly anxious to avoid giving any suggestion of his unique superiority, he would coach me carefully before the interview, priming me with questions to ask and observations to make.

On one occasion, for instance, he persuaded me to take him to an eminent psychiatrist. John himself played the part of a backward and neurotic child while I discussed his case with the professional man. This interview led to a course of treatment for John, and occasional meetings between the psychiatrist and myself to discuss progress. The poor man remained throughout ignorant that his small patient, seemingly so absorbed in his own crazy fantasies, was all the while experimenting on the physician, and that my own intelligent, though often provoking, questions had all originated in the mind of the patient himself.

Why did I let John use me thus? Why did I allow him to occupy so much of my time and attention, and to interfere so seriously with my career as a journalist? It could hardly be said that he was lovable. Of course, he was unique material for the journalist or the biographer, and I had already decided that some day I would tell the world all that I knew of him. But it is clear that even at this early stage the unfledged spirit of John exercised over me a fascination more subtle than that of novelty. I think I felt already that he was groping towards some kind of spiritual re-orientation which would put the whole of existence in a new light. And I hoped that I myself should catch some gleam of this illumination. Not till much later did I realize that his vision was essentially beyond the range of normal human minds.

For the present the only kind of illumination which came to John was apparently a devastating conviction of the futility of the normal species. To this discovery he reacted sometimes with mere contempt, sometimes with horror at the doom which awaited the human world, and with terror at his own entanglement in it. But on other occasions his mood was compassion, and on others again sardonic delight, and yet on others delight of a more serene kind in which compassion and horror and grim relish were strangely transmuted.

CHAPTER X

THE WORLD'S PLIGHT

I SHALL now try to give some idea of John's reactions to our world by setting down, more or less at random, some of his comments on individuals and types, institutions and movements, which he studied during this period.

Let us begin with the psychiatrist. John's verdict on this eminent manipulator of minds seemed to me to show both his contempt for *Homo sapiens* and his sympathetic appreciation of the difficulties of beings that are neither sheer animal nor fully human.

After our last visit to the consulting-room, indeed before the door was closed behind us, John indulged in a long chuckling laugh that reminded me of the cry of a startled grouse. "Poor devil!" he cried. "What else could he do anyhow? He's got to *seem* wise at all costs, even when he's absolutely blank. He's in the same fix as a successful medium. He's not just a quack. There's a lot of real sound stuff in his trade. No doubt when he's dealing with straightforward cases of a fairly low mental order, with troubles that are at bottom primitive, he fixes them up all right. But even then he doesn't really know *what* he's doing or *how* he gets his cures. Of course, he has his theories, and they're damned useful, too. He gives the wretched patient doses of twaddle, as a doctor might give bread pills, and the poor fool laps it all up and feels hopeful and manages to cure himself. But when another sort of case comes along, who is living habitually on a mental storey about six floors above our friend's own snug little flat, so to speak, there must be a glorious fiasco. How can a mind of his calibre possibly understand a mind that's at all aware of the really human things? I don't mean the highbrow things. I mean subtle human contacts, and world-contacts. He *is* a sort of highbrow, with his modern pictures and his books on the unconscious. But he's not human in the full sense, even according to the standards of *Homo sapiens*. He's not really grown up. And so, though he doesn't know it, the poor man is all at sea when he comes up against really grown-up people. For instance, in spite of his modern pictures, he hasn't a notion what art is after, though he thinks he has. And he knows less of philosophy, real philosophy, than an ostrich knows about the upper air. You can't blame him. His wings just wouldn't carry his big fleshy pedestrian mind. But that's no reason why he should make matters worse by burying his head in the sand and kidding himself he sees the foundations of human nature. When a really *winged* case comes along, with all sorts of troubles due to not giving his wings exercise, our friend hasn't the slightest perception what's the matter. He says in effect, 'Wings? What's wings? Just flapdoodle. Look at mine. Get 'em atrophied as quick as possible, and bury your head in the sand to make sure.' In fact he puts the patients into a sort of coma of the spirit. If it lasts, he's permanently 'cured,' poor man, and completely worthless. Often it *does* last, because your psychiatrist is an extremely good suggestionist. He could turn a saint into a satyr by mere sleight of mind. God! Think of a civilization that hands over the cure of souls to toughs like that! Of course, you can't blame him. He's a decent sort on his own plane, and doing his bit. But it's no use expecting a vet to mend a fallen angel."

If John was critical of psychiatry, he was no less so of the churches. It was not only with the purpose of studying *Homo sapiens* that he had begun to take an interest in religious practices and doctrines. His motive was partly (so he told me) the hope that some light might be thrown upon certain new and perplexing experiences of his own which might perhaps be of the kind that the normal species called religious. He actually attended a few services at churches and chapels. He always returned from these expeditions in a state of excitement, which found outlet sometimes in ribald jests about the proceedings, sometimes in almost hysterical exasperation and perplexity. Coming out from an emotional chapel service of the Bethel type he remarked, "Ninety-nine *per cent.* slush and one *per cent.*—something else, *but what?*" A tensity about his voice made me turn to look at him. To my amazement I saw tears in his eyes. Now John's lachrymatory reflexes were normally under absolute voluntary control. Since his infancy I had never known him weep except by deliberate policy. Yet these were apparently spontaneous tears, and he seemed unconscious of them. Suddenly he laughed and said, "This soul-saving! If one were God, wouldn't one laugh at it, or squirm! What *does* it matter whether we're saved or not? Sheer blasphemy to want to be, *I* should say. But what is it that *does* matter, and comes through all the slush like light through a filthy window?"

On Armistice Day he persuaded me to go with him to a service in a Roman Catholic cathedral. The great building was crowded. Artificiality and insincerity were blotted out by the solemnity of the occasion. The ritual was somehow disturbing even to an agnostic like me. One felt a rather terrifying sense of the power which worship in the grand tradition could have upon massed and susceptible believers.

John had entered the cathedral in his normal mood of aloof interest in the passions of *Homo sapiens*. But as the service proceeded, he became less aloof and more absorbed. He ceased to look about him with his inscrutable hawklike stare. His attention, I felt, was no longer concentrated on individuals of the congregation, or on the choir, or on the priest, but on the totality of the situation. An expression strangely foreign to all that I knew of him now began to flicker on his face, an expression with which I was to become very familiar in later years, but cannot to this day satisfactorily interpret. It suggested surprise, perplexity, a kind of incredulous rapture, and withal a slightly bitter amusement. I naturally assumed that John was relishing the folly and self-importance of our kind; but when we were leaving the cathedral he startled me by saying, "How splendid it might be, if only they could keep from wanting their God to be human!" He must have seen that I was taken aback for he laughed and said, "Oh, of course I see it's nearly all tripe. That priest! The way he bows to the altar is enough to show the sort he is. The whole thing is askew, intellectually and emotionally; but—well, don't *you* get that echo of something *not* wrong, of some experience that happened ages ago, and was right and glorious? I suppose it happened to Jesus and his friends. And something remotely like it was happening to about a fiftieth of that congregation. Couldn't you feel it happening? But, of course, as soon as they got it they spoilt it by trying to fit it all into the damned silly theories their Church gives them."

I suggested to John that this excitement which he and others experienced was just the sense of a great crowd and a solemn occasion, and that we should not "project" that excitement, and persuade ourselves we were in touch with something superhuman.

John looked quickly at me, then burst into hearty laughter. "My dear man," he said, and this I believe was almost the first time he used this devastating expression, "even if *you* can't tell the difference between being excited by a crowd and the other thing, I can. And a good many of your own kind can, too, till they let the psychologists muddle them."

I tried to persuade him to be more explicit, but he only said, "I'm just a kid, and it's all new to me. Even Jesus couldn't really say what it was he saw. As a matter of fact, he didn't try to say much about *it*. He talked mostly about the way it could change people. When he *did* talk about it, itself, he nearly always said the wrong thing, or else they reported him all wrong. But how do I know? I'm only a kid."

It was in a very different mood that John returned from an interview with a dignitary of the Anglican Church, one who was at the time well known for his efforts to revitalize the Church by making its central doctrines live once more in men's hearts. John had been away for some days. When he returned he seemed much less interested in the Churchman than in an earlier encounter with a Communist. After listening to a disquisition

on Marxism I said, "But what about the Reverend Gentleman?" "Oh, yes,
of course, there was the Reverend Gentleman, too. A dear man, so sensible
and understanding. I wish the Communist bloke could be a bit sensible,
and a bit dear. But *Homo sapiens* evidently can't be that when he has any
sort of fire in him. Funny how members of your species, when they do get
any sort of real insight and grasp some essential truth, like Communism,
nearly always go crazy with it. Funny, too, what a religious fellow that
Communist really is. Of course, he doesn't know it, and he hates the word.
Says men ought to care for Man and nothing else. A moral sort of cove,
he is, full of 'oughts.' Denies morality, and then damns people for not being communist saints. Says men are all fools or knaves or wasters unless
you can get 'em to care for the Class War. Of course, he tells you the Class
War is needed to emancipate the Workers. But what really *gets* him about
it isn't that. The fire inside him, though he doesn't know it, is a passion for
what he calls dialectical materialism, for the dialectic of history. The one
selfishness in him is the longing to be an instrument of the Dialectic, and
oddly enough what he really *means* by that, in his heart of hearts, is what
Christians so quaintly describe as the law of God, or God's will. Strange!
He says the sound element in Christianity was love of one's fellow men.
But *he* doesn't really love them, not as actual persons. He'd slaughter the
lot of them if he thought that was part of the Dialectic of History. What
he really shares with Christians, real Christians, is a most obscure but teasing, firing awareness of something super-individual. Of course, he thinks
it's just the mass of individuals, the group. But he's wrong. What's the
group, anyhow, but just everybody lumped together, and nearly all fools
or limps or knaves? It's not simply the *group* that fires him. It's justice,
righteousness, and the whole spiritual music that ought to be made by the
group. Damned funny that! Of course, I know all Communists are not
religious, some are merely—well, like that bloody little man the other day.
But this fellow *is* religious. And so was Lenin, I guess. It's not enough to
say his root motive was desire to avenge his brother. In a sense that's true.
But one can feel behind nearly everything he said a sense of being the
chosen instrument of Fate, of the Dialectic, of what might almost as well
be called God."

"And the Reverend Gentleman?" I queried. "The Reverend Gentleman? Oh, him! Well, he's religious in about the same sense as firelight is
sunshine. The coal-trees once lapped up the sun's full blaze, and now in
the grate they give off a glow and a flicker that snugs up his room nicely,
so long as the curtains are drawn and the night kept at arm's length. Outside, every one is floundering about in the dark and the wet, and all he
can do is to tell them to make a nice little fire and squat down in front
of it. One or two he actually fetches into his own beautiful room, and they
drip all over the carpet, and leave muddy marks, and spit into the fire.
He gets very unhappy about it, but he puts up with it nobly because,

though he hasn't a notion what *worship* is, he does up to a point try to love his neighbours. Funny, that, when you think of the Communist who doesn't. Of course, if people got really nasty, the Reverend would phone the police."

Lest the reader should suppose that John was not critical of the Communists, I will quote some of his comments on that other Communist, referred to above. "He knows in an obscure way that he's an utter waster, though he pretends to himself that he's noble and unfortunate. Of course he *is* unfortunate, frightfully unfortunate, in being the sort he is. And of course that's society's fault as much as his own. So the wretched creature has to spend his life putting out his tongue at society, or at the powers that be in society. He's just a hate-bag. But even his hate isn't really sincere. It's a posture of self-defence, self-justification, not like the hate that smashed the Tsar, and turned creative and made Russia. Things haven't got bad enough for that in England yet. At present all that can be done by blokes like this is to spout hate and give the other side a fine excuse for repressing Communism. Of course, hosts of well-off people and would-be-well-off people are just as ashamed of themselves subconsciously as that blighter, and just as full of hate, and in need of a scapegoat to exercise their hate upon. He and his like are a godsend to them."

I said there was more excuse for the have-nots to hate than for the haves. This remark brought from John a bit of analysis and prophecy that has since been largely justified.

"You talk," he said, "as if hate were rational, as if men only hated what they had reason to hate. If you want to understand modern Europe and the world, you have to keep in mind three things that are really quite distinct although they are all tangled up together. First there's this almost universal need to hate something, rationally or irrationally, to find something to unload your own sins on to, and then smash it. In perfectly healthy minds (even of your species) this need to hate plays a small part. But nearly all minds are damnably unhealthy, and so they must have something to hate. Mostly, they just hate their neighbours or their wives or husbands or parents or children. But they get a much more exalted sort of excitement by hating foreigners. A nation, after all, is just a society for hating foreigners, a sort of super-hate-club. The second thing to bear in mind is the obvious one of economic disorder. The people with economic power try to run the world for their own profit. Not long ago they succeeded, more or less, but now the job has got beyond them, and, as we all know, there's the hell of a mess. This gives hate a new outlet. The have-nots with very good reason exercise their hate upon the haves, who have made the mess and can't clean it up. The haves fear and therefore zestfully hate the have-nots. What people can't realize is that if there were no deep-rooted *need* to hate in almost every mind the social problem would be at least intelligently faced, perhaps solved. Then there's the third factor, namely, the growing sense that there's something all wrong with modern solely-scientific culture. I don't mean that people are intellectually doubtful about science. It's much deeper than that. They are simply finding that modern culture isn't enough to live by. It just doesn't work in practice. It has got a screw loose somewhere. Or some vital bit of it is dead. Now this horror against modern culture, against science and mechanization and standardization, is only just beginning to be a serious factor. It's newer than Bolshevism. The Bolshies, and all the socially left-wing people, are still content with modern culture. Or rather, they put all its faults down to capitalism, dear innocent theorists. But the essence of it they still accept. They're rationalistic, scientific, mechanistic, brass-tack-istic. But another crowd, scattered about all over the place, are having the hell of a deep revulsion against all this. They don't know what's the matter with it, but they're sure it's not enough. Some of them, feeling that lack, just creep back into church, specially the Roman Church. But too much water has passed under the bridge since the churches were alive, so that's no real use. The crowds who can't swallow the Christian dope are terribly in need of something, though they don't know what, or even know they're in need at all. And this deep need gets mixed up with their hate-need; and, if they're middle class, it gets mixed up also with their fear of social revolution. And this fear, along with their hate-need, may get played on by any crook with an axe to grind, or by any able man with an itch for bossing. That's what happened in Italy. That sort of thing will spread. I'd bet my boots that in a few years there'll be a tremendous anti-left movement all over Europe, inspired partly by fear and hate, partly by that vague, fumbling suspicion that there's something all wrong with scientific culture. It's more than an intellectual suspicion. It's a certainty of the bowels, call it a sort of brute-blind religious hunger. Didn't you *feel* the beginnings of it in Germany last year when we were there? A deep, still-unconscious revulsion from mechanism, and from rationality, and from democracy, and from sanity. That's it, a confused craving to be mad, possessed in some way. Just the thing for the well-to-do haters to use for their own ends. *That's* what's going to get Europe. And its power depends on its being a hotch-potch of self-seeking, sheer hate, and this bewildered hunger of the soul, which is so worthy and so easily twisted into something bloody. If Christianity could hold it in and discipline it, it might do wonders. But Christianity's played out. So these folk will probably invent some ghastly religion of their own. Their God will be the God of the hate-club, the nation. That's what's coming. The new Messiahs (one for each tribe) won't triumph by love and gentleness, but by hate and ruthlessness. Just because *that's* what you all really *want*, at the bottom of your poor diseased bowels and crazy minds. Jesus Christ!"

I was not much impressed by this tirade. I said the best minds had outgrown that old tribal god, and the rest would follow the best minds in the long run. John's laughter disconcerted me.

"The best minds!" he said. "One of the main troubles of your unhappy species is that the best minds can go even farther astray than the second best, much farther than the umpteenth best. That's what has been happening during the last few centuries. Swarms of the best minds have been leading the populace down blind alley after blind alley, and doing it with tremendous courage and resource. Your trouble, as a species, is that you can't keep hold of everything at once. Any one who is very wide awake toward one set of facts invariably loses sight of all the other equally important sets. And as you have practically no inner experience to orientate you, compass-wise, to the cardinal points of reality, there's no telling how far astray you'll go, once you start in the wrong direction."

Here I interjected, "Surely that is one of the penalties of being gifted with intelligence; it may lead one forward, but it may lead one badly astray."

John replied, "It's one of the penalties of being more than beast and less than fully human. Pterodactyls had a great advantage over the old-fashioned creepy crawly lizards, but they had their special dangers. Because they could fly a bit, they could crash. Finally, they were outclassed by birds. Well, I'm a bird."

He paused, and then said, "Centuries ago all the best minds were in the Church. In those days there was nothing to compare with Christianity for practical significance and theoretical interest. And so the best minds swarmed upon it, and generation after generation of them used their bright intelligences on it. Little by little they smothered the actual living spirit of religion, with their busy theorizing. Not only so but they also used their religion, or rather their precious doctrines, to explain all physical events. Presently there came along a generation of best minds that found all this ratiocination very unconvincing, and began watching how things really did happen in physical nature. They and their successors made modern science, and gave man physical power, and changed the face of the earth. All this was as impressive in its own way as the effects of religion had been, real live religion, in a quite different way, centuries earlier. So now nearly all the best minds buzzed off to science, or to the job of working out a new scientific view of the universe and a new scientific way of feeling and acting. And being so impressed by science and by industry and the business attitude to life, they lost whatever trace of the old religion they ever had, and also they became even more blind to their own inner nature than they need have been. They were too busy with science, or industry, or empire-building, to bother about interior things. Of course, a few of the best minds, and some ordinary folk, had mistrusted fashionable thought all the way through. But after the war mistrust became widespread. The war made Nineteenth Century culture look pretty silly, didn't it? So what happened? Some of the best minds (the *best* minds, mind you) tumbled helter-skelter back to the Churches. Others, the most social ones, declared that we ought all to live to improve mankind, or to make the future generations happy. Others, feeling that mankind was really past hope, just struck a fine attitude of despair, based either on contempt and hate of their fellows or on a compassion which was at bottom self-pity. Others, the bright young things of literature and art, set out to enjoy themselves as best they might in a crashing world. They were out for pleasure at any price, pleasure not entirely unrefined. For instance, though they demanded unrestrained sexual pleasure, it was to be highly conscious and discriminating. They also demanded æsthetic pleasure of a rather self-indulgent sort, and the thoroughly self-indulgent pleasure of tasting ideas, just for their spiciness or tang, so to speak. Bright young things! Yes, blowflies of a decaying civilization. Poor wretches! How they must hate themselves, really. But damn it, after all, they're mostly good stuff gone wrong."

John had recently spent some weeks studying the intelligentsia. He had made his entry into Bloomsbury by acting the part of a precocious genius, and allowing a well-known writer to exhibit him as a curio. Evidently he flung himself into the life of these brilliant and disorientated young men and women with characteristic thoroughness, for when he returned he was something of a wreck. I need not retail his account of his experiences, but his analysis of the plight of the leaders of our thought is worth reporting.

"You see," he said, "they really are in a sense the leaders of thought, or leaders of fashion in thought. What they think and feel to-day, the rest think and feel next year or so. And some of them really are, according to the standards of *Hom. sap.*, first-class minds, or might have been, in different circumstances. (Of course, most are just riff-raff, but they don't count.) Well, the situation's really very simple, and very desperate. Here is the centre to which nearly all the best sensibility and best intellect of the country gets attracted in the expectation of meeting its kind and enriching its experience; but what happens? The poor little flies find themselves caught in a web, a subtle mesh of convention, so subtle in fact that most of them are unaware of it. They buzz and buzz and imagine they are free fliers, when as a matter of fact each one is stuck fast on his particular strand of the web. Of course, they have the reputation of being the most unconventional people of all. The centre imposes on them a convention of unconventionality, of daring thought and conduct. But they can only be 'daring' within the limits of their convention. They have a sameness of intellectual and moral taste which makes them fundamentally all alike in spite of their quite blatant superficial differences. That wouldn't matter so much if their taste were really discriminate taste, but it's not, in most cases; and such innate powers of precision and delicacy as they actually have get dulled by the convention. If the convention were a sound one, all might be well, but it's not. It consists in trying to be 'brilliant' and 'original,' and in craving 'experience.' Some of them *are* brilliant and original according to the standards of your species; and some of them *have* the gift for experience. But when they do achieve brilliance and experience, this is *in spite* of the web, and consists at best in a certain flutter and agitation, not in flight. The influence of the all-pervading convention turns brilliance into brightness, originality into perversity, and deadens the mind to all but the cruder sorts of experience. I don't mean merely crudity in sex-experience and personal relations, though indeed their quite sound will to break the old customs and avoid sentimentality at all costs *has* led them in the end to a jading and coarsening extravagance. What I mean is crudity of—well, of spirit. Though they are often very intelligent (for your species) they haven't got any of the finer aspects of experience to use their intelligence *on*. And that seems to be due partly to a complete lack of spiritual discipline, partly to an obscure, half-conscious funk. You see they're all very sensitive creatures, very susceptible to pleasure and pain; and early in their lives, whenever they bumped into anything like a fundamental experience, they found it terribly upsetting. And so they formed habits of avoiding that sort of thing. And they made up for this persistent avoidance by drenching themselves in all sorts of minor and superficial (though sensational) experiences; and also by talking big about Experience with a capital E, and buzzing intellectually."

This analysis made me feel uncomfortable, for though I was not one of "them" I could not disguise from myself that the same sort of condemnation might apply to me. John evidently saw my thoughts, for he grinned, and moreover indulged in an entirely vulgar wink. Then he said, "Strikes home, old thing, doesn't it? Never mind, you're not *in* the web. You're an outsider. Fate has kept you safely fluttering in the backward North."

Some weeks after this conversation John's mood seemed to change. Hitherto he had been light-hearted, sometimes even ribald, both in the actual pursuit of his investigation and in his comments. In his more serious phases he displayed the sympathetic though aloof interest of an anthropologist observing the customs of a primitive tribe. He had always been ready to talk about his experiences and to defend his judgements. But now he began to be much less communicative, and, when he did condescend to talk, much more terse and grim. Banter and friendly contemptuousness vanished. In their place he developed a devastating habit of coldly, wearily pulling to pieces whatever one said to him. Finally this reaction also vanished, and his only response to any remark of general interest was a steady gloomy stare. So might a lonely man gaze at his frisking dog when the need of human intercourse was beginning to fret him. Had any one other than John treated one in that way, the act would have been offensive. Coming from John it was merely disturbing. It roused in me a painful self-consciousness, and an irresistible tendency to look away and busy myself with something.

Once only did John express himself freely. By appointment I had met

him in his subterranean workshop to discuss a financial project which I proposed to undertake. He was lying in his little bunk, swinging one leg
over the side. Both hands were behind his head. I embarked on my theme,
but his attention was obviously elsewhere. "Damn it, can't you listen?" I
said. "Are you inventing a gadget or what?" "Not inventing," he replied,
"discovering." There was such solemnity in his voice that a wave of irrational panic seized me. "Oh, for God's sake do be explicit. What's up with
you these days? Can't you tell a fellow?" He transferred his gaze from the
ceiling to my face. He stared. I started to fill my pipe.

"Yes, I'll tell you," he said, "if I can, or as much as I can. Some time ago
I asked myself a question, namely this. Is the plight of the world to-day a
mere incident, an illness that might have been avoided and may be cured?
Or is it something inherent in the very nature of your species? Well, I
have got my answer. *Homo sapiens* is a spider trying to crawl out of a
basin. The higher he crawls, the steeper the hill. Sooner or later, down he
goes. So long as he's on the bottom, he can get along quite nicely, but as
soon as he starts climbing, he begins to slip. And the higher he climbs the
farther he falls. It doesn't matter which direction he tries. He can make
civilization after civilization, but every time, long before he begins to be
really civilized, skid!"

I protested against John's assurance. "It *may* be so," I said, "but how
can you possibly *know*? *Hom. sap.* is an inventive animal. Might not the
spider some time or other contrive to make his feet sticky? Or—well, suppose he's not a spider at all but a beetle. Beetles have wings. They often
forget how to use them, but—aren't there signs that *Hom. sap.'s* present
climb is different from all the others? Mechanical power is a stickiness for
his feet. And I believe his wing-cases are stirring, too."

John regarded me in silence. Pulling himself together, he said, as if
from a great distance, "No wings. No wings." Then, in a more normal
voice, "And as for mechanical power, if he knew how to use it, it might
help him up a few steps farther, but he doesn't. You see, for every type
of creature there's a limit of *possible* development of capacity, a limit inherent in the ground plan of its organization. *Homo sapiens* reached his
limit a million years ago, but he has only recently begun to use his powers
dangerously. In achieving science and mechanism he has brought about a
state of affairs which cannot be dealt with properly save by capacity which
is much more developed than his. Of course, he *may* not slip just yet. He
may succeed in muddling through this particular crisis of history. But if
he does, it will only be muddling through to stagnation, not to the soaring
that even he in his own heart is desperately craving. Mechanical power,
you see, is indeed vitally necessary to the full development of the human
spirit; but to the sub-human spirit it is lethal."

"But, how *can* you know that? Aren't you being a bit too confident in
your own judgement?"

John's lips compressed themselves and assumed a crooked smile. "You're right," he said. "There's just one possibility that I have not mentioned. If the species as a whole, or a large proportion of the world population, were to be divinely inspired, so that their nature became truly human at a stride, all would soon be well."

I took this for irony, but he went on to say, "Oh, no, I'm quite serious. It's possible; if you interpret 'divinely inspired' to mean lifted out of their pettiness by a sudden and spontaneous access of strength to their own rudimentary spiritual nature. It happens again and again in individuals here and there. When Christianity came, it happened to large numbers. But they were a very small proportion of the whole, and the thing petered out. Short of that kind of thing, or rather something much more widespread and much more powerful than the Christian miracle, there's no hope. The early Christians, you see, and the early Buddhists and so on, remained at bottom what I should call sub-human, in spite of their miracle. In intelligence they remained what they were before the miracle; and in will, though they were profoundly changed by the new thing in them, the change was insecure. Or rather the new thing seldom managed to integrate their whole being into a new and harmonious order. Its rule was precarious. The new psychological compound, so to speak, was a terribly unstable compound. Or, putting it in another way, they managed to become saints, but seldom angels. The sub-human and the human were always in violent conflict in them. And so they mostly got obsessed with the idea of sin, and saving their souls, instead of being able to pass on to live the new life with fluency and joy, and with creative effect in the world."

At this point we fell silent. I relit my pipe, and John remarked, "Match number nine, you funny old thing!" It was true. There lay the eight burnt matches, though I had no recollection of using them. John from his position on the bed could not see the ash-tray. He must have noticed the actual re-lightings. It was simply that he observed whatever happened however engrossed he might be. "You funnier young thing!" I retorted.

Presently he began talking again. He kept his eye on me, but I felt that he was talking rather to himself than to me. "At one time," he said, "I thought I should simply take charge of the world and help *Homo sapiens* to remake himself on a more human plan. But now I realize that only what men call 'God' could do that. Unless perhaps a great invasion of superior beings from another planet, or another dimension, could do it. But I doubt if they would trouble to do it. They would probably merely use the Terrestrials as cattle or museum pieces or pets, or just vermin. All the same, if they wanted to make a better job of *Hom. sap.* I expect they could. But *I* can't do it. I believe, if I set my mind to it, I *could* fairly easily secure power and take charge of the normal species; and, once in charge, I could make a much more satisfactory world, and a much happier world; but always I should have to accept the ultimate limitations of capacity in the normal species. To make them try to live beyond their capacity would be like trying to civilize a pack of monkeys. There would be worse chaos than ever, and they would unite against me, and sooner or later destroy me. So I'd just have to accept the creature with all its limitations. And that would be to waste my best powers. I might as well spend my life chicken-farming."

"You arrogant young cub!" I protested. "I don't believe we are as bad as you think."

"Oh, don't you! Of course not, you're one of the pack," he said. "Look here, now! I've spent some time and trouble poking about in Europe, and what do I find? In my simplicity I thought the fellows who had come to the top, the best minds, the leaders in every walk, would be something like real human beings, fundamentally sane, rational, efficient, self-detached, loyal to the best in them. Actually they are nothing of the sort. Mostly they're even below the average. Their position has underminded them. Think of old Z (naming a Cabinet minister). You'd be amazed if you could see him as I have seen him. He simply can't experience anything clearly and correctly, except things that bear on his petty little self-esteem. Everything has to penetrate to him through a sort of eider-down of preconceived notions, *clichés,* diplomatic phrases. He has no more idea of the real issues in politics to-day than a mayfly has of the fish in the stream it's fluttering on. He has, of course, the trick of using a lot of phrases that *might* mean very important things, but they don't mean them to *him.* They are just counters for him, to be used in the game of politics. He's simply not *alive,* to the real things. That's what's the matter with him. And take Y, the Press magnate. He's just a nimble-witted little guttersnipe who has found out how to hoax the world into giving him money and power. Talk to him about the real things, and he just hasn't a notion what you're driving at. But it's not only that sort that terrify me with their combination of power and inanity. Take the real leaders, take young X, whose revolutionary ideas are going to have a huge effect on social thought. He's got a brain, and he's using it on the right side, and he has nerve, too. But— well, I've seen enough of him to spot his *real* motive, hidden from himself, of course. He had a thin time long ago, and now he wants to get his own back, he wants to make the oppressor frightened of him. He wants to *use* the have-nots to break the haves, for his own satisfaction. Well, *let* him get his own back, and good luck to him. But fancy taking that as your life's goal, even unconsciously! It has made him do damned good work, but it has crippled him, too, poor devil. Or take that philosopher bloke, W, who did so much toward showing up the old school with their simple trust in words. He's really in much the same fix as X. I know him pretty well, the perky old bird. And knowing him I can see the mainspring of all that brilliant work quite clearly, namely, the idea of *himself* as bowing to no man and no god, as purged of prejudice and sentimentality, as faithful to reason yet not blindly trustful of it. All that is admirable. But it obsesses him, and actually warps his reasoning. You can't be a real philosopher if you have an obsession. On the other hand, take V. He knows all about electrons and all about galaxies, and he's first class at his job. Further, he has glimmers of spiritual experience. Well, what's the mechanism this time? He's a kind creature, very sympathetic. And he likes to think that the universe is all right from the human point of view. Hence all his explorations and speculations. Well, so long as he sticks to science he is sound enough. But his spiritual experience tells him science is all very superficial. Right, again; but his is not very deep spiritual experience, and it gets all mixed up with kindliness, and he tells us things about the universe that are sheer inventions of his kindliness."

John paused. Then with a sigh he resumed. "It's no good going on about it. The upshot is simple enough. *Homo sapiens* is at the end of his tether, and I'm not going to spend my life tinkering a doomed species."

"You're mighty sure of yourself, aren't you?" I put in. "Yes," he said, "perfectly sure of myself in some ways, and still utterly unsure in others, in ways I can't explain. But one thing is stark clear. If I were to take over *Hom. sap.* I should freeze up inside, and grow quite incapable of doing what is my *real* job. *That* job is what I'm not yet sure about, and can't possibly explain. But it begins with something very *interior to me*. Of course, it's not just saving my soul. I, as an individual, might damn myself without spoiling the world. Indeed, my damning myself *might* happen to be an added beauty to the world. I don't matter on my own account, but I have it in me to do something that does matter. This I *know*. And I'm pretty sure I have to begin with—well, interior discovery of objective reality, in preparation for objective creation. Can you make anything of that?"

"Not much," I said, "but go on."

"No," he said, "I won't go on along that line, but I'll tell you something else. I've had the hell of a fright lately. And I'm not easily frightened. This was only the second time, ever. I went to the Cup Tie Final last week to see the crowd. You remember, it was a close fight (and a damned good game from beginning to end) and three minutes before time there was trouble over a foul. The ball went into goal before the referee's whistle had got going for the foul, and that goal would have won the match. Well, the crowd got all het up about it, as you probably heard. That's what frightened me. I don't mean I was scared of being hurt in a row. No, I should have quite enjoyed a bit of a row, if I'd known which side to be on, and there'd been something to fight about. But there wasn't. It clearly *was* a foul. Their precious, 'sporting instinct' ought to have kept them straight, but it didn't. They just lost their heads, went brute-mad over it. What got me was the sudden sense of being different from every one else, of being a human being alone in a vast herd of cattle. Here was a fair sample of the world's population, of the sixteen hundred millions of *Homo sapiens*. And this fair sample was expressing itself in a thoroughly characteristic way, an inarticulate bellowing and braying, and here was I, a raw, ignorant, blundering little creature, but human, *really* human, perhaps the only real human being in the world; and just because I was really human, and had in me the possibility of some new and transcendent spiritual achievement, I was more important than all the rest of the sixteen hundred million put together. That was a terrifying thought in itself. What made matters worse was the bellowing crowd. Not that I was afraid of *them,* but of the thing they were a sample of. Not that I was afraid as a private individual, so to speak. The thought was very exhilarating from that point of view. If they had turned on me I'd have made a damned good fight for it. What terrified me was the thought of the immense responsibility, and the immense odds against my fulfilling it."

John fell silent; and I was so stunned by his prodigious self-importance that I had nothing to say. Presently he began again.

"Of course I know, Fido old thing, the whole business must seem fantastic to you. But, perhaps, by being a bit more precise on one point I may make the thing clearer. It's already pretty common knowledge of course that another world-war is likely, and that if it does come it may very well be the end of civilization. But I know something that makes the whole situation look much worse than it's generally thought to be. I don't really *know* what will happen to the species in the long run, but I do know that unless a miracle happens there is *bound* to be a most ghastly mess in the short run for psychological reasons. I have looked pretty carefully into lots of minds, big and little, and it's devastatingly clear to me that in big matters *Homo sapiens* is a species with very slight educable capacity. He has entirely failed to learn his lesson from the last war. He shows no more practical intelligence than a moth that has fluttered through a candle-flame once and will do so again as soon as it has recovered from the shock. And again and yet again, till its wings are burnt. Intellectually many people realize the danger. But they are not the sort to act on the awareness. It's as though the moth *knew* that the flame meant death, yet simply couldn't stop its wings from taking it there. Then what with this new crazy religion of nationalism that's beginning, and the steady improvement in the technique of destruction, a huge disaster is simply inevitable, barring a miracle, which of course *may* happen. There *might* be some sort of sudden leap forward to a more human mentality, and therefore a world-wide social and religious revolution. But apart from that possibility I should give the disease fifteen to twenty years to come to a head. Then one fine day a few great powers will attack one another, and—phut! Civilization will have gone in a few weeks. Now, of course, if I took charge I could probably stave off the smash. But, as I say, it would mean chucking the really *vital* thing I can do. Chicken-farming is not worth such a sacrifice. The upshot is, Fido,

I'm through with your bloody awful species. I must strike out on my own, and, if possible, in such a way as to avoid being smashed in the coming disaster."

CHAPTER XI

STRANGE ENCOUNTERS

THE grave decision about the plight of *Homo sapiens* seems to have occurred at a time when John's own development had ripened him for a far-reaching spiritual crisis. Some weeks after the incident which I have just described he seemed to retire within himself more than ever, and to shun companionship even with those who had counted themselves among his friends. His former lively interest in the strange creatures among whom he lived apparently evaporated. His conversation became perfunctory; save on rare occasions when he flared up into hostile arrogance. Sometimes he seemed to long for intimacy and yet be quite unable to attain it. He would persuade me to go off with him for a day on the hills or for an evening at the theatre, and after a brave effort to restore our accustomed relationship, he would fall miserably silent, scarcely listening to my attempts at conversation. Or he would dog his mother's footsteps for a while, and yet find nothing to say to her. She was thoroughly frightened about his state, and indeed feared that "his brain was giving out," so blankly miserable and speechless could he be. One night, so she told me, she heard sounds in his room and crept in to see what was the matter. He was "sobbing like a child that can't wake from a bad dream." She stroked his head and begged him to tell her all about it. Still sobbing, he said, "Oh, Pax, I'm so *lonely*."

When this distressful state of affairs had lasted many weeks, John disappeared from home. His parents were well used to absences of a few days, but this time they received a post card, bearing a Scotch postmark, saying that he was going to have a holiday in the mountains, and would not be back "for quite a long time."

A month later, when we were beginning to feel anxious about him, an acquaintance of mine, Ted Brinston, who knew that John had disappeared, told me that a friend of his, McWhist, who was a rock-climber, had encountered "a sort of wild boy in the mountains of northern Scotland." He offered to put me in touch with McWhist.

After some delay Brinston asked me to dine with him to meet McWhist and his climbing companion, Norton. When the occasion arrived I was surprised and disconcerted to find that both men seemed reluctant to speak frankly about the incident that had brought us four together. Alcohol, however, or my anxiety about John, finally broke down their reluctance. They had been exploring the little-known crags of Ross and Cromarty, pitching their tent for a few days at a time beside a handy burn or loch. One hot day, as they were climbing a grassy spur of a mountain (which they refused to name) they heard a strange noise, apparently coming from the head of the glen to the right of them. They were so intrigued by its half-animal, half-human character that they went in search of its cause. Presently they came down to the stream and encountered a naked boy sitting beside a little waterfall and chanting or howling "in a way that gave me the creeps," said McWhist. The lad saw them and fled, disappearing among the birch-trees. They searched, but could not find him.

A few days later they told this story in a little public-house. A red-bearded native, who had not drunk too little, immediately retailed a number of yarns about encounters with such a lad—if it *was* a lad, and not some sort of kelpie. The good man's own sister-in-law's nephew said he had actually chased him and seen him turn into a wisp of mist. Another had come face to face with him round a rock, and the creature's eyes were as large as cannon balls, and black as hell.

Later in the week the climbers came upon the wild boy again. They had been climbing a rather difficult chimney, and had reached a point where further direct ascent seemed impossible. McWhist, who was leading, had just brought his second man up, and was preparing to traverse round a very exposed buttress in search of a feasible route. Suddenly a small hand appeared round the far side of the buttress, feeling for a hold. A moment later a lean brown shoulder edged its way round into view, followed by the strangest face that McWhist had ever seen. From his description I judged confidently that it was John. I was disturbed by the stress that McWhist laid on the leanness of the face. The cheeks seemed to have shrunk to pieces of leather, and there was a startling brightness about the eyes. No sooner had John appeared than his face took on an expression of disgust almost amounting to horror, and he vanished back round the buttress. McWhist traversed out to catch a view of him again. John was already half-way down a smooth face of rock which the climbers had attempted on the way up and then rejected in favour of the chimney. Recounting the incident, McWhist ejaculated. "God! The lad could climb! He *oozed* from hold to hold." When John reached the bottom of the bad pitch, he cut away to the left and disappeared.

Their final encounter with John was more prolonged. They were groping their way down the mountain late one evening in a blizzard. They were both wet through. The wind was so violent that they could hardly make headway against it. Presently they realized that they had missed their way in the cloud, and were on the wrong spur of the mountain. Finally they found themselves hemmed in by precipices, but they roped themselves and managed to climb down a gully or wide chimney, choked with fallen rocks. Half-way down, they were surprised to smell smoke, and saw it issuing from behind a great slab jammed in an angle of rocks beside their route. With considerable difficulty McWhist worked his way by rare and precarious holds over to a little platform near the smoking slab, and Norton followed. Light came from under it and behind it. A step or two of scrambling brought them to the illuminated space between one end of the slab and the cliff. The sides and opposite end of the slab were jammed in a mass of lesser rocks, and held in position by the two sides of the chimney. Stooping, they peered through the bright hole into a little irregular cave, which was lit by a fire of peat and heather. Stretched on a bed of dried grass and heather lay John. He was gazing into the fire, and his face was streaming with tears. He was naked, but there was a jumble of deer-skin beside him. By the fire was part of a cooked bird on a flat stone.

Feeling unaccountably abashed by the tears of this strange lad, the climbers quietly withdrew. Whispering together, however, they decided that they really must do something about him. Therefore, making a noise on the rocks with their boots as though in the act of reaching the cave, they remained out of sight while McWhist demanded, "Is anyone there?" No answer was given. Once more they peered through the tiny entrance. John lay as before, and took no notice. Near the bird lay a stout bone knife or dirk, obviously "home-made," but carefully pointed and edged. Other implements of bone or antler were scattered about. Some of them were decorated with engraved patterns. There was also a sort of pan-pipe of reeds and a pair of hide sandals or moccasins. The climbers were struck by the fact that there were no traces whatever of civilization, nothing, for instance, that was made of metal.

Cautiously they spoke again, but still John took no notice. McWhist crept through the entrance, noisily, and laid a hand on the boy's bare foot, gently shaking it. John slowly looked round and stared in a puzzled way at the intruder; then suddenly his whole form came alive with hostile intelligence. He sprang into a crouching posture, clutching a sort of stiletto made of the largest tine of an antler. McWhist was so startled by the huge glaring eyes and the inhuman snarl that he backed out of the cramping entrance of the cave.

"Then," said McWhist, "an odd thing happened. The boy's anger seemed to vanish, and he stared intently at me as though I were a strange beast that he had never seen before. Suddenly he seemed to think of something else. He dropped his weapon, and began gazing into the fire again with that look of utter misery. Tears welled in his eyes again. His mouth twisted itself in a kind of desperate smile."

Here McWhist paused in his narrative, looking both distressed and awkward. He sucked violently at his pipe. At last he proceeded.

"Obviously we couldn't leave the kid like that, so I asked cautiously if we could do anything for him. He did not answer. I crept in again, and squatted beside him, waiting. As gently as I could I put a hand on his knee. He gave a start and a shudder, looked at me with a frown, as if trying to get things straight in his mind, made a quick movement for the stiletto, checked himself, and finally broke into a wry boyish grin, remarking, 'Oh, come in, please. Don't knock, it's a shop.' He added, 'Can't you blighters leave a fellow alone?' I said we had come upon him quite by accident, but of course we couldn't help being puzzled about him. I said we'd been very struck with his climbing, the other day. I said it seemed a pity for him to be stuck up here alone. Wouldn't he come along with us? He shook his head, smiling, and said he was quite all right there. He was just having a bit of a rough holiday, and thinking about things. At first it had been difficult feeding himself, but now he'd got the technique, and there was plenty of time for the thinking. Then he laughed. A sudden sharp crackle it was that made my scalp tingle."

Here Norton broke in and said, "I had crawled into the cave by then, and I was terribly struck by the gaunt condition he was in. There wasn't a bit of fat on him anywhere. His muscles looked like skeins of cord under his skin. He was covered with scars and bruises. But the most disturbing thing was the look on his face, a look that I have only seen on some one that had just come out of the anæsthetic after a bad op.—sort of purified. Poor kid, he'd evidently been through it all right, but through what?"

"At first," said McWhist, "we thought he was mad. But now I'm ready to swear he wasn't. He was possessed. Something that we don't know anything about had got him, something good or bad, I don't know which. The whole business gave me the creeps, what with the noise of the storm outside, and the dim firelight, and the smoke that kept blowing back on us down the sort of chimney he'd made for it. We were a bit light-headed with lack of food, too. He offered us the rest of his bird, by the way, and some bilberries, but of course we didn't want to run him short. We asked if there wasn't *anything* we could do for him, and he answered, yes, there was, we could make a special point of not telling anyone about him. I said, couldn't we take a message to his people. He grew very serious and emphatic, and said, 'No, don't tell a soul, not a soul. Forget. If the papers get on to my tracks,' he said very slowly and coldly, 'I shall just have to kill myself.' This put us in a hole. We felt we really ought to do something and yet somehow we felt we *must* promise."

McWhist paused, then said crossly, "And we did promise. And then we cleared out, and floundered about in the dark till we reached our tent. We roped to get down the rock, and the lad went in front, unroped, to show us the way." He paused again, then added, "The other day when I happened to hear from Brinston about your lost lad, I broke my promise. And now I'm feeling damned bad about it."

I laughed, and said, "Well, no harm's done. *I* shan't tell the Press."

Norton spoke again. "It's not as simple as that. There's something McWhist hasn't told you yet. Go on, Mac."

"Tell him yourself," said McWhist, "I'd rather not."

There was a pause, then Norton laughed awkwardly, and said, "Well, when one tries to describe it in cold blood over a cup of coffee, it just sounds crazy. But damn it, if the thing *didn't* happen, something mighty queer must have happened to *us*, for we both saw it, as clearly as you see us now."

He paused. McWhist rose from his arm-chair and began examining the rows of books on shelves behind us.

Norton proceeded: "The lad said something about making us realize we'd come up against something big that we couldn't understand, said he'd give us something to remember, and help us to keep the secret. His voice had changed oddly. It was very low and quiet and composed. He stretched his skinny arm up to the roof, saying, 'This slab must weigh fifty tons. Above it there's just blizzard. You can see the raindrops in the doorway there.' He pointed to the cave entrance. 'What of it?' he said in a cold proud voice. 'Let us see the stars.' Then, my God, you won't believe it, of course, but the boy lifted that blasted rock upon his finger-tips like a trap door. A terrific gust of wind and sleet entered, but immediately died away. As he lifted he rose to his feet. Overhead was a windless, clear, starry sky. The smoke of the fire rose as a wavering column, illuminated at the base, and spreading dimly far above us, where it blotted out a few stars with a trail of darkness. He pushed the rock back till it was upright, then leaned lightly against it with one arm, crooking the other on his hip. 'There!' he said. In the starlight and firelight I could see his face as he gazed upwards. Transfigured, I should call it, bright, keen, peaceful.

"He stayed still for perhaps half a minute, and silent; then, looking down at us, he smiled, and said, 'Don't forget. We have looked at the stars together.' Then he gently lowered the rock into position again, and said, 'I think you had better go now. I'll take you down the first pitch. It's difficult by night.' As we were both pretty well paralysed with bewilderment we made no immediate sign of quitting. He laughed, gently, reassuringly, and said something that has haunted me ever since. (I don't know about McWhist.) He said, 'It was a childish miracle. But I am still a child. While the spirit is in the agony of outgrowing its childishness, it may solace itself now and then by returning to its playthings, knowing well that they are trivial.' By now we were creeping out of the cave, and into the blizzard."

There was a silence. Presently McWhist faced us again, and glared rather wildly at Norton. "We were given a great sign," he said, "and we have been unfaithful."

I tried to calm him by saying, "Unfaithful in the letter, perhaps, but not in the spirit. I'm pretty sure John wouldn't mind *my* knowing. And as to the miracle, I wouldn't worry about that," I said, with more confidence than I felt. "He probably hypnotized you both in some odd sort of way. He's a weird kid."

Toward the end of the summer Pax received a post card, saying "Home late to-morrow. Hot bath, please. John."

On the first opportunity I had a long talk with John about his holiday. It was a surprise to me to find that he was ready to talk with perfect frankness, and that he had apparently quite got over the phase of uncommunicative misery which had caused us so much anxiety before his flight from home. I doubt if I really understood what he told me, and I am sure there was a good deal that he didn't tell me because he knew I wouldn't understand. I had a sense that he was all the while trying to *translate* his actual thoughts into language intelligible to me, and that the translation seemed to him very crude. I can give only so much of his statement as I understood.

CHAPTER XII

JOHN IN THE WILDERNESS

JOHN said that when he had begun to realize the tragic futility of *Homo sapiens* he was seized with "a panicky sense of doom," and along with that "a passion of loneliness." He felt more lonely in the presence of others than in isolation. At the same time, apparently, something strange was happening to his own mind. At first he thought perhaps he was going mad, but clung to the faith that he was after all merely growing up. Anyhow he was convinced that he must cut right adrift and face this upheaval in himself undisturbed. It was as though a grub were to feel premonitions of dissolution and regeneration, and to set purposefully about protecting itself with a cocoon.

Further, if I understood him, he felt spiritually contaminated by contact with the civilization of *Homo sapiens*. He felt he must for a while at least strip away every vestige of it from his own person, face the universe in absolute nakedness, prove that he could stand by himself, without depending in any way whatever on the primitive and debased creatures who dominated the planet. At first I thought this hunger for the simple life was merely an excuse for a boyish adventure, but now I realize that it did have for him a grave importance which I could only dimly comprehend.

Of some such kind were the motives that drove him into the wildest region of this island. The thoroughness with which he carried out his plan amazed me. He simply walked out of a Highland railway station, had a good meal in an inn, strode up on to the moors toward the high mountains, and, when he judged himself safe from interruption, took off all his clothes, including his shoes, and buried them in a hole among the rocks. He then took his bearings carefully, so as to be able to recover his prop erty in due season, and moved away in his nakedness, seeking food and shelter in the wilderness.

His first days were evidently a terrible ordeal. The weather turned wet and cold. John, it must be remembered, was an extremely hardy creature, and he had prepared himself for this adventure by a course of exposure, and by studying beforehand all possible means of securing food in the valleys and moors of Scotland without so much as a knife or a piece of string to aid him. But fate was at first against him. The bad weather made shelter a necessity, and in seeking it he had to spend much time that might otherwise have been spent in the search for food.

He passed the first night under a projecting rock, wrapped in heather and grass that he had collected before the weather broke. Next day he caught a frog, dismembered it with a sharp stone, and ate it raw. He also ate large quantities of dandelion leaves, and other green stuff which from previous study he knew to be edible. Certain fungi, too, contributed to his diet on that day, and indeed throughout his adventure. On the second day he was feeling "pretty queer." On the third evening he was in a high fever, with a bad cough and diarrhœa. On the previous day, foreseeing possible illness, he had greatly improved his shelter, and laid by a store of such food as he considered least indigestible. For some days, he didn't know how long, he lay desperately sick, scarcely able to crawl to the stream for water. "I must have been delirious at one time," he said, "because I seemed to have a visit from Pax. Then I came to and found there wasn't any Pax, and I thought I was dying, and I loved myself desperately, knowing I was indeed a rare bright thing. And it was torture to be just wasted like that. And then that unspeakable joy came, that joy of seeing things as it were through God's eyes, and finding them after all *right,* fitting, in the picture." There followed a few days of convalescence, during which, he said, "I seemed to have lost touch completely with all the motives of my adventure. I just lay and wondered why I had been such a self-important fool. Fortunately, before I was strong enough to crawl back to civilization I lashed myself into facing this spiritual decay. For even in my most abject state I vaguely *knew* that somewhere there was another 'I,' and a better one. Well, I set my teeth and determined to go on with the job even if it killed me."

Soon after he had come to this decision some local boys with a dog came up the hill right on to his hiding-place. He leapt up and fled. They must have caught a glimpse of his small naked figure, for they gave chase, hallooing excitedly. As soon as he was on his feet he realized that his legs were like water. He collapsed. "But then," he said, "I suddenly managed to tap some deep reserve of vitality, so to speak. I simply jumped up and ran like hell round a corner of hillside, and farther, to a rocky place. There I climbed a pretty bad pitch into a hole I knew of and had counted on. Then I must have fainted. In fact, I think I must have lain unconscious for

almost twenty-four hours, for when I came to, the sun seemed to have gone
back to early morning. I was cold as death, and one huge ache, and so
weak I couldn't move from the twisted position I was in."

Later in the day he managed to crawl back to his lair, and with great
difficulty moved his bedding to a safer but less comfortable spot. The
weather was now hot and bright. For ten days or so he spent nearly all
his time creeping about in search of frogs, lizards, snails, birds' eggs and
green stuff, or just lying in the sun recovering his strength. Sometimes he
managed to catch a few fish by "tickling" them in a pool in the river. The
whole of one day he spent in trying to get a flame by striking sparks from
stones on a handful of dry grass. At last he succeeded, and began to cook
his meal, in an ecstasy of pride and anticipation. Suddenly he noticed a
man, far away but obviously interested in the smoke of his fire. He put
it out at once and decided to go much farther into the wilds.

Meanwhile, though his feet had been hardened with long practice at
home, they were now terribly sore, and quite unfit for "a walking tour."
He made moccasins out of ropes of twisted grass which he bound round
his feet and ankles. They kept in place for a while, but were always either
coming undone or wearing through. After many days of exploration, and
several nights without shelter, two of which were wet, he found the high
cave where later the climbers discovered him. "It was only just in time,"
he said. "I was in a pretty bad state. Feet swollen and bleeding, ghastly
cough, diarrhœa. But in that cave I soon felt snugger than I had ever felt
in my life, by contrast with the past few weeks. I made myself a *lovely*
bed, and a fireplace, and I felt fairly safe from intrusion, because mine was
a remote mountain, and anyhow very few people could climb those rocks.
Not far below there were grouse and ptarmigan; and deer. On my first
morning, sitting in the sun on my roof, positively happy, I watched a herd
of them crossing a moor, stepping so finely, ears spread, heads high."

The deer seem to have become his chief interest for a while. He was
fascinated by their beauty and freedom. True, they now depended for their
existence on a luxurious civilization; but equally they had existed before
there was any civilization at all. Moreover, he coveted the huge material
wealth that the slaughter of one stag would afford him. And he had apparently a queer lust to try his strength and cunning against a worthy
quarry. For at this time he was content to be almost wholly the primitive
hunter, "though with a recollection, away at the back of my mind, that
all this was just a process of getting clean in spirit for a very different
enterprise."

For ten days or so he did little but devise means for catching birds
and hares, and spent all spare time in resting, recuperating, and brooding
over the deer. His first hare, caught after many failures, he took by arranging a trap in its runway. A huge stone was precariously held in position
by a light stick, which the creature dislodged. Its back was broken. But

a fox ate most of it in the night. From its skin, however, he made a rough bow-string, also soles and thongs for his foot-gear. By splitting its thigh bones and filing them on the rock he made some fragile little knives to help him in preparing his food. Also he made some minute sharp arrow-heads. With a diversity of traps, and his toy bow and arrows, and vast patience and aptitude, he managed to secure enough game to restore him to normal strength. Practically his whole time was spent in hunting, trapping, cooking, making little tools of bone or wood or stone. Every night he rolled himself in his grass bedding dead tired, but at peace. Sometimes he took his bedding outside the cave and slept on a ledge of the precipice, under stars and driving cloud.

But there were the deer; and beyond them the spiritual problem which was the real motive of his adventure, and had not yet been consciously faced at all. It was clear that if he did not greatly improve his way of life, he would have no time for that concentrated meditation and spiritual exercise which he so greatly needed. The killing of the stag became a symbol for him. The thought of it stirred unwonted feelings in him. "It was as though all the hunters of the past challenged me," he said, "and as though, as though—well, as though the angels of God ordered me to do this little mighty deed in preparation for mightier deeds to come. I dreamt of stags, of their beauty and power and speed. I schemed and plotted, and rejected every plan. I stalked the herd, weaponless, intent only on learning their ways. One day I came upon some deer-stalkers, and I stalked them too, until they brought down a stag of ten; and how I despised them for their easy slaughter. To me they were just vermin preying upon *my* game. But when I had thought that thought, I laughed at myself; for *I* had no more right to the creatures than any one else."

The story of how John finally took his stag seemed to me almost incredible, yet I could not but believe it. He had marked down as his quarry the finest beast of the herd, an eight-year-old monarch, bearing besides his brow, bay and tray, "three on top" on the right, and four on the left. The weight of antler gave his head a superb poise. One day John and the stag met one another face to face round a shoulder of moor. They stood for full three seconds, twenty paces apart, gazing at one another, the stag's wide nostrils taking the scent of him. Then the beast swung round and cantered easefully away.

When John described that meeting, his strange eyes seemed to glow with dark fire. He said, I remember, "With my soul I saluted him. Then I pitied him, because he was doomed, and in the prime. But I remembered that I too was doomed. I suddenly knew that I should never reach my prime. And I laughed aloud, for him and for me, because life is brief and wild, and death too is in the picture."

John took long to decide on the method of his attack. Should he dig a pit for him, or lasso him with a cord of hide, or set a mighty stone to fell him, or pierce him with a bone-pointed arrow? Few of these devices seemed practicable; all but the last seemed ugly, and that last was not practicable. For some time he busied himself making dirks of various kinds, of wood, of the fragile bones of hares, of keen stone splinters from a neighbouring mountain. Patient experiment produced at last a preposterous little stiletto of hard wood pointed with bone, the whole "streamlined" by filing upon the rock. With this fantastic weapon and his knowledge of anatomy, he proposed to leap on the stag from a hiding-place and pierce its heart. And this in the end he did, after many days of fruitless stalking and waiting. There was a little glade where the deer sometimes grazed, and beside it a rock some ten feet high. On the top of this rock he secreted himself early one morning, when the wind was such that his scent would not betray him. The great stag came round the shoulder of hill, attended by three hinds. Cautiously they sniffed and peered; then, at last, lowered their heads and peacefully grazed. Hour after hour John lay, waiting for the right beast to stray below the rock. But it was as though the stag deliberately avoided the danger-spot. Finally the four deer left the glade. Two more days were spent in vain watching. Not till the fourth day did John leap from the rock upon the back of the grazing stag, bringing it down with its right flank to the ground. Before the creature could regain its feet John had thrust his primitive weapon home with all his weight. The stag half righted itself, wildly swung its antlers, tearing John's arm, then collapsed. And John, to his own surprise, behaved in a style most unseemly in a hunter. For the third time in his life, he burst into spontaneous tears.

For days afterwards he struggled to dismember the carcass with his inadequate implements. This task proved even more difficult than the killing, but in the end he found himself with a large quantity of meat, an invaluable hide, and the antlers, which, with desperate efforts, he smashed in pieces with a great stone and worked up as knives and other tools, by scraping them on the rocks.

At the end he could hardly lift his hands with fatigue, and they were covered with bleeding blisters. But the deed was accomplished. The hunters of all the ages saluted him, for he had done what none of them could have done. A child, he had gone naked into the wilderness and conquered it. And the angels of heaven smiled at him, and beckoned him to a higher adventure.

John's way of life now changed. It had become a fairly easy matter for him to keep himself alive, and even in comfort. He set his traps, and let fly his arrows, and gathered his green things; but all was now routine work. He was able to carry it out while giving his best attention to the strange and disturbing events which were beginning to occur within his own mind.

It is obviously quite impossible for me to give anything like a true account of the spiritual side of John's adventure in the wilderness. Yet to ignore it would be to ignore all that was most distinctive in John. I must at least try to set down as much of it as I was able to understand, for that little seems to me to have real significance for beings of my own species. Even if as a matter of fact I have merely misunderstood what he told me, my misunderstanding afforded at least to me a real enlightenment.

For a time he seems to have been chiefly concerned with art. He "sang against the waterfall." He made and played his pan-pipes, apparently adopting some weird scale of his own. He played strange themes and figures on the shores of the loch, in the woods, on the mountain-tops, and in his rock home. He decorated his tools with engraved angles and curves consonant with their form and use. On pieces of bone and stone he recorded symbolically his adventures with fish and birds; and with the stag. He devised strange shapes which epitomized for him the tragedy of *Homo sapiens,* and the promise of his own kind. At the same time he was allowing the perceptual forms with which he was surrounded to work themselves deeply into his mind. He accepted with insight the quality of moor and sky and crag. From the bottom of his heart he gave thanks for all these subtle contacts with material reality; and found in them a spiritual refreshment which we also find, though confusedly and grudgingly. He was also constantly, and ever surprisingly, illuminated by the beauty of the beasts and birds on which he preyed, a beauty significant of their power and their frailty, their vitality and their obtuseness. Such perceived organic forms seem to have moved him far more deeply than I could comprehend. The stag, in particular, that he had killed and devoured, and now daily used, seems to have had some deep symbolism for him which I could but dimly appreciate, and will not attempt to describe. I remember his exclaiming, "How I knew him and praised him! And his death was his life's crown."

This remark epitomized, I believe, some new enlightenment which John was now receiving about himself and about *Homo sapiens* and indeed about all living things. The actual nature of that enlightenment I find it impossible to conceive, but certain dim reflections of it I do seem able to detect, and must try to record.

It will be remembered that John had shown, even as an infant, a surprising detachment and strange relish in situations in which he himself was the sufferer. Referring to this, he now said, "I could always enjoy the 'realness' and the *neatness* of my own pains and griefs, even while I detested them. But now I found myself faced with something of quite a new order of horribleness, and one which I could not get into place. Hitherto my distresses had been merely isolated smarts and temporary frustrations, but now I saw my whole future as something at once much more vivid and much more painfully frustrated than anything I had conceived. You see, I knew so clearly by now that I was a unique being, far more awake than other people. I was beginning to understand myself and discover all sorts of new and exquisite capacities in myself; and at the same time I saw now all too clearly that I was up against a savage race which would never tolerate me or my kind, and would sooner or later smash me with its brute weight. And when I told myself that after all this didn't really matter, and that I was just a little self-important microbe making a fuss over nothing, something in me cried out imperiously that, even if *I* was of no account, the things I could *do,* the *beauty* I could make, and the *worship* that I was now beginning to conceive, did most emphatically matter, and *must* be brought to fruition. And I saw that there would be no fruition, that the exquisite things that it was my office to do would never be done. This was a sort of agony altogether different from anything that my adolescent mind had ever known."

While he was wrestling with this horror, and before he had triumphed over it, there came upon him the realization that for members of the normal species *every* pain, *every* distress of body and of mind, had this character of insurmountable hideousness which he himself had found only in respect of the highest reach of his experience, and was determined to conquer even there. It came as a shocking revelation to him that normal human beings were quite incapable of detachment and zest even in sufferings upon the personal plane. In fact he realized clearly for the first time the torture that lies in wait at every turn for beings who are more sensitive and more awakened than the beasts and yet not sensitive enough, not fully awakened. The thought of the agony of this world of nightmare-ridden half-men crushed him as nothing else had ever done.

His attitude to the normal species was undergoing a great change. When he had fled into the wilderness his dominant reaction was disgust. One or two of us he unreasonably cherished, but as a species he loathed us. He had recently seen too much, lived at too close quarters, been fouled and poisoned. His researches into the world of men had been too devastating for a mind which, though superior in quality, was immature and delicate. But the wild had cleansed him, healed him, brought him to sanity again. He could now put *Homo sapiens* at arm's length for study and appreciation. And he saw that, though no divinity, the creature was after all a noble and even a lovable beast, indeed the noblest and most lovable of them all; nay further, that its very repulsiveness lay in its being something more than beast, but not enough more. A normal human being, he now ungrudgingly admitted, was indeed a spirit of a higher order than any beast, though in the main obtuse, heartless, unfaithful to the best in himself.

Realizing all this, and realizing for the first time the incapacity of *Homo sapiens* to accept his pains and sorrows with equanimity, John was overwhelmed with pity, a passion which he had not hitherto experienced in any intensity; save on particular occasions, as when Judy's dog was run over by a car, and when Pax was ill and in great pain. And even then his pity was always tempered by his assumption that every one, even little Judy, could always "look at it from outside and enjoy it," as he himself could do.

For many days John seems to have been at grips with this newly realized problem of the absoluteness of evil, and the novel fact that beings that were tissues of folly and baseness could yet be pitiable and, in their kind, beautiful. What he sought was not an intellectual solution but an emotional enlightenment. And this, little by little, he seems to have gained. When I pressed him to tell me more of this strange enlightenment, he said it was just "seeing my own fate and the piteous plight of the normal species in the same way as I had always, since I was a kid, seen bumps and burns and disappointments. It was a case of delighting in their clear-cut form, and in their unity with the rest of things, and the way they—how shall I put it?—deepened and quickened the universe." Here, I remember, John paused, then repeated, "Yes, deepened and quickened the universe,—that's the main point. But it wasn't a case of *understanding* that they did so, but just *seeing* and *feeling* that they did so."

I asked him if what he meant was some kind of coming face to face with God. He laughed, and said, "What do I know about God? No more than the Archbishop of Canterbury, and that's nothing whatever."

He said that when McWhist and Norton came upon him in the cave he was "still desperately puzzling things out," and that their presence filled him just for a moment with the old disgust at their species, but that he had really done with all that long ago, and when he saw them there, looking so blank, he remembered his first close meeting with the stag. And suddenly the stag seemed to symbolize the whole normal human species, as a thing with a great beauty and dignity of its own, and a rightness of its own, so long as it was not put into situations too difficult for it. *Homo sapiens,* poor thing, *had* floundered into a situation too difficult for him, namely the present world-situation. The thought of *Homo sapiens* trying to run a mechanized civilization suddenly seemed to him as ludicrous and pathetic as the thought of a stag in the driving-seat of a motor-car.

I took this opportunity of asking him about the "miracle" with which he had so impressed his visitors. He laughed again. "Well," he said, "I had been discovering all sorts of odd powers. For instance I found that by a kind of telepathy I could get in touch with Pax and talk to her. It's true. You can ask her about it. Also I could sometimes feel what *you* were thinking about, though you were too dull to catch my messages and respond to me. And I had made queer little visits to events in my own past life. I just lived them again, with full vividness, as though they were 'now.' And in a telepathic way I had begun to get something very like evidence that after all I was not the only one of my kind in the world, that there were in fact quite a number of us scattered about in different countries.

And then again, when McWhist and Norton appeared in the cave I found that by looking at them I could read the whole of their past lives in their faces, and I saw how thoroughly sound they both were within the limitations of their kind! And I *think* I saw something about their future, something that I won't tell you. Then, when it was necessary to impress them, I suddenly got the idea of lifting the roof and clearing away the blizzard so that we could see the stars. And I knew perfectly well that I could do it, so I did it."

I looked at John with misgiving. "Oh yes," he said, "I know you think I'm mad, and that all I did was to hypnotize them. Well, put it that I hypnotized myself too, for I *saw* the whole thing as clearly as they did. But, believe me, to say I hypnotized us all is no more true and no less true than to say I actually shifted the rock and the blizzard. The truth of the matter was something much more subtle and tremendous than any plain little physical miracle could ever be. But never mind that. The important thing was that, when I did see the stars (riotously darting in all directions according to the caprice of their own wild natures, yet in every movement confirming the law), the whole tangled horror that had tormented me finally presented itself to me in its true and beautiful shape. And I knew that the first, blind stage of my childhood had ended."

I had indeed sensed a change in John. Even physically he had altered strikingly during his six months' absence. He was harder, more close-knit; and there were lines on his face suggestive of ordeals triumphantly passed. Mentally, though still capable of a most disconcerting impishness, he had also acquired that indefinable peacefulness and strength which is quite impossible to the adolescent of the normal species, and is very seldom acquired even by the mature. He himself said that his "discovery of sheer evil" had fortified him. When I asked, "how fortified?" he said, "My dear, it is a great strength to have faced the worst and to have *felt* it a feature of beauty. Nothing ever after can shake one."

He was right. By what magic he did it I do not know, but in all his future, and in the final destruction of all that he most cherished, he accepted the worst not with resignation, merely, but with a strange joy that must remain to the rest of us incomprehensible.

I will mention one other point that emerged in my long talk with John. It will be remembered that after performing his "miracle" he apologized for it. I questioned him on this matter, and he said something like this: "To enjoy exercising one's powers is healthy. Children enjoy learning to walk. Artists enjoy painting pictures. As a baby I exulted in the tricks I could do with numbers, and later in my inventions, and recently in killing my stag. And of course the full exercise of one's powers really is part of the life of the spirit. But it is only a part, and sometimes we are inclined to take it as the whole purpose of our existence, especially when we discover new powers. Well, in Scotland, when I began to come into all those queer powers that I mentioned just now, I was tempted to regard the exercise of them as the true end of my life. I said to myself, 'Now at last, in these wonderful ways, I shall indeed advance the spirit.' But after the momentary exaltation of lifting the rock I saw clearly that such acts were in no sense the goal of the spirit, but just a by-play of its true life, amusing, and sometimes useful, and often dangerous, but never themselves the goal."

"Then tell me," I said, perhaps rather excitedly, "what *is* the goal, the true life of the spirit?" John suddenly grinned like a boy of ten, and laughed that damnably disturbing laugh of his. "I'm afraid I can't tell you, Mr. Journalist," he said. "It is time your interview was concluded. Even if I *knew* what the true life of the spirit was, I couldn't put it into English, or any 'sapient' language. And if I could, you wouldn't understand." After a pause he added, "Perhaps we might safely say this much about it anyhow. It's not doing any one particular kind of thing, like miracles, or even good deeds. It's doing everything that comes along to be done, and doing it not only with all one's might but with—spiritual taste, discrimination, *full* consciousness of what one is doing. Yes, it's that. And it's more. It's—praise of life, and of all things in their true setting." Once more he laughed, and said, "What stuff! To describe the spiritual life, we should have to remake language from the foundations upwards."

CHAPTER XIII

JOHN SEEKS HIS KIND

FOR many weeks after his return from the wilderness John spent a good deal of his time at home, or in the neighbouring city. Apparently he was content to sink back into the interests of the normal adolescent. He resumed his friendship with Stephen, and with Judy. Often he took the child to a picture show, a circus, or any entertainment suited to her years. He acquired a motor-bicycle, on which, upon the very day of the purchase, Judy was treated to a wild ride. The neighbours said that John's holiday had done him good. He was much more normal now. With his brother and sister too, on the rare occasions when he met them, John became more fraternal. Anne was now married. Tom was a successful young architect. The two brothers had generally maintained a relation of restrained hostility to one another, but now hostility seemed to have mellowed into mutual tolerance. After a family reunion Tom remarked, "Our infant prodigy's positively growing up." Doc was delighted by John's new companionableness, and often talked to him at great length. Their main topic was John's future. Doc was anxious to persuade him to take to medicine and become "a greater Lister." John used to attend to these exhortations thoughtfully, seeming to be almost persuaded. Once Pax was present. She shook her head, smilingly but reprovingly at John. "Don't believe him, Doc," she said, "he's pulling your leg." In this period, by the way, John and Pax often went together to a theatre or concert. Indeed, mother and son were now seeing a great deal of each other. Pax's interest in the drama, and in "persons," seemed to afford him an unfailing common platform. Occasionally they even went up to London together for a week-end, "to see the shows."

There came a time when I began to feel a certain curiosity as to the meaning of this prolonged period of relaxation. John's behaviour seemed now almost completely normal. There was, indeed, one unusual but unobstrusive feature about it. In the midst of conversation or any other activity he would sometimes give a noticeable start of surprise. He would then perhaps repeat the immediately preceding remark, whether his own or the other person's; and then he would look around him with amused interest. I fancied that for some time after such an incident he was more alert than before it. Not that in the earlier stage he had seemed at all absent-minded. He was at all times thoroughly adjusted to his surroundings. But after these curious jerks the current of his life seemed to reach a higher tension.

One evening I accompanied the three Wainwrights to the local Repertory Theatre. During an interval, while we were drinking coffee in the foyer and discussing the play, John gave a more violent start than usual, spilling his coffee into the saucer. He laughed, and looked about him with surprised interest. After a moment's awkward silence, in which Pax regarded her boy with veiled solicitude, John continued his comments on the play, but (as it seemed to me) with new penetration. "My point is just this," he said. "The thing's too lifelike to be really alive. It's not a portrait but a death-mask."

Next day I asked him what had happened when he spilt his coffee. We were in my flat. John had come to inquire if the post had brought information about some patent or other. I was at my writing-table. He was standing at the window, looking out across the deserted promenade to the wintry sea. He was chewing an apple that he had picked up from a dish on my table. "Yes," he said, "it's time you were told, even if you can't believe. At present I am looking for other people more or less like me, and to do it I become a sort of divided personality. Part of me remains where my body is, and behaves quite correctly, but the other, the essential I, goes off in search of *them*. Or if you like, I stay put all the time, but *reach out* in search of them. Anyhow, when I come back, or stop the search, I get a bit of a jolt, taking up the threads of ordinary life again."

"You never seem to *lose* the threads," I said.

"No," he answered. "The incoming 'I' comes slick into possession of all the past experiences of the residential one, so to speak. But the sudden jump from God knows where to here gives a bit of a jar, all the same."

"And when you're away," I asked, "where do you go, what do you find?"

"Well," he said, "I had better begin at the beginning. I told you before that when I was in Scotland I used to find myself in telepathic touch with people, and that some of the people seemed queer people, or people in a significant way more like me than you. Since I came home I've been working up the technique for tuning in to the people I want. Unfortunately it's much easier to pick up the thoughts of folk one knows well than of strangers. So much depends on the general form of the mind, the matrix in which the thoughts occur, so to speak. To get you or Pax I have only to think of you. I can get your actual consciousness, and if I want to, I can get a good bit of the deeper layers of you too."

I was seized with horror, but I comforted myself with incredulity.

"Oh, yes, I can," said John. "While I've been talking, half your mind was listening and the other half was thinking about a quarrel you had last night with——" I cut him short with an expostulation.

"Righto, don't get excited," said John. "*You* haven't much to be ashamed of. And anyhow I don't want to pry. But just now,—well, you kept fairly shouting the stuff at me, because while you were attending to me you were thinking about it. You'll probably soon learn how to shut me out at will."

I grunted, and John continued: "As I was saying, it's much harder to get in touch with people one doesn't know, and at first I didn't know any of the people I was looking for. On the other hand, I found that the people of my sort make, so to speak, a much bigger 'noise' telepathically than the rest. At least they do when they want to, or when they don't care. But when they want *not* to, they can shut themselves off completely. Well, at last I managed to single out from the general buzz of telepathic 'noise,' made by the normal species, a few outstanding streaks or themes that seemed to have about them something or other of the special quality that I was looking for."

John paused, and I interjected, "What sort of quality?"

He looked at me for some seconds in silence. Believe it or not, but that prolonged gaze had a really terrifying effect on me. I am not suggesting that there was something magical about it. The effect was of the same kind as any normal facial expression may have. But knowing John as I did, and remembering the strange events of his summer in Scotland, I was no doubt peculiarly susceptible. I can only describe what I felt by means of an image. It was as though I was confronted with a mask made of some semi-transparent substance, and illuminated from within by a different and a *spiritually luminous* face. The mask was that of a grotesque child, half monkey, half gargoyle, yet wholly urchin, with its huge cat's eyes, its flat little nose, its teasing lips. The inner face,—obviously it cannot be described, for it was *the same* in every feature, yet wholly different. I can only say that it seemed to me to combine the august and frozen smile of a Buddha with the peculiar creepy grimness that the battered Sphinx can radiate when the dawn first touches its face. No, these images fail utterly. I cannot describe the symbolical intention that John's features forced upon me in those seconds. I can only say that I longed to look away and could not, or dared not. Irrational terror welled up in me. When one is under the dentist's drill, one may endure a few moments of real torture without flinching. But as the seconds pile up, it becomes increasingly difficult not to move, not to scream. And so with me, looked at by John. With this difference, that I was bound, and could not stir, that I had passed the screaming point and could not scream. I believe my terror was largely a wild dread that John was about to laugh, and that his laugh would annihilate me. But he did not laugh.

Suddenly the spell broke, and I leapt up to put more coal on the fire. John was gazing out of the window, and saying, in his normal friendly voice, "Well, of course I can't *tell* you what that special quality is, can I? Think of it this way. It's seeing each thing, each event, on its *eternal* side, instead of *merely* as a dated thing; seeing it as a living leaf on the tree Yggdrasill, flushed with the sap of eternity, and not *merely* as a plucked and dried and dated specimen in the book of history."

There was a long silence, then he continued his report. "The first trace of mentality like my own gave me a lot of trouble. I could only catch occasional glimpses of this fellow, and I couldn't make him take any notice of me. And the stuff that did come through to me was terribly incoherent and bewildering. I wondered whether this was the fault of my technique, or whether his was a mind too highly developed for me to understand. I tried to find out where he was, so that I could go and see him. He was evidently living in a large building with lots of rooms and many other people. But he had very little to do with the others. Looking out of his window, he saw trees and houses and a long grassy hill. He heard an almost continuous noise of trains and motor traffic. At least *I* recognized it as that, but it didn't seem to mean much to him. Clearly, I thought, there's a main line and a main road quite close to where he lives. Somehow I must find that place. So I bought the motor-bike. Meanwhile I kept on studying him. I couldn't catch any of his thoughts, but only his perceptions, and the way he felt about them. One striking thing was his music. Sometimes when I found him he was outside the house in a sloping field with trees between it and the main road; and he would be playing a pipe, a sort of recorder, but with the octave very oddly divided. I discovered that each of his hands had *five* fingers and a thumb. Even so, I couldn't make out how he managed all the extra notes. The kind of music he played was extraordinarily fascinating to me. Something about it, the mental pose of it, made me quite sure the man was really my sort. I discovered, by the way, that he had the not very helpful name of James Jones. Once when I got him he was out in the grounds and near a gap in the trees, so that he could see the road. Presently a bus flashed past. It was a 'Green Line' bus, and it was labelled 'BRIGHTON.' I noticed with surprise that these words apparently meant nothing to James Jones. But they meant a lot to me. I went off on the bike to search the Green Line routes out of Brighton. It took me a couple of days to find the right spot—the big building, the grassy hill, and so on. I stopped and asked someone what the building was. It was a lunatic asylum."

John's narrative was interrupted by my guffaw of relief. "Funny," he said, "but not quite unexpected. After pulling lots of wires I got permission to see James Jones, who was a relative of mine, I said. They told me at the Asylum that there was a family likeness, and when I saw James Jones I knew what they meant. He's a little old man with a big head and huge eyes, like mine. He's quite bald, except for a few crisp white curls above the ears. His mouth was smaller than mine (for the size of him) and it had a sort of suffering sweetness about it, specially when he let it do a peculiar compressed pout, which was a characteristic mannerism of his. Before I saw him they had told me a bit about him. He gave no trouble, they said, except that his health was very bad, and they had to nurse him a lot. He hardly ever spoke, and then only in monosyllables. He could understand simple remarks about matters within his ken, but it was often impossible to get him to attend to what was said to him. Yet oddly enough, he seemed to have a lively interest in everything happening around him. Sometimes he would listen intently to people's voices; but not, apparently, for their significance, simply for their musical quality. He seemed to have an absorbing interest in perceived rhythms of all sorts. He would study the grain of a piece of wood, poring over it by the hour; or the ripples on a duck-pond. Most music, ordinary music invented by *Homo sapiens,* seemed at once to interest and outrage him; though when one of the doctors played a certain bit of Bach, he was gravely attentive, and afterwards went off to play oddly twisted variants of it on his queer pipe. Certain jazz tunes had such a violent effect on him that after hearing one record he would sometimes be prostrate for days. They seemed to tear him with some kind of conflict of delight and disgust. Of course the authorities regarded his own pipe-playing as the caterwauling of a lunatic.

"Well, when we were brought face to face, we just stood and looked at one another for so long that the attendant found it uncomfortable. Presently James Jones, keeping his eyes on mine, said one word, with quiet emphasis and some surprise, 'Friend!' I smiled and nodded. Then I felt him catch a glimpse of my mind, and his face suddenly lit up with intense delight and surprise. Very slowly, as if painfully searching for each word, he said, 'You—are—not—mad, NOT MAD! We two, NOT MAD! But these—' (slowly pointing at the attendant and smiling) 'All mad, quite,

quite mad. But kind and clever. He cares for me. I cannot care for self. Too busy with—with——' The sentence trailed into silence. Smiling seraphically, he nodded slowly, again and again. Then he came forward and laid a hand for an instant on my head. That was the end. When I said yes, we were friends, and he and I saw things the same way, he nodded again; but when he tried to speak, an expression of almost comic perplexity came over his face. Looking into his mind, I saw that it was already a welter of confusion. He perceived, but he could not find any mundane significance in what he perceived. He saw the two human beings that confronted him, but he no longer connected my visible appearance with human personality, with the mind that he was still striving to communicate with. He didn't even see us as physical objects at all, but just as colour and shape, without any meaning. I asked him to play to me. He could not understand. The attendant put the pipe into his hand, closing the fingers over it. He looked blankly at it. Then with a sudden smile of enlightenment he put it to his ear, like a child listening to a shell. The attendant took it again, and played a few notes on it, but in vain. Then I took it and played a little air that I had heard him play before I found him. His attention was held. Perplexity cleared from his face. To our surprise he spoke, slowly but without difficulty. 'Yes, John Wainwright,' he said, 'you heard *me* play that the other day. I knew some *person* was listening. Give me my pipe.'

"He took it, seated himself on the edge of the table, and played, with his eyes fixed on mine."

John startled me with one sharp gasp of laughter. "God! it was music," he said. "If you could have heard it! I mean if you could have *really* heard it, and not merely as a cow might! It was lucid. It straightened out the tangles of my mind. It showed me just precisely the true, appropriate attitude of the adult human spirit to its world. Well, he played on, and I went on listening, hanging on to every note, to remember it. Then the attendant interrupted. He said this sort of noise always upset the other patients. It wasn't as if it was real *music,* but such crazy stuff. That was why J. J. was really only allowed to play out of doors.

"The music stopped with a squawk. J. J. looked with a kindly but tortured smile at the attendant. Then he slid back into insanity. So complete was his disintegration that he actually tried to eat the mouthpiece."

I believe I saw John shudder. He was now standing at the window once more, and he stood silent, while I wondered what to say. Then he exclaimed, "Where's your field-glass, quick! Damned if that's not a grey phalarope. Priceless little devil, isn't he!" In turn we watched the small silvery bird as it swam hither and thither in search of food, heedless of the buffeting wave-crests. Beside the gulls it was a yacht amongst the liners. "Yes," said John, answering my thought, "the way you feel when you watch that little blighter, just observant and delighted, and—well, curiously pious yet aloof,—yes, that's the starting-point, the very first moment, of what

J. J. was working out in his music. If you could hold that always, and fill
it out with a whole world of overtones, you'd be well on the way to 'us.'"

In the tone of John's "us" there was something of the shy audacity with
which a newly married couple first speak of "us." It began to dawn on me
that the discovery of his own kind, even in a lunatic asylum, must have
been for John a deeply moving experience. I began to realize that, having
lived for nearly eighteen years with mere animals, he had at last discovered
a human being.

John sighed, and took up his narrative. "Well, of course James Jones
was no good as a partner in the job of founding a new world. I've seen
him several times since, and he always plays to me, and I come away a little clearer in my head, and a little more grown up. But he's incurably mad,
all the same. So I started 'listening in' again; rather gloomily, for I was
afraid they might all turn out to be mad. And really the next one almost
cured me of looking any more. You see, I was trying to get in touch with
the near ones first, because they were handier. I had already spotted a strain
of French thinking that must be one of us, and also an Egyptian, and a
Chinese or Tibetan. But for the present I left these alone. Well, my next
was an infant more or less, the son of a crofter in South Uist (Outer Heb-
rides). He's a ghastly cripple; no legs, and arms like a newt's arms. And
there's something wrong with his mouth, so that he can't talk. And he's
always sick, because his digestion doesn't work properly. In fact he's the
sort any decent society would drown at birth. But the mother loves him
like a tigress; though she's scared stiff of him too, and loathes him. Neither
parent has any idea he's—what he is. They think he's just an ordinary
little cripple. And because he's a cripple, and because they treat him all
wrong, he's brewing the most murderous hate imaginable. Within the first
five minutes of my visit he spotted me as different from the others. He got
me telepathically. I got him too, but he shut his mind up immediately.
Now you'd think that finding a kindred spirit for the first time ever would
be an occasion for thanksgiving. But he didn't take it that way at all. He
evidently felt at once there wasn't room for him and me together on the
same planet. But he didn't let on he was going to do anything about it. He
kept his mind shut like an oyster, and his face as blank as a piece of paper.
I began to think I had made a mistake, that he was not one of us after all.
Yet all the circumstances corresponded with my earlier telepathic glimpses
of him,—the minute room with a flagged floor, the peat fire, his mother's
face, with one eye slightly bigger than the other, and traces of a moustache
at the corners of her lips. By the way, his parents were quite old people,
both grey. This made me curious, because the kid looked about a three-
year-old. I asked how old the baby was, but they seemed unwilling to say.
I tactfully said the child had a terribly wise face, not like a baby's. The
father blurted out that he was eighteen years old, and the mother gave a
high-pitched hysterical sort of laugh. Gradually I succeeded in making

friends with his parents. (I had told them, by the way, that I was on a fishing holiday with a party on the neighbouring island.) I flattered them by telling them I had read in a book that deformed children sometimes turned out to be great geniuses. Meanwhile I was still trying to get behind the kid's defences to see what his mind was like inside. It's impossible to give you a clear idea of the murderous trick he played on me. He must have made up his mind as soon as he saw me that he'd do me in. He chose the only effective weapon he had, and it was a diabolic one. It happened this way, so far as I can tell you. I had turned from his parents and was talking to him, trying to make friends. He just stared at me blankly. I tried harder and harder to open the oyster, and was just about ready to give up in disgust when, my God, the oyster opened wide, and I—well, this is the indescribable thing. I can only carry on with the image. The mental oyster opened wide and tried to swallow me into itself. And itself was—just the bottomless black pit of Hell. Of course, that sounds silly and romantic to you. But that's what it was like. I felt myself dropping plumb into the most appalling gulf of darkness, of mental and spiritual darkness, in which there was nothing whatever but eternally unsatisfied black hate; a sort of dank atmosphere of poison, in which everything that I had ever cared for seemed to moulder away into nastiness. I can't explain, I can't explain."

John had been sitting on the corner of my writing-table. He got up suddenly and walked to the window. "Thank God for light," he said, looking at the grey sky. "If there was some one who could understand, I could tell it all and be rid of it, perhaps. But half-telling it just makes it all come welling up again. And some say there's no Hell!"

He remained silent for some time, looking out of the window. Then he said, "Look at that cormorant. He's got a conger fatter than his own neck." I came up beside him, and we watched the fish writhing and lashing. Sometimes bird and prey disappeared together under water. Once the conger got away, but was speedily recovered. After many failures, the cormorant caught it by the head, and swallowed it, slick, so that nothing was to be seen of it but its tail, and a huge swelling in the bird's neck.

"And now," said John, "he'll be digested. That's what nearly happened to me. I felt my whole mind being disintegrated by the digestive juices of that Satanic young mollusc. I don't know what happened next. I remember seeing a perfectly diabolic expression on the kid's face; and then I must have saved myself somehow, for presently I found myself lying on the grass some way from the house, alone and in a cold sweat. The very sight of the house in the distance gave me the creeps. I couldn't think. I kept seeing that infantile grin of hate, and turning stupid again. After a while I realized I was cold, so I got up and walked toward the little bay where the boats were. Presently I began to ask myself what sort of a devil this baby Satan really was. Was he one of 'us,' or something quite different? But there was very little doubt in my mind, actually. Of course he was one of us, and probably a much mightier one than either J. J. or myself. But everything had gone wrong with him, from conception onwards. His body had failed him, and was tormenting him, and his mind was as crippled as his body, and his parents were quite unable to give him a fair chance. So the only self-expression possible to him was hate. And he had specialized in hate pretty thoroughly. But the oddest thing about it all was this. The further I got away from the experience, the more clearly it was borne in on me that his ecstasy of hate was really quite self-detached. He wasn't hating *for* himself. He hated himself as much as me. He hated everything, including hate. And he hated it all with a sort of sacred fervour. And why? Because, as I begin to discover, there's a sort of minute, blazing star of *worship* right down in the pit of his hell. He sees everything from the side of eternity just as clearly as I do, perhaps more clearly; but—how shall I put it?—he conceives his part in the picture to be the devil's part, and he's playing it with a combination of passion and detachment like a great artist, and for the glory of God, if you understand what I mean. And he's right. It's the only thing he *can* do, and he does it with style. I take off my hat to him, in spite of everything. But it's pretty ghastly, really. Think of the life he's living; just like an infant's, and with his powers! I dare say he'll manage to find some trick for blowing up the whole planet some day, if he lives much longer. And there's another thing. I've got to keep a sharp look out or he'll catch me again. He can reach me anywhere, in Australia or Patagonia. God! I can feel him now! Give me another apple, and let's talk about something else."

Crunching his second Cox, John became calm again. Presently he went on with his narrative. "I haven't done much since that affair. It took me some time to get my mind straight, and then I felt depressed about the chances of ever finding any one anywhere that was really my sort and yet also sane. But after ten days or so I began the search again. I found an old gipsy woman who was a sort of half-baked one of 'us.' But she's always having fits. She tells fortunes, and perhaps has some sort of glimpses of the future. But she's as old as the hills, and cares for nothing but fortune-telling and rum. Yet she's quite definitely one of us, up to a point; not intellectually, though she has the reputation of being damnably cunning, but in insight. She sees things on their eternal side all right, though not very steadily. Then there are several others in asylums, quite hopeless. And a hermaphrodite adolescent in a sort of home for incurables. And a man doing a life-sentence for murder. I fancy he might have been the real thing if he hadn't had a bit of his skull knocked in when he was a kid. Then there's a lightning calculator, but he doesn't seem to be anything else. He's not really one of us at all, but he's got just *one* of the essential factors in his make up. Well, that's all there is of *Homo superior* in these islands."

John began pacing the room, quickly, methodically, like a polar bear in its cage. Suddenly he stopped, and clenched his fists and cried out, "Cat-tle! Cattle! A whole world of cattle! My God, how they stink!" He stared at the wall. Then he sighed, and turning to me he said, "Sorry, Fido, old man! That was a lapse. What do you say to a walk before lunch?"

CHAPTER XIV

ENGINEERING PROBLEMS

NOT long after John told me of his efforts to make contact with other supernormals he took me into his confidence about his plans for the future. We were in the subterranean workshop. He was absorbed in a new inven-tion, a sort of generator-accumulator, he said. His bench was covered with test-tubes, jars, bits of metal, bottles, insulated wires, voltmeters, lumps of stone. He was so intent on his work that I said, "I believe you're regressing to childhood. This sort of thing has got hold of you again and made you forget all about—Scotland."

"No, you're wrong," he said. "This gadget is an important part of my plan. When I have finished this test I'll tell you." Silently he proceeded with the experiment. Presently, with a little shout of triumph, he said, "Got it, this time!"

Over a cup of coffee we discussed his plans. He was determined to search the whole world in the hope of discovering a few others of his kind, and of suitable age for joining with him in the founding of a little colony of supernormals in some remote part of the earth. In order to do this with-out loss of time, he said, he must have an ocean-going yacht and a small aeroplane, or flying machine of some kind, which could be stowed on the yacht. When I protested that he knew nothing about flying and less about designing planes, he replied, "Oh yes, I do. I learned to fly yesterday." It seems he had managed to persuade a certain brilliant young airman to give him not only a joy-ride but a long spell in control of the machine. "Once you get the feel of it," he said, "it's easy enough. I landed twice, and took off twice, and did a few stunts. But of course there's a good deal more to learn. As for designing, I'm on the job already, and on the yacht design too. But a lot depends on this new gadget. I can't explain it very well. At least, I can explain, in a way, but you just won't believe it. I've been look-ing into nuclear chemistry lately, and in the light of my Scotch experiences an idea struck me. Probably even you know (though you have a genius for keeping out of touch with science) that there's the hell of a lot of energy locked up in every atomic nucleus, and that the reason why you can't re-lease it is that the unlocking would take a fantastically powerful electric current, to overcome the forces that hold the electrons and protons, and so on, together. Well, I've found a much handier key. But it's not a physical key at all but a psychical one. It's no use trying to *overcome* those terrific interlocking forces. You must just *abolish* them for the time being; send them to sleep, so to speak. The interlocking forces, and the disruptive forces too, are just the spontaneous urges of the basic physical units, call them electrons and protons, if you like. What I do, then, is to hypnotize the little devils so that they go limp for a moment and loosen their grip on one another. Then when they wake up they barge about in hilarious freedom, and all you have to do is to see that their barging drives your machinery."

I laughed, and said I liked his parable. "Parable be damned," he said. "It's only a parable in the sense that the protons and electrons themselves are merely fictitious characters in a parable. They're not *really* independent entities at all, but determinations within a system—the cosmos. And they're not *really* just physical, but determinations within a psychophysical system. Of course if you take 'sapient' physics as God's truth, and not as an abstraction from a more profound truth, the whole idea seems crazy. But I thought it worth looking into, and I find it works. Of course there are difficulties. The main one is the psychological one. The 'sapient' mind could never do the trick; it's not awake enough. But the supernormal has the necessary influence, and practice makes the job reasonably safe and easy. The physical difficulties," he said, glancing at his apparatus, "are all connected with selecting the most favourable atoms to work on, and with tapping the flood of energy as it comes into action. I'm working on those problems now. Ordinary mud from the estuary is pretty good for the job. There's a minute percentage of a very convenient element in it."

With a pair of tweezers he took a pinch of mud from a test-tube and put it in a platinum bowl. He opened the trap-door of the workshop and placed the bowl outside, then returned, almost closing the trap-door. We both looked through the opening at the little bowl. Smiling, he said, "Now all you little electrons and protons go to sleep, and don't wake up till Mummy tells you." Turning to me, he added, "The patter, I may say, is for the audience, not for the rabbits in the conjurer's hat."

An expression of grave concentration came over his face. His breathing quickened. "Now!" he said. There was a terrific flash, and a report like a gun.

John wiped his forehead with a grubby pocket handkerchief, and remarked, "Alone I did it!" We returned to our coffee, and his plans.

"I've still got to find some really good way of bottling the energy till it's wanted. You can't be at one and the same time hypnotizing electrons *and* navigating a ship. I may simply have to use the energy to drive a dynamo and charge an accumulator. But there's a more interesting possibility. I *may* be able, when I have hypnotized the little beggars, to give them a sort of 'post-hypnotic suggestion,' so that they can only wake up and barge about again in response to some particular stimulus. See?"

I laughed. We both sipped our coffee. I may as well say at once that the "post-hypnotic" system turned out ultimately to be feasible, and was adopted.

"Well, you can see," he said, "there are great possibilities in this new dodge of mine. Now, while the yacht and plane are building, you are to come on the Continent with me. (I'm sure Bertha will be glad to have a holiday from you.) I want to do a bit of research. There's an obviously supernormal mind in Paris, and one in Egypt, and perhaps others, not too far away. When I have the yacht and plane I'll do the world tour in search of the rest. If I find a few suitable young things, I'll voyage in the Pacific to find a satisfactory island for the Colony."

During the next two months John was absorbed in the practical work of designing the yacht and the plane, perfecting the new power technique, and improving his flying.

At this time he was often to be seen "playing at boats" on the Park Lake or the more boisterous Estuary, like any ordinary boy. He was now over eighteen, but in appearance under fifteen. Thus his behaviour seemed quite normal. He produced a large number of models and fitted them out with electric motors or steam engines. These he dispatched across the lake in all weathers, observing their performance with great care. The design was largely determined by the necessity of stowing the plane on board, with wings folded, and by the need for extreme sea-worthiness. John's final choice was an extraordinary craft which local yachtsmen regarded as a mere caricature of a ship. John made a special three-foot model to this design, and fitted her out in great detail. In general shape she was ludicrously broad in the beam, and of shallow draft, in fact an exaggeration of the speed-boat hull; a sort of cross between a speed-boat and a life-boat, with a saucer somewhere in her ancestry, and perhaps a flat pebble of the "ducks and drakes" type. She was certainly a delightful toy; and I feel sure that John thoroughly enjoyed her simply as a toy, and had put much more work into her than was needed for mere experimentation. She represented a vessel the size of a small tug. No detail was omitted from her equipment. There were bunks for nine persons, but twenty could sleep on board at a pinch, and she could be handled comfortably by a single navigator. There was a realistic dining-saloon, with tables, chairs, cupboards. There was a latrine, glass portholes, minute navigation controls. These controls could be operated by some sort of radio device on shore. The engine was a fairly detailed replica of the sub-atomic engine that John intended for the actual ship.

Much entertainment was afforded by the antics which John made his model perform. On the Park Lake he would send her in leisurely pursuit of the terrified ducks. On the estuary, when the tide was in, he would stop her far out at sea, and persuade some kindly member of the sailing club to salvage her in a dinghy. When the sweating oarsman had reached the little derelict, and was putting out his hand to seize her, John (on shore, and half a mile away) would set her going for a yard or two and watch the man's repeated efforts to recover her. Finally he would let her out at full speed for the shore, and she would return to her master's hand like a well-trained dog.

John had also been at work on several model planes. He used to spend much time flying them; but in secret, for he feared that, if they were seen performing their surprising antics, they would attract too much attention. He therefore used to retire with them into the wilds of North Wales, by means of his motor-bike or my car. There he would try out his models in the fickle mountain winds, their sub-atomic power enabling them to perform feats which no elastic-driven model could possibly achieve.

His final choice was a surprising mechanism, made on the same scale as the model yacht, and capable of being dismantled and stowed on board. With this stub-winged instrument he would amuse himself and me by the hour, making it rise from the surface of a "llyn" (it had both wheels and floats), and climb heavenwards, till we had to use a field-glass to follow it. It maintained its equilibrium automatically, but was steered by radio from the ground. When he had become adept in the management of this mechanical bird, he sometimes used it for a modern sort of hawking, sending the sparrow-like little object in chase of curlews, buzzards and ravens. This sport needed very delicate perception as well as control. As a rule the quarry would hurry away as soon as it realized it was being chased. The plane would then chevy it, or even swoop upon its back. But one old raven turned to fight, and before John could bring his toy's superior speed into operation for escape, the raven's horny neb had slashed one of the silken wings, and the plane came tumbling to the heather.

The plans for the yacht and the plane were finished before John reached the age of nineteen. I need not describe how I negotiated with shipbuilders and aeroplane manufacturers, and finally placed orders for the actual construction. I gained the reputation of being a mad millionaire; for the designs appeared to be quite unworkable, and I would not consider any of the objections raised against them. The main trouble was that in both plane and yacht the space allotted to the generation of power was by all ordinary standards quite insufficient. Contracts for the generators and machinery were distributed among several engineering firms in such a manner as to arouse as little curiosity as possible.

CHAPTER XV

JACQUELINE

WHEN these problems of engineering had been solved, John was able to turn his attention once more to his telepathic researches. As he still looked too young to be wandering about the Continent by himself, he insisted on taking me with him to Paris. When we were approaching our destination he showed signs of eagerness. Well might he, for he expected to find a being who could meet him as an equal and afford him a far more satisfying companionship than any he had yet known. But when we had lodged ourselves in a little hotel in the rue Bertholet (off the avenue de Claude Bernard) he became almost disheartened. When I questioned him he laughed awkwardly, and said, "I'm having a new sensation. I'm feeling shy! She doesn't seem particularly keen on my coming. She won't help me to find her. I know she's somewhere in the Quartier Latin. She passes the end of this street quite often. I know she knows some one is looking for her, and yet she won't help. Also, she's evidently very old and wise. She remembers the Franco-Prussian War. I've been trying to see what she sees when she looks in a mirror, so as to get her face; but I can't catch her at the right time."

At that moment his head jerked, and he said without any pause, "While I was talking to you, I, the real I, was in touch with her. She's in a certain café. She'll be there for some time. Let's find her."

He had an obscure feeling that the café was near the Odéon, so thither we hastened. After some hesitation he selected a certain establishment, and we entered. As soon as he had passed through the door, he whispered excitedly, "This is it all right. This is the room she is seeing at the moment." He stood for a second or two, a queer little foreigner, jostled by waiters and a stream of guests. Then he made his way to an empty table at the far side of the room.

"There she is," said John, with surprise in his voice, almost with awe. Following his gaze I saw at a near table two women. One had her back to us, but I judged that she was under thirty, for her figure was slim and the curve of her cheek almost juvenile. The other was extravagantly old. Her face was a relief map; all ridges and valleys. I studied her with disappointment, for she had a dull and peevish face, and she was looking at John with offensive curiosity.

But now the other woman turned her head and looked about the room. There was no mistaking those large eyes. They were John's, though heavy-lidded. For a moment they rested on me, then on John. The drooping lids were lifted to reveal two black and lofty caverns more abysmal even than John's. The whole face lit up with intelligence and amusement. She rose, and advanced toward John, who also rose. They faced one another in silence. Then the woman said, "Alors c'est toi qui me cherches toujours!"

She was not what I had expected. In spite of the great eyes, she might almost have passed for a normal woman, an eccentric specimen of the normal species. Her head, though large, did not look noticeably out of proportion to her body, for she was tall, and the black hair which scarcely showed under her close-fitting hat added little to its size. Her ample mouth, I guessed, had been skilfully reduced by painting.

But though passably "human," according to the standards of *Homo sapiens,* she was strange. Were I an imaginative writer, and not merely a journalist, I might be able to suggest symbolically something of the almost "creepy" effect she had on me, something of its remote and sleepy power. As it is I can only record certain obvious features, and in general that curious combination of the infantile, or even the foetal, with the mature. The protruding brow, the short broad nose, the great distance between the great eyes, the surprising breadth of the whole face, the marked furrow from nose to lips—all these characters were definitely foetal; and yet the precisely chiselled lips themselves and the delicate moulding of the eyelids produced an expression of subtle experience suggestive of an ageless divinity. To me at least, prepared of course by familiarity with John's own strangeness, this strange face seemed to combine idiosyncrasy and universality. Here, in spite of a vaguely repulsive uncouthness, was a living symbol of womanhood. Yet here also was a being utterly different from any other, something unique and individual. When I looked from her to the most attractive girl in the room I was shocked to find that it was the normal beauty that was repulsive. With something like vertigo I looked once more at the adorable grotesque.

While I was watching her, she and John stood regarding one another in complete silence. Presently the New Woman, as I had already cynically named her for my private amusement, asked us to move to her table, which we accordingly did. Her real name was given as Jacqueline Castagnet. The old lady, introduced as Mme. Lemaître, regarded us with hostility, but had to put up with us. She was thoroughly commonplace; yet I was struck with certain points of likeness with Jacqueline, certain indescribable traits of expression and of voice. I guessed that the two women were mother and daughter. Later it turned out that I was right; and yet also quite wrong.

There followed a few aimless remarks, and then Jacqueline began speaking in a language quite unknown to me. For a second John looked surprised, then laughed, and answered, apparently in the same tongue. For half an hour or so they continued speaking, while I laboured to maintain conversation with Mme. Lemaître in very bad French.

Presently the old lady reminded Jacqueline that they were both due elsewhere. When the two women had left us, John and I remained at the table for a while. He was silent and absorbed. I asked what language they had been talking. "English," he said. "She wanted to tell me a lot about herself, and didn't want.the old one to know about it, so she started in on English-back-to-front. I've never tried that before, but it's quite easy, for us." There was a faint stress on the "us." John evidently knew that I felt "left out," for he continued: "I had better tell you the gist of what she said. The old lady is her daughter, but doesn't know it. Jacqueline was married to a man called Cazé eighty-three years ago, but she cleared out when the child was four. A few days ago she came across this old thing, and recognized her as her baby daughter, and made friends with her. Mme. Lemaître showed her a photograph 'of my mother who died when I was quite little—strangely like you, my dear. Perhaps you are some sort of great niece of mine.' Jacqueline herself was born in 1765."

John's account of the amazing life story of Jacqueline I can only summarize. It deserves to be recorded in a fat volume, but my concern is with John.

Her parents were peasants of that bleak country called "Lousy Champagne," between Châlons-sur-Marne and the Forest of Argonne. They were thrifty even to miserliness. Jacqueline, with her supernormal intelligence and sensibility and her ravenous capacity for life, was brought up in very cramping circumstances. This was probably a cause of the passion for pleasure and power which played so great a part in the earlier phases of her career. Like John, she took an unconscionable time a-growing up. This was a grievance to her parents, who were impatient for her to help in the house and on the land, and later were indignant that at an age when other girls were ready for marriage she was still a breastless child. The life which she was compelled to lead was physically healthy, but devastating to her spirit. She soon realized that she had capacities for all manner of subtle experience beyond the reach of her fellow mortals, and that the sane course was to devote herself to the exercise of these capacities; but her monotonous and dour existence made it impossible for her to detach herself from the less developed cravings of her nature, the increasing hunger for luxury and power. The fact that she inhabited a world of half-wits was borne in on her most obviously in the perception that the neighbouring peasants' daughters, though they eclipsed her in normal sexual appeal, were too stupid to make full use of this asset as a means to dominance.

Before adolescence had properly begun, when she was only nineteen, she had already determined to beat them all at their own game, and indeed to become a queen among women. In the neighbouring town of Ste. Menehould she sometimes saw fine ladies passing through in their coaches on their way to Paris, or breaking their journey at the local inn. She observed them with scientific care, and laid the foundations of her future technique.

When she was on the threshold of womanhood, her parents betrothed her to a neighbouring farmer. She ran away. Making full use of her only two weapons, sex and intelligence, she struggled through from the humblest and most brutish sort of prostitution to become the mistress of a wealthy Parisian merchant. For some years she lived upon him, latterly giving him nothing in return but the terrible charm of her society once a week at dinner.

When she had reached the age of thirty-five she fell in love, for the first time in her life, with a young artist, one of those who were preparing the way for the vital and triumphant movement of Parisian painting. This novel experience brought to a climax the great conflict which tormented her. She who had followed the most ancient profession without repugnance was now horrified at herself. For the young man had wakened in her those dormant capacities which had perforce been thwarted by her career. She used her technique to capture him, and easily succeeded. They lived together. For a few months both were happy.

Gradually, however, she came to realize that, after all, she was mated to something which, from her point of view, was little better than an ape. She had known, of course, that her peasant clients, her Parisian clients, and her amiable wealthy patron, were "subhuman"; the artist, she had persuaded herself, was an exception. Yet she still clung to her man. To break with the being to whom she had given her soul, even though in error, would, she felt, have killed her. Moreover, she still genuinely, though irrationally, loved him. He was her almost-human animal. She cared for him as a huntswoman and a spinster might care for her horse. He was *not* human, and could never be the mate of her spirit; but he was a noble animal and she was proud of his animal attainments, namely of his triumphs in the sphere of "subhuman" art. She entered into his work with enthusiasm. She was not merely his source of inspiration; increasingly she took command of his artistic faculty. The more she possessed him, the more clearly the unhappy man realized that his native genius was being overborne and suffocated by the flood of her fertile imagination. His was a complex tragedy. He seems to have recognized that the pictures which he produced under her influence were more daring and aesthetically more triumphant than anything he could produce without her; but he realized also that he was losing his reputation, that even the most sensitive of his follow-artists could not appreciate them. He made a stand for independence, and began to regain his self-respect and reputation. On her this turn of affairs had the effect of rousing all her suppressed disgust. Each was striving to be rid of the other, yet each craved the other. There was a quarrel, in which she played the part of the divinity who had come down to raise him to her own level, and was rejected. Next day he shot himself.

This tragedy evidently had a profound effect on her still juvenile mind. The finality of the deed bred in her a new tenderness and respect for the subhuman beings who surrounded her. Somehow this death lessened the distance between her and them. Though her passion for self-expression soon returned, and though she sometimes indulged it ruthlessly, it was tempered by the recollection that she had killed the one being in the world who for a whole month had seemed to her superior to herself.

For a few years after the death of the artist Jacqueline lived in great poverty on savings which she had accumulated in her association with the merchant. She tried to make a name for herself as a writer, under a masculine pseudonym; but the stuff which she produced was too remote to be appreciated, and she could not bring herself to write in a different vein. When she was in her forties, and still in the first flush of maturity, her obsessive craving for luxury and power returned with such insistence that, in a panic, she became a nun. She did not believe any of the explicit doctrines of the Church; but she made up her mind to pay lip service to all its superstitions for the sake of its flicker of genuine and corporate religious experience, which, she felt, she needed for the strengthening of her better nature. Her presence in the nunnery, however, very soon caused such an upheaval that the institution was finally disbanded, and Jacqueline, with bitter laughter in her heart, returned to her original calling.

But to her own surprise prostitution now afforded her something more than the means to wealth and power. Her experience in the nunnery had not been wholly barren. She had learned a good deal about the spiritual cravings of the subhuman kind; and this knowledge she now put to good use. Her motive in returning to prostitution had been purely self-regarding, but she soon discovered that the more human of her clients were suffering from an unconscious need for something more than carnal satisfaction. And she found exaltation in ministering to this essentially spiritual need. Carnal satisfaction she gave ungrudgingly. Her own initial distaste at intercourse with beings of a lowly order gave way to delight in her new office. Many a man whose real need was not merely copulation but intimacy with a sensitive yet fearless woman, many who needed moreover help in the seemingly hopeless task of "coming to terms with the universe," found in Jacqueline a well of strength. As her reputation grew, ever greater demands were made on her. Hoping to save herself from a breakdown, she chose disciples, young women who were ready to live her life and give themselves as she gave herself. Some of them were partially successful, but none could do as she had done. The strain increased until at last she fell seriously ill.

When she recovered, her old self-seeking passion was once more uppermost. Using all her prowess she fought her way up the social ladder of Europe, till, at fifty-seven and on the threshold of full maturity, she married a Russian prince. She did so knowing that he was a worthless creature and a half-wit, even by normal standards. So skilfully did she play her cards during the next fifteen years that she had a good prospect of setting him on the throne. Increasing disgust and horror, however, flung her into another mental disorder. From this she emerged once more her true self.

She cut adrift, disguised herself, and fled back to Paris to carry on her old profession. Occasionally she met one or other of her former clients, now well advanced in years. But as she herself had retained her youthful appearance, and indeed seemed to have the full flower of womanhood still ahead of her, she easily persuaded them that she was the former Jacqueline's young niece.

All this while she had never had a child, never conceived. In her early years she had taken precaution to avoid such a disaster; but in maturity, though she had felt no craving for motherhood, she had been less reluctant to risk it, and less cautious. As the decades passed and her remaining caution dwindled out, she came to suspect that she was sterile, and in the end she ceased to take any precautions at all. On her return from Russia an obscure sense that in missing motherhood she had missed a valuable experience developed into a definite hunger to have a baby of her own.

Not a few of her clients had tried to persuade her to accept marriage. Hitherto she had laughed at these suitors, but when she had passed her eightieth year, she began to be seriously attracted by the prospect of a spell of quiet married life. Among her clients was a young Parisian lawyer, Jean Cazé. Whether he was in fact the father of her child she did not know; but when, to her amazement, she found that she had conceived, she singled him out as a suitable husband. He, it so happened, had never thought of marrying her; but when she had slipped the idea into his mind, he pressed her ardently, overcame her feigned reluctance and carried her off in pride. After eleven months of pregnancy she bore her daughter, and very nearly died in the ordeal. Four years of maternal duties and of companionship with the faithful Cazé were enough for her. Jean, she knew, would treasure the infant; and indeed he did, to the extent of spoiling her for life. Jacqueline fled not only from Paris but from France, and started all over again in Dresden.

Throughout the last two-thirds of the nineteenth century Jacqueline appears to have had alternating spells of exalted prostitution and marriage. She counted among her husbands, she said, a British ambassador, a famous writer, and a West African negro who was a private in the French colonial army. Never again did she conceive. Probably John was right in surmising that she had the power of preventing conception by an act of volition, though she had no idea how she exercised this power.

Since the close of the nineteenth century Jacqueline had not indulged in marriage. She had preferred to carry on her profession, because of her "great affection for the dear children," by which she meant her clients. Hers must have been a strange life. Of course she gave herself for money, like any member of her profession, or of any other profession. Nevertheless, her heart was in her work, and she chose her clients, not according to their power to pay, but according to their needs and their capacity to benefit by her ministrations. She seems to have combined in her person the functions of harlot, psycho-analyst and priest.

During the war of 1914-18 she was drawn into overstraining herself once more. So many tragic cases came her way. And after the war, being wholly without national prejudices, she moved to Germany, where the need was greater. It was in Germany, in 1925, that she had once more collapsed, and was forced to spend a year in a "mental home." When we met her she was again established in Paris, and again at work.

On the day after our meeting in the café John had left me to amuse myself as best I could while he visited Jacqueline. He stayed away four days, and when he returned he was haggard and obviously in great distress. Not till long afterwards could he bring himself to tell the cause of his misery, and then he said only, "She's glorious, and hurt, and I can't help her, and she won't help me. She was terribly kind and sweet to me. Said she had never met any one like me, wished we'd met a hundred years ago. She says my work is going to be great. But *really* she thinks it's just schoolboy adventure, no more."

CHAPTER XVI

ADLAN

JOHN continued his search. I accompanied him. I shall not at this stage describe the few suitable supernormal youngsters whom he discovered and persuaded to prepare themselves for the great adventure. There was a young girl in Marseilles, an older girl in Moscow, a boy in Finland, a girl in Sweden, another in Hungary, and a young man in Turkey. Save for these, John found nothing but lunatics, cripples, invalids, and inveterate old vagabonds in whom the superior mentality had been hopelessly distorted by contact with the normal species.

But in Egypt John actually met his superior. This incident was so strange that I hesitate to record it, or even to believe it myself.

John had for long been convinced that a very remarkable mind was secreted somewhere in the Levant or the Nile Delta. From Turkey we took ship to Alexandria. Thence, after further investigation, we moved to Port Saïd. Here we spent some weeks. As far as I was concerned, they were weeks of idleness. There was nothing for me to do but to play tennis, bathe and indulge in mild flirtations. John himself seemed to be idling. He bathed, rowed in the harbour, wandered about the town. He was unusually absent-minded, and sometimes almost irritable.

When Port Saïd was beginning to bore me excessively, I suggested that we should try Cairo. "Go yourself," said John, "if you want to, but I'm staying here. I'm busy." I therefore took him at his word, and crossed the Delta by train. Long before we reached Cairo the Great Pyramids came into view, overtopping the palm trees and the unseen city. I shall not forget that first glimpse of them, for later it seemed to symbolize the experience that John himself was passing through in Port Saïd. They were grey-blue, in the blue sky. They were curiously simple, remote, secure.

I took a room at Shepheard's Hotel, and gave myself over to sight-seeing. One day, about three weeks after I left Port Saïd, a telegram came from John. It said merely, "Home, John." Nothing loath, I packed my traps and took the next train for Port Saïd.

As soon as I arrived, John made me book accommodation for *three* to Toulon by an Orient boat that was due to pass through the Canal a few days later. The new member of the party, he said, was on his way from Upper Egypt, and would join us as soon as he could. Before giving details of our future fellow passenger I must try to report what John told me of the very different being with whom he was in contact during my absence in Cairo.

"You see," he said, "the fellow I was after (Adlan, by name) turned out to have died thirty-five years ago. He was trying to get me from his place in the past, and at first I didn't realize. When at last we effected some sort of communication, he managed to show me what he was seeing, and I noticed that the steamers in the harbour were all little low old things with yards on their masts. Also there wasn't any Canal Company's Building where it ought to have been. (You know, the green-domed thing.) You can imagine how exciting this was. It took me a long time to get myself into the past instead of his coming to me in the present."

John's story must be condensed. In order to secure a less precarious footing in the past, John, under Adlan's direction, made the acquaintance of a middle-aged Englishman, a ship-chandler, who had spent much of his childhood in Port Saïd in Adlan's time. This Anglo-Egyptian, Harry Robinson, was easily persuaded to talk about his early experiences, and to describe Adlan, whom he used at one time to meet almost daily. John soon made himself familiar with Robinson's mind to such an extent that he was able to reach back and establish himself quite firmly in the child Harry and in the Port Saïd that had long since vanished.

Seen through Harry's eyes, Adlan turned out to be an aged and pov-erty-stricken native boatman. His face, John said, was like a mummy's, black and pinched and drawn, but very much alive, with a frequent and rather grim smile. His gigantic head bore upon its summit a fez which was ridiculously small for it. When, as occasionally happened, this covering fell off, his cranium was seen to be perfectly bald. John said it reminded him of a dark and polished and curiously moulded lump of wood. He had the typical great eyes, one of which was bloodshot, and running with yellow mucus. Like so many natives, he had suffered from ophthalmia. His bare brown legs and feet were covered with scars. Several toe-nails had been lost. Adlan made his living by ferrying passengers between the liners and the shore, and by transporting European residents to and from the "bath-houses"—wooden erections built out over the sea on angle-irons. The Robinson family hired Adlan and his boat several times a week to row them across the harbour to their "bath house." He had to wait while they bathed and lunched. Then he would row them back to the town. It was while Adlan was tugging at the oars in his long-prowed and gaily painted boat, and while Harry was prattling to his parents or his sister or even to Adlan himself, that John, regarding the scene through Harry's eyes, carried on his telepathic conversations with the unique Egyptian.

John's projection of his mind into the past took him back to the year 1896. At this time Adlan claimed that he was three hundred and eighty-four years old. John would have been less inclined to believe this before he met Jacqueline, but by now he was ready to accept it. Adlan, then, was born in 1512, somewhere in the Soudan. Most of his first century was spent as the wise man of his tribe, but in the end he resolved to exchange his primitive environment for something more civilized. He travelled down the Nile, and settled in Cairo, where in time he gained a reputation as a sorcerer. During the seventeenth century he played an active part in the turbulent political life of Egypt, and was at one time the power behind the throne. But political activities could not satisfy him. He was drawn into them much as an intelligent spectator might be drawn into a game of chess played by blockheads. He could not help seeing how the game might be played most effectively, and presently he found himself playing it. Toward the end of the eighteenth century, he became more and more absorbed in the development of his "occult" powers, and chiefly his most recent art, that of projecting himself into the past.

A few years before Napoleon's Egyptian expedition Adlan broke with his political life entirely by faking a suicide. For some years he continued to live in Cairo, but in complete obscurity and very humble circumstances. He made his living as a water-carrier, driving his ass, laden with swollen and dripping skins, along the dusty streets. Meanwhile he continued to improve his supernormal powers, and would sometimes use them to practise psycho-therapy upon his fellow-proletarians. But his chief interest was exploration of the past. At this time the knowledge of Ancient Egypt was extremely scanty, and Adlan's passion was to gain direct experience of the great race of long ago. Hitherto his powers had only enabled him to reach a few years back, to events which occurred in an environment similar to his own. But presently he determined to bury himself in some obscure village and till the soil of the Delta, entering into the life of the primitive agriculturalists whose customs and culture had probably changed little since the days of the Pharaohs. For many decades he wielded the hoe and the shadoof; and in due course he learned to be almost as familiar with ancient Memphis as with modern Cairo.

In the second quarter of the nineteenth century, however, when he was still in appearance no more than middle-aged, he conceived the need to explore other cultures. For this purpose he settled in Alexandria, and took up his old profession of water-carrier. Here, with less ease and less success than in his study of Ancient Egypt, he made his entry into Ancient Greece, learning to project himself into the era of the great Library, and even into Greece itself of the age of Plato.

Not till the last quarter of the nineteenth century did Adlan ride his donkey along the strip of sand between Lake Menzaleh and the sea, and settle in Port Saïd, once more as a water-carrier. He did not practise his old profession exclusively. Sometimes he would hire out his donkey to a European passenger, ashore for the day. Then he would run barefoot behind the tall white ass, affectionately whacking its hind-quarters, and crying "Haa! Haa!" Once, when his beast, which he called "Two Lovely Black Eyes," was stolen, he ran thirty miles in chase of it, following its footprints on the moist shore. When at last he overtook the thief, he battered him, and returned in triumph on the ass. Sometimes he would board the liners and amuse the passengers with conjuring tricks with rings and balls and restless little yellow chicks. Sometimes he would sell them silk or jewellery.

Adlan's object in moving to Port Saïd had been to put himself into touch with contemporary European life and thought, and if possible to make some kind of contact with India and China. The Canal was by now the most cosmopolitan spot in all the world. Levantines, Greeks, Russians, Lascars, Chinese firemen, Europeans on their way to the East, Asiatics on their way to London and Paris, Moslem pilgrims on their way to Mecca, —all passed through Port Saïd. Scores of races, scores of languages, scores of religions and cultures jostled one another in that most flagrantly mongrel town.

Adlan soon learned how to get the best out of his new environment. His methods were diverse, but all depended chiefly on telepathy and extreme intelligence. He constructed little by little in his own mind a very clear picture of European, and even Indian and Chinese culture. He did not, indeed, find any culture ready to hand in the minds of the beings with whom he made contact in Port Saïd, for they, residents and passengers alike, were nearly all quite philistine. But by a brilliant process of inference from the meagre and incoherent traces of thought in these migrants he was able to reconstruct the cultural matrix in which they had developed. This method he supplemented by reading books lent him by a shipping agent who had a liking for literature. He learned also to extend his telepathic reach to such an extent that, by conjuring up all that he knew of

John Ruskin (let us say), he could make contact with that didactic sage in his remote home by Coniston Water.

Presently it became evident to Adlan that the really interesting period of European thought lay in the future. Could he, then, explore the future as he had explored the past? This proved a far more difficult task, and one which he could never have performed at all effectively had he not, by great good luck, discovered John, a mind of somewhat the same calibre as his own. He conceived the idea of teaching that fellow-supernormal to reach back into the past to him, so that he himself might learn about the future without the precarious and dangerous labour of projecting himself into it.

I was surprised to hear from John, that, though only a few weeks had passed since our arrival in Egypt, he had in that period spent many months with Adlan. Or perhaps I should say that his interviews with Adlan (through the mind of Harry) were distributed over a period of many months in Adlan's life. Day after day the old man would ferry the Robinsons to their bathhouse, pulling steadily at his battered oars, and prattling in kitchen Arabic to Harry about ships and camels. And at the same time he would be carrying on a most earnest and subtle telepathic conversation with John about relativity or the quantum theory or the economic determination of history. John was soon convinced that he had encountered a mind which either through native superiority or though prolonged meditation was far in advance of his own, even in ability to cope with Western European culture. But Adlan's brilliance made his way of life seem all the more perplexing. With some complacency John assured himself that if he were to live as long as Adlan he would not have to spend his old age toiling for a pittance from *Homo sapiens*. But before he parted from Adlan he began to take a humbler view of himself and a more respectful attitude to Adlan.

The old man was greatly interested in John's biological knowledge, and its bearing upon himself and John. "Yes," he said, "we are very different from other men. I have known it since I was eight. Indeed these creatures that surround us are scarcely men at all. But perhaps, my son, you take that difference too seriously. No, I should not say that. What I mean is that though for you this project of founding the new species is the true way, for me there is another way. And each of us must serve Allah in the way that Allah demands of him."

It was not, John explained, that Adlan threw cold water on his great adventure. On the contrary he entered into it with sympathy and made many helpful suggestions. Indeed one of his favourite occupations, as he plied his oars, was to expound to John with prophetic enthusiasm the kind of world that "John's New Men" would make, and how much more vital and more happy it would be than the world of *Homo sapiens*. This enthusiasm was undoubtedly sincere, yet, said John, there was a delicate mockery behind it. It was not wholly unlike the zeal with which grown men enter into the games of children. One day John deliberately challenged him by referring to his project as the greatest adventure that man could ever face. Adlan was resting on his oars before crossing the harbour, for an Austrian Lloyd steamer was passing into the Canal. Harry was intent upon the liner, but John induced him to turn his eyes on the old boatman. Adlan was looking gravely at the lad. "My son, my dear son," he said, "Allah wills of his creatures two kinds of service. One is that they should toil to fulfil his active purpose in the world, and that is the service which you have most at heart. The other is that they should observe with understanding and praise with discriminate delight the excellent form of his handiwork. And this is my service, to lay at Allah's feet such a life of praise that no man, not even you, my very dear son, can give him. He has fashioned you in such a manner that you may serve him best in action, though in action inspired always by deep-searching contemplation. But me he has fashioned such that I must serve him directly through contemplation and praise, though for this end I had first to pass through the school of action."

John protested that the end of praise would be far better served by a world of the New Men than by a few isolated lofty spirits in a world of subhuman creatures; and that, therefore, the most urgent of all tasks was to bring such a world into being.

But Adlan replied, "It seems so to you, because you are fashioned for action, and because you are young. And indeed it *is* so. Spirits of my kind know well that in due season spirits of your kind will in fact create the new world. But we know also that for us there is another task. It may even be that part of my task is actually to peer so far into the future that I may see and praise those great deeds which you, or some other, are destined to perform."

When John had reported this speech to me he said, "Then the old man broke off his communication with me, and also ceased prattling to Harry. Presently he thought to me again. His mind embraced me with grave tenderness, and he said, 'It is time for you to leave me, you very dear and godlike child. I have seen something of the future that lies before you. And though you could bear the foreknowledge without faltering from the way of praise, it is not for me to tell you.' Next day I met him again, but he was uncommunicative. At the end of the trip, when the Robinsons were stepping out of the boat, he took Harry in his arms and set him on the land, saying in the lingo that passed as Arabic with European residents, "'L hwaga swoia, quaïs ketír!' (the little master, very nice). To me he said in his thoughts, 'To-night, or perhaps to-morrow, I will die. For I have praised the past and the present, and the near future too, with all the insight that Allah has given me. And peering into the farther future I have been able to see nothing but obscure and terrible things which it is not in me to praise. Therefore it is certain that I have fulfilled my task, and may now rest.' "

Next day another boat took Harry and his parents to the bath-houses.

CHAPTER XVII

NG-GUNKO AND LO

IT will be remembered that we booked passages for three persons by Orient to Toulon and England. The third member of the party turned up three hours before the ship sailed.

John explained that in discovering this amazing child, who went by the name of Ng-Gunko, he had been helped by Adlan. The old man in the past had been in touch with this contemporary of John's, and had helped the two to make contact with one another.

Ng-Gunko was a native of some remote patch of forest-clad mountain in or near Abyssinia; and though only a child he had at John's request found his way from his native country to Port Saïd by a series of adventures which I will not attempt to describe.

As time advanced and he failed to appear, I became more and more sceptical and impatient, but John was confident that he would arrive. He turned up at our hotel as I was trying to shut my cabin trunk. He was a grotesque and filthy little blackamoor, and I resented the prospect of sharing accommodation with him. He appeared to be about eight years old, but was in fact over twelve. He wore a long, blue and very grubby caftan and a battered fez. These clothes, we subsequently learned, he had acquired on his journey, in order to attract less attention. But he could not help attracting attention. My own first reaction to his appearance was frank incredulity. "There ain't no such beast," I said to myself. Then I remembered, that, when a species mutates, it often produces a large crop of characters so fantastic that many of the new types are not even viable. Ng-Gunko was decidedly viable, but he was a freak. Though his face was a dark blend of the negroid and the semitic with an unmistakable reminiscence of the Mongolian, his negroid wool was not black but sombre red. And though his right eye was a huge black orb not inappropriate to his dark complexion, his left eye was considerably smaller, and the iris was deep blue. These discrepancies gave his whole face a sinister comicality which was borne out by his expression. His full lips were frequently stretched in a grin which revealed three small white teeth above and one below. The rest had apparently not yet sprouted.

Ng-Gunko spoke English fluently but incorrectly, and with an uncouth

pronunciation. He had picked up this foreign tongue on his six-weeks'
journey down the Nile valley. By the time we reached London his English
was as good as our own.

The task of making Ng-Gunko fit for a trip on an Orient liner was
arduous. We scrubbed him all over and applied insecticide. On his legs
there were several festering sores. John sterilized the sharpest blade of his
penknife and cut away all the bad flesh, while Ng-Gunko lay perfectly
still, but sweating, and pulling the most hideous grimaces, which expressed
at once torture and amusement. We purchased European clothes, which,
of course, he detested. We had him photographed for his passport, which
John had already arranged with the Egyptian authorities. In triumph we
took him off to the ship in his new white shorts and shirt.

Throughout the voyage we were busy helping him to acquire European ways. He must not pick his nose in public, still less blow it in the
natural manner. He must not take hold of his meat and vegetables with
his hands. He had to acquire the technique of the bathroom and the watercloset. He must not relieve himself in inappropriate places. He must not,
though a mere child, saunter into the crowded dining-saloon without his
clothes. He must not give evidence that he was excessively intelligent. He
must not stare at his fellow-passengers. Above all, he must, we said, restrain
his apparently irresistible impulse to play practical jokes on them.

Though frivolous, Ng-Gunko was certainly of superior intelligence.
It was, for instance, remarkable that a child who had lived his fourteen
years in the forest should easily grasp the principle of the steam turbine,
and should be able to ask the chief engineer (who showed us round the
engine room) questions which made that experienced old Scot scratch his
head. It was on this expedition that John had to whisper fiercely to the
little monster, "If you don't take the trouble to bottle up your blasted
curiosity I'll pitch you over-board."

When we reached our northern suburb Ng-Gunko was installed in
the Wainwright household. As we did not want him to cause more of a
sensation than need be, we dyed his hair black and made him wear spec-
tacles with a dark glass for one eye. Only in the house might he be without them. Unfortunately he was too young to be able to resist the temptation
of startling the natives. Walking along the street with John or me, muffled
to the eyes against the alien climate, duly spectacled and demure, he would
sometimes drop a pace behind as we were approaching some old lady or
child. Then, projecting his chin above his scarf, he would whip off his
glasses and assume a maniacal grin of hate. How often he did this without
being caught I do not know; but on one occasion he was so successful that
the victim let out a scream. John turned upon his protégé and seized him
by the throat. "Do that again," he said, "and I'll have that eye of yours
right out, and step on it." Never again did Ng-Gunko play the trick when

John was present. But with me he did, knowing I was too amiable to report him.

In a few weeks, however, Ng-Gunko began to enter more seriously into the spirit of the great adventure. The conspiratorial atmosphere appealed to him. And the task of preparing himself to play his part gradually absorbed his attention. But he remained at heart a little savage. Even his extraordinary passion for machinery suggested the uncritical delight of the primitive mind in its first encounter with the marvels of our civilization. He had a mechanical gift which in some ways eclipsed even John's. Within a few days of his arrival he was riding the motor-bicycle and making it perform incredible "stunts." Very soon he took it to pieces and put it together again. He mastered the principles of John's psycho-physical power unit, and found, to his intense delight, that he could perform the essential miracle of it himself. It began to be taken for granted that he would be the responsible engineer of the yacht, and of the future colony, leaving John free for more exalted matters. Yet in all Ng-Gunko's actions, and in his whole attitude to life, there was an intensity and even a passion which was very different from John's invariable calm. Indeed I sometimes wondered whether he was emotionally a true supernormal, whether he had anything unusual in his nature beyond brilliant intelligence. But when I suggested this to John he laughed. "Ng-Gunko's a kid," he said, "but Ng-Gunko's all right. Amongst other things he has a natural gift for telepathy, and when I have trained him a bit he may beat me in that direction. But we are both beginners."

Not long after our return from Egypt another supernormal arrived. This was the girl whom John had found in Moscow. Like others of her kind, she looked much younger than she was. She seemed a child, not yet on the threshold of womanhood, but was actually seventeen. She had run away from home, taken a job as stewardess on a Soviet steamer, and slipped ashore at an English port. Thence, equipped with a sufficiency of English money, which she had secured in Russia, she had found her way to the Wainwrights.

Lo was at first glance a much more normal creature than either Ng-Gunko or John. She might have been Jacqueline's youngest sister. No doubt her head was strikingly large, and her eyes occupied more of her face than was normal, but her features were regular, and her sleek black hair was long enough to pass for a "shingle." She was clearly of Asiatic origin, for her cheek bones were high, and her eyes, though great, were deeply sunk within their half-closed and slanting lids. Her nose was broad and flat, like an ape's, her complexion definitely "yellow." She suggested to me a piece of sculpture come to life, something in which the artist had stylized the human in terms of the feline. Her body, too, was feline, "so lean and loose," said John. "It feels breakable, and yet it's all steel springs covered with loose velvet."

During the few weeks which passed before the sailing of the yacht, Lo occupied the room which had once belonged to Anne, John's sister. Relations between her and Pax were never easy, yet always amicable. Lo was exceptionally silent. This, I am sure, would not trouble Pax, for she was generally drawn to silent persons. Yet with Lo she seemed to feel constantly an obligation to talk, and an inability to talk naturally. To all her remarks Lo would reply appropriately, even amiably, yet whatever she said seemed to make matters worse. Whenever Lo was present, Pax would seem ill at ease. She would make silly little mistakes in her work, putting things into wrong drawers, sewing buttons on in the wrong place, breaking her needle, and so on. And everything took longer than it should.

I never discovered why Pax was so uncomfortable with Lo. The girl was, indeed, a disconcerting person, but I should have expected Pax to be more, not less, able to cope with her than others were. It was not only Lo's silence that was so disturbing, but also her almost complete lack of facial expression, or rather of changes of expression for her very absence of expression was itself expressive of a profound detachment from the world around her. In all ordinary social situations, when others would show amusement or pleasure or exasperation, and Ng-Gunko would register intense emotion, Lo's features remained unmoved.

At first I imagined that she was simply insensitive, perhaps dull-witted; but one curious fact about her soon proved that I was wrong. She discovered a passion for the novel, and most of all for Jane Austen. She read all the works of that incomparable authoress over and over again, indeed so often that John, whose interest ran in very different channels, began to chaff her. This roused her to deliver her one long speech. "Where I come from," she said, "there is nothing like Jane Austen. But in me there is something like that, and these old books are helping me to know myself. Of course, they are only 'sapient,' I know; but that is half the fun. It's so interesting to transpose it all to suit *us*. For instance, if Jane could understand me, which she couldn't, what, I ask myself, would she say about me? I find the answer extraordinarily enlightening. Of course, our minds are quite outside her range, but her *attitude* can be applied to us. Her attitude to her little world is so intelligent and sprightly that it gives it a significance that it could never have discovered in itself. Well, I want to regard even us, even our virtuous Colony, in a Jane-like manner. I want to give it a kind of significance that would have remained hidden even from its earnest and noble leader. You know, John, I fancy *Homo sapiens* has still quite a lot to teach you about personality. Or if you are too busy to learn, then I must, or the colony will be intolerable."

To my surprise John replied by giving her a hearty kiss, and she remarked, demurely, "*Odd* John, you have indeed a lot to learn."

This incident may suggest to the reader that Lo was lacking in humour. She was not. Indeed she had a gift of not unkindly wit. Though she seemed incapable of smiling, she often roused others to laughter. And yet, as I say, she was mysteriously disconcerting to most of us. Even John was sometimes uncomfortable in her presence. Once when he was giving me some instructions about finance he broke off to say, "That girl's laughing at me, in spite of her solemn face. She never laughs at all, and yet she's always laughing. Now tell me, Lo, *what's* amusing you." Lo replied, "Dear and important John, it is you who are laughing, at your own reflection in me."

Lo's chief occupation during her few weeks in England was to master the science and art of medicine, and to make herself acquainted with all the most advanced work on the subject of embryology. The reason for this I did not learn till much later. Her vocational training she pursued partly by means of an intensive study under an embryologist of some distinction at the local university, partly by prolonged discussion with John.

As the time approached when the yacht was to be ready and the adventure to begin, Lo's studies became more and more exacting. She began to show signs of strain. We urged her to take a holiday for a few days. "No," she said, "I *must* get to the end of this business before we sail. Then I will rest." We asked if she was sleeping all right. She was evasive. John became suspicious. *"Do* you sleep, ever?" he asked. She hesitated, then replied, "Not *ever,* if I can help it. In fact it is some years since I last slept. And then I slept for ages. But I will *never* sleep again if I can help it." Her first answer to John's incredulous "Why?" was a shudder; then she added as an afterthought, "It is a waste of time. I do go to bed, but I read all night; or just think."

I forget whether I mentioned that all the other supernormals were brief sleepers. John, for instance, was satisfied with four hours a night, and could comfortably do entirely without sleep for three nights at a stretch.

A few days after this incident I learned that Lo had not come down to breakfast, and that Pax had found her still in bed, and asleep. "But it's all wrong," said Pax, "It's more like a fit. She's lying there with her eyes tight shut and awful expressions of horror and rage passing over her face; and she keeps muttering Russian or something, and her hands keep clawing at her chest."

We tried to wake her, but could not. We sat her upright. We put cold water on her. We shouted at her. We shook her and pricked her, but it was no good. That evening she began to scream. She kept it up, off and on, all that night. I stayed with the Wainwrights, though I could do nothing. But somehow I couldn't go. The whole street was kept awake. It was sometimes just an inarticulate screech like an animal beside itself with pain and fury, sometimes a torrent of Russian, shouted at the top of her voice, but so blurred that John could make nothing of it.

Next morning she quietened down, and for more than a week she slept without stirring. One morning she came down to breakfast as though nothing had happened, but looking, so John said, "like a corpse animated by a soul out of Hell." As she sat down she said to John, *"Now* do you understand why I like Jane Austen, better for instance than Dostoievski?"

It took her some time to regain her strength and her normal equanimity. One day, when she had settled down to work again, she told Pax a bit about herself. Away back in her infancy, before the Revolution, when her people lived in a small town beyond the Urals, she used to sleep every night; but she often had bad dreams, which she said were extremely terrifying, and completely indescribable in terms of any normal experience. All she could say of them was that she felt herself turn into a mad beast or a devil, yet that inwardly she always remained her sane little self, an impotent spectator of her own madness. As she grew older, these infantile terrors left her. During the Revolution and the years immediately following it her family experienced terrible sufferings from civil war and famine. She was still in appearance an infant but mentally well able to appreciate the significance of events going on around her. She had, for instance, already reached a conviction that, though both sides in the civil war were equally capable of brutality and generosity, the spirit of the one was on the whole right, the other wrong. Even at that early age she felt, vaguely but with conviction, that the horror of her life, the bombardments, the fires, the mass executions, the cold, the hunger, must somehow be embraced, not shunned. Triumphantly she did embrace them. But there came a time when her town was sacked by the Whites. Her father was killed. Her mother fled with her in a refugee train crowded with wounded men and women. The journey was, of course, desperately fatiguing. Lo fell asleep, and was plunged once more into her nightmare, with the difference that it was now peopled with all the horrors of the civil war, and she herself was forced to watch impotently while her other self perpetrated the most hideous atrocities.

Ever since those days any great strain was liable to bring sleep upon her, with all its horrors. She reported, however, that the attacks were now much less frequent; but that on the other hand the content of her dreams was more terrible, because—she couldn't properly explain—because it was more universal, more metaphysical, more cosmically significant, and at the same time more definitely an expression of something Satanic (her own word) within her very self.

CHAPTER XVIII

THE *SKID'S* FIRST VOYAGE

HENCEFORTH Pax was more at ease with Lo. She had nursed her, received her confidence, and found occasion to pity her. All the same it was
clear that the continued presence of Lo was a strain on Pax. When the
yacht was launched, John himself said to me, "We must get away as soon
as possible now. Lo is killing Pax, though she does her best not to. Poor
Pax! She's being driven into old age at last." It was true. Her hair was
fading, and her mouth drawn.

It was with mixed feelings that I learned that I was not to take part
in the coming voyage in search of additional members for the colony. I
could live my own life. I could marry and settle down, holding myself in
readiness to serve John when he should need me. But how could I live
without John? I tried to persuade him that I was necessary to him. A
saucer-like craft wandering the oceans with a crew of three children would
attract less attention if she carried one adult. But my suggestion was dismissed. John claimed that he no longer looked a child, and further declared
that he could touch up his face so as to appear at least twenty-five.

I need not describe in detail the preparations which these three young
eccentrics undertook in order to fit themselves for their adventure. Both
Ng-Gunko and Lo had to learn to fly; and all three had to become familiar
with the mannerisms of their own queer aeroplane and their own queer
yacht. The vessel was launched on the Clyde by Pax, and christened *Skid,*
under which odd but appropriate name she was duly registered. I may
mention that for the Board of Trade inspection she was fitted with a normal motor-engine, which was subsequently removed to make room for the
psycho-physical power unit and motor.

When both yacht and plane were ready for use, a trial trip was made
among the Western Isles. On this trip I was tolerated as a guest. The experience was enough to cure me of any desire for a longer voyage in such
a diabolical vessel. The three-foot model had somehow failed to make me
imagine the discomforts of the actual boat. Her great beam made her fairly
steady, but she was so shallow, and therefore low in the water, that every
considerable wave splashed over her, and in rough weather she was always
awash. This did not greatly matter, as her navigating controls were all
under cover in a sort of stream-lined deck-house reminiscent of a sporting
saloon motor-car. In fine weather one could stretch one's legs on deck, but
below deck there was scarcely room to move, as she was a mass of machinery, bunks, stores. And there was the plane. This strange instrument,

minute by ordinary standards, and folded up like a fan, occupied a large
amount of her space.

After emerging from Greenock we skidded comfortably down the
Clyde, past Arran, and round the Mull of Kintyre. Then we struck heavy
weather, and I was violently sick. So also, much to my satisfaction, was
Ng-Gunko. Indeed, he was so ill that John decided to make for shelter,
lest he should die. But quite suddenly Ng-Gunko learned to control his
vomiting reflexes. He stopped being sick, lay still for ten minutes, then
leapt from his bunk with a shout of triumph, only to be hurled into the
galley by a lurch of the ship.

The trials were said to be entirely successful. When she was going
full speed the *Skid* lifted the whole fore part of herself right out of the
water and set up a mountain-range of water and foam on either side of
her. Though the weather was rather wild, the plane also was tested. It
was heaved out aft on a derrick and unfolded while afloat. All three members of the crew took a turn at flying it. The most surprising thing about
it was that, owing to its cunning design and its immense reserve of power,
it rose straight from the water without taxi-ing.

A week later the *Skid* set out on her first long voyage. Our farewells
were made at the dock. The Wainright parents reacted very differently to
the departure of their youngest son. Doc was genuinely anxious about the
dangers of the voyage in such a vessel, and mistrustful of the abilities of
the juvenile crew. Pax showed no anxiety, so complete was her confidence
in John. But clearly she found it difficult to face his departure without
showing distress. Hugging her, he said, "Dear Pax," then sprang on board.
Lo, who had already made her farewells, came back to Pax, took both her
hands, and said, actually smiling, "Dear mother of important John!" To
this odd remark Pax replied simply with a kiss.

My slender knowledge of the voyage is derived partly from John's
laconic letters, partly from conversation after his return. The programme
was determined by his telepathic researches. Distance, apparently, made
no difference to the ease with which he could pick up the psychic processes
of other supernormals. Success depended entirely on his ability to "tune
in" to their mental "setting" or mode of experience, and this depended on
the degree of similarity of their mode to his own. Thus he was already in
clear communication with a supernormal in Tibet, and two others in
China, but for the rest he could only make the vaguest guesses as to the
existence and location of possible members of the colony.

Letters told us that the *Skid* had spent an unprofitable three weeks on
the West Coast of Africa. John had flown into the hinterland, pursuing
traces of a supernormal in some oasis in the Sahara. He struck a sand
storm of peculiar violence, and made a forced landing in the desert, with
his engine choked with sand. "When the wind had dropped I cleaned her

guts," said John, "and then flew back to the *Skid*, still chewing sand."
What epic struggles were involved in this adventure I can only guess.

At Cape Town the *Skid* was docked, and the three young people set
off to comb South Africa, following up certain meagre traces of the supernormal mentality. Both John and Lo soon returned empty-handed. In his
letter John remarked, "Delicious to watch the Whites treating the Blacks
as an inferior species. Lo says it reminds her of her mother's stories of
Tsarist Russia."

John and Lo waited impatiently for some weeks while Ng-Gunko,
doubtless revelling in his return to native conditions, nosed about in the
remote woodlands and saltpans of Ngamiland. He was in telepathic communication with John, but there seemed to be some mystery about his activities. John grew anxious, for the lad was dangerously juvenile, and
possibly of a less balanced type than himself. At last he was driven to tell
Ng-Gunko that if he did not "chuck his antics" the *Skid* would sail without him. The reply was merely a cheerful assurance that he would be
starting back in a day or two. A week later came a message that combined
a cry of triumph and an S.O.S. He had secured his prey, and was making
his way through the wilds to civilization, but had no money for the return
railway journey. John therefore set out to fly to the spot indicated, while
Lo, single handed, took the *Skid* round to Durban.

John had already been waiting some days at the primitive settlement
when Ng-Gunko appeared, dead beat, but radiant. He removed a bundle
from his back, uncovered the end of it, and displayed to the indignant
John a minute black infant, immature, twitching and gasping.

Ng-Gunko, it seems, had traced the telepathic intimations to a certain
tribe and a certain woman. His African experiences had enabled him to
detect in this woman's attitude to the life of the forest something akin to
his own. Further investigation led him to believe that though she herself
was in some slight degree supernormal, the main source of those obscure
hints which he had been pursuing was not the mother but her unborn
child, in whose pre-natal experiences Ng-Gunko recognized the rudiments
of supernormal intensity. It was indeed remarkable that before birth a mind
should have any telepathic influence at all. The mother had already carried her baby for eleven months. Now Ng-Gunko knew that he himself
had been born late, and that his mother had not been delivered of him
till certain incentives had been used upon her by the wise women of the
tribe. This treatment he persuaded the black matron to undergo, for she
was weary to death. As best he could, Ng-Gunko applied what he knew of
the technique. The baby was born, but the mother died. Ng-Gunko fled
with his prize. When John asked how he had fed the baby on the long
journey, Ng-Gunko explained that in his Abyssinian days he and other
youngsters used to milk wild antelopes. They stalked them, and by means
of a process that reminded me of "tickling" trout, they persuaded the

mothers to let themselves be milked. This trick had served on the journey. The infant, of course, had not thrived, but it was alive.

The kidnapper was pained to find that his exploit, far from being applauded, was condemned and ridiculed. What on earth, John demanded, could they possibly do with the creature? And anyhow, was he really at all worth bothering about? Ng-Gunko was convinced that he had secured an infant superman who would outclass them all; and in time John himself was impressed by his telepathic explorations of the new-comer.

The plane set out for Durban with the baby in Ng-Gunko's arms. One would have expected the care and maintenance of it to fall to Lo, but her attitude toward it was aloof. Moreover, Ng-Gunko himself made it clear that he would bear all responsibility for the new-comer, who somehow acquired the name Sambo. Ng-Gunko became as devoted to Sambo as a mother to her first-born or a schoolboy to his white mice.

The *Skid* now headed for Bombay. Somewhere north of the Equator she ran into very heavy weather. This was a matter of small importance to a craft of her seaworthiness, though it must have greatly increased the discomfort of her crew. At a much later date I learned of a sinister incident that occurred in those wild days, an incident to which John made no reference in his letters. The *Skid* sighted a small British steamer, the *Frome,* in distress. Her steering engine was out of action, and she was labouring broadside-on to the storm. The *Skid* stood by, till, when the *Frome's* plight was obviously hopeless, the crew took to the two remaining boats. The *Skid* attempted to take them both in tow. This operation was evidently very dangerous, for a sea flung one of the boats bodily on to the after deck of the yacht, thrusting her stern under water, and threatening to sink her. Ng-Gunko, who was dealing with the tow rope, had a foot rather badly crushed. The boat then floated off, and capsized. Of her crew only two were rescued, both by the *Skid.* The other boat was successfully taken in tow. A few days later the weather improved, and the *Skid* and her charge made good progress toward Bombay. But now the two strangers on board the *Skid* began to show great curiosity. Here were three eccentric children and a black baby cruising the ocean in a most eccentric craft driven by some unintelligible source of power. The two seamen were loud in praise of their rescuers. They assured John that they would speak up for him in the public inquiry which would be held over the loss of the *Frome.*

This was all very inconvenient. The three supernormals discussed the situation telepathically, and agreed that drastic action was demanded. John produced an automatic pistol and shot the two guests. The noise caused great excitement in the boat. Ng-Gunko slipped the tow rope, and John cruised round while Ng-Gunko and Lo, lying on the deck with rifles, disposed of all the *Frome's* survivors. When this grim task was finished, the corpses were thrown to the sharks. The boat was scrubbed of blood stains, and then scuttled. The *Skid* proceeded to Bombay.

Long afterwards, when John told me about this shocking incident, I was as much perplexed as revolted. Why, I asked, if he dared not risk a little publicity, had he been willing to risk destruction in the work of rescuing the ship's boats? And how did he fail to realize, during that operation, that publicity was inevitable? And was there, I demanded, any enterprise whatever, even the founding of a new species, that could justify such cold butchery of human beings? If this was the way of *Homo superior,* I said, thank God I was of another species. We might be weak and stupid, but at least we were able sometimes to feel the sanctity of human life. Was not this piece of brutality on exactly the same footing as the innumerable judicial murders, political murders, religious murders, that had sullied the record of *Homo sapiens?* These, I declared, had always seemed to their perpetrators righteous acts, but were regarded by the more human of our kind as barbarous.

John answered with that mildness and thoughtfulness with which he treated me only on those rare occasions when I gave him matter for serious consideration. He first pointed out that the *Skid* had still to spend much time in contact with the world of *Homo sapiens.* Her crew had work to do in India, Tibet and China. It was certain, therefore, that if their part in the *Frome* incident became public, they would be forced to give evidence at the inquiry. He insisted, further, that if they were discovered, their whole venture would be ruined. Had they at that early stage known all that they knew later about hypnotically controlling the humbler species, they might indeed have abolished from the minds of the *Frome's* survivors all memory of the rescue. "But you see," he said, "we could not do it. We had deliberately risked publicity, as we had risked destruction by the storm, *hoping* to avoid it. We *tried* to set up a process of 'oblivifaction' in our guests, but we failed. As for the wickedness of the act, Fido, it naturally revolts you, but you are leaving something out of account. Had we been members of your species, concerned only with the dreamlike purposes of the normal mind, what we did would have been a crime. For to-day the chief lesson which your species has to learn is that it is far better to die, far better to sacrifice even the loftiest of all 'sapient' purposes, than to kill beings of one's own mental order. But just as you kill wolves and tigers so that the far brighter spirits of men may flourish, so we killed those unfortunate creatures that we had rescued. Innocent as they were, they were dangerous. Unwittingly they threatened the noblest practical venture that has yet occurred on this planet. Think! If *you,* and Bertha, had found yourselves in a world of great apes, clever in their own way, lovable too, but blind, brutish, and violent, would you have refused to kill? Would you have sacrificed the founding of a human world? To refuse would be cowardly, not physically, but spiritually. Well, if we could wipe out your whole species, frankly, we would. For if your species discovers us, and realizes at all what we are, it will certainly destroy us. And we know, you must remember, that *Homo sapiens* has little more to contribute to the music of this planet, nothing in fact but vain repetition. It is time for finer instruments to take up the theme."

When he had done, John looked at me almost pleadingly. He seemed to long for my approval, the approval of a half-human thing, his faithful hound. Did he, after all, feel guilty? I think not. I think this strong desire to persuade me sprang simply from affection. For my part, such is my faith in John, that though I cannot approve, I cannot condemn. There must surely be some aspect that I am too stupid or insensitive to grasp. John, I feel, *must* be right. Though he did what would have been utterly wrong if it had been done by any of us, I have an almost passionate faith that, done by John, and in John's circumstances, the terrible deed was right.

But to return to the story. At Bombay John and Lo spent some time studying Indian and Tibetan languages, and otherwise preparing themselves for contact with Eastern races. When at length they left the *Skid,* and Bombay, Ng-Gunko remained behind to nurse Sambo and his damaged foot. The two explorers set out together in the plane; but Lo, disguised as a Nepalese boy, was put down at an Indian hill station. There, it was hoped, she might develop a telepathic contact which was thought to indicate a supernormal in some such environment. John himself continued his flight over the great mountains to Tibet to meet the young Buddhist monk with whom he had often been in communication.

In his brief letter describing his expedition to Tibet John scarcely mentioned the actual journey, though the flight over the Himalayas must have been an exacting task even for a superman in a superplane. He said only, "She took the jump splendidly, and then was blown right back again into India, head over heels, too. She dropped my thermos flask. Coming back I saw it on the ridge, but let it lie."

As the Tibetan monk was able to guide him telepathically, he found the monastery quite easily. John described Langatse as a supernormal of forty years, physically but little advanced beyond the threshold of manhood. He had been born without eyes. Blindness had forced him to concentrate on his telepathic powers, which he had developed far beyond John's own attainment. He could always see telepathically what other people were seeing; consequently, for reading he had simply to use some one else's eyes. The other would cast his eye over the page while Langatse followed telepathically. He had trained several young men to perform this task for him so well that he could read almost as quickly as John. One curious effect of his blindness was that, since he could use many pairs of eyes at a time, and could see all round an object at once, his mental imagery was of a kind quite inconceivable to ordinary persons. As John put it, he *grasped* things visually, instead of merely having a single aspect of them. He saw things mentally from every point of view at once.

John had originally hoped to persuade Langatse to join his great adventure, but he soon found that this was out of the question. The Tibetan regarded the whole matter much as Adlan had done. He was interested, encouraging, but aloof. To him the founding of a new world, though it must indeed some day be accomplished by some one, was not a matter of urgency, and must not tempt him from his own more lofty spiritual services. Nevertheless he consented gladly to be the spiritual adviser of the colony, and meanwhile he would impart to John all that he knew of the telepathic technique and other supernormal activities. At one time Langatse suggested that John should give up his enterprise and settle in Tibet to share the more exacting and more exalted spiritual adventures on which he himself was engaged. But, finding that John was not to be easily persuaded, he soon desisted. John stayed at the monastery a week. During his return flight he received a message from Langaste to the effect that, after grave spiritual exercise, he had decided to help John by seeking out and preparing any young supernormals that were in Asia and suited to the adventure.

John received a communication also from Lo. She had discovered two remarkable sisters, both younger than herself. They would join the expedition; but as the elder was just now in a very poor state of health, and the younger a little child, they must stay where they were for the present.

The *Skid* now set her course for the China Seas. In Canton John met Shên Kuo, the Chinese supernormal boy with whom he had already had some communication. Shên Kuo readily agreed to make his way inland to join the two other boys and two girls whom Langatse had discovered in the remote Eastern Province of Sze Chwan. Thence the five would journey to Tibet to Langatse's monastery, to undergo a course of spiritual discipline in preparation for their new life. Langatse reported that he had also secured three Tibetan boys and a girl for the colony, and that these also would be prepared at the monastery.

One other convert was made. This was a half-caste Chinese American girl resident in San Francisco. This child, who went by the name of Washingtonia Jong, was also discovered by Langatse telepathically. The *Skid* crossed the Pacific to pick her up, and she straightway became a member of the crew. I did not meet her till a much later date; but I may as well say at once that "Washy," as she was called, appeared to me at first a quite normal young person, a keen little American flapper with rather Chinese eyes and black cropped hair. But I was to find that there was more in her than that.

John's next task was to discover a suitable island for the colony. It must have a temperate or subtropical climate. It must have a fertile soil, and be well situated for fishing. It must be remote from any frequented steamer route. This last requirement was extremely important, for complete secrecy was essential. Even the most remote and unconsidered island would certainly be visited sooner or later; so John had thought out certain steps to prevent ships from reaching his island, and certain others to ensure that any visitors who should make a landing should not spread news of the colony among the normal species. Of these devices I shall speak in due season.

The *Skid* crossed the Equator and began a systematic exploration of the South Seas. After many weeks of cruising a suitable though minute island was discovered somewhere in the angle between the routes from New Zealand to Panama and New Zealand to Cape Horn, and well away from both courses. This discovery was an incredible stroke of luck, indeed it might well have been an act of Providence. For the island was one which was not marked on any charts, and there were clear signs that it had only within the last twenty years or so been thrown up by sub-oceanic disturbance. There were no non-human mammals on it, and no reptiles. Vegetation was still scanty and undiversified. Yet the island was inhabited. A small native group had taken possession of it, and were living by fishing around its coasts. Many varieties of plants and trees they themselves had brought over from their original home and established on the island.

I did not hear about these original inhabitants till much later, when I visited the island. "They were simple and attractive creatures," said John, "but, of course, we could not allow them to interfere with our plans. It might have been possible to obliterate from their minds every recollection of the island and of ourselves, and then to transport them. But though I had learned much from Langatse, our technique of oblivifaction was still unreliable. Moreover, where could we have deposited the natives without rousing protests, and curiosity? We might have kept them alive on the island, as domestic animals, but this would have wrecked our plans. It would also have undermined the natives spiritually. So we decided to destroy them. One bit of hypnotic technique (or magic, if you like) I felt sure I could now perform successfully on normal minds in which there were strong religious convictions. This we decided to use. The natives had welcomed us to their island and arranged a feast for us. After the feast there were ritual dances and religious rites. When the excitement was at a climax I made Lo dance for them. And when she had done, I said to them, in their own language, that we were gods, that we needed their island, that they must therefore make a great funeral pyre for themselves, mount it together, lie down together, and gladly die. This they did, most gladly, men, women and children. When they had all died we set fire to the faggots and their bodies were burnt."

I cannot defend this act. But I may point out that, had the invaders been members of the normal species, they would probably have baptised the natives, given them prayer books and European clothes, rum and all the diseases of the White Man. They would also have enslaved them economically, and in time they would have crushed their spirits by confronting them at every turn with the White Man's trivial superiority. Finally, when all had died of drink or bitterness, they would have mourned for them. Perhaps the only defence of the psychological murders which the supernormals committed when they took possession of the island would run as follows. Having made up their minds that at all costs the island must be theirs, and unencumbered, they did not shirk the consequences of their decision. With open eyes they went about their task, and fulfilled it in the cleanest possible way. Whether the end which they so ruthlessly pursued did in fact justify the means, I simply do not feel competent to decide. All my sympathies lie with the view that murder can never be justified, however lofty the end at stake. Certainly, had the killing been perpetrated by members of my own kind, such a deed would have deserved the sternest condemnation. But who am I that I should judge beings who in daily contact with me constantly proved themselves my superiors not only in intelligence but in moral insight?

When the five superior beings, John and Lo, Ng-Gunko and Washingtonia and the infant Sambo, had taken possession of the island, they spent some weeks resting from their travels, preparing the site for future settlement, and conferring with Langatse and those who were under his guidance. It was arranged that as soon as the Asiatics were spiritually equipped they should find their way as best they could to one of the French Polynesian islands, whence the *Skid* would fetch them. Meanwhile, however, the *Skid* would make a hurried trip to England *via* the Straits of Magellan to secure materials for the founding of the colony, and to fetch the remaining European supernormals.

CHAPTER XIX

THE COLONY IS FOUNDED

THE *Skid* reached England three weeks before the date on which I was to be married. As she had no radio, and her voyage had been speedy, she arrived unannounced. Bertha and I had been shopping. We called at my flat to deposit some parcels before going out for the evening. Arm in arm, we entered my sitting-room, and found the *Skid's* crew snugly installed, eating my apples and some chocolates which I kept for Bertha's entertainment. We stood for a moment in silence. I felt Bertha's arm tighten on mine. John was enjoying his apple in an easy chair by the fire. Lo, squatting on the hearth rug, was turning over the pages of the *New Statesman*. Ng-Gunko was in the other easy chair, chewing sweets and bending over Sambo. I think he was helping the infant to readjust the thick and unfamiliar clothes without which he could not have faced the English climate.

Sambo, all head and stomach, with limbs that were mere buds, cocked an inquisitive eye at me. Washingtonia, whom I had not seen before, struck me at that moment as reassuringly commonplace among those freaks.

John had risen, and was saying with his mouth full, "Hullo, old Fido, hullo, Bertha! You'll hate me, Bertha, but I *must* have Fido to help me for a few weeks, buying stores and things." "But we're just going to get married," I protested. "Damn!" said John. Then to my surprise I assured John that of course we would put it off for a couple of months. Bertha wilted on to a chair with a voiceless "Of course." "Good," cried John cheerfully. "After this affair I may not bother you any more." Unexpectedly my heart sank.

The following weeks were spent in a whirl of practical activities. The *Skid* had to be reconditioned, the plane repaired. Tools and machinery, electric fittings and plumbing materials must be bought and shipped to Valparaiso to await transhipment. Timber must be sent from the South American forests to the same port. General stores must be purchased in England. My task was to negotiate all these transactions, under John's direction. John himself prepared a list of books which I must somehow procure and dispatch. There were to be scores of technical works on various biological subjects, tropical agriculture, medicine and so on. There were to be books on theoretical physics, astronomy, philosophy, and a rather intriguing selection of purely literary works in many languages. Most difficult to procure were many scores of Asiatic writings with titles suggestive of the occult.

Shortly before the *Skid's* next sailing-date the additional European members of the party began to arrive. John himself went to Hungary to fetch Jelli, a mite said to be seventeen years old. She was no beauty. The frontal and the occipital regions of her head were repulsively over-developed, so that the back of her head stretched away behind her, and her brow protruded beyond her nose, which was rudimentary. In profile her head suggested a croquet mallet. She had a hare-lip and short bandy legs. Her general appearance was that of a cretin; yet she had supernormal intelligence and temperament, and also hyper-sensitive vision. Not only did she distinguish two primary colours within the spectrum-band that we call blue, but also she could see well down into the infra-red. In addition to this colour-discrimination, she had a sense of form that was, so to speak, much finer-grained than ours. Probably there were more nerve-endings in her retinae than in normal eyes, for she could read a newspaper at twenty yards' distance, and she could see at a glance that a penny was not accurately circular. So sensitive was she to form that, if the parts of a puzzle picture were flung down before her, she took in their significant relations at a glance, and could construct the picture without a pause. This amazing percipience often caused her distress, for no man-made article appeared to her to achieve the shape that its maker intended. And in the sphere of art she was excruciated, not merely by inaccuracy of execution but also by crudity of conception.

Besides Jelli, there was the French girl, Marianne Laffon, quite normal in contrast with Jelli, and rather pretty with her dark eyes and olive skin. She was seemingly a repository of the whole of French culture, and could quote any passage of any classic, and, by some magic of her own, so amplify it that one seemed to plumb the author's mind.

There was also a Swedish girl, Sigrid, whom John called the Comb-Wielder, "because she has such a gift for combing out tangled minds till they're all sleek and sane." She had been a consumptive, but had apparently cured herself by some sort of mental "immunizing" of her tissues. Even after her cure she retained the phthisic's cheerfulness. A great-eyed, fragile thing, she combined her wonderful gift of sympathy and insight with a maternal tenderness toward brute strength. When she found it being brutal, she censured but still loved it. She was moved to send it away howling with its tail between its legs, but at the same time she "felt all sloppy about it, as though it were just a delicious little naughty boy."

Several young male supernormals turned up, one by one, to join the *Skid*. (The Wainwrights' house became at this time a shocking slum.) There was Kemi, the Fin, a younger John; Shahîn, the Turk, a few years older than John, but well content to be his subordinate; and Kargis from the Caucasus.

Of these, Shahîn was from the normal point of view the most attractive, for he had the build of a Russian dancer and in social intercourse a lightness of touch which one took according to one's mood, either as charming frivolity or as sublime detachment.

Kargis, who was not much younger than John, arrived in a state bordering on mania. He had had a very trying journey in a tramp steamer, and his unstable mind had failed to stand the strain. In appearance he was of John's type, but darker and less hardy. I found it very difficult to form a consistent idea of this strange being. He oscillated between excitement and lethargy, between passion and detachment. The cause of these fluctuations was not, I was assured, anything in his body's physiological rhythm, but external events which were hidden from me. When I inquired what kind of events, Lo, who was trying to help me, said, "He's like Sigrid in having a great sense of personality. But he regards persons rather differently from her way. She just loves them, and laughs at them too, and helps them, and cures them. But for him each person is like a work of art, having a particular quality or style, or ideal form which he embodies well or ill. And when a person is jarringly untrue to his peculiar style or ideal form, Kargis is excruciated."

The ten young people and one helpless infant set sail in the *Skid* in August of 1928.

John kept in communication with us by the ordinary mail. As I shall explain later, the *Skid,* and sometimes the plane, had occasion to make frequent voyages among the Islands or to Valparaiso. Thus it was possible to post John's brief and guarded letters. From these documents we learned first that the voyage out had been uneventful; that they had called at Valparaiso to load as much of the stores as possible; that they had reached the island; that the *Skid,* manned by Ng-Gunko, Kemi and Marianne, was plying to and from Valparaiso to transport the rest of the stores; that the building of the settlement was now well under way; that the Asiatic members had arrived, and were "settling in nicely," that a hurricane had struck the island, destroying all the temporary buildings, depositing the damaged *Skid* on a little hill beside the harbour, and hurting one of the Tibetan boys; that they had sowed large tracts of fruit and vegetables; that they had built six canoes for fishing; that Kargis had fallen seriously ill of some digestive disease and was expected to die; that he had recovered; that the remains of a Galapagos lizard had been washed up on the shore after God knows how long a journey; that Sigrid had tamed an albatross, and that it stole the breakfast; that the Colony had suffered its first tragedy, for Yang Chung had been caught by a shark, and Kemi had been seriously mauled in the vain attempt to rescue him, that Sambo was spending all his time reading, but could not yet sit upright; that they had made for themselves pipes on the James Jones model, but with special attachments so that they could be played by normal five-fingered hands; that Tsomotre (one of the Tibetans) and Shahîn were composing wonderful music; that Jelli had developed acute appendicitis and Lo had operated successfully; that Lo herself had been working too hard on some embryological experiments and had fallen into one of her terrible nightmares; that she was awake again; that Marianne and Shên Kuo had gone to live on the far side of the Island "because they wanted to be alone for a bit"; that "Washy" was going mad, for she complained of feeling hate for Lankor (a Tibetan girl) who had won the heart of Shahîn; that "Washy" had tried to kill Lankor and herself; that Sigrid, in spite of prolonged and patient efforts, had failed to cure "Washy," and was now herself showing signs of strain; that both girls were not being cured from afar by Langatse's telepathic influence; that the Colonists had completed their stone library and meeting-house, and the observatory was being started; that Tsomotre and Lankor, who were evidently the most expert telepathists, were now able to provide the colony with the news of the world in daily bulletins; that the more advanced members of the party, under the direction of Langatse, were undergoing severe exercises in spiritual discipline, which in time should raise them to a new plane of experience; that a severe earthquake had caused the whole island to sink nearly two feet, so that they had to lay several new courses of stone on the quays, and would henceforth need to keep the *Skid* in readiness for a sudden exodus, in case the island should disappear.

As the months protracted themselves into years, John's letters became less frequent and more brief. He was evidently entirely absorbed in the affairs of the colony; and as the party became more and more concerned with supernormal activities, he found it increasingly difficult to give us an intelligible account of their life.

In the spring of 1932, however, I was greatly surprised to receive a long letter from John, the main purport of which was to urge me to visit the island as soon as possible. I quote the essential passage. "You will laugh when I tell you I want you to come and use your journalistic prowess upon us. In fact I want you to write that threatened biography after all, not for our sakes but for your own species. I must explain. We have made a wonderful start. Sometimes it was a bit grim, but now we have worked out a very satisfactory life and society. Our practical activities run smoothly, delightfully, and we are able at last to join in a great effort to reach the higher planes of experience. Already we are very different mentally from what we were when we landed. Some of us have seen far and deep into reality, and we have at least gained a clear view of the work we have undertaken. But a number of signs suggest that before very many months have passed the colony will be destroyed. If your species discovers us, it will certainly try to smash us; and we are not yet in a position to defeat it. Langatse has urged us (and he is right) to push on with the spiritual part of our work, so as to complete as much as possible of it before the end. But also we may as well leave records of our little adventure as an example for any future supernormals who may attempt to found the new world, and for the benefit of the more sensitive members of *Homo sapiens*. Langatse will take charge of the record for supernormals; the record for your species entails only normal powers and can be done satisfactorily by yourself."

I was now a tolerably successful free-lance journalist, and I had a full programme before me. I was married, and Bertha was expecting a child. Yet I eagerly accepted the invitation. That afternoon I made inquiries about steamers for Valparaiso, and replied to John (*post restante* at that city), telling him when to expect me.

Guiltily, I broke my news to Bertha. She was hard hit by it, but she said, "Yes, if John wants you, of course you must go." Then I went round to the Wainwrights'. Pax greatly surprised me, for no sooner had I begun to tell her about the letter than she interrupted me. "I know," she said, "for some weeks he has been giving me little stray visions of the island, and even talking to me. He *said* he would be asking for you."

CHAPTER XX

THE COLONY IN BEING

WHEN I arrived at Valparaiso the *Skid* was waiting for me, manned by Ng-Gunko and Kemi. Both lads had appreciably matured since I had last seen them, nearly four years earlier. Those crowded years seemed to have speeded up the slow growth natural to their kind. Ng-Gunko, in particular, who was actually sixteen and might have been taken for twelve, had acquired a grace and a seriousness which I never expected of him. Both seemed in a great hurry to put to sea. I asked if there was any special engagement to keep on the island. "No," said Ng-Gunko, "but we may have less than a year to live, and we love the island, and all our friends. We want to go home."

As soon as my baggage and some cases of books and stores had been transhipped in the *Skid's* dinghy, we got under way. Ng-Gunko and Kemi promptly divested themselves of their clothes, for it was a hot day. Kemi's fair skin had been burnt to the colour of the teak woodwork of the *Skid*.

When we had come within about forty miles of the island, Kemi, who was at the helm, said, glancing from the magnetic to the gyroscopic compass, "They must be using the deflector. That means some ship has come too close, and they're heading her off." He went on to explain that on the island they had an instrument for deflecting a magnetic compass at any range up to about fifty miles. This was the fourth occasion for its use.

At last we sighted the island, a minute grey hump on the horizon. As we approached, it rose and displayed itself as a double mountain. Even when we were quite close to land I failed to detect any sign of habitation. Ng-Gunko explained that the buildings had all been placed in such a manner as to escape detection. Not till the island had opened out its little harbour to embrace us did I see the corner of one wooden building protruding from behind some trees. Not till we had entered the inner harbour did the whole settlement appear. It consisted of a score or more of small wooden buildings, with a larger stone building behind them and slightly higher up the slope. Most of the little wooden buildings, I was told, were the private houses of the residents. The stone building was the library and meeting-house. There were also buildings on the quayside, including a stone power-station. Somewhat remote from the rest of the settlement was a collection of wooden sheds which were said to be temporary labs.

The *Skid* was moored alongside the lowest of three stone quays, for the tide was out. The colonists were waiting to receive us and unload. They were a bunch of naked, sunburnt youngsters of both sexes and very diverse appearance. John sprang on board to greet me, and I found myself tongue-tied. He had become a dazzling figure, at least to my faithful eyes. There was a new firmness and a new dignity about him. His face was brown and smooth and hard like a hazel nut. His whole body was like shaped and bees-waxed oak. His hair was bleached to a dazzling whiteness. I noted among the party several unfamiliar faces, the Asiatics, of course, from China, Tibet and India. Seeing all these supernormals together, I was struck by a pervading Chinese or Mongolian expression about them. They had come from many lands, but they had a family likeness. John might well be right in guessing that all had sprung from a single "sporting point" centuries ago, probably in Central Asia. From that original mutation, or perhaps from a number of similar mutations, successive generations of offspring had spread over Asia, Europe, Africa, interbreeding with the normal kind, but producing occasionally a true supernormal individual.

Subsequently I learned that Shên Kuo's direct researches in the past had confirmed this theory.

I had been dreading life in this colony of superior persons. I expected to feel unwanted, to be as useless and distracting as a dog at a highbrow concert. But my reception reassured me. The younger members accepted me gaily and carelessly, treating me much as nieces and nephews might treat an uncle whose special office it was to make a fool of himself. The elders of the party were more restrained, but genial.

I was assigned one of the wooden cottages or shacks as my private residence. It was surrounded by a verandah. "You may prefer to have your bed out here," said John. "There are no mosquitoes." I noticed at once that the cottage had been made with the care and accuracy of fine cabinet-making. It was sparsely furnished with solid and simple articles of waxed wood. On one wall of the sitting-room was a carved panel representing in an abstract manner a boy and a girl (of the supernormal type) apparently at sea in a canoe, and hunting a shark. In the bedroom was another carving, much more abstract, but vaguely suggestive of sleep. On the bed were sheets and blankets, woven of rough yarns unknown to me. I was surprised to see electric light, an electric stove, and beyond the bedroom a minute bathroom with hot and cold taps. The water was heated by an electric contrivance in the bathroom itself. Fresh water was plentiful, I was told, for it was distilled from the sea as a sort of by-product of the psycho-physical power-station.

Glancing at the small electric clock, let into the wall, John said, "There'll be a meal in a few minutes. That long building is the feeding-house, with the kitchen alongside of it." He pointed to a low wooden building among the trees. In front of it was a terrace, and on the terrace, tables.

I shall not forget my first meal on the island. I was seated between John and Lo. The table was crowded with unfamiliar eatables, especially tropical and sub-tropical fruits, fish, and a queer sort of bread, all served in vessels made of wood or of shell. Marianne and the two Chinese girls seemed responsible for the meal, for they kept disappearing into the kitchen to produce new dishes.

Looking at the slight naked figures of various shades from Ng-Gunko's nigger-brown to Sigrid's rich cream, all seated round the table and munching with the heartiness of a school treat, I felt that I had strayed into an island of goblins. This was in the main an effect of the two rows of large heads and eyes like field-glass lenses, but was accentuated by the disproportionately large hands which were busy with the food. The islanders were certainly a collection of young freaks, but one or two of them were freakish even in relation to the standards of the group itself. There was Jelli with her hammer-head and hare-lip, Ng-Gunko with his red wool and discrepant eyes, Tsomotre, a Tibetan boy, whose head seemed to grow straight out of his shoulders without the intervention of a neck, Hwan Tê, a Chinese youngster, whose hands outclassed all the others in size, and bore, in addition to the normal set of fingers, an extra and very useful thumb.

Since the death of Yang Chung the party comprised eleven youths and boys (including Sambo) and ten girls, of whom the youngest was a little Indian child. Of these twenty-one individuals, three lads and a girl were Tibetan, two youths and two girls were Chinese, two girls were Indian. All the others were of European origin, except Washingtonia Jong. I was to discover that of the Asiatics the outstanding personalities were Tsomotre, the neckless expert in telepathy, and Shên Kuo, a Chinese youth of John's age who specialized in direct research into the past. This gentle and rather frail young man, who, I noticed, was given specially prepared food, was said to be in some ways the most "awakened" member of the colony. John once said half seriously, "Shên Kuo is a reincarnation of Adlan."

On my first afternoon John took me for a tour of inspection round the island. We went first to the power-house, a stone building on the quay. Outside the door the infant Sambo lay upon a mat, kicking with his crooked black legs. Curiously, he seemed to have changed less than the other supernormals. His legs were still too weak to support him. As we passed, he piped to John, "Hi! What about a bit of a talk? I've got a problem." John replied without checking his progress, "Sorry, too busy just now." Within we found Ng-Gunko, his back shining with sweat, shovelling sand, or rather dried ooze, into a sort of furnace. "Convenient," I said, laughing, "to be able to burn mud." Ng-Gunko paused, grinning, and wiping his brow with the back of his hand.

John explained. "The element that we use now is particularly easy to disintegrate by the psychical technique, but also it occurs only in very small quantities. Of course, if we disintegrated *all* this mass of stuff and let it go off with a bang, the whole island would be blown up. But only about a millionth part of the raw material is the element we want. The furnace merely frees the desired atoms as a sort of ash, which has to be refined out of the other ash, and stored in that hermetically sealed container."

He now led the way into another room, and pointed to a much smaller and very solid-looking bit of mechanism. "That," he said, "is where the real business is done. Every now and then Ng-Gunko puts a pinch of the stuff on a sticky wafer, pops it in there, and 'hypnotizes' it. That makes it go invisible and intangible and *materially* non-existent, at least for ordinary purposes; because, you see, it has gone to sleep and can't take *any* effect on anything. Well, either Ng-Gunko wakes it up again at once, and it sends the hell of a blast of power into that engine, to drive the dynamos; or it is taken away for use on the *Skid,* or elsewhere."

We passed into a room full of machinery, a mass of cylinders, rods, wheels, tubes, dials. Beyond that were three big dynamos, and beyond them the plant for distilling sea-water.

We then moved over to the laboratory, a rambling collection of wooden buildings rather apart from the settlement. There we found Lo and Hwan Tê working with microscopes. Lo explained that they were "trying to spot a bug that's got at the maize plantation." The place was much like any ordinary lab., crowded with jars, test-tubes, retorts and so on. It evidently served for work on both the physical and the biological sciences, but the biological was preponderant. On one side of the room was an immense cupboard, or rather series of small cupboards. These, I learned, were incubators for use in embryological work. I was to hear more of this later.

The library and meeting-room was a stone erection which had evidently been built to last, and to delight the eye. It was quite a small building of one storey, and I was not surprised to learn that most of the books were still housed in wooden sheds. But the shelves of the library itself were already filled with all the most prized volumes. When we entered the room, we found Jelli, Shên Kuo and Shahîn surrounded by piles of books. The smaller half of the building was occupied by the meeting-room, which was panelled with strange woods and decorated with much-stylized carvings. Of these works, some repelled and intrigued me, others moved me not at all. The former, John said, had been done by Kargis, the latter by Jelli. It was plain that Jelli's creations had a significance unperceived by me, for John was evidently held by them, and to my surprise we found Lankor, the Tibetan girl, standing motionless before one of them, her lips moving. When he saw her, John said, lowering his voice, "She's far away, but we mustn't risk disturbing her."

After leaving the library we walked through a big kitchen garden, where several of the young people were at work, and thence up the valley between the island's two mountains. Here we passed through fields of maize and groves of baby orange-trees and shaddock, which, it was hoped, would some day bear a rich crop. The vegetation of the island ranged from tropical to subtropical and even temperate. The extinct native pioneers had introduced much valuable tropical vegetation, such as the ubiquitous and invaluable coco-palm, and also bread-fruit, mango, and guava. Owing to the saltness of the air none but the coco-palm had really prospered until the supernormals had invented a spray to counteract the salt. When we had climbed out of the valley by a little track amongst a tangle of aromatic bushes, we presently emerged upon a tract of bare hillside consisting of rock, covered in places with dried sub-oceanic ooze. Here and there a wind-borne seed had alighted and prospered, and founded a little colony of vegetation. On a shoulder of the mountain John pointed out "the island's main attraction for sightseers." It was the keel and broken ribs of a wooden vessel evidently wrecked and sunk before the island rose from the bottom of the Pacific. Within it were bits of crockery and a human skull.

On the top of the little mountain we came upon the unfinished observatory. Its walls had risen only a foot from the ground, yet the whole place had a deserted look. To my question John replied, "When we found out how short a time lay before us, we abandoned all work of that kind, and concentrated on undertakings that we could bring to some sort of conclusion. I'll tell you more about them, some day."

I have reached the part of my narrative that I intended to present with most detail and greatest effect, but several attempts to tackle it have finally convinced me that the task is beyond my powers. Again and again I have tried to plan an anthropological and psychological report on the colony. Always I have failed. I can give only a few incoherent observations. I can say, for instance, that there was something incomprehensible, something "inhuman," about the emotional life of the islanders. In all normal situations, though of course their behaviour varied from the exuberance of Ng-Gunko and the fastidiousness of Kargis to the perfect composure of Lo, their emotions seemed on the whole normal. Doubtless, even in the most hearty expression of normal emotion in everyday situations, there was a curious self-observation and a detached relish, which seemed to me not quite "human." But it was in grave and exceptional situations and particularly in disaster that the islanders revealed themselves as definitely of a different texture from that of *Homo sapiens*. One incident must serve as an example.

Shortly after my arrival Hsi Mei, the Chinese girl, commonly called May, was seized with a terrible fit, and in disastrous circumstances. In her, apparently, the supernormal nature, though highly developed, was very precariously established. Her fit was evidently caused by a sudden reversion to the normal, but to the normal in a distorted and savage form. One day she was out fishing with Şhahîn, who had recently become her mate. She had been strange all the morning. Suddenly she flew at him and began tearing him with nails and teeth. In the scuffle the boat capsized, and the inevitable shark seized May by the leg. Fortunately Shahîn wore a sheath-knife, for use in cleaning fish. With this he attacked the shark, which by good luck was a young one. There was a desperate struggle. Finally the brute released its prey and fled. Shahîn, mauled and exhausted, succeeded with great difficulty in bringing May back to land. During the following three weeks he nursed her constantly, refusing to allow anyone to relieve him. What with her almost severed leg and her mental disorder, she was in a desperate plight. Sometimes her true self seemed to reappear, but more often she was either unconscious or maniacal. Shahîn was hard put to it to restrain her from doing serious hurt to herself or to him. When at last she seemed to be recovering, Shahîn was ecstatically delighted. Presently, however, she grew much worse. One morning, when I took his breakfast over to their cottage, he greeted me with a gaunt but placid face, and said, "Her soul is torn too deeply now. She will never mend. This morning she knows me, and has reached out her hand for me. But she is not herself, she is frightened. And very soon she will not know me ever again. I will sit with my dear this morning as usual, but when she is asleep I must kill her." Horrified, I rushed to fetch John. But when I had told him, he merely sighed and said, "Shahîn knows best."

That afternoon, in the presence of the whole colony, Shahîn carried the dead Hsi Mei to a great rock beside the harbour. Gently he laid her down, gazed at her for a moment with longing, then stepped back among his companions. Thereupon John, using the psycho-physical technique, caused a sufficient number of the atoms of her flesh to disintegrate, so that there was a violent outpouring of their pent-up energies, and her whole body was speedily consumed in a dazzling conflagration. When this was done, Shahîn passed his hand over his brow, and then went down with Kemi and Sigrid to the canoes. The rest of the day they spent repairing the nets. Shahîn talked easily, even gaily, about May; and laughed, even, over the desperate battle of her spirit with the powers of darkness. And sometimes while he worked, he sang. I said to myself, "Surely this is an island of monsters."

I must now try to convey something of my vivid impression that strange and lofty activities were all the while going on around me on the island although I could not detect them. I felt as though I were playing blind man's buff with invisible spirits. The bodily eye watched unhindered the bright perceived world and the blithe physical activities of these young people; but the mind's eye was blindfold, and the mind's ear could gather only vague hints of incomprehensible happenings.

One of the most disconcerting features of life on the island was that much of the conversation of the colonists was carried on telepathically. So far as I could judge, vocal speech was in process of atrophy. The younger members still used it as the normal means of communication, and even among the elders it was often indulged in for its own sake, much as we may prefer to walk rather than take a bus. The spoken language was prized chiefly for its aesthetic value. Not only did the islanders make formal poems for one another as frequently as the cultured Japanese; they also delighted sometimes to converse with one another in subtle metre, assonance and rhyme. Vocal speech was used also for sheer emotional expression, both deliberately and inadvertently. Our civilization had left its mark on the island in such ejaculations as "damn" and "blast" and several which we do not yet tolerate in print. In all reactions to the personality of others, too, speech played an important part. It was often a vehicle for the expression of rivalry, friendship and love. But even in this field all finer intercourse, I was told, depended on telepathy. Speech was but an obbligato to the real theme. Serious discussion was always carried on telepathically and in silence. Sometimes, however, emotional stress would give rise to speech as a spontaneous but unconsidered accompaniment of telepathic discourse. In these circumstances vocal activity tended to be blurred and fragmentary like the speech of a sleeper. Such mutterings were rather frightening to one who could not enter into the telepathic conversation. At first, by the way, I had been irrationally disturbed whenever a group of the islanders, working in silence in the garden or elsewhere, suddenly began to laugh for no apparent reason though actually in response to some telepathic jest. In time I came to accept these oddities without the "nervy" creepiness which they used to arouse in me.

There were happenings on the island far more strange than the normal flow of telepathic conversation. On my third evening, for instance, all the colonists gathered in the meeting-room. John explained that this was one of the regular twelfth-day meetings "to review our position in relation to the universe." I was advised to come, but to go away when I was bored. The whole party sat in the carved wooden chairs round the walls of the room. There was silence. Having had some experience of Quaker meetings, I was not at first ill at ease. But presently a rather terrifying absolute stillness came upon the company. Not only gross fidgetings, but even those almost imperceptible movements which characterize all normal living, ceased, and became noticeable through their absence. I might have been in a roomful of stone images. On every face was an expression of intent but calm concentration which was not solemn, was even perhaps faintly amused. Suddenly and with keen scrutiny, all eyes turned upon me. I was seized with a sudden panic; but immediately there came over all the intent faces a reassuring smile. Then followed an experience which I can only describe by saying that I felt directly the presence of those supernormal minds, felt telepathically a vague but compelling sense of their immature majesty, felt myself straining desperately to rise to their level, felt myself breaking under the strain, so that I had finally to flee back into my little isolated and half-human self, with the thankfulness of one who falls asleep after great toil, but with the loneliness of an exile.

The many eyes were now turned from me. The young winged minds had soared beyond my reach.

Presently Tsomotre, the neckless Tibetan, moved to a sort of harpsichord, tuned to the strange intervals which the islanders enjoyed. He played. To me his music was indescribably unpleasant. I could have screamed, or howled like a dog. When he had done, a faint involuntary murmur from several throats seemed to indicate deep approval. Shahîn rose from his seat, looking with keen inquiry at Lo, who hesitated, then also rose. Tsomotre began playing once more, tentatively. Lo, meanwhile, had opened a huge chest, and after a brief search she took from it a folded cloth, which when she had shaken it out was revealed as an ample and undulatory length of silk, striped in many colours. This she wrapped around her. The music once more took definite form. Lo and Shahîn glided into a solemn dance, which quickened presently to a storm of wild movement. The silk whirled and floated, revealing the tawny limbs of Lo; or was gathered about her with pride and disdain. Shahîn leapt hither and thither around her, pressed toward her, was rejected, half accepted, spurned again. Now and then came moments of frank sexual contact, stylized and knit into the movement-pattern of the dance. The end suggested to me that the two lovers, now clinging together, were being engulfed in some huge catastrophe. They glanced hither and thither, above, below, with expressions of horror and exaltation, and at one another with gleams of triumph. They seemed to thrust some invisible assailant from them, but less and less effectively, till gradually they sank together to the ground. Suddenly they sprang up and apart to perform slow marionette-like antics which meant nothing to me. The music stopped, and the dance. As she returned to her seat, Lo flashed a questioning, taunting look at John.

Later, when I had described this incident in my notes, I showed my account of it to Lo. When she had glanced at it, she said, "But you have missed the point, you old stupid. You've made it into a love story. Of course, what you say is all right—but it's all wrong too, you poor dear."

After the dance the company relapsed into silence and immobility. Ten minutes later I slipped away to refresh myself with a walk. When I returned, the atmosphere seemed to have changed. No one noticed my entrance. There was something indescribably eerie in the spectacle of those young faces staring with adult gravity at nothing. Most disturbing of all was Sambo, sitting like a little black doll in his ample chair. Tears were trickling down his cheeks, but his soft little mouth seemed to have grown hard and proud and old. After a few minutes I fled.

Next morning, though the meeting had not ended till dawn, the normal life of the colony was afoot once more. I asked John to explain what had been happening at the meeting. He said they had at first merely been looking into their motives. The young especially had still a lot to learn in this respect. Both young and old had also done a good deal of work upon their deeper mutual relations, relations which in the normal species would have been far below the threshold of consciousness.

All the colonists, John said, had been engaged in making themselves known to one another as fully as possible. They had also, all of them, been disciplining themselves, making their minds more seemly and more effective. This they had performed in the presence of Langatse, their spiritual adviser, and of course under his guidance. With him they had also meditated deeply about metaphysics. In addition to all this, said John, they had been learning to expand their "now" to embrace hours, days; and narrowing it also to distinguish the present and the past strokes of a gnat's wing. "And we explored the remote past," he said, "helped greatly by Shên Kuo, whose genius moves in that sphere. We attained also a kind of astronomical consciousness. Some of us at least glimpsed the myriads of peopled worlds, and even the minds of stars and of nebulae. We saw also very clearly that we must soon die. And there were other things which I must not tell you."

Life on the island did not consist entirely of this exalted corporate activity. The islanders had to do a good deal of hard work of a much more practical kind. Every day two or three canoes would go out fishing. Nets and boats and harpoons had to be repaired. There was constant work in the garden and fruit-groves, and in the maize-fields. Hitherto there had been endless building operations in wood and stone, but when the islanders had discovered their impending fate, such work was abandoned. A good deal of minor woodwork was still afoot. Much of the "crockery" was made of wood, and the rest of shell or gourd. The machinery needed constant attention, and so did the *Skid*. I was surprised to learn that the *Skid* had made many voyages among the Polynesian Islands, actually bartering some of the handicrafts of the colony for native produce. Later I found that these voyages had another purpose.

All this manual work was entered into rather as sport than as toil, for it had never been a tyranny. The most serious attention of every member was given to very different matters. The younger islanders spent much time in the library and the lab., absorbing the culture of the inferior species. The elders were concerned with a prolonged research into the physical and mental attributes of their own kind. In particular they were grappling with the problem of breeding. At what age might their young women safely conceive? Or should reproduction be ectogenetic? And how could they ensure that the offspring should be both viable and supernormal? This research was evidently the chief work of the laboratory. Originally its aim had been mainly practical, but even after the discovery of their impending doom the islanders continued these biological experiments for their theoretical interest.

When we entered the labs we found several persons at work. Lo, Kargis and the two Chinese boys were apparently in charge of the research. Delicate experiments were being carried out on the germ cells of molluscs, fishes and specially imported mammals. Still more difficult work was in progress upon human ova and spermatozoa, both normal and supernormal. I was shown a series of thirty-eight living human embryos, each in its own incubator. These startled me considerably, but the story of their conception and capture startled me even more. Indeed, it filled me with horror, and with violent though short-lived moral indignation. The eldest of these embryos was three months old. Its father, I was told, was Shahîn, its mother a native of the Tuamotu Archipelago. The unfortunate girl had been seduced, brought to the island, operated upon, and killed while still under the anaesthetic. The more recent specimens, however, had been secured by milder methods, for Lo had invented a technique by which the fertilized ovum could be secured without violence to the mother. In all the more recent cases the mothers had yielded up their treasure unwittingly, and without leaving their native islands. They were merely persuaded to agree to comply with certain instructions given by the supernormal father. The technique apparently combined physical and psychical methods, and was imposed upon the girls as a sublime religious ritual.

There was also a series of five much younger and ectogenetically fertilized ova. In these cases both father and mother were members of the colony. Lo herself had contributed one specimen. The father was Tsomotre. "You see," she said, "I am rather young for gestation, but my ova are all right for experimental purposes." I was puzzled. I knew well that sexual intercourse was practised on the island. Why then had the *fertilization* of this ovum been carried out artificially? As tactfully as I could, I stated my difficulty. Lo answered with some asperity, "Why, of course, because I was not in love with Tsomotre."

Since I am on this subject of sex I had better pursue it. The younger members of the colony, such as Ng-Gunko and Jelli, were only on the threshold of adolescence. Nevertheless, they were very sensitive to one another, both physically and mentally. Moreover, though physically backward, they were (so to speak) imaginatively precocious, as John had been. Consequently the mental side of sexual love was surprisingly developed among them.

Among the elder members there were, of course, more serious attachments. As they had discovered how to bring conception under direct voluntary control, their unions were followed by no practical difficulties. They had, however, produced a crop of emotional stresses.

From what I was told, I gathered that there must have been a subtle difference between the love experiences of the islanders and those of normal persons. So far as I can tell, the difference was caused by two characteristics of the supernormal, namely, more discriminate awareness of self and of others, and greater detachment. The greater accuracy of self- and other-consciousness was of course responsible for a high degree of mutual understanding, tolerance and sympathy in ordinary relations. It seems to have rendered the loves of these strange beings at once exceptionally vivid and in most cases exceptionally harmonious. Occasionally some surge of crude and juvenile emotion would threaten to blot out this insight, but then detachment would normally supervene to prevent disaster. Thus between the very different spirits of Shahîn and and Lankor there arose a passionate relationship in which there were frequent conflicts of desire. With beings like us this would have produced endless strife. But in them mutual insight and self-detachment seems to have kindled in each the spirit of the other, so that the result was not strife but the mental aggrandizement of both. On the other hand, when the unhappy Washingtonia found herself forsaken by Shahîn, primitive impulses had triumphed in her to such an extent that, as I have reported, she hated her rival. Such an irrational emotion was from the supernormal point of view sheer insanity. The girl herself was terrified at her own derangement. A similar incident occurred when Marianne favoured Kargis rather than Huan Tê. But the Chinese youth apparently cured himself without help. Yet not strictly without help, for all the islanders had formed a habit of recounting their amatory experiences to Jacqueline, far away in France; and she had often played the part of the wise woman, comforting them, helping these complicated and inexperienced young creatures to make effective spiritual contact with one another.

When the young people had enjoyed one another promiscuously for a period of many months, they seem to have passed into a new phase. They gradually sorted themselves out into more or less constant couples. In some cases a couple would actually build for themselves a single cottage, but as a rule they were content to make free of each other's private homes. In spite of these permanent "marriages" there were many fleeting unions, which did not seem to break up the more serious relationship. Thus at one time or other nearly every lad was mated with nearly every lass. This statement may suggest that the islanders lived in a ceaseless round of promiscuous sexual activity. They did nothing of the sort. The sexual impulse was not violent in them. But though coitus was on the whole a rare event on the island, it was always permitted when both parties desired it. Moreover, though the culminating sexual act was rare, much of the normal social life of the island was flushed, so to speak, with a light-hearted and elegant sexuality.

I believe that there were only one male and one female who had never spent a night in one another's arms, and indeed had never embraced at all. These, surprisingly, and in spite of their long connexion and deep mutual intimacy and respect, were John and Lo. Neither of them had a permanent mate. Each had played a part in the light-hearted promiscuity of the colony. Their seeming detachment from one another I attributed at first to sheer sexual indifference. But I was mistaken. When I remarked to John in my blundering way that I was surprised that he never seemed to be in love with Lo, he said simply, "But I *am* in love with Lo, always." I concluded that she was not attracted by him, but John read my thoughts, and said, "No, it's mutual all right." "Then *why?*" I demanded. John said nothing until I had pressed him again. He looked away, like any bashful adolescent. Just as I was about to apologize for prying, he said, "I just don't know. At least, I half know. Have you noticed that she never lets me so much as touch her? And I'm frightened of touching her. And sometimes she shuts me right out of her mind. That hurts. I'm frightened even of trying to make telepathic contact with her, unless she begins it; in case she doesn't want it. And yet I know her so well. Of course, we are very young, and though we have both had many loves and have learnt a lot, I think we mean so much to one another that we are afraid of spoiling it all by some false step. We are frightened to begin until we have learned much more about the art of living. Probably if we were to live another twenty years—but we shall *not.*" That "not" sounded with an undercurrent of grief which shocked me. I did not believe John would ever be shaken by purely personal emotion.

I decided to make an opportunity for asking Lo about her relations with John. One day, while I was meditating a tactful approach, she discovered my intention telepathically, and said, "About me and John—I keep him away because I know, and he knows too, that we are not in a position yet to give our best to one another. Jacqueline advised me to be careful, and she's right. You see, John is amazingly backward in some ways. He's cleverer than most of us, but quite simple about some things. That's why he's—*Odd* John. Though I'm the younger, I feel much older. It would never do to go all the way with him before he's really grown up. These years on the island with him have been very beautiful, in their kind. In another five we might be ready. But of course, since we have to die soon, I shall not wait too long. If the tree is to be destroyed, we must pluck the fruit before it is ripe."

When I had written and revised the foregoing account of life on the island, I realized that it failed almost completely to convey even so much of the spirit of the little community as I myself had been able to appreciate. But, try as I may, I cannot give concrete embodiment to that strange combination of lightness and earnestness, of madness and superhuman sanity, of sublime common sense and fantastic extravagance, which characterized so much on the island.

I must now give up the attempt, and pass on to describe the sequence of events which led to the destruction of the colony, and the death of all its members.

CHAPTER XXI

THE BEGINNING OF THE END

WHEN I had been on the island nearly four months a British surveying vessel discovered us. We knew beforehand from telepathic sources that she was likely to come our way, for she had orders to study the oceanic conditions of the South-east Pacific. We knew also that she had a gyroscopic compass. It would be difficult to lead her astray.

This vessel, the *Viking,* strayed about the ocean for some weeks, following the dictates of research. With innumerable zigzags she approached the island. When she came within range of our deflector her officers were perplexed by the discrepancy between the magnetic and gyroscopic compasses, but the ship maintained her true course. On one of her laps she passed within twenty miles of the island, but at night. Would she on the next lap miss us entirely? No! Approaching from the south-west, she sighted us far away on the port bow. The effect was unexpected. Since no island had any business to be in that spot, the officers concluded that the gyro was wrong after all, although their observation of the sun had seemed to confirm it. This island, then, must be one of the Tuamotu Group. The *Viking,* therefore veered away from us. Tsomotre, our chief telepathist, reported that the officers of the *Viking* were feeling very much like people lost in the dark.

A month later the *Viking* sighted us again. This time she changed her course and headed for the island. We saw her approaching, a minute toy vessel, white, with buff funnel. She plunged and swayed, and grew larger. When she was within a few miles of the island, she cruised round it, inspecting. She came a mile or two nearer and described another circle, at half speed, using the lead. She anchored. A motor-launch was lowered. It left the *Viking* and nosed along the coast till it found the entrance to our harbour. In the outer harbour it came to shore and landed an officer and three men. They advanced inland among the brushwood.

We still hoped that they might make a perfunctory examination and then return. Between the inner and the outer harbours, and along the slopes of the outer harbour itself, there was a dense wilderness of scrub, which would give pause to any explorer. The actual channel to the inner harbour had been concealed with a curtain of vegetation hung from a rope which stretched from shore to shore.

The invaders wandered about in the comparatively open space for a while, then turned back to the launch. Presently one of them stooped and picked up something. John, who was in hiding beside me, watching both the bodies and the minds of the four men, exclaimed, "God! He's found one of your bloody cigarette-ends—a fresh one, too." In horror I sprang to my feet, crying, "Then he must find me." I plunged down the hillside, shouting. The men turned and waited for me. As I approached, naked, dirty and considerably scratched by the scrub, they gaped at me in astonishment. Panting, I poured out an impromptu story. I was the sole survivor of a schooner, wrecked on the island. I had smoked my last cigarette today. At first they believed me. While we made our way toward the launch, they fired questions at me. I played my part tolerably well, but by the time we reached the *Viking,* they were growing suspicious. Though superficially dirty after my stampede, I was quite decently groomed. My hair was short, I was beardless, my nails were cut and clean. Under cross-examination by the Commander of the vessel I became confused; and finally, in despair, I told them the whole truth. Naturally they concluded that I was mad. All the same, the Commander determined to make further investigations on the island. He himself came with the party. I was taken, too, in case I should prove useful.

I now feigned complete idiocy, hoping they might still find nothing. But they discovered the camouflage curtain, and forced the launch through it it into the inner harbour. The settlement was now in full view. John and the others had decided that it was useless to hide, and were standing about on the quay, waiting for us. As we came alongside, John advanced to greet us. He was an uncouth but imposing figure, with his dazzling white hair, his eyes of a nocturnal beast, and his lean body. Behind him the others waited, a group of unclad boys and girls with formidable heads. One of the *Viking's* officers was heard to exclaim, "Jesus Christ! What a troupe!"

The invaders were fluttered by the sight of naked young women, several of whom were of the white race.

We took the officers to the feeding-house terrace, and gave them light refreshments, including our best Chablis. John explained to them rather fully about the colony; and though, of course, they could not appreciate the more subtle aspect of the great adventure, and were frankly though politely incredulous of the "new species" idea, they were sympathetic. They appreciated the sporting aspect of the matter. They were also impressed by the fact that I, the only adult and the only normal human figure among these juvenile freaks, was obviously a quite unimportant person on the island.

Presently John took them to see the power-station, which they just wouldn't believe, and the *Skid,* which impressed them more than anything else. To them she was a subtle blend of the crazy and the shipshape. There followed a tour of the other buildings and the estate. I was surprised that John was so anxious to show everything, more surprised that he made no attempt to persuade the Commander not to report on the island and its inhabitants. But John's policy was more subtle. After the tour of inspection he persuaded the Commander to allow all his men to leave the launch and come to the terrace for refreshments. There the party spent another half-hour. John and Lo and Marianne talked to the officers. Other islanders talked to the men. When at last the party made its farewells on the quay, the Commander assured John that he would make a full report on the island, and give high praise to its inhabitants.

As we watched the launch retreating, several of the islanders showed signs of mirth. John explained that throughout the interview the visitors had been subjected to an appropriate psychological treatment, and that by the time they reached the *Viking* their memory of recent events on the island would be so obscure that they would be quite unable to produce a plausible report, or even to give their shipmates an account of their ad-venture. "But," said John, "this is the beginning of the end. If only we could have treated the whole ship's company thoroughly, all might have been well. As it is, some distorted information is sure to get through and rouse the curiosity of your species."

For three months the life of the island proceeded undisturbed. But it was a changed life. Knowledge that the end could not be far off produced a fresh intensity of consciousness in all personal relations and social activi-ties. The islanders evidently discovered a new and passionate love of their little society, a kind of poignant and exalted patriotism, such as must have been felt in Greek city-states when the enemy was at the gates. But it was a patriotism curiously free from hate. The impending disaster was regarded less as an attack by human enemies than as a natural catastrophe, like destruction by an avalanche.

The programme of activities on the island was now altered consider-ably. All work that could not bear fruit within the next few months was abandoned. The islanders told me that they had certain supreme tasks on hand which must if possible be finished before the end. The true purpose of the awakened spirit, they reminded me, is twofold, namely to help in the practical task of world-building, and to employ itself to the best of its capacity in intelligent worship. Under the first head they had at least created something glorious though ephemeral, a miscrocosm, a world in little. But the more ambitious part of their practical purpose, the founding of the new species, they were destined never to fulfil. Therefore they were concentrating all their strength upon the second aim. They must appre-hend existence as precisely and zestfully as they could, and salute That in the universe which was of supreme excellence. This purpose, with the aid of Langatse, they might yet advance to a definite plane of achievement which at present still lay beyond them, though their most mature minds had already glimpsed it. With their unique practical experience and their consciousness of approaching doom they might, they said, within a few months offer to the universal Spirit such a bright and peculiar jewel of worship as even the great Langatse himself, alone and thwarted, could not create.

This most exalting and most exacting of all tasks made it necessary for them to give up all but the necessary daily toil in the fields and in the canoes. Not that very much of their time could be devoted to their spiritual exercises, for there was danger of overstraining their powers. It was necessary therefore to secure plentiful relaxation. Much of the life of the colony during this period seemed to consist of recreation. There was much bathing in the shark-free harbour, much love-making, much dancing and music and poetry, and much aesthetic juggling with colour and form. It was difficult for me to enter into the aesthetic appreciation of the islanders, but from their reactions to their own art in this period I judged that the pervading sense of finality had sharpened their sensibility. Certainly in the sphere of personal relations the knowledge that the group would soon be destroyed produced a passion of sociality. Solitariness lost its charm.

One night Chargut, who was on duty as telepathic look-out, reported that a British light cruiser was under orders to make a search for the mysterious island which had somehow temporarily undermined the sanity of so many of the *Viking's* crew.

Some weeks later the vessel entered the zone of our deflector, but had little difficulty in keeping her course. She had expected some sort of craziness on the part of the magnetic needle, and trusted only to her gyroscopic compass. After some groping, she reached the island. This time the islanders made no attempt at concealment. From a convenient shoulder of the mountain we watched the grey ship drop anchor and heave slowly in the swell, displaying her red bottom-colour. A launch left her. When it was near enough, we signalled it round to the harbour entrance. John received the visitors on the quay. The lieutenant (in white duck and stiff collar) was inclined to stand on his dignity as the representative of the British Navy. The presence of naked white girls obviously increased his hauteur by upsetting his equilibrium. But refreshments on the terrace, combined with secret psychological treatment, soon produced a more friendly atmosphere. Once more I was impressed by John's wisdom in keeping a store of good wine and cigars.

I have not space to give details of this second encounter with *Homo sapiens*. There was unfortunately much coming and going between the cruiser and the shore, and it was impossible to administer a thorough hypnotic inoculation to every man who saw the settlement. A good deal was achieved, however, and the visit of the Commander himself, a grizzled and a kindly gentleman of the sea, was particularly satisfactory. John soon discovered telepathically that he was a man of imagination and courage, and that he regarded his calling with unusual detachment. Therefore, seeing that a number of the naval men had escaped with only slight psychological treatment, it seemed best not to administer "oblivifaction" to

the Commander, but instead to attempt the more difficult enterprise of rousing in him an overmastering interest in the colony, and loyalty to its purpose. The Commander was one of those exceptional seamen who spend
a good deal of their time in reading. His mind had a background of ideas
which rendered him susceptible to the technique. His was not, indeed, a
brilliant intellect, but he had dabbled in popular science and popular philosophy, and his sense of values was intuitively discriminate, though un-
cultivated.

The cruiser remained for some days off the island, and during this
time the Commander spent much of his time ashore. His first official act
was to annex the island to the British Empire. I was reminded of the way
in which robins and other birds annex gardens and orchards, regardless of
human purposes. But alas in this case the robin represented a Great Power
—the power, indeed, of the jungle over this minute garden of true humanity.

Though the Commander alone was to be allowed clear memory of
his experiences on the island, all the visitors were treated in such a way
as to help them to appreciate the colony as well as it was in them to do.
Some were of course impervious, but many were affected to some extent.
All were forced to use every ounce of their imagination to envisage the
colony at least as a gay and romantic experiment. In most cases, doubtless,
the notion that they conceived of it was extremely crude and false; but in
one or two, besides the Commander, all sorts of rudimentary and inhibited
spiritual capacities were roused into unfamiliar and disturbing activity.

When at last the time came for the visitors to leave the island, I
noticed that their demeanour was different from what it had been on their
arrival. There was less formality, less of a gulf between officers and men,
less strict discipline. I noticed, too, that some who had formerly looked at
the young women with disapproval or lust or both, now bade them farewell
with friendly courtesy, and with some appreciation of their uncouth beauty.
I noticed also on the faces of the more sensitive a look of anxiety, as though
they did not feel altogether "at home" in their own minds. The Commander himself was pale. As he shook hands with John, he muttered, "I'll
do my best, but I'm not hopeful."

The cruiser departed. Events on board her were followed by our telepathists with intense interest. Tsomotre and Chargut and Lankor reported
that amnesia for all events on the island was rapidly spreading; that some
of those who still had clear recollection were so tortured by their spiritual
upheaval, and the contrast between the island and the ship, that they were
losing all sense of discipline and patriotism; that two had committed suicide;
that a vague panic was spreading, a sense that madness was afoot amongst
them; that, apart from the Commander, none who had been in close contact
with the islanders could now recall more than the most confused and incredible memories of the island; that those who escaped severe psycho-

logical treatment were also very confused, but that they remembered enough to make them a source of grave danger; that the Commander had addressed the whole ship's company, ordering them, imploring them, to keep strict silence ashore on the subject of their recent experiences. He himself must of course report to the Admiralty, but the crew must regard the whole matter as an official secret. To spread incredible stories would only cause trouble, and get the ship into disgrace. Privately, of course, he intended to make a perfectly colourless and harmless report.

Some weeks later the telepathists announced that fantastic stories of the island were current in the Navy; that a reference had been made in a foreign paper to "an immoral and communistic colony of children on a British island in the Pacific"; that foreign secret services were nosing out the truth, in case it should prove diplomatically useful; that the British Admiralty was holding a secret inquiry; that the Commander of the cruiser had been dismissed from the Service for making a false report; that the Soviet Government had collected a good deal of information about the island, and intended to embarrass Britain by organizing a secret expedition to make contact with the colony; that the British Government had learnt of this intention, and was determined to evacuate the island at once. We were told also that the world at large knew practically nothing of the matter. The British Press had been warned against making any reference to it. The Foreign Press had not given serious attention to the vague rumour which one paper had published.

The visit of the second cruiser ended much as the previous incident, but at one stage it entailed desperate measures. The second Commander had perhaps been chosen for his uncompromising character. He was in fact a bit of a bully. Moreover, his instructions were emphatic, and he had no thought but to carry them out promptly. He sent a launch to give the islanders five hours to pack up and come aboard. The lieutenant returned "in a state of nerves" and reported that the instructions were not being carried out. The Commander himself came ashore with a party of armed men. He was determined to stand no nonsense. Refusing offers of hospitality, he announced that all the islanders must come aboard at once.

John asked for an explanation, trying to lead the man into normal conversation. He also pointed out that most of the islanders were not British subjects, and that the colony was doing no harm to any one. It was no use. The Commander was something of a sadist, and the sight of unclad female flesh had put him in a mood of ruthlessness. He merely ordered the arrest of every member of the colony.

John intervened in a changed and solemn voice. "We will not leave the island alive. Any one that you seize will drop down dead."

The Commander laughed. Two tars approached Chargut, who happened to be the nearest. The Tibetan looked around at John, and, at the first touch of the sailors' hands, he dropped. The sailors examined him. There was no sign of life.

The Commander was flustered; but, pulling himself together, he repeated his order. John said, "Be careful! Don't you see yet that you're up against something you can't understand? Not one of us will be taken alive." The sailors hesitated. The Commander snapped out, "Obey orders. Better begin on a girl, for safety." They approached Sigrid, who turned with her bright smile to John, and extended a hand behind her to feel for Kargis, her mate. One of the sailors laid a gentle and hesitating paw on her shoulder. She collapsed backwards into the arms of Kargis, dead.

The Commander was now thoroughly upset, and the sailors were showing signs of insubordination. He tried to reason with John, assuring him that the islanders would be well treated on the ship; but John merely shook his head. Kargis was sitting on the ground with the dead Sigrid in his arms. His own face looked dead. After a moment's contemplation of Kargis the Commander said, "I shall consult with the Admiralty about you. Meanwhile you may stay here." He and his men returned to their boat. The cruiser departed.

On the island the two bodies were laid upon the great rock by the harbour. For some time we all stood round in silence, while the seagulls cried. One of the Indian girls, who had been attached to Chargut, fainted. But Kargis showed now no sign of grief. The desolate expression that had come over his face when Sigrid fell dead in his arms had soon cleared. The supernormal mind would never for long succumb to emotion that must perforce be barren. For a few moments he stood gazing on the face of Sigrid. Suddenly he laughed. It was a John-like laugh. Then Kargis stooped and kissed the cold lips of his mate, gently but with a smile. He stepped aside. Once more John availed himself of the psycho-physical technique. There was a fierce blaze. The bodies were consumed.

Some days later I ventured to ask John why he had sacrificed these two lives, and indeed why the islanders could not come to terms with Britain. No doubt the colony would have to be disbanded, but its members would be allowed to return to their respective countries, and each of them might expect a long life of intense experience and action. John shook his head and replied, "I cannot explain. I can only say that we are one together now, and there is no life for us apart. Even if we were to do as you suggest and go back into the world of your species, we should be watched, controlled, persecuted. The things that we live for beckon us to die. But we are not ready yet. We must stave off the end for a while so that we may finish our work."

Shortly after the departure of the second cruiser an incident occurred which gave me fresh understanding of the mentality of the islanders. Ng-Gunko had for some time been absorbed in private researches. With the self-importance and mysteriousness of a child he announced that he would rather not explain until he had finished his experiments. Then one day, grinning with pride and excitement, he summoned the whole company to the laboratory and gave a full account of his work. His speech was tele-pathic; so also were the subsequent discussions. My report is based on information given me by John, and also by Shên Kuo and others.

Ng-Gunko had invented a weapon which, he said, would make it im-possible for *Homo sapiens* ever again to interfere with the island. It would project a destructive ray, derived from atomic disintegration, with such effect that a battleship could be annihilated at forty miles' distance, or an aeroplane at any height within the same radius. A projector placed on the higher of the two mountain-tops could sweep the whole horizon. The designs were complete in every detail, but their execution would involve huge co-operative work, and certain castings and wrought-steel parts would have to be ordered secretly in America or Japan. Smaller weapons, however, could be laboriously made at once on the island, and fitted to the *Skid* and the plane to equip them for dealing with any attack that might be expected within the next few months.

Careful scrutiny proved that the invention was capable of doing all that was claimed for it. The discussion passed on to the detailed problems of constructing the weapon. But at this point, apparently, Shên Kuo inter-posed, and urged that the project should be abandoned. He pointed out that it would absorb the whole energy of the colony, and that the great spiritual task would have to be shelved, at any rate for a very long time. "Any resistance on our part," he said, "would bring the whole force of the in-ferior species against us, and there would be no peace till we had conquered the world. That would take a long time. We are young, and we should have to spend the most critical years of our lives in warfare. When we had finished the great slaughter, should we be any longer fit mentally for our real work, for the founding of a finer species, and for worship? No! We should be ruined, hopelessly distorted in spirit. Violent practical under-takings would have blotted out for ever such insight as we have now gained into the true purpose of life. Perhaps if we were all thirty years older we should be sufficiently mature to pass through a decade of warfare without becoming too impoverished, spiritually, for our real work. But as things are, surely the wise course is to forego the weapon, and make up our minds to fulfil as much as possible of our accepted spiritual task of worship before we are destroyed."

I could tell by merely watching the faces of the islanders that they were now in the throes of a conflict of wills such as they had never before experienced. The issue was not merely one of life and death; it was one of fundamental principle. When Shên Kuo had done, there was a clamour of protest and argument, much of which was actually vocal; for the islanders were deeply moved. It was soon agreed that the decision should be post-poned for a day. Meanwhile there must be a solemn meeting in the meeting-room, and all hearts must be deeply searched in a most earnest effort to reach mental accord and the right decision. The meeting was silent. It lasted for many hours. When it was over I learned that all, including Ng-Gunko and John himself, had accepted with conviction and with gladness the views of Shên Kuo.

The weeks passed. Telepathic observation informed us that, when the second cruiser had left us, considerable amnesia and other mental derangements had occurred among those of the crew who had landed on the island. The Commander's report was incoherent and incredible. Like the first Commander, he was disgraced. The Foreign Offices of the world, through their secret services, ferreted out as much as possible of this latest incident. They did not form anything like an accurate idea of events, but they procured shreds of truth embroidered with fantastic exaggeration. There was a general feeling that something more was at stake than a diplomatic coup, and the discomfiture of the British Government. Something weird, something quite beyond reckoning was going on on that remote island. Three ships had been sent away with their crews in mental confusion. The islanders, besides being physically eccentric and morally perverse, seemed to have powers which in an earlier age would have been called diabolic. In a vague subconscious way *Homo sapiens* began to realize that his supremacy was challenged.

The Commander of the second cruiser had informed his Government that the islanders were of many nationalities. The Government, feeling itself to be in an extremely delicate position in which a false step might expose it as guilty of murdering children, yet feeling that the situation must be dealt with firmly and speedily before the Communists could make capital out of it, decided to ask other Powers to co-operate and share responsibility.

Meanwhile the Soviet vessel had left Vladivostok and was already in the South Seas. Late one afternoon we sighted her, a small trading-vessel of unobtrusive appearance. She dropped anchor and displayed the Red Flag, with its golden device.

The Captain, a grey-haired man in a peasant blouse, who seemed to me to be still inwardly watching the agony of the Civil War, brought us a flattering message from Moscow. We were invited to migrate to Russian territory, where, we were assured, we should be left free to manage our colony as we wished. We should be immune from persecution by the Capitalist Powers on account of our Communism and our sexual customs. While he was delivering himself of this speech, slowly, but in excellent English, a woman who was apparently one of his officers was making friendly advances to Sambo, who had crawled toward her to examine her boots. She smiled, and whispered a few endearments. When the Captain had finished, Sambo looked up at the woman and remarked. "Comrade, you have the wrong approach." The Russians were taken aback, for Sambo was still in appearance an infant. "Yes," said John, laughing, "Comrades, you have the wrong approach. Like you, we are Communists, but we are other things also. For you, Communism is the goal, but for us it is the beginning. For you the group is sacred, but for us it is only the pattern made up of individuals. Though we are Communists, we have reached beyond Communism to a new individualism. Our Communism is individualistic. In many ways we admire the achievements of the New Russia; but if we were to accept this offer we should very soon come into conflict with your Government. From our point of view it is better for our colony to be destroyed than to be enslaved by any alien Power." At this point he began to speak in Russian, with great rapidity, sometimes turning to one or other of his companions for confirmation of his assertions. Once more the visitors were taken aback. They interjected remarks, they began arguing with each other. The discussion seemed to become heated.

Presently the whole company moved to the feeding terrace, where the visitors were given refreshments, and their psychological treatment was continued. As I cannot understand Russian I do not know what was said to them; but from their expressions I judged that they were greatly excited, and that, while some were roused to bewildered enthusiasm, others kept their heads so far as to recognize in these strange beings a real danger to their species and more particularly to the Revolution.

When the Russians departed, they were all thoroughly confused in mind. Subsequently, we learned from our telepathists that the Captain's report to his Government had been so brief, self-contradictory and incredible, that he was relieved of his command on the score of insanity.

News that the Russian expedition had occurred, and that it had left the islanders in possession, confirmed the worst fears of the Powers. Obviously, the island was an outpost of Communism. Probably it was now a highly fortified base for naval and aerial attack upon Australia and New Zealand. The British Foreign Office redoubled its efforts to persuade the Pacific Powers to take prompt action together.

Meanwhile the incoherent stories of the crew of the Russian vessel had caused a flutter in the Kremlin. It had been intended that when the islanders had been transported to Russian territory the story of their persecution by Britain should be published in the Soviet Press. But such was the mystery of the whole matter that the authorities were at a loss, and decided to prevent all reference to the island.

At this point they received a diplomatic note protesting against their interference in an affair which concerned Britain alone. The party in the Soviet Government which was anxious to prove to the world that Russia was a respectable Power now gained the upper hand. The Russian reply to Britain was a request for permission to take part in the proposed international expedition. With grim satisfaction Britain granted the request.

Telepathically the islanders watched the little fleet converging on it from Asia and America. Near Pitcairn Island the vessels assembled. A few days later we saw a tuft of smoke on the horizon, then another, and others. Six vessels came into view, all heading toward us. They displayed the ensigns of Britain, France, the United States, Holland, Japan, and Russia; in fact, "the Pacific Powers." When the vessels had come to anchor, each dispatched a motor-launch, bearing its national flag in the stern.

The fleet of launches crowded into the harbour. John received the visitors on the quay. *Homo superior* faced the little mob of *Homo sapiens,* and it was immediately evident that *Homo superior* was indeed the better man. It had been intended to effect a prompt arrest of all the islanders, but an odd little hitch occurred. The Englishman, who was to be spokesman, appeared to have forgotten his part. He stammered a few incoherent words, then turned for help to his neighbour the Frenchman. There followed an anxious whispered discussion, the rest of the party crowding round the central couple. The islanders watched in silence. Presently the Englishman came to the fore again, and began to speak, rather breathlessly. "In the name of the Governments of the Pacif—" He stopped, frowning distractedly and staring at John. The Frenchman stepped forward, but John now intervened. "Gentlemen," he said, pointing, "let us move over to the shady end of that terrace. Some of you have evidently been affected by the sun." He turned and strode away, the little flock following him obediently.

On the terrace, wine and cigars appeared. The Frenchman was about to accept, when the Japanese cried, "Do not take. It is perhaps drugged." The Frenchman paused, withdrew his hand and smiled deprecatingly at Marianne, who was offering the refreshments. She set the tray on the table.

The Englishman now found his tongue, and blurted out in a most unofficial manner, "We've come to arrest you all. You'll be treated decently, of course. Better start packing at once."

John regarded him in silence for a moment, then said affably, "But please tell us, what is our offence, and your authority?"

Once more the unfortunate man found that the power of coherent speech had left him. He stammered something about "The Pacific Powers" and "boys and girls on the loose," then turned plaintively to his colleagues for help. Babel ensued, for every one attempted to explain, and no one could express himself. John waited. Presently he began speaking. "While you find your speech," he said, "I will tell you about our colony." He went on to give an account of the whole venture. I noticed that he said almost nothing about the biological uniqueness of the islanders. He affirmed only that they were sensitive and freakish creatures who wanted to live their own life. Then he drew a contrast between the tragic state of the world and the idyllic life of the islanders. It was a consummate piece of pleading, but I knew that it was really of much less importance than the telepathic influence to which the visitors were all the while being subjected. Some of them were obviously deeply moved. They had been raised to an unaccustomed clarity and poignancy of experience. All sorts of latent and long-inhibited impulses came to life in them. They looked at John and his companions with new eyes, and at one another also.

When John had finished, the Frenchman poured himself out some wine. Begging the others to fill their glasses and drink to the colony, he made a short but eloquent speech, declaring that he recognized in the spirit of these young people something truly noble, something, indeed, almost French. If his Government had known the facts, it would not have participated in this attempt to suppress the little society. He submitted to his colleagues that the right course was for them all to leave the island and communicate with their Governments.

The wine was circulated and accepted by all, save one. Throughout John's speech the Japanese representative had remained unmoved. Probably he had not understood well enough to feel the full force of John's eloquence. Possibly, also, his Asiatic mind was not to be mastered telepathically by the same technique as that which applied to his colleagues. But the main source of his successful resistance, so John told me later, was almost certainly the influence of the terrible Hebridean infant, who, ever desiring to destroy John, had contrived to be telepathically present at this scene. I had seen John watching the Jap with an expression in which were blended amusement, anxiety and admiration. This dapper but rather formidable little man now rose to his feet, and said, "Gentlemen, you have been tricked. This lad and his companions have strange powers which Europe does not understand. But we understand. I have felt them. I have fought against them. I have not been tricked. I can see that these are not boys and girls; they are devils. If they are left, some day they will destroy us. The world will be for them, not for us. Gentlemen, we must obey our orders. In the name of the Pacific Powers I—I——" Confusion seized him.

John intervened and said, almost threateningly, "Remember, any one of us that you try to arrest, dies."

The Japanese, whose face was now a ghastly colour, completed his sentence, "I arrest you all." He shouted a command in Japanese. A party of armed Japanese sailors stepped on to the terrace. The lieutenant in command of them approached John, who faced him with a stare of contempt and amusement. The man came to a stand a few yards from him. Nothing happened.

The Japanese Commander himself stepped forward to effect the arrest. Shahîn barred his way, saying, "You shall take me first." The Jap seized him. Shahîn collapsed. The Jap looked down at him with horror, then stepped over him and moved toward John. But the other officers intervened. All began talking at once. After a while it was agreed that the islanders should be left in peace until the representatives of *Homo sapiens* had communicated with their Governments.

Our visitors left us. Next morning the Russian ship weighed anchor and sailed. One by one the others followed suit.

CHAPTER XXII

THE END

JOHN was under no illusion that the colony had been saved; but if we could gain another three months' respite, he said, the immediate task which the islanders had undertaken would be finished. A minor part of this work consisted in completing certain scientific records, which were to be entrusted to me for the benefit of the normal species. There was also an amazing document, written by John himself, and purporting to give an account of the whole story of the Cosmos. Whether it should be taken as a plain statement of fact or a poetic fantasy I do not know. These various documents were now being typed, filed and packed in wooden cases; for the time had come for my departure. "If you stay much longer," John said, "you will die along with the rest of us, and our records will be lost. To us it matters not at all whether they are saved or not, but they may prove of interest to the more enlightened members of your own species. You had better not attempt to publish them till a good many years have passed, and the Governments have ceased to feel sore about us. Meanwhile, if you like, you can perpetuate the biography—as fiction, of course, since no one would believe it."

One day Tsomotre reported that a party of toughs was being secretly equipped for our destruction by agents of certain governments which I will not name.

The wooden chests were loaded on to the *Skid* along with my baggage. The whole colony assembled on the quay to bid me farewell. I shook hands with them all in turn; and Lo, to my surprise, kissed me. "We do love you, Fido," she said. "If they were all like you, domestic, there'd have been no trouble..Remember, when you write about us, that we loved you." Sambo, when his turn came, clambered from Ng-Gunko's arms to mine, then hurriedly back again. "I'd go with you if I wasn't so tied up with these snobs that I couldn't live without them."

John's parting words were these. "Yes, say in the biography that I loved you very much." I could not reply.

Kemi and Marianne, who were in charge of the *Skid*, were already hauling in the mooring lines. We crept out of the little harbour and gathered speed as we passed between the outer headlands. The double pyramid of the island shrank, faded, and was soon a mere cloud on the horizon.

I was taken to one of the least important of the French islands, one on which there were no Europeans. By night we unloaded the baggage in the dinghy and set it on a lonely beach. Then we made our farewells, and very soon the *Skid* with her crew vanished into the darkness. When morning came I went in search of natives and arranged for the transport of my goods and myself to civilization. Civilization? No, that I had left behind for ever.

Of the end of the colony I know very little. For some weeks I hung about in the South Seas trying to pick up information. At last I came upon one of the hooligans who had taken part in the final scene. He was very reluctant to speak, not only because he knew that to blab was to risk death, but also because the whole affair had evidently got on his nerves. Bribery and alcohol, however, loosened his tongue.

The assassins had been warned to take no risks. The enemy, though in appearance juvenile, was said to be diabolically cunning and treacherous. Machine-guns might be useful, and it would be advisable not to parley.

A large and well-armed party of the invaders landed outside the harbour, and advanced upon the settlement. The islanders must have known telepathically that these ruffians were too base to be dealt with by the technique which had been used on former invaders. Probably it would have been easy to destroy them by atomic disintegration as soon as they landed; though I remember being told that it was much more difficult to disintegrate the atoms of living bodies than of corpses. Apparently no attempt was made to put this method in action. Instead, John seems to have devised a new and subtler method of defence; for according to my informant the landing-party very soon "began to feel there were devils in the place." They were apparently seized with a nameless horror. Their flesh began to creep, their limbs to tremble. This was all the more terrifying because it was broad daylight, and the sun was beating heavily down on them. No doubt the supernormals were making their presence felt telepathically in some grim and formidable manner unintelligible to us. As the invaders advanced hesitatingly through the brushwood, this terrifying sense of some overmastering presence became more and more intense. In addition they began to experience a crazy fear of one another. Every man cast sidelong glances of fright and hate at his neighbour. Suddenly they all fell upon one another, using knives, fire-arms, teeth and fingers. The brawl lasted only a few minutes, but several were killed, many wounded. The survivors took to their heels, and to the boats.

For two days the ship lay off the island, while her crew debated violently among themselves. Some were for abandoning the venture; but others pointed out that to return empty-handed was to go to certain destruction; for the great ones who had sent them had made it clear that, though success would be generously rewarded, failure would be punished ruthlessly. There was nothing for it but to try again. Another landing-party was organized, and fortified with large quanties of rum. The result was much the same as on the former occasion; but it was noticed that those who were most drunk were least affected by the sinister influence.

The assassins took three more days to screw up their courage for another landing. The bodies of their dead comrades were visible upon the hill-side. How many of the living were destined to join that ghastly company? The party made itself so drunk that it could hardly row the boats. It braced itself with uproarious song. Also it carried the brave liquor with it in a keg. After the landing the gruesome influence was again felt, but this time the invaders answered it with reinforcements of rum and revelry. Reeling, clinging together, dropping their weapons, tripping over roots and one another's feet, but defiantly singing, they advanced over the spur of hill, and saw the harbour and the settlement beneath them. They floundered down the slope. One of them accidentally discharged a pistol into his own thigh. He collapsed, yelling, but the others rushed on.

They stumbled into the presence of the supernormals, who were gathered near the power-station. There the reeling assailants sheepishly came to a stand. By now the effects of the rum were somewhat abated; and the sight of those strange beings, motionless, with their great calm eyes, seems to have dismayed the assassins. Suddenly they fled.

For some days they wrangled among themselves, and kept to their ship. They dared not land again; they dared not sail.

One afternoon, however, they were amazed to see a prodigious and dazzling spread of flame rise from behind the hill, and light up land and sea. There followed a muffled roar which echoed from the clouds like thunder. The blaze died down, but it was followed by an even more alarming phenomenon. The whole island began to sink. Waves appeared to be clambering up the hills. Presently the ship's anchor released itself from the sinking bottom, and she was cast adrift. The island continued to descend, and the sea swept in upon it, bearing the gyrating vessel over the tops of the sunken trees. The twin peaks were submerged. Converging currents met above their heads and reared a great spout of ocean. This liquid horn, descending, drove hills of water outwards in all directions. The ship was overwhelmed. Her top-hamper, boats, and most of her deck-houses were torn away. Half the crew were lost overboard.

This cataclysm apparently occurred on the 15th December 1933. It may, of course, have been an effect of purely physical causes. Even when I first heard of it, however, I was inclined to think that it was not. I suspected that the islanders had been holding their assailants at bay in order to gain a few days for the completion of their high spiritual task, or in order to bring it at least to a point beyond which there was no hope of further advancement. I liked to believe that during the few days after the repulse of the third landing-party they accomplished this aim. They then decided, I thought, not to await the destruction which was bound sooner or later to overtake them at the hands of the less human species, either through these brutish instruments or through the official forces of the Great Powers. The supernormals might have chosen to end their career by simply falling dead, but seemingly they desired to destroy their handiwork along with themselves. They would not allow their home, and all the objects of beauty with which they had adorned it, to fall into subhuman clutches. Therefore they deliberately blew up their power-station, thereby destroying not only themselves but their whole settlement. I surmised further that this mighty convulsion must have spread downwards into the precarious foundations of the island, disturbing them so violently that the whole island collapsed.

As soon as I had gleaned as much information as possible, I hurried home with my documentary treasures, wondering how I should give the news to Pax. It did not seem to me likely that she would have learnt it already from John. When I landed in England, she and Doc met me. Her face showed me that she was prepared. At once she said, "You need not break the news gently, because we know the main part of it. John gave me visions of it. I saw those tipsy brutes routed by his power. And in a few days afterwards I saw many happy things on the island. I saw John and Lo, walking together on the shore, like lovers at last. One day I saw all the young people sitting in a panelled room, evidently their meeting-room. I heard John say that it was time to die. They all rose and went away, in couples and little groups; and presently they gathered round the door of a stone building that must have been their power-station. Ng-Gunko went through the door, carrying Sambo. Suddenly there was blinding light and noise and pain, then nothing."

SIRIUS

A FANTASY OF LOVE AND DISCORD

BY

OLAF STAPLEDON

DOVER PUBLICATIONS, INC.
NEW YORK

Contents

I should like to acknowledge my debt to Mr. J. Herries McCulloch's delightful study, *Sheep Dogs and Their Masters*. He must not, however, be held in any way responsible for my sheer fantasies.

FIRST MEETING

PLAXY and I had been lovers; rather uneasy lovers, for she would never speak freely about her past, and sometimes she withdrew into a cloud of reserve and despond. But often we were very happy together, and I believed that our happiness was striking deeper roots.

Then came her mother's last illness, and Plaxy vanished. Once or twice I received a letter from her, giving no address, but suggesting that I might reply to her "care of the Post Office" in a village in North Wales, sometimes one, sometimes another. In temper these letters ranged from a perfunctory amiability to genuine longing to have me again. They contained mysterious references to "a strange duty," which, she said, was connected with her father's work. The great physiologist, I knew, had been engaged on very sensational experiments on the brains of the higher mammals. He had produced some marvelously intelligent sheep-dogs, and at the time of his death it was said that he was concerned with even more ambitious research. One of the colder of Plaxy's letters spoke of an "unexpectedly sweet reward" in connection with her new duty, but in a more passionate one she cried out against "this exacting, fascinating, dehumanizing life." Sometimes she seemed to be in a state of conflict and torture about something which she must not explain. One of these letters was so distraught that I feared for her sanity. I determined therefore to devote my approaching leave to walking in North Wales in the hope of finding her.

I spent ten days wandering from pub to pub in the region indicated by the addresses, asking everywhere if a Miss Trelone was known in the neighbourhood. At last, in Llan Ffestiniog, I heard of her. There was a young lady of that name living in a shepherd's cottage on the fringe of the moor somewhere above Trawsfynydd. The local shopkeeper who gave me this information said with an air of mystery, "She is a strange young lady, indeed. She has friends, and I am one of them; but she has enemies."

Following his directions, I walked for some miles along the winding Trawsfynydd road and then turned to the left up a lane. After another mile or so, right on the edge of the open moor, I came upon a minute cottage built of rough slabs of shale, and surrounded by a little garden and stunted trees. The door was shut, but smoke rose from a chimney. I knocked. The door remained shut. Peering through a window, I saw a typical cottage kitchen, but on the table was a pile of books. I sat down on a rickety seat in the garden and noted the neat rows of cabbages and peas. Away to my right, across the deep Cynfal gorge, was Ffestiniog, a pack of slate-grey elephants following their leader, the unsteepled church, down a spur of hill towards the valley. Behind and above stood the Moelwyn range.

I was smoking my second cigarette when I heard Plaxy's voice in the distance. It was her voice that had first attracted me to her. Sitting in a café I had been enthralled by that sensitive human sound coming from some unknown person behind me. And now once more I heard but did not see her. For a moment I listened with delight to her speech, which, as I had often said, was like the cool sparkling talk of small waves on the pebbly shore of a tarn on a hot day.

I rose to meet her, but something strange arrested me. Interspersed with Plaxy's remarks was no other human voice but a quite different sound, articulate but inhuman. Just before she came round the corner of the house she said, "But, my dear, don't *dwell* on your handlessness so! You have triumphed over it superbly." There followed a strange trickle of speech from her companion; then through the gate into the garden came Plaxy and a large dog.

She halted, her eyes wide with surprise, and (I hoped) with joy; but her brows soon puckered. Laying a hand on the dog's head, she stood silent for a moment. I had time to observe that a change had come over her. She was wearing rather muddy corduroy trousers and a blue shirt. The same grey eyes, the same ample, but decisive mouth, which had recently seemed to me to belie her character, the same shock of auburn, faintly carroty hair. But instead of a rather pale face, a ruddy brown one, and a complete absence of make-up. No lip-stick, even. The appearance of rude health was oddly contradicted by a darkness under the eyes and a tautness round the mouth. Strange how much one can notice in a couple of seconds, when one is in love!

Her hand deserted the dog's head, and was stretched out to me in welcome. "Oh well," she said smiling, "since you have nosed us out, we had better take you into our confidence." There was some embarrassment in her tone, but also perhaps a ring of relief. "Hadn't we, Sirius," she added, looking down at the great dog.

Then for the first time I took note of this remarkable creature. He was certainly no ordinary dog. In the main he was an Alsatian, perhaps with a dash of Great Dane or Mastiff, for he was a huge beast. His general build was wolf-like, but he was slimmer than a wolf, because of his height. His coat, though the hair was short, was superbly thick and silky, particularly round the neck, where it was a close turbulent ruff. Its silkiness missed effeminacy by a hint of stubborn harshness. Silk wire, Plaxy once called it. On back and crown it was black, but on flanks and legs and the under surface of his body it paled to an austere greyish fawn. There were also two large patches of fawn above the eyes, giving his face a strangely mask like look, or the appearance of a Greek statue with blank-eyed helmet pushed back from the face. What distinguished Sirius from all other dogs was his huge cranium. It was not, as a matter of fact, quite as large as one would have expected in a creature of human intelligence, since, as I shall explain later, Trelone's technique not only increased the brain's bulk but also produced a refinement of the nerve fibres themselves. Nevertheless, Sirius's head was far loftier than any normal dog's. His high brow combined with the silkiness of his coat to give him a look of the famous Border Collie, the outstanding type of sheep-dog. I learned later that this brilliant race had, indeed, contributed to his make-up. But his cranium was far bigger than the Border Collie's. The dome reached almost up to the tips of his large Alsatian ears. To hold up this weight of head, the muscles of his neck and shoulders were strongly developed. At the moment of our encounter he was positively leonine, because the hair was bristling along his spine. Suspicion of me had brushed it up the wrong way. His grey eyes might have been wolf's eyes, had not the pupils been round like any dog's, not slits like the wolf's. Altogether he was certainly a formidable beast, lean and sinewy as a creature of the jungle.

Without taking his gaze off me, he opened his mouth, displaying sierras of ivory, and made a queer noise, ending with an upward inflection like a question. Plaxy replied, "Yes, it's Robert. He's true as steel, remember." She smiled at me deprecatingly, and added, "And he may be useful."

Sirius politely waved his amply feathered tail, but kept his cold eyes fixed on mine.

Another awkward pause settled upon us, till Plaxy said, "We have been working on the sheep out on the moor all day. We missed our dinner and I'm hungry as hell. Come in and I'll make tea for us all." She added as we entered the little flagged kitchen, "Sirius will understand everything you say. You won't be able to understand him at first, but I shall, and I'll interpret."

While Plaxy prepared a meal, passing in and out of the little larder, I sat talking to her. Sirius squatted opposite me, eyeing me with obvious anxiety. Seeing him, she said with a certain sharpness fading into gentleness, "Sirius! I tell you he's all right. Don't be so suspicious!" The dog rose, saying something in his strange lingo, and went out into the garden. "He's gone to fetch some firewood," she said; then in a lowered voice, "Oh, Robert, it's good to see you, though I didn't want you to find me." I rose to take her in my arms, but she whispered emphatically, "No, no, not now." Sirius returned with a log between his jaws. With a sidelong glance at the two of us, and a perceptible drooping of the tail, he put the log on the fire and went out again. "Why not now?" I cried, and she whispered, "Because of Sirius. Oh, you'll understand soon." After a pause she added, "Robert, you mustn't expect me to be wholly yours ever, not fully and single-heartedly yours. I'm too much involved in—in this work of my father's." I expostulated, and seized her. "Nice human Robert," she sighed, putting her head on my shoulder. But immediately she broke away, and said with emphasis, "No, *I* didn't say that. It was just the female human animal that said it. What *I* say is, I can't play the game you want me to play, not wholeheartedly."

Then she called through the open door, "Sirius, tea!" He replied with a bark, then strode in, carefully not looking at me.

She put a bowl of tea for him on a little table-cloth on the floor, remarking, "He has two meals generally, dinner at noon and supper in the evening. But to-day is different." Then she put down a large crust of bread, a hunk of cheese, and a saucer with a little lump of jam. "Will that keep you going?" she asked. A grunt signified approval.

Plaxy and I sat at the table to eat our bread and rationed butter and war-time cake. She set about telling me the history of Sirius. Sometimes I put in an occasional question, or Sirius interrupted with his queer speech of whimper and growl.

The matter of this and many other conversations about the past I shall set down in the following chapters. Meanwhile I must say this. Without the actual presence of Sirius I should not have believed the story; but his interruptions, though canine and unintelligible, expressed human intelligence by their modulation, and stimulated intelligible answers from Plaxy. Obviously he was following the conversation, commenting and watching my reaction. And so it was not with incredulity, though of course with amazement, that I learned of the origin and career of Sirius. I listened at first with grave anxiety, so deeply involved was Plaxy. I began to understand why it was that our love had always been uneasy, and why when her mother died she did not come back to me. I began to debate with myself the best way of freeing her from this "inhuman bondage." But as the conversation proceeded I could not but recognize that this strange relationship of girl and dog was fundamentally beautiful, in a way sacred. (That was the word I used to myself.) Thus my problem became far more difficult.

At one point, when Plaxy had been saying that she often longed to see me again, Sirius made a more sustained little speech. And in the middle of it he went over to her, put his fore-paws on the arm of her chair, and with great gentleness and delicacy kissed her cheek. She took the caress demurely, not shrinking away, as human beings generally do when dogs try to kiss them. But the healthy glow of her face deepened, and there was moisture in her eyes as she stroked the shaggy softness under his neck, and said to me, while still looking at him, "I am to tell you, Robert, that Sirius and Plaxy grew up together like the thumb and forefinger of a hand, that he loves me in the way that only dogs can love, and much more now that I have come to him, but that I must not feel bound to stay with him, because by now he can fend for himself. Whatever happens to him ever,

I—how did you say it, Sirius, you foolish dear?" He put in a quick sentence, and she continued, "Oh, yes, I am the scent that he will follow always, hunting for God."

She turned her face towards me with a smile that I shall not forget. Nor shall I forget the bewildering effect of the dog's earnest and almost formal little declaration. Later I was to realize that a rather stilted diction was very characteristic of him, in moments of deep feeling.

Then Sirius made another remark with a sly look and a tremor of the tail. She turned back to him laughing, and softly smacked his face. "Beast," she said, "I shall not tell Robert that."

When Sirius kissed her I was startled into a sudden spasm of jealousy. (A man jealous of a dog!) But Plaxy's translation of his little speech roused more generous feelings. I now began to make plans by which Plaxy and I together might give Sirius a permanent home and help him to fulfil his destiny, whatever that might be. But, as I shall tell, a different fate lay in store for us.

During that strange meal Plaxy told me that, as I had guessed, Sirius was her father's crowning achievement, that he had been brought up as a member of the Trelone family, that he was now helping to run a sheep farm, that she herself was keeping house for him, and also working on the farm, compensating for his lack of hands.

After tea I helped her to wash up, while Sirius hovered about, jealous, I think, of my handiness. When we had finished, she said they must go over to the farm to complete a job of work before dark. I decided to walk back to Ffestiniog, collect my baggage and return by the evening train to Trawsfynedd, where I could find accommodation in the local pub. I noticed Sirius's tail droop as I said this. It drooped still further when I announced that I proposed to spend a week in the neighbourhood in the hope of seeing more of Plaxy. She said, "I shall be busy, but there are the evenings."

Before I left she handed over a collection of documents for me to take away and read at leisure. There were scientific papers by her father, including his journal of Sirius's growth and education. These documents, together with a diary of her own and brief fragmentary records by Sirius himself, all of which I was given at a much later date, form the main "sources" of the following narrative; these, and many long talks with Plaxy, and with Sirius when I had learnt to understand his speech.

I propose to use my imagination freely to fill out with detail many incidents about which my sources afford only the barest outline. After all, though a civil servant (until the Air Force absorbed me) I am also a novelist; and I am convinced that with imagination and self-criticism one can often penetrate into the essential spirit of events even when the data are superficial. I shall, therefore, tell the amazing story of Sirius in my own way.

CHAPTER II

THE MAKING OF SIRIUS

PLAXY'S father, Thomas Trelone, was too great a scientist to escape all publicity, but his work on the stimulation of cortical growth in the brains of mammals was begun while he was merely a brilliant young research worker, and it was subsequently carried on in strict secrecy. He had an exaggerated, a morbid loathing of limelight. This obsession he justified by explaining that he dreaded the exploitation of his technique by quacks and profit-mongers. Thus it was that for many years his experiments were known only to a few of his most intimate professional colleagues in Cambridge, and to his wife, who had a part to play in them.

Though I have seen his records and read his papers, I can give only a layman's account of his work, for I am without scientific training. By introducing a certain hormone into the blood-stream of the mother he could affect the growth of the brain in the unborn young. The hormone apparently had a double effect. It increased the actual bulk of the cerebral cortices, and also it made the nerve-fibres themselves much finer than they normally are, so that a far greater number of them, and a far greater number of connections between them, occurred in any given volume of brain. Somewhat similar experiments, I believe, were carried out in America by Zamenhof; but there was an important difference between the two techniques. Zamenhof simply fed the young animal with his hormone; Trelone, as I have said, introduced his hormone into the foetus through the mother's blood-stream. This in itself was a notable achievement, because the circulatory systems of mother and foetus are fairly well insulated from each other by a filtering membrane. One of Trelone's difficulties was that the hormone caused growth in the maternal as well as the foetal brain, and since the mother's skull was adult and rigid there must inevitably be very serious congestion, which would lead to death unless some means were found to insulate her brain from the stimulating drug. This difficulty was eventually overcome. At last it became possible to assure the unborn animal a healthy maternal environment. After its birth Trelone periodically added doses of the hormone to its food, gradually reducing the dose as the growing brain approached what he considered a safe maximum size. He had also devised a technique for delaying the closing of the sutures between the bones of the skull, so that the skull might continue to expand as required.

A large population of rats and mice was sacrificed in the attempt to perfect Trelone's technique. At last he was able to produce a number of remarkable creatures. His big-headed rats, mice, guinea-pigs, rabbits, though their health was generally bad, and their lives were nearly always cut short by disease of one kind or another, were certainly geniuses of their humble order. They were remarkably quick at finding their way through mazes, and so on. In fact they far excelled their species in all the common tests of animal intelligence, and had the mentality rather of dogs and apes than of rodents.

But this was for Trelone only the beginning. While he was improving his technique so that he could ensure a rather more healthy animal, he at the same time undertook research into methods of altering the tempo of its life so that it should mature very slowly and live much longer than was normal to its kind. Obviously this was very important. A bigger brain needs a longer life-time to fulfil its greater potentiality for amassing and assimilating experience. Not until he had made satisfactory progress in both these enterprises did he begin to experiment on animals of greater size and higher type. This was a much more formidable undertaking, and promised no quick results. After a few years he had produced a number of clever but seedy cats, a bright monkey that died during its protracted adolescence, and a dog with so big a brain that its crushed and useless eyes were pushed forward along its nose. This creature suffered so much that its producer reluctantly destroyed it in infancy.

Not till several more years had elapsed, had Trelone perfected his technique to such an extent that he was able to pay less attention to the physiological and more to the psychological aspect of his problem. Contrary to his original plan, he worked henceforth mainly on dogs rather than apes. Of course apes offered the hope of more spectacular success. They were by nature better equipped than dogs. Their brains were bigger, their sight was more developed, and they had hands. Nevertheless from Trelone's point of view dogs had one overwhelming advantage. They were capable of a much greater freedom of movement in our society. Trelone confessed that he would have preferred to work on cats, because of their more independent mentality; but their small size made them unsuitable. A certain absolute bulk of brain was necessary, no matter what the size of the animal, so as to afford a wealth of associative neural paths. Of course a small animal did not need as large a brain as a large animal of the same mental rank. A large body needed a correspondingly large brain merely to work its machinery. A lion's brain had to be bigger than a cat's. An elephant's brain was even larger than a much more intelligent but smaller man's. On the other hand, each rank of intelligence, no matter what the size of the animal, required a certain degree of complexity of neural organization, and so of brain bulk. In proportion to the size of the human body a man's brain was far *bigger* than an elephant's. Some animals were large enough to accommodate the absolute bulk of brain needed for the human order of intelligence; some were not. A large dog could easily do so, but a cat's organization would be very gravely upset by so great an addition. For a mouse anything of the sort would be impossible.

Not that Trelone had at this stage any expectation of raising any animal so far in mental stature that it would approach human mentality. His aim was merely to produce, as he put it, "a rather super-sub-human intelligence, a missing-link mind." For this purpose the dog was admirably suited. Human society afforded for dogs many vocations requiring intelligence at the upper limit of the sub-human range. Trelone chose as the best vocation of all for his purpose that of the sheep-dog. His acknowledged ambition was to produce a "super-sheep-dog."

One other consideration inclined him to choose the dog; and the fact that he took this point into account at all in the early stage of his work shows that he was even then toying with the idea of producing something more than a missing-link mind. He regarded the dog's temperament as on the whole more capable of development to the human level. If cats excelled in independence, dogs excelled in social awareness; and Trelone argued that only the social animal could make full use of its intelligence. The independence of the cat was not, after all, the independence of the socially aware creature asserting its individuality; it was merely the blind individualism that resulted from social obtuseness. On the other hand he admitted that the dog's sociality involved it, in relation to man, in abject servility. But he hoped that with increased intelligence it might gain a measure of self-respect, and of critical detachment from humanity.

In due course Trelone succeeded in producing a litter of big-brained puppies. Most of them died before reaching maturity, but two survived, and became exceptionally bright dogs. This result was on the whole less gratifying than disappointing to Trelone. He carried out further experiments, and at last, from an Old English Sheep-dog bitch, produced a big-brained family, three of which survived, and reached a definitely super-canine level of mentality.

The research continued for some years. Trelone found it necessary to take more trouble about the "raw material" to which his technique was to be applied. He could not afford to neglect the fact that the most capable of all the canine races is the Border Collie, bred through a couple of centuries for intelligence and responsibility. All modern champions are of this breed, and all are descendants of a certain brilliant animal, named Old Hemp, who was born in Northumberland in 1893. The Border Collie of to-day is hardy, but rather small. Trelone, therefore, decided that the best raw material would be a cross between some outstanding champion of the International Sheep-Dog Trials and another intelligent but much heavier animal. The Alsatian was the obvious choice. After a good deal of negotiation with owners of champion sheep-dogs and enthusiasts for Alsatians, he produced several strains, which blended the two types in various proportions. He then applied his improved technique to various expectant mothers of these types, and in due season he was able to provide several of his friends with animals of "almost missing-link intelligence" as house-dogs. But there was nothing spectacular about these creatures; and unfortunately all were delicate, and all died before their somewhat protracted adolescence was completed.

But at last further improvements in his technique brought him real success. He achieved several very bright animals with normally strong constitutions, predominantly Alsatian in appearance.

He had persuaded his wife Elizabeth that, if ever he succeeded to this extent, they should take a house in a sheep district in Wales. There she and the three children and the forthcoming baby would live, and he himself would spend the vacations and week-ends. After much exploration they found a suitable old farm-house not far from Trawsfynedd. Its name was "Garth." A good deal of work had to be done to turn it into a comfortable family home. Water-closets and a bathroom had to be installed. Some of the windows were enlarged. Electricity was laid on from the village. An out-house was converted into a palatial kennel.

Some time after the fourth baby had been born, the family moved. They were accompanied by Kate, the long-established servant, who had somehow become practically a member of the family. A village girl was engaged as her assistant. There was also a nursemaid, Mildred; and, of course, the children, Thomasina, Maurice, Giles, and the baby Plaxy. Thomas took with him two canine families. One consisted of a bitch and four hardy little animals that he intended to train as "super-sheep-dogs." The other family of four were orphans, the mother having died in giving birth to them. They had therefore to be hand-nursed. The brains of these animals were very much bigger than the brains of the other family, but unfortunately three of them were much less healthy. Two died shortly after the removal to Wales. Another was subject to such violent fits that it had to be destroyed. The fourth, Sirius, was a healthy and cheerful little creature that remained a helpless infant long after the other litter were active adolescents. For months it could not even stand. It merely lay on its stomach with its bulgy head on the ground, squeaking for sheer joy of life; for its tail was constantly wagging.

Even the other litter matured very slowly for dogs, though far more rapidly than human children. When they were nearly adult all but one of them were disposed of to neighbouring farms. The one was kept as the family dog. Most of the local farmers had proved very reluctant to take on these big-headed animals even as gifts. But a neighbour, Mr. Llewelyn Pugh of Caer Blai, had entered into the spirit of the venture, and he subsequently bought a second pup as a colleague for the first.

The production of these super-sheep-dogs and others which followed formed a camouflage for Thomas's more exciting venture, of which Sirius was at present the only outcome. The public would be led to believe that super-sheep-dogs and other animals of missing-link mentality were his whole concern. If the little Alsatian really developed to human mental stature, few people would suspect it. Thomas was always morbidly anxious that it should not be exploited. It must grow up in decent obscurity, and mature as naturally as possible.

The super-sheep-dogs, on the other hand, were allowed to gain notoriety. The farmers who had accepted them mostly with great reluctance soon found that fate had given them pearls of great price. The animals learned their technique surprisingly quickly, and carried out their orders with unfailing precision. Commands had seldom to be repeated. Sheep were never hustled, and yet never allowed to break away. Not only so, but Trelone's dogs had an uncanny way of understanding instructions and carrying them out with no human supervision. They attached the right meanings to the names of particular pastures, hill-sides, valleys, moors. Told to "fetch sheep from Cefn" or from Moel Fach or what not, they succeeded in doing so while their master awaited them at home. They could also be sent on errands to neighbouring farms or villages. They would take a basket and a note to a particular shop and bring back the required meat or haberdashery.

All this was very useful to the farmers, and extremely interesting to Trelone, who was of course allowed every chance of studying the animals. He found in them a startlingly high degree of practical inventiveness, and a rudimentary but remarkable understanding of language. Being after all sub-human, they could not understand speech as we do, but they were incomparably more sensitive than ordinary dogs to familiar words and phrases. "Fetch wood from shed," "Take basket to butcher and baker," and all such simple familiar orders could be distinguished and obeyed, as a rule without distraction. Thomas wrote a monograph on his super-sheep-dogs, and consequently scientists from all over the world used to turn up at Garth to be shown the animals at work. Throughout the district their fame was fully established among farmers, and there were many demands for puppies. Very few could be supplied. Some farmers refused to believe that the offspring of these bright animals would not inherit their parents' powers. Naturally, all attempts to breed super-sheep-dogs from super-sheep-dogs without the introduction of the hormone into the mother were a complete failure.

But it is time to return to the little Alsatian, in fact, to Sirius. Trelone was from the first very excited about this animal. The longer it remained a helpless infant, the more excited he became. He saw in it the possibility of the fulfilment of his almost wildest hopes. Discussing it with Elizabeth, he fired her imagination with the prospects of this canine infant, and unfolded his plan before her. This animal must have as far as possible the same kind of psychological environment as their own baby. He told her of an American animal-psychologist and his wife who had brought up a baby chimpanzee in precisely the same conditions as their own little girl. It was fed, clothed, cared for, exactly as the child; and with very interesting results. This, Thomas said, was not quite what he wanted for little Sirius, because one could not treat a puppy precisely as a baby without violating its nature. Its bodily organization was too different from the baby's. But what he did want was that Sirius should be brought up to feel himself the social equal of little Plaxy. Differences of treatment must never suggest differences of biological or social rank. Elizabeth had already, he said, proved herself an ideal mother, giving the children that precious feeling of being devotedly loved by a divinely wise and generous being, yet fostering their independence and making no greedy emotional claims on them. This was the atmosphere that Thomas demanded for Sirius; this and the family environment. And their family, he told her, had taught him a very important truth. Unfortunate experiences in his own childhood had led him to regard family as a hopelessly bad institution, and one which ought to be abolished. She would remember his wild ideas of experimenting with their own children. She had tactfully and triumphantly resisted every attempt to remove her own first two children from her; and before the third was born Thomas was already convinced that a really good family environment was the right influence for a growing child. No doubt she had made mistakes. Certainly he had made many. No doubt they had to some extent unwittingly damaged their children. There was Tamsy's occasional mulishness and Maurice's diffidence. But on the whole—well it would be false modesty and unfair to the children not to recognize that they were all three fine specimens, friendly, responsible, yet independent and critical. This was the ideal social tradition in which to perform the great experiment with baby Sirius. Dogs, Thomas reminded Elizabeth, were prone to servility; but this vice was probably not due to something servile in their nature; it sprang from the fact that their great social sensitivity was forced to take a servile turn by the tyranny of the more developed species which controlled them. A dog with human intelligence, brought up to respect itself, would probably not be servile at all, and might quite well develop a superhuman gift for true social relationship.

Elizabeth took some time to consider her husband's suggestion, for the responsibility would be mainly hers. Moreover, she was naturally anxious about the effects of the experiment on her own baby. Would her little Plaxy suffer in any way? Thomas persuaded her that no harm would be done, and indeed that the companionship of child and super-canine dog must be beneficial to both. With fervour he insisted that the most valuable social relationships were those between minds as different from one another as possible yet capable of mutual sympathy. It is perhaps remarkable that Thomas, who was not himself gifted with outstanding personal insight or sympathy, should have seen intellectually the essential nature of community. It would be very interesting, he said, to watch the growth of this difficult but pregnant companionship. Of course it might never develop. There might be mere antagonism. Certainly Elizabeth would have to exercise great tact to prevent the child from overpowering the dog with its many human advantages. In particular the little girl's hands and more subtle eyesight would be assets which the puppy could never attain. And the whole human environment, which was inevitably alien and awkward for the dog, might well breed neurosis in a mind that was not human but humanly sensitive. Everything possible must be done to prevent Sirius from becoming either unduly submissive or defiantly arrogant in the manner so familiar in human beings suffering from a sense of inferiority.

One other principle Thomas wanted Elizabeth to bear in mind. It was, of course, impossible to know beforehand how the dog's nature would develop. Sirius might, after all, never reach anything like human mental stature. But everything must be done on the assumption that he would do so. Hence it was very important to bring him up not as a pet but as a person, as an individual who would in due season live an active and independent life. This being so, his special powers must be fostered. While he was still, as Thomas put it, a "schoolboy," his interests would, of course, be "schoolboy" interests, physical, primitive, barbarian; but being a dog, his expression of them would necessarily be very different from a real schoolboy's. He would have to exercise them in normal canine occupations, such as desultory roaming and hunting and fighting. But later, as his intelligence opened up the human world to him, he would want some kind of persistent "human" activity; and obviously sheep could provide him with a career, even if he far excelled the typical super-sheep-dog mentality. With this in view, and whatever his destiny, he must be brought up "as hard as nails and fit as hell." This had always been Elizabeth's policy with her own children; but Sirius would some time need to face up to conditions far more Spartan than those of the most Spartan human family. It would not do simply to force him into such conditions. Somehow she must wile him into wanting them, for sheer pride in his own nature, and later for the sake of his work. This, of course, would not apply to his childhood, but in adolescence he must begin of his own free will to seek hardness. Later still, when his mind was no longer juvenile, he would perhaps drop the sheep-dog career entirely and give his mind to more adult pursuits. Even so, the hard practical life of his youth would not have been in vain. It would endow him with permanent grit and self-reliance.

Elizabeth was a good deal more sceptical than her husband about the future of Sirius. She expressed a fear, which did not trouble Thomas, that such a disunited being as Sirius might be doomed to a life of mental torture. Nevertheless, she finally made up her mind to enter into the spirit of the experiment, and she planned accordingly.

CHAPTER III

INFANCY

WHILE he was still unable to walk, Sirius showed the same sort of brightness as Plaxy in her cot. But even at this early stage his lack of hands was
a grave disadvantage. While Plaxy was playing with her rattle, he too
played with his; but his baby jaws could not compete with Plaxy's baby
hands in dexterity. His interest even in his earliest toys was much more
like a child's than like the ordinary puppy's monomania for destruction.
Worrying his rattle, he was attentive to the sound that it made, alternately
shaking it and holding it still to relish the contrast between sound and
silence. At about the time when Plaxy began to crawl, Sirius achieved a
staggering walk. His pride in this new art and his joy in the increased
scope that it gave him were obvious. He now had the advantage over Plaxy,
for his method of locomotion was far better suited to his quadruped structure than her crawl to her biped form. Before she had begun to walk he
was already lurching erratically over the whole ground floor and garden.
When at last she did achieve the upright gait, he was greatly impressed,
and insisted on being helped to imitate her. He soon discovered that this
was no game for him.

Plaxy and Sirius were already forming that companionship which was
to have so great an effect on both their minds throughout their lives. They
played together, fed together, were washed together, and were generally
good or naughty together. When one was sick, the other was bored and
abject. When one was hurt, the other howled with sympathy. Whatever
one of them did, the other had to attempt. When Plaxy learned to tie a
knot, Sirius was very distressed at his inability to do likewise. When Sirius
acquired by observation of the family's super-sheep-dog, Gelert, the habit
of lifting a leg at gate-posts to leave his visiting card, Plaxy found it hard
to agree that this custom, though suitable for dogs, was not at all appropriate to little girls. She was deterred only by the difficulty of the operation.
Similarly, though she was soon convinced that to go smelling at gate-posts
was futile because her nose was not as clever as Sirius's, she did not see
why the practice should outrage the family's notions of propriety. Plaxy's
inability to share in Sirius's developing experience of social smelling, if I
may so name it, was balanced by his clumsiness in construction. Plaxy was
the first to discover the joy of building with bricks; but there soon came
a day when Sirius, after watching her intently, himself brought a brick
and set it clumsily on the top of the rough wall that Plaxy was building.
His effort wrecked the wall. This was not Sirius's first achievement in con-

struction, for he had once been seen to lay three sticks together to form a triangle, an achievement which caused him great satisfaction. He had to learn to "handle" bricks and dolls in such a way that neither his saliva nor his pin-point teeth would harm them. He was already enviously impressed by Plaxy's hands and their versatility. The normal puppy shows considerable inquisitiveness, but no impulse to construct; Sirius was more persistently inquisitive and at times passionately constructive. His behaviour was in many ways more simian than canine. The lack of hands was a handicap against which he reacted with a dogged will to triumph over disability.

Thomas judged that his weakness in construction was due not only to handlessness but to a crudity of vision which is normal in dogs. Long after infancy he was unable to distinguish between visual forms which Plaxy would never confuse. For instance, it took him far longer than Plaxy to distinguish between string neatly tied up in little bundles and the obscure tangle which, at Garth as in so many homes, composed the general content of the string-bag. Again, for Sirius, rather fat ovals were no different from circles, podgy oblongs were the same as squares, pentagons were mistaken for hexagons, angles of sixty degrees were much the same as right angles. Consequently in building with toy bricks he was apt to make mistakes which called forth derision from Plaxy. Later in life he corrected this disability to some extent by careful training, but his perception of form remained to the end very sketchy.

In early days he did not suspect his inferiority in vision. All his failures in construction were put down to lack of hands. There was indeed a grave danger that his handlessness would so obsess him that his mind would be warped, particularly during a phase when the infant Plaxy was apt to laugh at his helplessness. A little later she was brought to realize that poor Sirius should not be ragged for his misfortune, but helped whenever possible. Then began a remarkable relationship in which Plaxy's hands were held almost as common property, like the toys. Sirius was always running to ask Plaxy to do things he could not manage himself, such as opening boxes and winding up clock-work toys. Sirius himself began to develop a surprising "manual" dexterity, combining the use of fore-paws and teeth; but many operations were for ever beyond him. Throughout his life he was unable to tie a knot in a piece of cotton, though there came a time when he could manage to do so in a rope or stout cord.

Plaxy was the first to show signs of understanding speech, but Sirius was not far behind. When she began to talk, he often made peculiar little noises which, it seemed, were meant to be imitations of human words. His failure to make himself understood often caused him bitter distress. He would stand with his tail between his legs miserably whining. Plaxy was the first to interpret his desperate efforts at communication, but Elizabeth in time found herself understanding; and little by little she grew able to equate each of the puppy's grunts and whines with some particular elementary sound of human speech. Like Plaxy, Sirius began with a very simple baby-language of monosyllables. Little by little this grew into a canine, or super-canine, equivalent of educated English. So alien were his vocal organs to speech, that even when he had perfected the art no outsider would suspect his strange noises of being any human language at all. Yet he had his own equivalent of every vocal sound. Some of his consonants were difficult to distinguish from one another, but Elizabeth and Plaxy and the rest of the family came to understand him as easily as they understood each other. I described his speech as composed of whimpers and grunts and growls. This perhaps maligns it, though essentially true. He spoke with a notable gentleness and precision, and there was a fluid, musical quality in his voice.

Thomas was, of course, immensely elated by the dog's development of true speech, for this was a sure sign of the fully human degree of intelligence. The baby chimpanzee that was brought up with a human baby kept level with its foster-sister until the little girl began to talk, but then dropped behind; for the ape never showed any sign of using words.

Thomas determined to have a permanent record of the dog's speech. He bought the necessary apparatus for making gramophone discs, and reproduced conversations between Sirius and Plaxy. He allowed no one to hear these records except the family and his two most intimate colleagues, Professor McAlister and Dr. Billing, who were influential in procuring funds for the research, and knew that Thomas's secret ambition soared far above the production of super-sheep-dogs. On several occasions Thomas brought the distinguished biologists to see Sirius.

There was a time when it seemed that these gramophone records would be the sole lasting and tangible evidence of Thomas's triumph. In spite of inoculation, Sirius developed distemper and almost succumbed. Day after day, night after night, Elizabeth nursed the wretched little animal through this peculiarly noisome disease, leaving her own child mainly to Mildred, the nursemaid. Had it not been for Elizabeth's skill and devotion, Sirius would not have come through with his powers unimpaired. Probably he would have died. This incident had two important results. It created in Sirius a passionate and exacting affection for his foster-mother, so that for weeks he would scarcely let her out of his sight without making an uproar; and it bred in Plaxy a dreadful sense that her mother's love was being given wholly to Sirius. In fact Plaxy became lonely and jealous. This trouble was soon put right when Sirius had recovered, and Elizabeth was able to give more attention to her child; but then it was the dog's turn to be jealous. The climax came when Sirius, seeing Elizabeth comforting Plaxy after a tumble, rushed savagely at her and actually nipped her little bare leg. There was then a terrible scene. Plaxy screamed and screamed. Elizabeth was for once really angry. Sirius howled with remorse for what he had done; and actually, out of a sense that retribution was needed, made a half-hearted attempt to bite his own leg. Then matters were made much worse by the family's super-sheep-dog, Gelert, who rushed to the scene of uproar. Seeing Plaxy's bleeding leg, and Elizabeth being very angry with the puppy, Gelert assumed that this was a case for severe punishment, and set upon the abject culprit. Sirius was bowled over and none too gently mauled by the furiously growling Gelert. The puppy's remorse gave place to fright, and his whimpers to screams of terror, to which the weeping Plaxy added screams of fear for her beloved friend. The other children rushed upon the scene, followed by Kate and Mildred with brooms and a rolling pin. Even the infant Plaxy seized Gelert by the tail and tried to drag him off. But it was Elizabeth herself who snatched Sirius from the jaws of death (as it seemed to him) and roundly cursed the officious Gelert.

This incident seems to have had several important results. It made both Sirius and Plaxy realize how much, after all, they cared for one another. It persuaded Plaxy that her mother had not discarded her for Sirius. And it proved to Sirius that Elizabeth loved him even when he had been very wicked. The unfortunate Gelert alone gained no comfort.

The only further punishment inflicted on Sirius was deep disgrace. Elizabeth withdrew her kindness. Plaxy, in spite of her secret knowledge that Sirius was very dear, was filled with self-pity once more when he had been rescued, and treated him with cold self-righteousness. To punish Sirius, Plaxy showed a violent affection for the kitten, Tommy, who had recently been imported from a neighbouring farm. Sirius, of course, was tortured with jealousy, and was afforded good practice in self-control. He succeeded all the better because on the one occasion when he did attack Tommy, he discovered that the kitten had claws. Sirius was very sensitive to neglect and censure. When his human friends were displeased with him he lost interest in everything but his misery. He would not play, he would not eat. On this occasion he set himself to win Plaxy over by many little attentions. He brought her a beautiful feather, then a lovely white pebble, and each time he timidly kissed her hand. Suddenly she gave him a hearty hug, and both broke into a romp. Towards Elizabeth, Sirius was less bold. He merely eyed her askance, his tail timorously vibrating when he caught her glance. So comic was this spectacle that she could not help laughing. Sirius was forgiven.

At a stage in his puppyhood shortly after this incident Sirius conceived a respectful admiration for Gelert. The slightly older and biologically quite adult super-sub-human animal treated him with careless contempt. Sirius followed Gelert about and mimicked all his actions. One day Gelert by great good fortune caught a rabbit and devoured it, growling savagely when Sirius approached. The puppy watched him with mingled admiration and horror. The spectacle of that swift pursuit and capture roused in him the hunting impulses of the normal dog. The scream of the rabbit, its struggle, sudden limpness and hideous dismemberment, shocked him deeply; for he had a sympathetic and imaginative nature, and Elizabeth had brought up her family in a tradition of tenderness towards all living things. But now a conflict arose which was to distress him throughout his life, the conflict between what he later called his "wolf-nature" and his compassionate civilized mentality.

The immediate result was a strong and guilty lust for the chase and an intensified, awed passion for Gelert. He became obsessed by the rabbit-warren. He was for ever sniffing at the entrances to the burrows, whimpering with excitement. For a while Plaxy was almost forgotten. Vainly she tried to win him back into partnership in her games. Vainly she hung about the burrows with him, bored and cross. In her presence he once caught a frog and disgustingly mangled it in an attempt to eat it. She burst into tears. His hunting impulse was suddenly quenched, and horror supervened. He rushed whimpering to his darling and covered her face with bloody kisses.

Many times henceforth he was to suffer the torturing conflict between his normal canine impulses and his more developed nature.

His admiration of Gelert was gradually damped down by the discovery that the older dog had no interest in anything but hunting and eating. Once more there was a conflict. Hunting now gripped Sirius as the main joy of life; but it was a guilty joy. He felt its call almost as a religious claim upon him, the claim of the dark blood-god for sacrifice; but he was also disgusted with the sacrifice, and deeply disturbed by Plaxy's horror. Moreover, after his first obsession he began to recover interest in the many activities which he shared with Plaxy. These were of no interest to Gelert.

The final disillusionment came when Sirius began to realize that Gelert not merely would not but could not talk. This suspicion had long haunted Sirius, but he had believed that Gelert's unresponsiveness was merely due to his haughty disposition. There came a day, however, when this theory ceased to be possible. Young Sirius, whose four-foot locomotion was far more developed than Plaxy's running, had been trying to keep up with Gelert at the outset of a hunting expedition. They came upon a sheep with a broken leg. Though Gelert was not in the sheep-tending profession, he knew very well that sheep were things to be cherished. He knew also that Mr. Pugh of Caer Blai was in this case the responsible man. He therefore hurried off to Caer Blai, far outstripping the loose-limbed puppy. When at last Sirius arrived in the farmyard, he found Gelert making an inarticulate fuss around Pugh, vainly trying to persuade him to come up the hill. Sirius knew that he himself could not make Pugh understand, but he knew also that he could explain to any member of his own family. He therefore set off to find one of them and encountered Giles on his way home from school. He pantingly told Giles the story, and the two hurried to Caer Blai. Giles momentarily forgot the great family taboo about "not telling people about Sirius," and said to Pugh, "Sirius says there's a sheep with a broken leg in Nant Twll-y-cwm, and it may get drowned." Pugh looked at him with incredulity, but was impressed by the boy's earnestness and the antics of the dogs. He accompanied them up the valley, and there was the sheep. After this incident Sirius regarded Gelert as a nit-wit, and the farmer suspected Sirius of being an altogether "super" super-sheep-dog.

The discovery that Gelert could not speak, and was in other respects also a half-wit, was a shock to Sirius. Gelert excelled him in all those ways in which he outshone his human friends, in speed, in endurance, in scent and in hearing. For some time he had taken Gelert as his model. Mimicking Gelert's taciturnity, he had even tried not to talk. So successful had he been that Elizabeth in one of her letters to Thomas said that Sirius's human mentality seemed to be waning. The realization that the older dog simply could not talk changed the puppy's attitude. Suddenly he became garrulous, and showed an increased desire to keep pace with Plaxy in acquiring all sorts of human skills. Also he devised an amusing way of ridiculing Gelert. He would hold imaginary conversations with the super-sheep-dog, pretending that Gelert's silence was due to deliberate taciturnity. The older animal would at first ignore the garrulous puppy; but presently, particularly if the spectators laughed, his super-canine though sub-human mind would begin to suspect that Sirius was making a fool of him. He would look very self-conscious and perplexed, and sooner or later drive the insolent youngster away, or seize him and chastise him.

Plaxy was by now being taught to read and write. Her mother devoted an hour a day to this task. Sirius had at first shown a mild curiosity about the queer business, but under the influence of Gelert he had thrown it over for the sake of hunting. Elizabeth made no effort to compel him to carry on his studies. Either his distaste was a passing phase, soon to be outgrown, or his mind was after all not sufficiently super-canine to persist in this alien occupation, in which case compulsion would be disastrous. However, when his idol had fallen, he reverted to the game of reading and writing. He had missed a good deal, so Elizabeth undertook to coach him up to Plaxy's standard. Of course his handlessness made it impossible for him ever to write save with some special apparatus. It was also discovered that, apart from his obvious disability for writing, his reading also was doomed to be very seriously hampered, so crude was his perception of visual form. Plaxy used to spell out simple words with her box of letters, but Sirius found it very difficult to distinguish between C, G, D, O and Q, and also between B, P, R, and K. He was also greatly confused by E and F, by S and Z, by A and H, by H and K. At a later stage, when Plaxy was mastering the lower-case letters, and these in small type, Sirius was still more handicapped. Sometimes it almost seemed that his intelligence was after all sub-human. Elizabeth, who, in spite of her triumphant impartiality towards her child and her foster-child, had always a secret desire for Plaxy to excel, now wrote to Thomas that after all Sirius was not much better than a moron. But Thomas, whose secret desire was the reverse of his wife's, replied with a dissertation on the poor vision of dogs, and urged her to encourage Sirius by telling him of this canine disability, to praise his enterprise in learning to read and write at all, and to remind him that he had great advantages over human beings in other spheres. Encouragement tapped a surprising fund of doggedness in Sirius, for he spent hours every day by himself practising reading. Great progress was made, but after a week or so Elizabeth felt bound to intervene because of symptoms of mental breakdown. She praised him and petted him, and persuaded him that he would learn more quickly and permanently if he tried a bit less hard.

Sirius recognized, of course, that in writing he could not possibly reach Plaxy's standard, but he was determined not to be entirely without this valuable art. It was he himself that invented a way out of his disability. He persuaded Elizabeth to make him a tight leather mitten for his right paw. On the back of the mitten was a socket into which a pen or pencil could be inserted. When this article was completed, he made his first experiment in writing. He was very excited. Lying in the "couchant" position with his left foreleg on the paper to hold it in place, he kept his right elbow on the ground, and was able to scrawl out DOG, CAT, PLAXY, SIRIUS, and so on. The neural organization of his leg and the motor-centres of his brain were probably not at all well adapted to this activity; but once more his doggedness triumphed. Long practice brought him after some years the skill to write a letter in large, irregular but legible characters. In later life, as I shall tell, he even ventured on the task of writing books.

Thomas was more impressed than Elizabeth by Sirius's achievement, because he probably appreciated more fully the difficulties that the puppy had overcome.

So far as possible, Sirius took part in all the simple lessons that Elizabeth gave to Plaxy. He was never very good at arithmetic, perhaps because of his poor visual powers; but he managed to avoid being outclassed by Plaxy, who was none too good herself. His spelling, too, was very bad, probably for the same reason. But at an early age he showed a great interest in language and the art of precise expression. Poetry had sometimes a deep effect on him. In spite of his visual weakness he read a good deal, and he often begged members of the family to read aloud to him. This they did very frequently, knowing how great a boon it was for him.

But to return to his puppyhood. There came a time when it seemed desirable for Plaxy to attend the village school. Sirius, of course, could not do so. It was sometimes with thankfulness for his freedom, but sometimes with envy, that he watched his little foster-sister set off with her books in the morning. He was now of an age to do a great deal of free roaming, and the passion for the scents and adventures of the countryside was now strong in him. But the thought that Plaxy was outstripping him in knowledge of the great world of men worried him sorely. In the afternoons, when she returned from school, she often assured him that lessons were a bore; but he could tell from her tone that she felt important and proud, and that a good deal that happened at school was great fun. He made a habit of gleaning from her the most useful bits of information that she had acquired during the day. It became a regular custom with her to do her homework with him, to the profit of them both. Meanwhile Elizabeth continued Sirius's education in a desultory but stimulating way. Often he was able to pay his debt to Plaxy by passing on to her the fruits of his own lessons, though she generally adopted a superior attitude to his tit-bits. Sometimes he told her about conversations with Thomas, who had made a habit of taking Sirius for walks on the hills and telling him all sorts of significant scraps of science or world-history. Plaxy herself, of course, was sometimes present on these walks. But generally Thomas needed vigorous exercise at the week-ends, and his little daughter could not keep up with him as well as Sirius. During his puppyhood Sirius often came home tired after long expeditions with Thomas, but when he reached mid-adolescence he used to look forward with pleasure to the almost weekly trek over Arenig, the Rhinogs or Moelwyn, listening to the far-ranging flow of Thomas's thought, or probing him with questions. These the great physiologist answered with all the patience and care which he was accustomed to give to his students. This was Sirius's main intellectual education, this frequent contact with a mature and brilliant mind. Often the two would discuss Sirius's future, Thomas encouraging him to believe that a great work lay before him. But of this later. I have let myself pass beyond the dog's puppyhood, and now I must return to it.

Not only in reading and writing but in another way also Sirius was inevitably inferior to Plaxy, and indeed to nearly all human beings. He was entirely colour-blind. I understand that there is still doubt about colour-sensitivity in dogs. Dissection, I believe, has revealed that they have approximately the same equipment of "rods and cones" in their retinae as that of human beings. But psychological experiments have not yet proved that dogs are in fact sensitive to colour. Possibly the truth is that, though some dogs are aware of colour, the incidence of colour-blindness in the canine species is much greater than in man. However that may be, it is certain that Sirius was completely colour-blind. Until quite late in his puppyhood, long after he had learned to talk, he himself had no suspicion that his seeing lacked any qualities possessed by Plaxy's. Thomas had told Elizabeth that dogs were almost certainly colour-blind, but she refused to believe it of Sirius, insisting that he could distinguish between her differently coloured dresses. "No," said Thomas, "he probably does it by scent or the touch of his sensitive tongue. Besides, haven't you noticed that he goes

badly adrift in his use of the names of colours? Anyhow, let's test him."
For this purpose Thomas bought a child's box of wooden picture-blocks,
and covered the faces of the cubes with paper of different colours very
carefully selected so that their tone values and tactual and olfactory qualities should be identical. Any differences of odour that might be due to differences of pigment he blotted out by drenching the blocks in eau-de
Cologne. He then presented the "box of bricks" to Plaxy and Sirius. Plaxy
at once produced a chequer of pink and blue squares. Sirius was obviously
uninterested in the blocks, but he was persuaded to copy Plaxy's chequer.
He put the pieces together quite at random. It was soon obvious even to
Sirius himself that Plaxy saw something which he missed. He at once set
about the same kind of self-education which he had undertaken in order
to read. With Plaxy's aid he must discover the thing that had escaped him
in the bricks, and then strengthen his powers of seeing it. Plaxy displayed
coloured objects to him one after another, naming their colours. She showed
him a coloured print and a monochrome photograph. Giles produced a
flash-light with red and green glasses. But all was in vain. Sirius was quite
unable to discover what colour was.

He was at first greatly distressed, but Thomas comforted him by assuring him that all dogs were colour-blind, and probably all mammals but
apes and men. And he reminded Sirius that dogs were at any rate far
superior in hearing and smelling. Sirius had long known that human
noses were very poor instruments. He had often been contemptuous because Plaxy could not smell out her mother's track in the garden, or tell
with her nose whether a certain footprint was Gelert's or another dog's.
Moreover at an early age he was surprised and disappointed at her obtuseness to all the mysterious and exciting smells of the countryside after rain.
While she mildly enjoyed an indiscriminate freshness and fragrance, he
would analyse the messages of the breeze with quivering nostrils, gasping
out words between the sniffs. "Horse," he would say; then after another
sniff, "And not a horse I have smelt before." Or, "Postman! Must be coming up the lane." Or perhaps, "Sea-smell to-day," though the sea was several miles away behind the Rhinogs. A slight veering of the wind might
bring him whiffs of a distant waterfall, or more fragrant odours of the
moor, or peat or heather or bracken. Sometimes, gripped by some strange
enticing scent, he would rush off to trace it. Once he came trotting back
after a few minutes of exploration and said, "Strange bird, but I couldn't
see him properly." On another occasion he suddenly rushed out of the
house, sniffed the breeze, raced off up the moor, cast about till he picked
up a trail, and then streamed along it round the hill shoulder. After an
hour or so he returned in great excitement, made Plaxy fetch out the animal book and turn the pages till she came to The Fox. "That's him!" he
cried, "Gosh, what a smell!" Once in the middle of a romping game in
the garden he came to a sudden halt, sniffing. His hair bristled, his tail

curled under his belly. "Let's go inside," he said, "there's some dreadful thing up wind." Plaxy laughed, but he seemed so disturbed that she consented. Twenty minutes later Giles arrived from school, full of the news that he had seen a menagerie pass along the road to Ffestiniog.

Giles was so tickled by Sirius's reaction that he clamoured for Sirius to be taken to see the wild beasts with the rest of the family, arguing that the little coward had better learn that bad smells were not really dangerous. After much persuasion Sirius consented to go. The experience had a lasting effect on him. As he entered the enclosure the appalling confusion of odours, some enticing, some formidable, tore his nerves as though (as he said long afterwards) all the instruments of an orchestra were tuning up together at full blast. With tucked-in tail and scared eyes he kept close to Elizabeth as the party moved from cage to cage. Many of the animals roused his hunting impulse; but the great carnivora, the abject and mangy lion, tiger, and bear, forlornly pacing their narrow cages, tortured him, partly by their terrifying natural smell, partly by their acquired odour of ill-health and misery. The slit-eyed wolf, too, greatly affected him with its similarity to himself. While he was gazing with fascination at this distant cousin, the lion suddenly roared, and Sirius, shivering with fright, shrank up against Elizabeth's legs. Stimulated by the lion, the rest of the animals started to give tongue. When the elephant rent the air with a blast of his trumpet, Sirius took to his heels and vanished.

The world of odour was one in which Plaxy had only slight experience. In the world of sound she was not so completely outclassed, but she was far behind Sirius. He could hear approaching footsteps long before Plaxy or any other human being could detect them, and he could unfailingly tell who it was that was coming. The cry of a bat, entirely beyond the range of most human ears, was described by Sirius as a sharp needle of sound. Both Elizabeth and Plaxy soon discovered that he was incredibly sensitive to their tone of voice. He could distinguish unerringly between spontaneous praise and mere kindly encouragement, between real condemnation and censure with an undertone of amusement or approval. Not only so, but he seemed able to detect changes of temper in them before they themselves had noticed them. "Elizabeth," he would suddenly ask, "why are you sad?" She would reply, laughing, "But I'm *not!* I'm rather pleased because the bread has risen nicely." "Oh, but you *are* sad, underneath," he would answer. "I can hear it quite well. You are only pleased on top." And after a pause she would have to say, "Oh, well, perhaps I am. I wonder why."

His nose, too, gave him a lot of information about people's emotional states. He sometimes spoke of a "cross smell," a "friendly smell," a "frightened smell," a "tired smell."

So sensitive was he to odour and to sound, that he found human speech quite inadequate to express the richness of these two universes. He

once said of a certain odour in the house, "It's rather like the trail of a
hare where a spaniel has followed it, and some time ago a donkey crossed
it too." Both scent and sound had for him rich emotional meaning, innate
and acquired. It was obvious that many odours that he encountered for
the first time roused a strong impulse of pursuit, while others he sought to
avoid. It was obvious, too, that many odours acquired an added emotional
meaning through their associations. One day when he was out on the moor
by himself one of his paws was badly cut on a broken bottle. It happened
that while he limped home there was a terrifying thunderstorm. When
at last he staggered in at the front door, Elizabeth mothered him and
cleaned up his foot with a certain well-known disinfectant. The smell of it
was repugnant to him, but it now acquired a flavour of security and kindliness which was to last him all his life.

Many sounds stirred him violently. Thunder and other great noises
terrified him. The tearing of calico made him leap with a purely physiological fright, and set him barking in merry protest. Human laughter he
found very infectious. It roused in him a queer yelping laughter which
was all his own. The tones of the human voice not only told him of the
emotional state of the speaker but also stimulated strong emotional responses in himself. The odours of emotion had a similar effect.

Like many dogs, young Sirius found human music quite excruciating.
An isolated vocal or instrumental theme was torture enough to him; but
when several voices or instruments combined, he seemed to lose control
of himself completely. His fine auditory discrimination made even well-
executed solos seem to him badly out of tune. Harmony and the combination of several themes resulted for him in hideous cacophony. Elizabeth
and the children would sometimes sing rounds, for instance when they were
coming down the moor after a picnic. Sirius invariably had to give up
his usual far-ranging course and draw into the party to howl. The indignant children would chase him away, but as soon as the singing began
again he would return and once more give tongue. On one occasion Tamsy,
who was the most seriously musical member of the family, cried implor-
ingly, "Sirius, do either keep quiet or keep away! Why can't you let us
enjoy ourselves?" He replied, "But how can you like such a horrible jar-
ring muddle of sweet noises? I have to come to you because they're so sweet,
and I have to howl because it's a mess, and because—oh because it might
be so lovely." Once he said, "If I were to paint a picture could you just
keep away? Wouldn't you go crazy because of the all-wrongness of the
colour? Well, sounds are far more exciting to me than your queer colour
is to you."

The family refused to admit that their singing was a mess. Instead,
they determined to "teach Sirius music." He accepted his fate with doglike
docility and fortitude. After all, painful as the process must be, it would
help him to find out more about human beings; and even at a very early

age he had begun to be curious about the difference between himself and his friends.

The whole family gathered in the sitting-room to "teach Sirius music." Elizabeth produced her cherished but now neglected violin. On the few earlier occasions when she had played on it within earshot of Sirius, he always came hurrying to her, howling. If the door was shut, he gave tongue outside. Otherwise he rushed into the room and leapt up at her till she had to stop. On this occasion he at first made some effort to keep a hold on himself during the painful operation that his family were determined to perform on him. But excitement soon overcame him. Tamsy was at the piano. Maurice and Giles were ready, if wanted, with their recorders. Plaxy sat on the floor with her arms around the resigned but rather mischievous Sirius, "to keep him from going mad on us." For it was clear that Sirius was going to be difficult. When Plaxy let him escape, he bounded from instrument to instrument, making mock attacks on each. His tail thrashed from side to side in a conflict of agony and delight, knocking the bow from Elizabeth's hand, and sending a recorder flying across the room. Even when Plaxy held him, he turned the experiment to chaos by giving tongue with such vigour and virtuosity that the simple tones of the instrument were drowned. When at last he was persuaded to co-operate seriously, it was soon found that he had at any rate a far better ear for pitch than any of the family. When Elizabeth moved her finger so slightly on the string that none of the children could hear any difference, Sirius detected a change. Elizabeth was amazed to find that he could also sing accurately in tune. Once when she played a single tone and he could not restrain himself from giving tongue, the main element in his wail was obviously in tune with the violin. With a little encouragement he produced the pure note without any trimmings. When Maurice played a scale on his recorder, Sirius sang in unison with it, keeping perfectly in tune even with the inaccurate tones produced by the young musician on an imperfect instrument.

With his usual doggedness Sirius set about conquering this excruciating thing, music. He showed surprising aptitude for singing, soon outstripping Plaxy in reproducing the family songs. Sometimes he sang without words; sometimes he used his own canine equivalent of the English words of the song. (His lingo, being simply mispronounced English, rhymed and scanned appropriately.)

With practice he became less tortured by human music. In fact he actually came to like it, so long as it was not too badly out of tune. He would often join in singing the rounds that had formerly tormented him. Sometimes when Elizabeth played her violin he would come to listen. In certain moods he would retire to a favourite point of vantage on the moor and spend hours singing to himself. He would go over and over the songs that Elizabeth had so often sung about the house.

It was a tune-loving family. Under Elizabeth's influence it had de-

veloped an amusing system of musical calls which served the function of
bugle-calls. A certain little tune meant "Time to get up," another "Breakfast is ready," another "All is now prepared for starting on the expedition,"
and so on. Plaxy and Sirius, the two youngest members of the family, invented a number of private calls of their own. One of these, for instance,
meant "Come and help me!" Another said, "Something interesting here.
Come and investigate"; another "Come and play with me!" One little
trickle of sound meant, "I am going to pee." To this there were two possible musical answers. One said, "Right oh! So am I," and the other "Nothing doing by me." It was curious, by the way, that if one of them made
water the other had always to follow suit on the same spot, in the approved canine manner. Always? No! Plaxy soon found that she could not
keep pace with Sirius in this etiquette of leaving tokens.

When Thomas heard of Sirius's habit of retiring on to the moor to
practise singing, he feared lest his precious animal should become notorious
as "the singing dog," and be exploited. It was indeed startling for the
natives to hear the sweet, accurate, but inarticulate and inhuman voice, and
to come upon a large dog squatting on his haunches melodiously giving
tongue. Thomas, it was rumoured, had sinister powers. He could put de-
mons into dogs. Fortunately the farther these rumours spread, the less they
were believed. No craze equivalent to the case of the talking mongoose or
the Loch Ness monster developed over the singing dog.

In his puppyhood Sirius sang only human music. Throughout his life
he was deeply interested in the great classical achievements of man's musical genius, but as he had always found the fundamental structure of human
music crude, and inadequate to his interest in sound-form and the emotions
which sought musical expression, he began to experiment with new scales,
intervals, and rhythms, suited to his more sensitive hearing. He made use
of the quarter-tone and even the eighth-of-a-tone. Sometimes, in his purely
canine mood, his melodies divided the octave in quite a different manner
from any human musical mode. Thus to the human listener his most distinctive music became less recognizably musical and more like the baying
of a dog, though a strangely varied and disturbing baying.

A supple and mellow voice was Sirius's only medium of expression.
He often longed to play some instrument, so as to be able to introduce
harmony into his experiments, but his tragic lack of hands prevented him.
Sometimes he sat at the piano trying to finger out a two-note accompaniment to his singing, but his paws were far too clumsy to do even this
properly. For long spells he would give up music entirely because his handlessness prevented him from doing what he wanted with it. At these times
he would wander about with tail and head low, refusing comfort. The
mingled sense of helplessness and talent tormented him. But presently his
buoyant spirits would revive, and he would resolve that, if instrumental
music must remain for ever impossible to him, he would do new and mar-

vellous things with his voice. Throughout his life Sirius alternated between self pity on account of his disabilities and a surprisingly detached and humorous acceptance of his nature and his environment, issuing in a zestful will to triumph in spite of everything.

CHAPTER IV

YOUTH

IN the foregoing chapter I should have written only about Sirius as a puppy, but in dealing with his disabilities and powers I was inevitably led on to speak of his later life. His serious musical adventures, for instance, did not begin till puppyhood was well over. I must now concentrate more definitely on his adolescence and early maturity, preparing the way for an account of that part of his life with which my own life became for a while closely entangled.

Already in adolescence Sirius was larger than most sheep-dogs. But though tall, he was at this time very slight and lanky, and it was often said that he had "overgrown his strength." He was also far from courageous. His caution in his encounters with other dogs was increased by his discovery in sundry minor brawls that his large cranium made his head unwieldly and his seizing of his opponent rather less slick than it might have been. This weakness was largely overcome when he reached full maturity, for constant exercise developed the muscles of his neck sufficiently to cope with his extra weight of head. In youth, however, he was no match for the smaller but more experienced collies that tended the sheep. One of these, unfortunately a near neighbour, formed a habit of persecuting Sirius when-ever possible. There came a day when he was ignominiously chased home by this animal, who bore the appropriate name Diawl Du, black devil. It was the school-girl Plaxy who seized the yard broom and drove off the black devil with blows and shrill curses. Later Sirius heard Plaxy telling her mother about the incident. She ended the story with, "I'm afraid poor Sirius hasn't much spunk." Sirius did not know the word "spunk," but he detected in Plaxy's voice, which she intended to be merely amused, a note of deep mortification. He sneaked off to find a dictionary. With some trouble and much use of his wet tongue for turning the "India paper" pages he found the word; and he didn't like the idea that Plaxy thought him lacking in spunk. For "spunk" according to the Oxford Concise Dictionary meant "courage, mettle, spirit, anger," and was connected with "spark." Somehow he must regain Plaxy's respect, but how?

That same day Plaxy seemed to turn her attention away from Sirius

towards the young cat, Trix, successor to Tommy. This impulse to make
much of cats was a common reaction with her when she was at all alienated from Sirius. She would cuddle Trix in front of him and remark on
her lovely tortoise-shell coat or her dainty nose. Also, Sirius noted, she
would become strangely catlike herself, sitting about in lofty silence and
indolence, "hugging herself," as he sometimes put it.

Shortly after his defeat by Diawl Du, Sirius got himself into serious
disgrace over Trix. The cat was contemplating a leap into Plaxy's lap when
Sirius lost control of himself and attacked his minute rival with noisy rage.
She arched her back and stood firm, slashing Sirius's face, so that he retreated, yelping. Plaxy's scream turned into a laugh. Reviling Sirius for a
bully and a coward, she snatched up Trix and lavished endearments on
her. Sirius slunk away in shame and misery.

A fortnight later it was remarked in the family that Sirius had developed an unexpected craze for worrying an old spade-handle which had
been lying in the outhouse. Whenever possible he would persuade some
sturdy human being, preferably Maurice, who was home from boarding
school, to join in the game. Boy and dog would hang on to opposite ends
of the piece of ash and swing hither and thither about the garden, each
trying to shake off his opponent. Towards the end of the holidays Maurice
remarked, "Sirius is getting damned strong. You can't tear the thing from
him; you can't twist it from him." All this time Sirius had been carefully
avoiding Diawl Du, but at last he felt ready. Though he was confident that
his grip was much more powerful than it had been, and his head movements quicker and more precise, he would not trust to physical powers
alone; cunning must be his mainstay. His strategy was planned with great
care. He studied his chosen battle-ground, and rehearsed the crucial action
which was to give him victory in the very scene of his former discomfiture,
and under the eyes of Plaxy.

One afternoon when Plaxy had returned from school he hurried over
to Glasdo, the farm where Diawl Du lived, and ostentatiously hung about
till his enemy issued like a black avalanche from the farmyard gate. Sirius
at once took to his heels, bolting for home. To reach the front door of
Garth, which was ostensibly his objective, he had to make a right-angled
turn through the yard gate. (Garth, it will be remembered, was an old
farm-house.) As he checked himself to do this and swing through the gate,
he glanced behind to see that Diawl Du was at the correct distance. Then
he raced round the yard in a great curve, arriving back at the gate, but at
right angles to his original course through it, and hidden from Diawl Du
by the wall. At that moment the collie swerved through the gate in pursuit,
and Sirius with great momentum crashed into him on the left flank. Diawl
Du rolled over with Sirius on top of him. Sirius gripped his throat, his
teeth finding a much firmer hold than on the hard old spade handle. He
hung on desperately, fearing that if he once let go the superior skill of the

other dog would be his undoing. The collie's throttled screams and Sirius's own continuous muffled growl soon brought out the inmates of the house. Out of the corner of his eye, as he rolled over and over with his enemy, Sirius caught sight of Plaxy. The warm blood seeped into his mouth and threatened to choke him, but he hung on, coughing for breath. The saltness and odour of Diawl Du's blood, he afterwards said, turned him mad. Some pent up energy and fury in him was released for the first time. At the height of the struggle the thought flashed upon him, "This is real life, this is what I am for, not all that human twaddle." He gripped and tugged and worried, while Diawl Du's struggles became weaker, and the horrified human beings did their best to loosen his grip. They beat him, they threw pepper in his face so that he sneezed violently, but he did not let go. They fell upon him in a mass to hold him quiet while they tried to prise his jaws open with a stick. His own blood mixed with the collie's in his mouth, and he was surprised at the different flavour of it. Nothing that the family could do made him loosen his grip. Plaxy, desperate with horror, did her best to force her hands into his mouth. Then suddenly beside herself, she screamed. At last Sirius let go, and Diawl Du lay inert on the ground.

The victor stalked away, licking his blood-slippery lips, his spine still bristling. After taking a drink at the trough under the yard pump, he lay down with his chin on his paws to watch the proceedings. Elizabeth sent the children into the house for warm water, disinfectants, bandages, while she examined the wound. Presently Plaxy was holding the unconscious dog's head, while Elizabeth applied a large cotton-wool pad and wound the bandage round his neck. After a while Diawl Du showed signs of life, moving his head slightly in Plaxy's hands. He produced the ghost of a growl, which ended in a whimper. Then they carried him inside and laid him before the kitchen fire with a drink of water beside him.

No one took any notice of Sirius, who still lay in the yard, stiff and sore; triumphant, but also rather bewildered and resentful. If she wanted him to have spunk, why didn't she come and praise him and pet him?

Presently Elizabeth came and started up the little car. When she had backed it into the road, she went in and, with Maurice's help, brought out Diawl Du in her arms, while the others prepared a place for him on the back seat of the car. When he was comfortably laid on a rug on the seat, she drove off to Glasdo.

The children turned towards Sirius. "Gosh!" said Maurice, "you've done it this time!" And Tamsy, "They'll have you shot as a dangerous animal." Giles contributed, "It was just murder." Plaxy said nothing but "Oh, Sirius!" He stared at her in silence, trying to analyse her tone of voice. Mainly it spoke reproach, and horror. But there was something else in it, perhaps exultation at his prowess, perhaps mere human superiority. Anyhow, what did he care? He lay still for a little longer with chin on paws, staring at Plaxy. At that moment Trix, the cat, came and rubbed herself against Plaxy's legs. Plaxy picked her up and hugged her. Sirius rose, his back once more bristling, and with a low noise between a snort and a growl he stalked with conscious dignity out through the gate.

The fight with Diawl Du was a turning point in the career of Sirius. He had tasted victory. He had got his own back. Never again would he be cowed by half-wit persecutors. But something more had happened than a calculated triumph. His deeper nature, his unconscious nature, had found expression. He had discovered something far more satisfying than human sophistication. These thoughts were not clear in his mind at the time; but looking back on the incident from a much later period, this was the form that he gave them.

Elizabeth warned him that, if he attempted murder again, there might be serious trouble. "Remember," she said, "to outsiders you are only a dog. You have no legal rights at all. If someone decides that you are a nuisance and shoots you, he won't be had up for murder; he'll merely get into trouble for destroying a bit of our property. Besides," she added, "how *could* you do it? It was horrible, just animal." Sirius gave no response to this taunt; but taunt he felt it to be. He could both smell and hear her contemptuous hostility. Probably some suppressed and unacknowledged hate for her canine foster-child had found a sudden outlet. Sirius saw the folly and danger of his action clearly enough, but her last remark filled him with rage. In his heart he said, "To hell with them all!" Outwardly he gave no sign that he was even listening. He was sitting in front of the kitchen fire, and after Elizabeth's taunt he cocked up a hind leg and carefully, ostentatiously, groomed his private parts, a habit which he often used with great effect to annoy his women folk.

As the months piled up into years Sirius's self-confidence in relation to other dogs was greatly augmented. His increasing weight and strength combined with superior intelligence to give him not only freedom from persecution but acknowledged superiority over all the sheep-dogs of the countryside, who were all much smaller than the young Alsatian. His combination of size and cunning put him in a class apart. As for "spunk", the truth seems to be that throughout his life he remained at heart a timid creature who rose to a display of boldness only in desperation or when the odds were favourable, or on those rare occasions when the dark god of his blood took possession of him.

I cannot deal with his relations with animals of his own biological type without giving some account of his sexual adventures. Long before the fight with Diawl Du he had begun to be perplexedly interested in any bitch in heat that he happened to come across. Mostly they would have nothing to do with him, regarding him, presumably, as an overgrown puppy. But there was one large and rather elderly black bitch who seemed to find the callow young giant very attractive. With her he periodically indulged in a great deal of desultory love play. Thomas observed the antics of the couple with keen interest, because it soon became obvious that Sirius lacked the ordinary dog's intuitive aptitude for making full use of his opportunities. The two animals would race around, tumbling over one another in mock battle, obviously relishing the delectable contact of their bodies. But after a while Sirius would stand about foolishly wagging his tail, wondering what to do next. This aimlessness was of course a normal stage in the sexual development of dogs, but normally it soon led to copulation. Sirius, however, who as it happened had never observed another canine pair copulating, seemed permanently at a loss. It was not till he came upon his own beloved in the act of being taken by another dog, far younger than himself but more instinctive and more physiologically mature, that he discovered what it was that his body wanted to do.

Henceforth his amours were brought to a point in the normal manner. Physiologically he was still merely in the "school-boy" phase, and not very attractive to mature bitches. Nor was sex at this stage an obsessive passion with him. It was more important as a symbol of maturity than as an end in itself. Its natural seductiveness was much enhanced by its being "the done thing" for grown-up dogs. In comparison with Plaxy and even the elder children Sirius seemed sexually precocious, simply because his unrestricted amours afforded him experience and technique, while to the children everything of the sort remained for a long while almost unexplored territory.

In one respect Sirius found his love affairs miserably unsatisfactory, throughout his life. For the beloved of the hour, however delectable in odour and appearance and in bodily contact, was invariably from his point of view something less than a half-wit. She could not speak, she could not understand his spoken endearments. She could not share the adventures of his wakening mind. And when her heat was over she became devastatingly frigid and unattractive. The fragrance was gone; the moron mentality remained.

Thomas was greatly interested in Sirius's accounts of his love affairs; about which, by the way, he showed no reticence. To the question, "What is it that attracts you in her?" young Sirius could only reply, "She smells so lovely." Later in life he was able to say more. Some years later I myself discussed the matter with him, and he said, "Of course it's mostly the luscious smell of her. I can't possibly make you understand the power of it, because you humans are so bad at smells. It's as though your noses were not merely feeble but colour-blind. But think of all that your poets have ever said about the delectable curves and colours of the beloved, and how her appearance seems to express a lovely *spirit* (often deceptively), and then imagine the whole thing done in terms of fragrance. Morwen's fragrance when she wants me is like the scent of the morning, with a maddening tang in it for which there are no words. It is the scent of a very gentle and fragrant *spirit,* but unfortunately the spirit of Morwen is nine-tenths asleep, and always will be. But she smells like what she *would* be if she *were* really awake."

"But what about her appearance?" I said. "Doesn't that attract you?" "It attracts *me* a lot," he replied, "but ordinary dogs take little notice of it. With them it's smell that counts, and of course the touch of her, too. But it's the smell that enthrals one, the maddening, stinging, sweet smell, that soaks right through your body, so that you can't think of anything else day or night. But her looks? Yes *I* certainly do care about her looks. She's so sleek and slim and slick. Also her looks help a lot to express the spirit that she *might* have been if she had been properly awake, like me. But then you see *I* have been made to notice appearances so much by being with you sharp-eyed creatures. All the same, even for me her voice is really more important than her looks. She can't talk, of course; but she can say the sweetest, tenderest things with the tone and rhythm of her voice. Of course she doesn't really and clearly *mean* them. She says in her sleep, so to speak, things that she *would* mean if she were awake."

But to return to Sirius's adolescence. Elizabeth had brought up her children in the modern tradition. Living in the country they were bound to learn a bit about sex from watching beasts and birds. But since there was none of the still very common guiltiness attached to sex in their minds, their interest in sex was very desultory, and they took a surprisingly long time to tumble to it. When Sirius achieved his first love affair, the two younger members of the family, who were not yet at boarding school, suspected nothing; but presently he began to talk about it with obvious pride. Elizabeth had to use all her tact and humour to establish the convention that what was perfectly right and proper for Sirius was not to be indulged in by human children until they were grown up; and that anyhow one didn't talk about these things outside the family; and above all, not in Wales. The whole affair, she confessed to Thomas, was really rather awkward, and she only hoped she hadn't done more harm than good.

Plaxy had of course already had numerous childhood romances. Very early in her schooldays she had been violently in love with a little Welsh girl at the village school. Whether this should be regarded as a sexual sentiment or not, it was certainly an obsession. Sirius, for the first time in his life, found himself unwanted. Plaxy suddenly had no time for the games they used to play when school and homework were over; for she had always promised to do something with Gwen. She would not let him come with her when she went out with her friend, for (she said) Gwen would soon find out that Sirius could talk; and it was the whole family's most sacred taboo that outsiders must not discover yet that Sirius was something more than a super-sheep-dog. This was the secret which they had learnt to cherish as a tribal mystery. No one but the six members of the family knew about it, except Kate, who had long ago been accepted into the tribe. The other two members of the domestic staff, Mildred the nurse-

maid and the local girl, had both been regretfully dismissed in order that
the secret might not be endangered. Sirius therefore saw the force of Plaxy's
argument; but something in her voice told him that she was glad to have
such a plausible excuse for leaving him behind. The sudden loss of Plaxy's
companionship and confidence weighed heavily on the puppy. He did
nothing but mope about the house and garden waiting for her return.
When she arrived he treated her with effusive affection, but in her response
there was often a note of absentmindedness or even indifference.

After a while this early romance faded out, and Sirius was reinstated.
But other romances followed. When she was twelve Plaxy lost her heart to
the local blacksmith's boy, Gwilim, who was eighteen. This was a one-
sided affair, and Plaxy saw little of him. She made Sirius her confidant, and
he comforted her by protesting that Gwilim must be stupid not to love
such a nice girl. Once he said, "Anyhow, Plaxy, *I* love you." She hugged
him and said, "Yes, I know, and I love you. But I do love Gwilim. And
you see he's my *kind,* and you're not. I love you differently; not less, but
differently."

It was while Plaxy was pining for her brawny young blacksmith that
Sirius himself began to be seriously interested in the females of his own
kind. Suddenly Plaxy found that her faithful confidant, who had always
been ready to listen and sympathize, save during brief hunting expeditions,
was no longer available. Often when she came back from school he was
nowhere to be found. He failed to turn up either for homework or games
or even meals. Or if he was present, he was mentally far away, and perfunctory in his sympathy. Once when she was telling him how marvellously
Gwilim swung the hammer on to the red-hot iron, and how he smiled at
her afterwards, Sirius suddenly sprang to his feet, stood for a moment
sniffing the air, then bolted. Bitterly mortified, she said to herself, "He's
not a real friend, after all. He's just a brute beast." (This expression she
had recently learnt at school.) "He doesn't really understand, he doesn't
really care." All this she knew to be quite untrue.

After her intermittent and always unrequited passion for Gwilim had
dragged on for eighteen months, causing her much sweet sorrow and self-
importance, she happened to come one day upon Sirius in the very act of
love with his fragrant darling of the moment. On one occasion recently she
had seen two dogs behaving in this odd way, but she had not seen Sirius
doing it. She was surprised to find that it was a horrid shock to her. She
hurried away, feeling unreasonably outraged and lonely.

It was two or three years after the affair with Gwilim that she made
her first conquest. Conwy Pritchard, the postmaster's son, was a much more
responsive lover than the always friendly but never sentimental Gwilim.
Conwy had a fight with another boy about her. This was very thrilling.
She let herself be wholly monopolized by him. Sirius was once more neglected. When he himself happened to have an affair on, or was crazy about

hunting, he did not mind at all. At other times he was often very lonely. Moreover, during this enthralling intimacy with Conwy, Plaxy's manner to Sirius sometimes showed an unwonted harshness. It was as though she had not merely forgotten about him, but resented his existence. Once he came upon the youthful lovers walking in a lane, hand in hand. When she saw him, Plaxy withdrew her hand and said in the way one speaks to a mere dog, "Go home, Sirius!" Conwy remarked, "Why does your father have to breed these fat-headed brutes?" Plaxy laughed nervously, and said in a rather squeaky voice, "Oh, but Sirius is a nice dog, really. Now off with you, Sirius. We don't want you now." While the dog stood still in the road, trying to analyse Plaxy's tone, to discover her precise emotional state, Conwy made a move as though to pick up a stone, and shouted, "Go home you tyke." The strong silky mane rose along Sirius's neck and shoulders, and he stalked ominously towards Conwy, with head down, ears back, and the ghost of a snarl. Plaxy cried out in a startled voice, "Sirius! Don't be crazy!" He looked at her coldly, then turned and walked off down the lane.

That evening Plaxy tried hard to make friends with Sirius, but he would not respond. At last she said, and he could tell that she was nearly in tears, "I'm terribly sorry about this afternoon. But what could I do? I *had* to pretend you were just an ordinary dog, hadn't I?" His reply disconcerted her. "You wish I really was one, don't you!" A tear spilled out of her eye as she answered, "Oh, Sirius, I don't. But I'm growing up, and I must be like other girls." "Of course," he answered, "just as I must be like other dogs, even though I'm not really one of them, and there's no one of my sort in the whole world." He began to move off, but she suddenly seized him and hugged him, and said, "Oh, oh, you and I will be friends always. Even if each of us wants to be away living another life sometimes, we'll always, always, come back to one another afterwards, and tell about it." "If it could be like that," he said, "I should not be lonely even when you were away." She smiled and fondled him. "Plaxy," he said, "in spite of you being a girl and me a dog, you are nearest of all creatures to lonely me." Sniffing lightly at her neck, he added, "And the smell of you is more lovely really than the crazy-making scents of bitches." Then with his little whimpering laugh he said, "Nice human bitch!" Plaxy blushed, but she too laughed. She silently considered the phrase; then said, "If Conwy called me a bitch he'd mean something horrid, and I'd never speak to him again. When you say it, I suppose it's a compliment." "But you *are* a bitch," he protested. "You're a bitch of the species *Homo sapiens,* that Thomas is always talking about as though it was a beast in the Zoo."

After the incident in the lane, Plaxy's affair with Conwy went all awry. She saw him in a new light. He was an attractive enough human animal, but he was nothing more. Apart from his looks and his confident irresistible love-making, there was nothing to him. The dog Sirius was far more human.

For a while Plaxy and Sirius maintained a very close intimacy. She even persuaded him to walk to school in the morning and bring her back in the afternoon, "to keep Conwy from being a nuisance." Indeed the two were always together, and never at a loss for talk. When Plaxy went to a party at the village school, where there was to be dancing, Sirius was of course lonely and bored, but he did not really mind. She would come back. When Sirius went off for the day with Thomas, it did not matter. Plaxy was lonely, but busy. And when he came back he would tell her all about it. Even when he went crazy over a new bitch she did not fundamentally mind. She was secretly and unexpectedly jealous; but she laughed at herself, and she kept her jealousy hidden. His love affairs, she told herself, were no concern of hers, and they did not really matter. Anyhow they were soon over; and she herself was beginning to be interested in a boy she had met at the dance, a young student, on holiday from Bangor.

At this time Plaxy was already (so I was told) developing that rather queer gracefulness which became so striking in her maturity. Whether by native composition or by constant companionship with a non-human creature, or both, she earned the remark of the local doctor's wife, "That child is going to be a charmer, but somehow she's not quite human." At school she was often called "Pussy," and there was indeed a cat-like quality about her. Her soft hair and very large greenish blue eyes, her rather broad face, with its little pointed chin and flat nose, were obviously feline; so was her deliberate, loose-limbed walk. Sometimes when she was moody, and inaccessible to her own kind, her mother would call her "The cat that walked by itself." Not till long after I had married her did I tell her my own theory of her peculiar grace. It was, of course, the influence of Sirius, I said, that had created her "scarcely human" manner; but it was her latent antagonism to Sirius that had turned that manner cat-like. It was this character that enthralled him and exasperated him, and indeed all her admirers, from Conwy Pritchard to myself. There was one characteristic about her which particularly suggested an unconscious protest against Sirius, one which tended to be exaggerated whenever she was in conflict with him. This was the extraordinary delicacy and precision of the movements of her hands, both in practical operations and in gesture. It was as though her consciousness of herself was chiefly centred in her hands, and to a lesser degree in her eyes. This character of elegant "handedness" was something far stronger than mere felinity. It was reminiscent of those Javanese dancers who use their hands with such exquisite effect. It was at once human and "parahuman," so that she seemed to me not so much cat as fay. She was indeed at once cat, fawn, dryad, elf, witch.

This description really applies to Plaxy in her early maturity, when I first met her; no doubt in childhood her peculiar charm was only nascent.

But even at fifteen or sixteen the "scarcely human" grace was appearing, and was strongly attractive to the young males of her own species.

It was in this period, in fact when Plaxy was sixteen, that Elizabeth suggested to Thomas that it was high time for the child to go to boarding school. The others had gone at a much earlier age. Plaxy had been kept back partly to be an intelligent companion for Sirius. "But now," said Elizabeth, "she's much too wrapped up in him. She won't grow up properly this way. She's cloistered here in this lonely place. She needs to see more of her own kind." Thomas had been secretly planning not to send Plaxy to boarding school at all, partly for Sirius's sake, but also because the other three, he felt, had been rather deadened by it. "Cloistered!" he cried, "what about that damned nunnery where Tamsy was?" Elizabeth admitted that it had turned out rather badly, and added, "Anyhow, I thought we might send Plaxy to a more modern place, preferably co-educational. She doesn't mix enough with the boys."

Strange, or perhaps not strange at all, that both parents, though consciously modern in outlook, and on friendly terms with their children, were kept completely in the dark about their children's love affairs. They scarcely guessed that such things occurred!

I am inclined to think that there was another reason why Thomas was reluctant to send Plaxy away from home, a reason which, I suspect, Thomas himself did not recognize. Perhaps my guess is wrong, but on the few occasions when I saw father and daughter together, I felt that behind his detached and ostentatiously "scientific" interest in her lay a very strong feeling for his youngest child. And I suspect that he could not bring himself to face week-ends at Garth in her absence. Plaxy, on her side, was always rather aloof from her father, though quite friendly with him. She sometimes teased him about his mannerisms, for instance his habit of pursing his lips when he was puzzled. She was never infected by his passion for science, but when he was criticized she sometimes defended him with surprising ardour. For this reason, and in the light of subsequent events, it may be inferred that Thomas's submerged passion for her was reciprocated. Yet many years later, when Plaxy and I were married, and I was planning out this biography of Sirius with her, she ridiculed my suggestion that there was any strong feeling between her and her father, arguing that, like so many amateur psychologists, I was "always looking for a parent complex."

This book is about Sirius, not Plaxy. I should not mention the problem of Plaxy's relation with Thomas did I not feel that it may throw some light on her extraordinarily deep, though conflicting, feelings about Sirius, who was Thomas's crowning work, and the apple of his eye.

However this may be, Thomas was not easily persuaded to let Plaxy go to boarding school. When at last he agreed in principle, and both parents began to search for a suitable school, he found weighty objections against all of them. However, in the end he accepted a certain co-educational and temperately modern establishment, situated conveniently near Cambridge.

The whole matter had, of course, been discussed with Plaxy herself, who was not easily reconciled to the prospect of what she called "going to prison." So great an upheaval in her life was bound to intimidate her. Moreover the thought came to her, "What will Sirius do without me?"

As though answering this unexpressed question, her mother said, "We think it's time for Sirius to get away for a bit too. He is to begin learning to be a sheep-dog."

Plaxy was in the end reconciled to going; and once she had made up her mind to it, she found herself sometimes strangely eager. This eagerness she could not help tracing to the prospect of being wholly a normal girl among other girls and boys. Evidently she was already suffering from a serious conflict over Sirius.

It was Thomas who talked to Sirius about the great change that was being planned. He began by saying that the time seemed to have come for Sirius to have an active life away from home. "I know quite well, of course, that I have no right to treat you as a mere dog, and that you yourself must settle your career; but you are young. In physical and mental growth, as in years, you are level with Plaxy, about sixteen. So the advice of an older mind may be helpful. Naturally I have my own ideas about your future. You are quite as intelligent as most human adolescents, and you have special advantages. I see you becoming one of the world's great animal psychologists and working with my crowd at Cambridge. But you mustn't get into the limelight yet. It would be very bad for you; and anyhow you have not had the right training yet, and of course mentally you are still too young. I think what you need now is a whole-time job as a sheep-dog, say for a year. I'll put you across as my 'super-super-sheep-dog.' I think I can fix you up with Pugh, and he will certainly treat you decently. You'll have a hard life, of course, but you need that. And the whole experience should be interesting, and very useful to you later on. You must be careful not to give it away that you can talk; but you have had some practice at that game already. I'm afraid the job will be terribly dull at times, but most jobs are. For intellectual interest you will have to depend on your own resources. There'll be no chance of reading, but you will be able to make some very interesting observations of animal and human behaviour."

Sirius listened intently to this long harangue as he walked with Thomas on the crest of the Moel. At last he spoke, slowly and carefully; for Thomas was less practised than the others at understanding him. "Yes," he said, "I'm ready to have a shot at it. Do you think I should be able to come home fairly often?"

"Oh yes," Thomas replied, in an altered voice. "You probably haven't yet heard that Plaxy is going to boarding school. I'll tell Pugh the whole family will be very disappointed if you are not with us a lot during the holidays, because you are the family-dog, now that Gelert is dead. Pugh will arrange that all right." He added, "I'm afraid you and Plaxy will miss one another badly at first. But you will both get used to it. And after all you must live your lives separately some day, so you had better begin practising now."

"Yes, of course," said Sirius, but his tail drooped and he fell silent for a long time.

In fact only once did he speak. He suddenly asked, "Why did you make only one of me? It's going to be lonely being me."

Thomas told him that there had been a litter of "four of you," and that he alone had survived. "We have tried again many times," he said. "It's fairly easy to produce the Gelert sort, but you are a very different kettle of fish. We have two promising puppies coming on now, but they are too young yet for us to size up their powers. And there's a super-chimp, though of course she's no good to you. She's a problem, sometimes a nit-wit and sometimes too clever by half."

There was always a great bustle in the house when a child was being made ready for school. When it was the child's first term, the preparations were even more prolonged. Clothes had to be bought or made. Books, writing materials, sports gear, had all to be procured. As the day approached, Plaxy became more and more absorbed in her urgent affairs. Sirius wondered at her cheerfulness. It was supposed to be a gallant pose in the face of impending sorrow, but often it "smelt" genuine. There was little for him to do in the preparations, save for occasional messages, so he had far too much time to brood on the future. Plaxy's cheerfulness was, indeed, partly a cloak to cover her desolation at the prospect of leaving home and all that she loved. Had she been younger she might not have felt the break so badly. On the morning of her departure she happened to meet Sirius alone on the landing. She surprised him by dropping her bundle of clothes and kneeling down to hug him. With schoolgirl senti-mentality but with underlying sincerity of feeling, she said, "Whatever becomes of me I shall always belong to you. Even when I have been un-kind to you I belong to you. Even if—even if I fall in love with someone and marry him some day, I shall belong to you. Why did I not know it properly until to-day?" He said, "It is I that am yours until I die. I have known it ever so long—since I bit you." Looking into his grey eyes and fondling the dense growth on his shoulder, she said, "We are bound to hurt one another so much, again and again. We are so terribly different." "Yes," he said, "But the more different, the more lovely the loving."

CHAPTER V

SHEEP-DOG APPRENTICE

ON the day after Plaxy went to boarding school Thomas took Sirius over to Pugh at Caer Blai. On the way he talked a great deal to the dog about his future, promising that when he had been with Pugh a year he should see something of the human world beyond the sheep country, and possibly settle in Cambridge. Sirius listened and consented; but he was an anxious and a sorrowing animal, and his tail would not stay proud.

One source of solid comfort lay in the fact that he knew Pugh for a decent sort. Sirius classified human beings in respect of their attitude to dogs; and even in later life he found this a useful touchstone of human character. There were those who were simply indifferent to dogs, lacking sufficient imagination to enter into any reciprocal relation with them. There were the "dog-lovers," whom he detested. These were folk who sentimentalized dogs, and really had no accurate awareness of them, exaggerating their intelligence and loveableness, mollycoddling them and over-feeding them; and starving their natural impulses of sex, pugnacity and hunting. For this sort, dogs were merely animate and "pathetically human" dolls. Then there were the dog-detesters, who were either too highbrow to descend to companionship with a dumb animal or too frightened of their own animal nature. Finally there were the "dog-interested," who combined a fairly accurate sense of the difference between dog and man with a disposition to respect a dog *as a dog,* as a rather remote but essentially likeminded relative. Pugh was of this sort.

At the farm they were greeted with an uproar by the two super-sheep-dogs at present in Pugh's possession. The farmer issued from the byre. He was a fresh-complexioned middle-aged man with a scrubby reddish moustache and blue eyes with a permanent twinkle. Sirius rather liked the smell of him. He guessed the man must do a lot of laughing. They were taken into the kitchen, where drinks were provided by Mrs. Pugh, while the two men talked. Pugh had a good look at Sirius, who was squatting on the floor by Thomas. "He's really far too big for a sheep-dog, Mr. Trelone," said Pugh in his singing Welsh voice. "He should be herding rhinoceroses, or not the little Welsh mountain sheep, anyhow. But, my! What a head he has on him! If it's brain that counts, Mr. Trelone, he must be a genius, isn't it! I can see it's he that'll be running this farm and me running after the sheep for him. Pity I'm so rheumatic!" Thomas admitted that Sirius was pretty bright, for a dog. "He'll be useful. But don't expect *too* much. After all, he's only a dumb animal." "Of course," said Pugh, and then surprisingly he winked at Sirius. "I have had experience of your dogs, Mr. Trelone, and fine animals they are. There's Idwal here now. He's full of strength, though he is twelve, which is very unusual for a hard-working sheep-dog. Then there's the bitch you sent me two years ago. Juno, we call her. My! She was quick to learn the tricks of the trade! And now she has had that litter of six by old Idwal. But the magic did not go into them from the parents. They are six little fools. But I have sold them all for a good price." "Well," said Thomas, "I told you not to expect anything from the second generation." Pugh replied with a sigh. "Yes, indeed, and you did, Mr. Trelone. I told the purchasers what you said, but they would not believe it, whatever; so what could I do but take the good price and tell them they were fools." After lighting his pipe Pugh asked, "And how old is this one, Mr. Trelone?" Thomas hesitated, then said, "Fifteen, aren't you, Sirius?" The dog let slip a "Yes," but Pugh apparently did not notice anything unusual in his sudden grunt. "Fifteen! Holy Moses, Mr. Trelone, but most dogs are dead long before that, and this one is not much more than a puppy." Thomas reminded him that longevity had been one of the aims of the experiment. "Well," said Pugh laughing, "if he will stay on with me he shall marry my daughter Jane and take over the farm when I am gone. But what is the name he answers to, Mr. Trelone, did you say?" "I call him Sirius," said Thomas. Pugh pursed his mouth and frowned. "That is not a handy name for calling across the valley, is it!" He paused, puffing at his pipe, then added, "Perhaps, Mr. Sirius, you will permit me to call you by some other name. How would Bran do?" Sirius had tilted his head over on one side, as though he were vainly trying to understand this remark, obviously addressed to him. Thomas said, "That's fine. He'll pick it up in no time."

Sirius's despondency was increased by the discovery that even his name was to be taken from him. Surely, he thought, he would be changed into a new being. Nothing whatever of the old life was to be left to him but the memory of it. At home, though he had grown up in the custom of sharing ownership of most things with Plaxy, each of the two young creatures had possessions of their own. Nearly all their toys had been held in common, but when Plaxy had gone to the village school she had also begun to acquire personal property connected with her new life—books, pens, pencils and many little nondescript treasures gained through intercourse with her fellows. Sirius also had begun to collect a few personal possessions, though far fewer than Plaxy; for, owing to his lack of hands, there were few things that he could use. There were certain ancient treasures preserved on a shelf in the minute room that had been allotted him—a rubber bone, a lump of gleaming white quartz, a sheep's skull, several picture books. And there were later-acquired possessions—more books, and music, his three writing gloves and several pens and pencils.

In his new life he had to be even more propertyless than St. Francis, for he was just a dog, and whoever heard of a dog with property? Fortunately property meant little to him; he had a propensity towards communism, due perhaps to his strong canine sociality. It should be remembered, however, that though dogs in many ways show a far more social disposition than human beings, in some respects they have a keen sense of personal ownership, for instance over bones, bitches, human friends, and localities. For Sirius, at any rate, to be completely stripped, even of his precious writing gloves, was indeed to be reduced to the status of a brute-beast. And now they intended to take away his very name. Speech, too, was of course stolen from him by the simple fact that no one on the farm could understand him. Nor was he to be able as a rule to understand them, for among themselves the Pughs talked Welsh.

Sirius's attention had wandered from the conversation, but it was recalled when Thomas rose to leave. All three went out into the yard. Thomas shook hands with Pugh, then patted Sirius, and said "Good-bye, old man. You stay there." Sirius feigned perplexity, made as if to follow Thomas, was shooed back and retreated with a puzzled whimper.

In the afternoon Pugh took Sirius and Idwal to a high valley, on the slopes of which some of his sheep were grazing. He gave a word of command in Welsh. Idwal raced off and began to round up the sheep. Sirius looked anxiously at Pugh. The command was repeated, this time along with his new name, "Bran." He shot away to help Idwal, who was moving round behind the sheep in a great semi-circle, so as to bunch them towards Pugh down in the valley. Sirius tumbled to the situation at once, and decided to start at the opposite horn of the semi-circle and meet Idwal in the middle. Automatically each dog took charge of his own arc. Idwal's, however, was much wider than Sirius's, partly because the less experienced dog had to spend time in retrieving sheep that he had allowed to slip away up the hill, partly because Idwal was the faster animal. The operation continued till all the sheep on the hillside had been brought down into the hollow where Pugh was standing. He said a Welsh word, and Idwal at once squatted, panting. Sirius followed suit, anxiously trying to fix the word in his memory.

Pugh then put the two dogs through sundry manoeuvres with the sheep, folding them in a stone pen, fetching them out, taking them in a bunch along the valley, separating them into two equal groups, scattering them again, picking out a particular individual at which Pugh pointed with his stick. All this was done with commands in Welsh, aided by various kinds of whistling. After a while he issued commands to Idwal alone, keeping Sirius at his side. Idwal was made to single out a particular wether and hold it with his eye. He crept up to within a few feet of it, flat on the ground like a snake, all the while staring fixedly at it. Then he lay still, belly to earth, legs ready for sudden action, nose stretched out on the grass in front of him, tail on the grass behind him. The wether stared back, or made incipient movements, which Idwal checked by mere gestures. The animal just stood patiently waiting, or fidgeted with mild exasperation. Obviously it was not really afraid. It was used to this sort of game, and it recognized in Idwal's eye a command that must be obeyed.

Sirius knew that he was witnessing the famous sheep-dog trick of control by "the eye." Idwal evidently had developed "the eye" almost to perfection.

Idwal was then put through other manœuvres, which Sirius anxiously watched. Presently it was his turn to perform. The novice had strained every nerve to follow the proceedings, but he found himself badly at sea. Not only did the sheep constantly slip past him, causing Pugh to bellow with amiable rage, but also he found that fatigue was preventing him from managing his body with precision, so that he often stumbled over rocks or into holes. His great head became increasingly heavy, so that any slight slip might bowl him over like a shot rabbit. In addition to all this there was the language difficulty. Again and again Sirius found himself completely at a loss while Pugh repeated some strange Welsh noise in a frantic *crescendo,* and Idwal whimpered impatiently at his side. If only the man would talk English, thought Sirius.

But when it came to the exercise of holding the sheep by the power of the eye, Sirius found to his delight that he was by no means incompetent. Of course the process needed perfecting. Once or twice the sheep nearly broke away. It evidently did not feel itself as masterfully held as it did under Idwal, but it recognized Sirius's authority. Pugh was obviously pleased.

Presently Pugh worked the two dogs together again, but issued different commands to each by name, and also in a different tone of voice for each. Sirius had to get accustomed to acting promptly to the shriller tone, whether his name, Bran, was mentioned or not; and to ignore the deeper tone which was meant for Idwal.

At last the lesson was over. Pugh walked back along the grassy valley with the two dogs at his heels. Sirius was more tired than he had ever been before, "dog-tired," as we say. His tail hung, his head almost touched the ground. The under surface of his body was caked with bog-mud. His feet were sore, his head ached. With despair he looked forward to a whole year of this sort of thing, with no companion but the sub-human dogs and the remote Pugh. Perhaps he would forget language altogether, and when he met Plaxy again he would indeed be a dumb animal. But, worn out and despondent as he was, he was able to summon his fundamental doggedness, and promise himself that he would not be beaten by this new life. And when he caught Pugh's eye quizzing him with friendly ridicule because of his abject appearance, he stuck up his tail and wagged it, at the same time grinning, as though to say, "Oh, I have spunk all right, you'll see." This unmistakably human response startled Pugh, and set him thinking.

When they reached the farm, the two dogs were given the remains of the family midday dinner. After they had devoured this they were put into an outhouse for the night. Under the straw bedding there was a rough stone floor. It seemed to Sirius that he had hardly lain down and gone to sleep when he woke up to the sound of Idwal whining at the shut door. Sunlight streamed through the chinks.

During the following weeks Sirius was given constant work with the sheep, and he soon began to get the hang of the job. With practice he wasted less energy on retrieving his mistakes, and arrived home less tired. He was successfully learning not only the Welsh commands but the names of the fields. One day Pugh took both dogs far up among the hills to inspect the sheep on the remote high pastures and teach Sirius the names of the hillsides, streams and cwms. Here he was in familiar country, for he had often walked in this direction with Thomas. At one point the tour brought him to a bwlch within a couple of miles of his home. He even seemed to catch a faint characteristic whiff of it on the wind, but this was probably a delusion.

It did not take long for Sirius to gain sufficient experience to carry out orders unattended. For instance he could be sent to search all the bracken areas for sick sheep; for when sheep feel ill they grow fearful of their disapproving fellows, and so they hide themselves in the bracken, where, if they are not found, they may die through lack of attention. Sirius knew also how to help a bogged or crag-bound sheep to free itself. He would carefully tug at it, till the extra force enabled it to struggle into safety. And he could catch a sheep and throw it, and hold it down for Pugh or his man to inspect.

The power of his "eye", too, was greatly improving. In this matter dogs vary between excessive gentleness towards the sheep and excessive ruthlessness. Idwal was on the whole ruthless, sometimes making the sheep unduly nervous and restless. Sirius, on the other hand, was often too mild by disposition, so that his authority was not established until he had deliberately learnt a firmer policy. The difference of natural style appeared also in the whole method of the two dogs. Idwal was of the "obstinate" type, insisting on doing everything in his own way. If Pugh prevented him he would raise his tail defiantly and simply trot off the field of action, "refusing to play." It was to Pugh's credit that on these occasions he generally gave in, with humorous vituperation, knowing well that Idwal could be trusted to do the job efficiently in his own style. Sirius, on the other hand, was of the "biddable" type. He was desperately anxious to learn, and had little faith in his own intuition. Shepherds regard this type of dog as less brilliant in the long run than the other, since they lack the conviction of genius; but it soon became clear to Pugh that Bran's docility was not due to a servile disposition. When he had learnt his lesson he often introduced novelties which greatly improved the method. Yet even when he had become an expert with sheep, he was always ready to pick up new tips from observation of other dogs at work.

Sirius could be sent out into the hills alone to select a required bunch of sheep from the flock, whether young ewes or "hoggs" (young sheep before their first shearing) or wethers; and he could bring them down from the hills to the farm without human aid. All this was real super-sheep-dog work. In order to make full use of his clever animals Pugh had arranged all his gates with latches that a dog could open or shut.

As autumn neared, the time came for bringing groups of lambs or of old or unhealthy ewes down from the mountains to be taken away for sale. This task Pugh entrusted almost entirely to Idwal and Sirius, helped sometimes by Juno. But that bright creature was of a distressingly unstable nature, and was often incapacitated by convulsions. The dogs would travel over the high moors, picking out the appropriate animals, sometimes losing them again in the cloud, and recovering them by scent, finally bringing them in a bunch along the turfy track in the high valley. All Pugh's sheep bore a red mark on the rump, but this, of course, was invisible to the colour-blind dogs. In addition the sheep bore three little slits in the left ear to mark them as Pugh's. This was invaluable to Idwal and Sirius, as a confirmation of the distinctive smell of the Caer Blai flock. Any sheep that had strayed into Caer Blai territory from a neighbouring run was soon detected and piloted home. In addition to the common smell of the flock, by the way, each individual sheep had its own peculiar odour. It did not take Sirius more than a few weeks to recognize every sheep in the flock by its smell, or even by its voice. Occasionally the dogs found a sheep that had been damaged, and then one of them had to set out to the farm to fetch Pugh. There was a recognized way of barking to signify "damaged sheep"; another, less excited, meant "sheep undamaged but crag-bound and inaccessible"; yet another meant "dead sheep."

The collecting of sheep for sale was a process which occurred now and again over many weeks. When the lambs or ewes had been brought down from the moors they had to be taken by train, or in lorries hired for the purpose, to the auction sales in the lower country. The dogs accompanied them, and Sirius thoroughly enjoyed these excursions into the great world. It was a pleasure merely to hear the English language spoken again, and to find that he could still understand it.

When the sales were over and autumn was well under way, the main task of the dogs was to guard the high valley pastures from the sheep. It is often the custom of mountain sheep to sleep on the heights and come down in the morning to the richer grazing; but in the autumn they must be prevented from doing this because the valley grass will be more urgently needed in the winter. In the autumn, too, the ewes must be prevented from grazing in marshy places, lest they should become infected by liver fluke. And autumn is a time for dipping the whole flock. As Pugh had many hundreds of sheep, this was a great undertaking, and the dogs were desperately hard worked for many days, bringing the sheep down in batches and driving them into the pen, where Pugh or one of his helpers could seize each animal in turn and force it into the dip. Sirius was pleased to find that he stood up to the strain of this great undertaking as well as Idwal, though he was not at this stage quite so fast or quite so agile.

Presently came another task. The ewe lambs had to be collected and sent to a lowland farm so that they might escape the grim conditions on the mountains during winter, the savage weather and poor food. Not till the following May would they be brought home.

In spite of all this hard work, there were days when the dogs had nothing to do but hang about the yard or accompany Pugh on his rounds, or run messages to the village. A little stationery-cum-newspaper shop in the village used to attract Sirius. Outside were posters from which he gained the most sensational news. Sometimes he put his paws on the windowsill and read the headlines of the papers displayed within, or the titles of the little rank of cheap novels. In the village he met other dogs. They gave him no trouble, because he was by now very large and "hard as nails." Out of loyalty to Thomas he tried to study the psychology of these animals; but apart from simple temperamental differences, they were mentally all depressingly alike. The most obvious differences between them had been imposed by human conditioning. Some were disposed towards friendliness with all human beings, some were cold to strangers but obsessively devoted to their masters, some habitually fawned, some cringed.

One day in the village Sirius came upon a fine young bitch in heat, a red setter. Suddenly life was worth living once more. Her odour and touch intoxicated him. In their love-play they careered about the open space in the village while Pugh was in the pub. (Pugh seems to have had an idea that super-sheep-dogs would be cruelly bored if they were forced to sit with him inside.) The consummation of this union took place under the lascivious eyes of two schoolboys and an unemployed quarryman.

Henceforth Sirius had a constant hunger for the village and the bitch. He was tempted to run away from the farm and have all he could of her while she was still in the mood; but he did not, because he had once seen a dog on a neighbouring farm thrashed for absenting himself from duty. Sirius was determined that he would never do anything to incur such an indignity. He had never been thrashed in his life, though occasionally hit or kicked in anger. To be deliberately thrashed seemed to him to be a mortal insult to his dignity as an intelligent and self-respecting person. If Pugh ever tried it on him, Pugh must be killed on the spot, whatever the consequences. But Pugh never did. Pugh belonged to the school of sheep-dog owners who pride themselves on obtaining obedience by kindness rather than ferocity. Sirius never saw him use violence on any dog. Probably he would never have beaten Sirius even if Sirius had given him serious provocation, for he had a firm though vague conviction that the new dog was somehow more than a dog, even more than a super-dog.

Several incidents had aroused this suspicion. Once he sent Sirius to the village with a basket and a ten-shilling note to fetch a pair of boots which the cobler had repaired. The dog duly brought back the boots and the change. When he arrived in the yard, Pugh, who was in the darkness of an outhouse, saw Sirius take out the boots and study the money in the basket. After looking puzzled for some time he trotted back along his tracks, nosing the ground. Presently he came on a small object which he managed with great difficulty to pick up. With obvious satisfaction he brought it back with him. When he dropped it into the basket it was visible to Pugh as a small brown disc, in fact a penny. Sirius then brought the basket to Pugh. It contained the boots, the receipted bill and the change, which consisted of two half-crowns, a florin, and seven pennies. Pugh was not so fanciful as to suppose that the dog had actually counted the change and checked it by the bill, but at least he must have spotted the difference between six pennies and seven.

Another incident made Pugh suspect that there was something "human" (as he put it) about this dog. The farmer had a few cows and a fine young bull. Sirius had once been prodded by a cow, and he had heard alarming stories about bulls. From time to time a cow was brought from one or other of the neighbouring farms to be served by the Caer Blai bull. On these occasions the dogs had to enter the paddock, round up the bull, and bring it down the lane into the farmyard for its love-making. When the deed had been done, the dogs drove the bull back to its paddock. Sirius was always very nervous, and did his stuff very badly. Idwal would face the bull with fierce persistence, and slip away from its lowered horns in the nick of time; but Sirius was far too anxious to keep his distance. The bull discovered that Sirius was a coward, and formed a habit of chasing him.

Pugh, by the way, was struck with the different ways in which the two dogs behaved when bull and cow were brought together in the farm-yard, generally surrounded by a small group of interested men and boys, while the women kept discreetly indoors. Idwal nosed about the yard or lay down to rest. Sirius watched the whole performance with the same cheerful interest as the human spectators. It was evident that his interest was sexual, for when the bull effected his clumsy embrace, the dog himself gave unmistakable signs of sexual excitement.

But the incident which impressed Pugh most, and made him suspect that Sirius's intelligence was as quick as a man's, occurred in connection with the bull's habit of taking the offensive against the cowardly Sirius. Pugh had gone to the village with Idwal. Owen, the hired man, was ploughing in a remote field. Somehow the bull managed to break out of its paddock into the lane. It trotted down into the yard, saw Jane with a basket of washing, and approached her, snorting. Always a nervous girl, she screamed, dropped the basket and slipped into the stable. The bull spent a few minutes tossing the clothes, then made off down the lane. Meanwhile Mrs. Pugh had made a tentative sortie from the house. Then Sirius appeared, and raced down the lane after the bull. He did not overtake it till after it had reached the main road. Then he silently rushed at it, and seized its tail. With a roar the bull swung round, but Sirius had let go, and was retreating towards the lane, barking. The bull followed him, and he led it back to the farmyard and into its field. It was now rather blown, but Sirius led it round and round the field, till its ardour was cooled. The less anxious it was to follow him, the more bold grew Sirius. When it came to a standstill, he rushed in and nipped its hind leg. The reinfuriated beast chased him once more, but was soon exhausted. This process was repeated several times, till Sirius noticed that the two women had put some strands of barbed wire across the gap in the hedge. Then he retreated, with a proud tail, leaving a bull that was thoroughly cowed. Henceforth Sirius was always able to deal with the bull or any other cattle.

Some time after this incident Sirius did something which was far beyond super-sheep-dog capacity.

Throughout his first term he was desperately lonely. He longed for his own people, and most of all for Plaxy. If only he could write a letter! But he had no writing-glove, and no stationery. And anyhow the task of putting a stamp on a letter had always defeated him.

He knew he could write a few words very badly by holding a pencil in his mouth; if he could find one, and paper. He had once seen Pugh take out pen, ink and paper from the drawer in the oak dresser. One day, when Mrs. Pugh and Jane were milking, he slipped into the kitchen, opened the drawer, and found in it several sheets of paper, also envelopes, a pen, an ink-pot, and a pencil with a broken point. He stole a sheet and an envelope. Pen and ink seemed too complicated, and the pencil was useless, so he left these, and took merely an envelope and paper to the dog's outhouse. He put them in an old packing case under some straw.

There was now nothing for it but to wait until someone should need to sharpen the pencil. He seized every opportunity to sneak into the kitchen and look into the drawer. Meanwhile he spent much thought in planning exactly how he would write his letter, and what he would say. Sometimes he practised. Holding a splinter of slate in his mouth, he scribbled on the slate doorstep. The process was difficult, because his nose was always in the way, and he could not see what he was doing; and generally the slate-splinter snapped.

At last, after many days, he found that the pencil had been sharpened. He took it away to the outhouse.

Not till several days later did Sirius find an opportunity of writing his letter. In spidery capitals it said, "Dear Plaxy, I hope you are happy.

I am lonely without you, terribly. Love, Sirius." With great care he addressed the envelope, hoping that his memory was trustworthy. He had
serious difficulty in folding the paper and putting it into the envelope.
Then he licked the gummy-edge, closed it, and held his paw on it. He
had intended to post it unstamped; but the thought that Plaxy would have
to pay threepence, double postage, on it distressed him so much that he
decided to wait in the hope of finding some stamps in the drawer. When
at last a sheet of six three-halfpenny stamps appeared, he ran off with
them and set about trying to detach one. First he held the sheet between
his paws and pulled with his teeth. The stamp tore across the middle, and
the bit in his mouth stuck to his wet teeth, so that he could not get rid of
it. Flustered by this experience, he decided to think the problem out more
carefully. He hit on a plan. He held the envelope down with his paw and
licked the right-hand top corner. Then with extreme care he took up the
stamp-sheet in his teeth and laid it on the envelope so that one of the corner stamps was roughly in the right position. This was difficult, because
as usual his nose was in the line of sight. He let go, and inspected the
result. The stamp was crooked, and not wholly on the envelope. Hastily
he lifted it off again and replaced it, well on the envelope. Again he inspected it, then carefully pulled it into better position. Then he pressed it
on with his paw. When he thought the gum was dry, he held the sheet
of stamps down with his paw and gently pulled the letter with his teeth.
The letter came away, with the stamp intact, and part of the next one
projecting over the edge. This he trimmed off with his teeth. He then restored the mangled sheet of stamps to the drawer. Not till he came back
to the letter did he notice that the stamp was upside down.

He hid his letter under the straw and waited till his next errand to
the village. This did not occur till some days later. It was fairly common
for him to be sent with letters to the post, but on this occasion his own
was the only one. He trotted off with his basket and an order for the
grocer; and his letter. He went straight to the post office, put down his
basket, took out the letter, raised himself against the wall, and slipped the
precious document into the box.

This was no unusual sight in the village. Dr. Huw Williams, who was
passing, scarcely noticed it; but when, next day, he met Mr. Pugh and
wished him good day, he mentioned the incident, complimenting him on
his dog's intelligence. Now Pugh had sent off no letter that day. He wondered whether his wife had written to her mother in Bala, or if Jane had
entrusted Bran with a love-letter. This possibility disturbed him, for though
by nature a friendly man, prone to treat people with respect and trust, he
was no modern parent. When he reached home he made inquiries. Mrs.
Pugh and Jane both denied that they had given Bran a letter. Pugh went
to the drawer and saw that the stamps had been badly mauled. One was
missing, and two others were torn. In a burst of indignation he charged

his daughter with clandestine correspondence, theft, lying and clumsiness. Jane defended herself with vigour, and added, "Go and ask Bran whose letter it was." That sarcasm put a wild idea into Pugh's head. He went to the drawer again and picked up the pencil. There were toothmarks on it—Bran's or his own? Fantastic doubt!

CHAPTER VI

BIRTH-PANGS OF A PERSONALITY

TO Sirius, Plaxy's first term at boarding school seemed endless, but in due season the holidays loomed near. Sirius had counted the days by putting a pebble a day in the old packing-case. One day, when he had collected almost the right number of pebbles but was expecting two or three more days of labour, he returned with Pugh and the other dogs from the moors, with early snow on Pugh's hat and the dogs' backs, and encountered Thomas in the yard. Sirius rushed at him and nearly knocked him down with a wild welcome. After both men had shaken the worst of the snow from their clothes, Pugh took Thomas into the kitchen. Sirius knew that he was not supposed to go into the house when he was in a mess; but, after a violent shake, in he went. Mrs. Pugh smiled indulgently.

Thomas asked Pugh about Sirius's success as a sheep-dog, and was given a good report. Sirius had proved himself as hardy as Idwal, and far more cunning and responsible. But he was not always quite "on the spot." He was a bit of a day-dreamer. He was sometimes caught napping. A sheep might escape from the flock and run away before Sirius woke to the situation. It was "as though he had been thinking of something else." After making the report Pugh nodded knowingly at Thomas, who merely changed the subject. Before they parted, Pugh insisted on handing over to Thomas ten shillings less fourpence halfpenny. This sum he described as Bran's earnings, "less a small item of expenditure." Saying his, he stared hard at Sirius and winked. The dog hastily looked away, but could not prevent a snort of surprise and a tremor of the tail. Thomas tried to refuse the money, but Pugh insisted.

The journey home through driving sleet was a journey to heaven. Thomas explained that he and Elizabeth had come home a couple of days early to get the house ready before Plaxy and Giles arrived from boarding school. Tamsy and Maurice, both of them undergraduates, were visiting friends.

Sirius recounted some of his experiences. "It has all been very good for me, I know, but I really don't think I *can* go on with that life any longer. I should go mad with loneliness. No talk, no books, no music. And all the while knowing the world is so big and strange beyond the farm. Plaxy will leave me far behind."

This speech came as a shock to the not very imaginative Thomas. He remarked cautiously, "Oh, it's not quite as bad as all that, is it? Anyhow, we must talk it over carefully." Sirius knew from his tone that he was rather put out about it, and that there would be trouble.

Elizabeth greeted Sirius as one of her children, hugging him and kissing him. He showed none of his former boisterousness, but gave a tremulous little whine of painful joy.

Next day Giles arrived, and in the evening Plaxy. Thomas took the car to the station to meet her, Sirius sitting beside him. Out of the train stepped the long-legged schoolgirl in her school hat and coat. Having kissed her father, no doubt with her customary rather distant affection, she squatted down to hug Sirius. "I got your letter," she whispered, "but I couldn't answer, could I?" Of course she couldn't. Sirius savoured the well-known voice with delight; but with an undertone of anxiety, for school life had changed it.

During the first part of the holidays Sirius simply enjoyed being home again. He scarcely noticed the two disquieting facts that had obtruded themselves right at the beginning. Thomas would not let him off his sheep-dog apprenticeship; Plaxy was changed.

For a week or so he was content to live the old family life, which, though by no means entirely harmonious, did afford to every member the invaluable experience of belonging to a true community. There was always talk going on, and Sirius after his long isolation felt a great need for conversation. There were many walks with members of the family, and several long expeditions up Moelwyn, the Rhinogs, Arenig. But what Sirius now craved most was indoor life, with reading, music, talk, and all the little affairs that fill the day.

After a day or two of almost entirely social life he began to take up once more some of his old private occupations. Not only did he read as much as his eyesight would let him, and experiment a good deal in music; he also contrived adventures in his private art of odour. This he did by collecting all kinds of materials that had striking or significant smells, and blending them in saucers. Sometimes, much to the amusement of the family, he laid his materials out in a long trail round the garden path, and then followed it from beginning to end, giving tongue in a weird diversified chant that was neither human nor canine. After these olfactory adventures he was often very silent and remote. Sometimes they seemed to put him in the mood for hunting, for he would disappear for many hours, returning tired and dirty. Not infrequently he brought back a rabbit or hare, or even a wild duck or grouse, handing it over to Giles to prepare for cooking. But often he brought nothing, and behaved as though he himself had gorged.

Not much of his time was spent in solitary occupations, for he craved social intercourse more than ever, chiefly with Plaxy. Gradually it dawned on him that when she and he were out together they did not always find the careless intimacy which formerly had never failed them. Sometimes neither of them seemed able to think of anything to say; sometimes Sirius found himself bored with Plaxy's stories of school life; sometimes she seemed to have lost interest in all the things that formerly they had enjoyed together. Sirius expected not only that she would have out-distanced him in knowledge of school subjects, which of course she had, but also that she would be more keenly and persistently interested in the life of the mind. But she was nothing of the sort. She was mainly absorbed, it seemed, in her school companions, with all their loves and hates; and in the teachers, male and female, who were playing so large a part in her new life. When he asked her to teach him some of the wonderful things that she must have learnt during the term, she said she would, some time; but always she found some excuse to postpone the lesson. At last there came a time when no excuse was available. She was idling in an easy chair petting the cat, Smut, who was purring heartily. Sirius, whose thirst for knowledge was at this time more insistent than discriminate, suggested that she should tell him what she had learnt during the term about the Cavaliers and Roundheads. Cornered, she blurted out, "Oh, I just *can't* swot in the holidays." He did not ask her again.

It was not that they were any less fond of one another. On the contrary, each craved the other's society; but always there was a faint mist of remoteness between them. And occasionally open antagonism occurred, as when Plaxy ostentatiously doted upon Smut, half in jest, half in earnest, calling him "my black panther," affirming that she was a witch, and witches always had black cats as their companions, and never clumsy dogs. But antagonism was rare. More often there was a faintly awkward friendliness. At this time Plaxy developed a maiden shyness in relation to Sirius. He was bewildered, for instance, by her new and to him quite inexplicable reluctance to respond to their familiar urinary tune by singing the antistrophe that signified assent, and crouching to relieve herself. Although this new shyness was only a passing phase, it was to recur whenever Plaxy was feeling too much involved with Sirius.

In fact her estrangement from him was partly a reaction against her deep-rooted entanglement with him. But he, who was far more conscious of her aloofness than she was herself, attributed it to the fact that she had outstripped him both in learning and in experience of human people, while he had stagnated at Caer Blai. Once or twice, however, when she had gently twitted him with being interested in nothing but learning, he wondered whether it was she that was stagnating. He had conceived a real passion for learning, for finding out about the great world, and understanding the miracle of human nature and the minor miracle of his own unique nature. The arid weeks behind him and the arid weeks to come filled him with a thirst not only for intelligent companionship but also for intellectual life. His proximity to the sub-human perhaps made him over-anxious to prove that even the loftier ranges of the human spirit were not beyond him.

It was during these holidays that another and a long-established source of alienation between Plaxy and Sirius took on a new form and a more disturbing effect. Even in earlier days Plaxy had developed a peculiarly keen interest in seeing. As a child she had often shown disappointment and exasperation with Sirius for his failure to share this delight with her. She would rhapsodize over the colour and shape of a speedwell, or of hills receding hazily one behind the other in a cadence of russet to purple. Once she had innocently called upon him to admire the golden elegance of her own young arm. On all such occasions his response was perfunctory, since vision was never for him a gateway to heaven. Even of Plaxy's arm he could say only, "Yes, it's lovely because it has the look of a handy tool. And it smells good, like the rest of you, and it's good to lick." From childhood onwards Plaxy had amused herself with pencil and paint box, and at school her gift for colour and shape had won her much praise from the drawing mistress. In the holidays she spent a good deal of time looking at reproductions of famous pictures, and in discussing art with her mother. Even more absorbed was she in drawing schoolgirls in blatantly graceful poses, and in painting the view of the Rhinogs from her bedroom window. Sirius found all this fuss over the looks of things very boring. He had tried hard to develop a taste for pictorial art, but had failed miserably. Now that Plaxy was so absorbed in it, he felt "left out." If he took no notice of her creations she was disappointed. If he praised them, she was irritated, knowing quite well that he could not really appreciate them. Yet all this visual interest, which at bottom, no doubt, was a protest against Sirius, she also longed to share with him. Thus did these two alien but fundamentally united creatures torture one another and themselves.

As the end of the holidays approached, Sirius's anxiety about his future increased. He took every opportunity of tackling Thomas on the subject. But Thomas always managed to turn the talk in some other direction. When at last the time came for Plaxy to return to school, it was assumed that Sirius would return to Caer Blai. When Plaxy said good-bye to him, she begged him to go back with a good grace. She herself, she said, hated leaving home. But he knew quite well from her voice and her tingling smell that, though in a way she did hate it, in another way she was glad and excited. But he—well, in a way he too was glad, surprised though he was at this discovery. He was glad to get away from the mist that had come between him and Plaxy; and also because a mist had come between

him and the whole of his beloved home life. What was it? Why was there
this remoteness? What was it that kept rising between him and all his
dearest things, making him defiant and wild? Was it just that he wanted
a fragrant bitch, a sweet though stupid companion of his own kind, instead of these stinking humans? Or did he need something more? Was it
the ancestral jungle beast that sometimes woke in him? His farewell to
Plaxy was seemingly all affection and sorrow. She never guessed that another and an alien Sirius was at that moment yawning himself awake,
finding her company tiresome and her smell unpleasant.

There followed a term of bitter weather and heavy work with the
sheep. All the dogs were now kept busy stopping the sheep from going
up to the heights for the night, for fear of snow. This meant staying with
them till dark whenever snow seemed likely. Sometimes, without warning,
heavy snow would fall on the tops during the night, and then dogs and
men would have to go up in the morning to bring the flock down into
the valleys. Generally there is far less snow in Wales than in the more
northerly mountain districts, but a run of severe winters caused the dogs
much toil and a good deal of danger. On several occasions, up and down
the district, dogs and even men were lost in the snow. Sometimes sheep
were completely buried under snowdrifts. Only a dog could then find
them; and often only a man with a spade could rescue them. Sometimes
the snow covered both high and low pastures. So long as it remained soft,
the sheep could scrape it away with their feet and feed on the grass below.
But when the surface was hardened by frost following thaw, this was impossible, and then hay had to be taken out to them. This was a job for
Pugh or his man with a cart and the old mare, Mab. But the dogs, being
super-dogs, were expected to report on the condition of the snow. If it was
hard, they would come home to scratch and whine at Pugh's feet.

Sometimes when Sirius was out in the hills alone in the winter dawn,
examining the condition of the snow and looking for sheep in distress, the
desolation of the scene would strike him with a shivering dread of existence. The universal carpet of snow, the mist of drifting flakes, the miserable dark sheep, pawing for food, the frozen breath on his own jaws,
combined to make him feel that after all *this* was what the world was
really like; that the warm fireside and friendly talk at Garth were just a
rare accident, or perhaps merely a dream. "The whole world is just a dreary
accident, with a few nice accidents mixed up in the mass." He had still
to learn that there was something far worse than bitter weather with the
near prospect of food and comfort, far worse even than his bitter loneliness
at Caer Blai; and that the most horrible things in the world were all man-
made. It was perhaps well that he did not yet realize the depth of man's
folly and heartlessness, for if he had done so he might have been turned
against the dominant species for ever. As it was, he attributed all evil to
accident or "fate," and in fate's very indifference he sometimes found a

certain exhilaration. Plodding home through the snow one day (so he told me long afterwards) he had a kind of inner vision of all living things, led by man, crusading gallantly against indifferent or hostile fate, doomed in the end to absolute defeat, but learning to exult in the battle, and snatching much delight before the end. And he saw himself as a rather lonely outpost in this great war, in which victory was impossible, and the only recompense was the sheer joy of the struggle. But by the very next day, so he said, his mood had changed from self-dramatization to an amused acceptance of his littleness and impotence.

Before the lambing season Pugh went over all his ewes to cut locks of wool away from their udders, so that their lambs should not swallow wool and clog their stomachs. This simple process itself meant a great deal of work for men and dogs, but the actual lambing meant a great deal more. The flock had to be met at dawn on its way down from the heights. During the day the men would be hard at work, but the dogs would often be idle. Pugh noticed that Bran was far more interested than ordinary dogs and even super-sheep-dogs in the process of birth. This was one of the many signs that convinced him that Bran was really a sort of man-dog. Pugh had gradually formed a habit of giving Bran fairly detailed instructions in English, and they were always accurately carried out. He still had no idea that Bran himself could talk, and he kept his convictions about the dog's nature strictly to himself. But he increasingly treated him as an assistant rather than as a chattel, an assistant who was particularly bright and responsible, but lamentably clumsy through lack of hands. All Sirius's clever arrangements for fetching and carrying, for pouring from tins and bottles, and so on, failed to compensate for his grievous handlessness. One useful operation that needed dexterity he could do. He could drive Mab, the old mare, whether with the spring cart, the heavy cart, the roller or the harrow. Ploughing inevitably remained beyond him. And of course he could not load a cart with turnips or hay or manure, and so on. Nor could he manage the simple task of harnessing the mare. Buckles defeated him.

When, at the end of the school term, Elizabeth came to fetch Sirius home, his joy was tempered by a self-important doubt as to how Pugh would manage without him.

During these holidays he busied himself in intellectual work. Taxing his eyesight, he even plunged into Wells's *Outline of History* and *The Science of Life*. He also pestered members of the family to read poetry aloud to him, and passages from the Bible. He was very sensitive to the rhythm of verse and prose, and of course to the musical quality of words; but vast tracts of literature meant nothing to him, save as verbal music, because his subconscious nature had not the necessary human texture to respond to them emotionally, nor had he the necessary associations in his experience. His strong feeling for personality led him at one time into an obsession with Browning. Later came a more lasting interest in what he called "the poetry of self and universe." Hardy at one time fascinated him. The early Eliot intoxicated him with new rhythms and with a sense of facing the worst in preparation for a new vision. But the vision never came. Instead came orthodoxy. Sirius longed for that vision. He hoped for it from the younger moderns; but though he was even younger than any of them, they meant little to him.

Music was ever for Sirius a more satisfying art than poetry. But it tortured him, because the texture of his own musical sensibility remained alien to the human. He felt that he had to choose between two evils. Either he must express himself with full sincerity but in utter loneliness, unappreciated by dogs or men; or, for the sake of his underlying brotherhood with man, he must violate his finer canine sensibility, and discipline himself to the coarser human modes, in the hope that somehow he might express himself adequately to man in man's own musical language. For this end he was anxious to absorb as much human music as possible.

His relations with Plaxy at this time were uneasy. While he was obsessed with the life of the mind, she was obsessed with personal relations. The loves and hates of school were still far more important to her than book-learning. And her school life was utterly different from Sirius's hard and anxious life on the farm. It might have been expected that in these circumstances dog and girl would find little in common; and indeed superficially there was little enough. On their walks they were often silent, while each pursued a private train of thought. Sometimes one or the other would hold forth at some length, and the soliloquy would be punctuated by sympathetic but rather uncomprehending comments by the listener. Occasionally this mutual incomprehension caused exasperated outbursts.

Their discord was often increased by a tendency on Plaxy's part to express her vague sense of frustration in subtle little cruelties. Very often the cattish torture of Plaxy's behaviour was unconscious. For instance, at times when she was subconsciously resentful of his emotional hold over her, the affectionate ragging which they sometimes indulged in would change its character. Not knowing what she did, she would twist his ear too violently, or press his lip upon his teeth too hard. Then, realizing that she had hurt him, she would be all contrition. More often her felinities were mental. Once, for example, when they were coming down the moel during a brilliant sunset, and Plaxy was deeply stirred by the riot of crimson and gold, of purple and blue and green, she said, not remembering how it must wound her colour-blind companion, "Sunsets in pictures are so tiresome, but only boors and half-wits are not stirred by real sunsets."

Apart from this infrequent and often thoughtless exposure of her claws, Plaxy kept up the manner of friendliness even when secretly she was straining away from him; for fundamentally each respected the other's life and was thankful for the other's society. The roots of these two alien beings were so closely intertwined that in spite of their divergence each needed the other. One unifying subject of common interest they always had, and they often talked about it. Both these sensitive young creatures were beginning to puzzle about their own nature as persons. Both, for very different reasons, were revolting against the purely scientific assumptions of their home, according to which a person was simply the psychological aspect of a very complex physical organism. Plaxy was feeling that persons were the most real of all things. Sirius was more than ever conscious of the inadequacy of his canine body to express his super-canine spirit. The word "spirit" seemed to them to epitomize the thing that science left out; but what precisely ought to be meant by the word they could not decide. Plaxy had come under the influence of a member of the school staff for whom she had conceived a great admiration. This quick-witted and sensitive young woman taught biology, but was also a lover of literature. It seems to have been her influence, by the way, that first made Plaxy clearly feel that, however important science was, for herself not science but literature was the way to full mental life. The young teacher had once said, "I suppose I ought to believe that Shakespeare was *just* a highly developed mammal, but I can't *really* believe it. In some sense or other he was—well, a spirit." This remark was the source of Plaxy's juvenile dalliance with the word "spirit"; and then of Sirius's.

The young dog was now seriously worrying about his future. Sheep-farming was not without interest, now that he was helping Pugh in a more human way; but it was not what he was *for*. What was· he for? Was he *for* anything? He remembered his desolate impression on the snow-clad moors that the whole world was just a purposeless accident. Now, he somehow could not believe it. Yet the all-wise Thomas said no one was *for* anything, they just *were*. Well, what could a unique creature like him, a sheer freak, find to *be*? How could he discover peace of mind, of spirit? Thomas did not see why he should worry. Thomas had a nice slick programme for him.

One evening when the others had gone to bed, man and dog were left in the sitting-room in the course of one of those long talks which had been so great a factor in the education of Sirius. They were sitting before the fire, Thomas in one of the easy chairs, Sirius luxuriating on the couch. Thomas had been telling him of the progress of his research, and explaining the latest theory about the localization of mental powers in the brain-centres. He was pleased at the dog's shrewd questions, and had said so. Sirius, after a pause in which he absently licked a paw while gazing into the fire, said, "Even by human standards I really am fairly bright, am I?" "Indeed you are," was the prompt reply. Sirius continued, "You see, I don't seem able to think properly. My mind keeps wandering. I start out to think about something, and then suddenly, with a jolt I wake up to find I've been thinking about something else instead; and often I can't even remember what it was, or even what the first subject was. It's frightening. Do you think I'm going mad? It's like—going off on the trail of a rabbit and then being led aside by a hare, and then streaking off on the smell of a fox, and twisting and doubling on the trail till all of a sudden you find yourself up against water, and no trail at all. And then you say to yourself, 'How on earth did I get here? What in hell was I doing?' Human beings don't think that way, do they?" Thomas laughed with delight. "Don't they!" he said. "I certainly think that way myself, and I'm not exceptionally scatter-brained." Sirius sighed with relief, but continued, "Then there's another thing. Sometimes I managed to follow a trail of thought quite well for a long time, in and out, up and down, but always with my mind's nose on the trail; and then suddenly I find—well, the weather has changed and given it all a different meaning. It was warm and bright, but now it's cold and dank. No, worse than that! It was fox, and now it's cat, so to speak, or just dull cow, or horrible menagerie tiger. No, *it's* the same but *I* have changed. I wanted it desperately, and now I don't. There's an entirely new me. That's frightening, too." Thomas reassured him. "Don't worry, old thing!" he said. "It's just that you're a rather complicated person, really, and there's too much diversity in you to be easily systematized."

Sirius once more licked his paw, but soon stopped to say, "Then I really am a *person*, not just a laboratory animal?" "Of course," said Thomas, "and a very satisfactory person, too; and an excellent companion for *this* person, in fact the best I have, apart from one or two colleagues." Sirius added for him, "And Elizabeth, I suppose." "Of course, but that's different. I meant man-to-man companionship." Sirius pricked his ears at that phrase, and Thomas laughed at himself. Said the dog, "Then why apprentice me to a sub-human job, which is bound to dehumanize me?" "My dear Sirius," replied Thomas with some heat, "we have had all that out before, but let's try to settle it now, once for all. It's true you have a first-class human intelligence, but you are not a man, you are a dog. It's useless to train you for some human trade, because you can't do it. But it's immensely important to give you some responsible practical work until the time comes for you to join us at Cambridge. You are not to be an imitation man. You are a super-super-dog. This sheep-dog life is very good for you. Remember you are not yet seventeen. There's no hurry. Your pace is Plaxy's, not Idwal's. If you grow up too quick, you'll fossilize too quick. Stick to sheep. There's a lot in that job, if you give your mind to it. When you come to us at the lab we want you to have had experience of a normal dog's way of life."

Inwardly Sirius said, "Blast the lab!" but to Thomas he said, "I *have* been putting my mind into the job. And as a matter of fact it's not just sheer dog's work now. Pugh has been giving me a lot of man's work to do. He knows I am different from Idwal. But—well, that sort of work, though it *is* largely man's work, does deaden the mind. And the mind—is *me*.

I'm not human, but also I'm not canine. Fundamentally I'm just the sort of thing you are yourself. I have a canine clothing, just as you have a human clothing, but *I*—I am"—he paused and looked warily at Thomas— "a spirit, just as you are." Thomas snorted, and presently his smell went rather sour. Then almost in the tone of a liberal-minded parent expostulating with a child that had said something "rude," he remarked, "Why use that silly meaningless word? Besides, who has been putting such ideas into your head?"

Sirius did not answer this last question. Instead, he said, "There's something in me very different from my canine body. If *you* had a dog's body instead of a man's, you would grasp that as clearly as I do. You couldn't help it. You would feel like someone trying to typewrite on a sewing machine, or make music with a typewriter. You would never mistake the sewing machine for *you, yourself.*"

"I see what you mean," said Thomas, "but the conflict is not really between your spirit and your canine body; it's between the canine part of your body and the super-canine part, that I gave you."

There was silence in the room for a full minute. Then Sirius yawned, and felt the warmth of the fire on his tongue. He said, "That sounds so sensible; and yet, though I'm only seventeen and only a dog, I can smell there's something wrong with it. It's only just a bit more true than the 'soul' dope that the parsons give—the Rev. Davies, for instance, when he called on us, and tried to convert you to Methodism, while you tried to convert him to scientific method. Do you remember? He caught me staring too interestedly at him, and he said I looked as if I was more open to persuasion than you were yourself, and it was a pity, almost, that God hadn't given *me* a soul to be saved."

Thomas smiled, and rose to go to bed. As he passed Sirius he gave his ear a friendly pull, and said, "Oh, well, nearly all great questions turn out in the end to be misconceived. Probably both our answers are wrong."

Sirius, getting down from the couch, suddenly realized that he had been once more side-tracked from his purpose, which was to discuss his future. "One thing is sure," he said, "My job is not just sheep, and it's not to alternate between being a sheep-dog and being a super-laboratory-animal. It's the spirit."

Thomas came to a halt. "Oh, very well," he said gently, respectfully, but with a faint ridicule that did not escape Sirius. "Your job's the spirit." Then after a pause he added with friendly sarcasm, "We must send you to a theological college."

Sirius gave a snort of indignation. He said, "Of course I don't want the old religious dope. But I don't want just the new science dope either. I want the truth." Then, realizing that he had said the wrong thing, he touched his master's hand. "I'm afraid I'm not working out according to plan," he said. "But if I am really a *person* you shouldn't expect me to.

Why did you make *me* without making a world for me to live in. It's as though God had made Adam and not bothered to make Eden, nor Eve. I think it's going to be frightfully difficult being me."

Thomas laid his hand on the dog's head. The two stood gazing into the dying fire. The man said to the dog, "It's my fault that you are more than a dog. It's my meddling that woke the 'spirit' in you, as you call it. I'll do my best for you, I promise. And now let's go to bed."

CHAPTER VII

WOLF SIRIUS

THOMAS succeeded in persuading Sirius to complete his year with Pugh, assuring him with Machiavellian subtlety that it would be an invaluable "spiritual training." And it was. It was a Spartan, an ascetic life; for Sirius accepted all the ordinary sheep-dog conditions. At times it was a life of grim hardship and overwork. Men and dogs returned from their labour dead tired, and fit for nothing but supper and sleep. But there were other times when there was little to be done that did not necessitate human hands. Then Sirius used to lie about pretending to sleep, but in fact trying desperately to think about man and himself, and the identity of the spirit in them, a task in which he was singularly unsuccessful.

Since Pugh was by now fairly well in the know about Sirius, Thomas had arranged that during his last term the dog should have more or less regular hours, like a human worker, so that he could frequently go home and put in a little study. The word "study," of course, was not mentioned, but Pugh agreed with a knowing wink.

Expeditions over the high hills were becoming rather much for the ageing Welshman, so he handed over more and more responsibility to Sirius. He arranged with the saddler to make two pairs of small panniers which could be strapped on to the dogs' flanks. These he filled with lotions, medicines, bandages. Sirius could now travel far afield and doctor sick sheep without Pugh having to accompany him. He would set off with Idwal, who now accepted him as a leader, and spend the day inspecting the whole flock. When they had rounded up a bunch of sheep into some remote moorland pen, Sirius would examine each one of them for foot-rot or fly-strike. Any animal that showed restlessness, or kept trying to nibble at its own back, was probably infected with fly-strike. Sirius was sufficiently human to dislike exposing the grubs with his own teeth, and cleaning out the superficial wound with his tongue; but the work had to be done. By keeping a sharp watch on the flock, and tackling the earliest symptoms himself, he was able to reduce to a minimum the number of advanced cases which demanded attention from man's exploring fingers. But inevitably a few were not found till they were deeply infected. These had to be taken away for human treatment. Very rarely Sirius came on sheep lying down, neither ruminating nor sleeping, and with great open wounds seething with grub. For these he had to fetch human aid at once, or they would soon die. Pugh, by the way, had put all the drugs and ointments into tins with clip-on lids which Sirius could open without excessive difficulty.

When the shearing season arrived the whole flock had to be brought down in batches, and put into pens to be tackled each in turn by one of the half-dozen shearers who were going the round of all the flocks in the district. The actual shearing was a job which Sirius would never be able to do. Nothing but human hands or some mechanical device could ever divide a sheep from its fleece. Sirius would stand about watching the manual dexterity of the shearers with fascination and sadness. The sheep, on its haunches between the knees of the man, would sometimes struggle, generally when its skin was nipped and little red stains appeared on the cream of its inner wool; but in the main the blades peeled off its coat as though merely undressing the creature. The gleaming inner surface of the fleece, as it was rolled back upon its own drab exterior, was a wave of curd. When the operation was over, the naked, angular beast would spring away bleating with bewilderment.

Throughout the last few months of his year with Pugh, Sirius was much absorbed in his work; but also he was in a state of suppressed excitement, and of conflict. He delighted in the prospect of release from this servitude, yet in spite of himself he regretted that the connection must be broken. He had become thoroughly interested, and he had a real affection for Pugh. It seemed mean to desert him. And though Cambridge promised novelty and a great diversity of human contacts, he was sufficiently imaginative to realize that town life might not suit him at all.

There was also another and a deeper conflict in his mind, one which was increasingly troubling him. It was the endless conflict over his relations with the dominant species of the planet. Never did he cease to feel that man and he were at once poles asunder and yet in essential nature identical. At this early stage the trouble had not come clear to him. He could not yet focus it. But to explain his obscure and still largely inarticulate distress, his biographer must set forth Sirius's plight with a clarity which he himself had not yet attained. Men were many and he was one. They had walked the eartth for a million years or more, and they had finally possessed it entirely. And he? Not only was he himself a unique product of their cunning, but the whole race of dogs were their creation. Only the wolf was independent. And wolves were now no more than a romantic relic that man would never again seriously fear. Little by little, through their million years, men had worked out their marvellous human way of living, culminating in civilization. With those enviable hands of theirs they had built themselves their first crude forest shelters, then settlements of huts, then good stone houses, cities, railways. With nicely correlated hand and eye they had made innumerable subtle implements, from microscopes to battleships and aeroplanes. They had discovered so much, from electrons to galaxies. They had written their millions of books, which they could read as easily as he could follow a trail on a damp morning. And some few of those books even he must read, because they had the truth in them, a bit of it. He, by contrast, with his clumsy paws and imprecise vision, could never do anything worthy of the brain that Thomas had given him. Everything worth while in him had come from mankind. His knowledge, such as it was, they had taught him. His love of the arts, of wisdom, of the "humanities!" God! Would that wisdom lay rather in "caninities!" For him there was no possible life-aim except to help on in some minute way the great human enterprise, whether through the humble work of sheep-tending or the career that Thomas had planned for him as a museum piece and a tenth-rate scientist. For him there could be no wisdom but man's alien wisdom; just as for him there could be no real loving but the torturing business of loving these infinitely alien human creatures. Or would Thomas some day produce others of his kind for him to love? But they would be so young.

It was indeed mankind that had shown him what love was, with their gently ministering and caressing hands and their consoling voices. His ever-trusted and caninely revered foster-mother had loved him always as her own child; or only with so slight a difference that neither she herself nor her Plaxy but only he with his keen ears and nose could detect it. For this difference he could feel no resentment. It was not indeed strictly a difference of love at all but of animal maternal attraction. Then Thomas, yes Thomas also had shown him what love was, but in a different aspect, in the aspect of "man-to-man" intelligent companionship. Of course Thomas really loved his science far more. Probably he would be ready to submit his creature to any torture, physical or spiritual, for the advancement of his science, of his creative work. But this was as it should be. God himself, if there was a God, might be like that. Might he? Might he? Anyhow, Sirius could understand this attitude. It was not with Thomas nor with Elizabeth but with Plaxy that he had found the essence of love, the close mutual dependence and sharing. Yet strangely it was often the thought of Plaxy that wakened the other mood in him, in which he rebelled against humanity's dominance.

Throughout the summer at the farm he brooded a great deal about his relationship with Plaxy. When the term was over and they met again, he found that time and difference of experience had increased the gulf between them. They still needed one another and gravitated towards each other, but they ever strained apart for the fulfilling of their divergent lives. Strange indeed was his relation to Plaxy! So alien were they in native propensity, yet so united in common history and in essential spirit. But now so divergent, like stars that have swung very near together out of space to fly apart towards opposite poles of the heaven. Altogether, how he loved her; and how, in another mood even while loving, he hated her!

The native odours of Plaxy were not naturally attractive to him, as was the intoxicating scent of a bitch. In nature, in the jungle, the characteristic human smell would probably have repelled him, like the stink of a baboon. Certainly it was an acquired taste, but he had acquired it so long ago and so thoroughly that the love of it had become a second and fuller nature to him; so that by now, though the sweet maddening smell of a bitch might at any time irresistibly draw him away from Plaxy, always he must return to her. She, he felt, must ever be the centre of his life and he of hers; and she knew it. Yet their lives must inevitably fall apart. There was no common future for them. Even now, how tiresome was her schoolgirl prattle, how boring her unfulfilled schoolgirl romances! (Why ever had the human race developed this ridiculous attitude to sex? How it disgusted him!) And those heartless artificial scents that she had begun to use, perversely wishing to cover her wholesome, and to him by now lovely, natural odour!

But there were times when the natural odour of Plaxy filled him with disgust. Then, all human beings stank in his nostrils, but Plaxy his darling most of all. Sometimes when he was lying in the yard waiting for orders, watching the old cock treading one of his harem, or Jane setting off in her best clothes to Dolgelly, or Mrs. Pugh carrying pails of milk to the dairy, or one of the hired men shifting muck out of the pigstye, he tried hard to analyse his feelings about the human species, and the causes of his own fluctuation between adoration and contemptuous resentment. He recognized that the species that had produced him (more or less for fun) had on the whole treated him pretty well. The specimens that he knew best had on the whole been kindly. All the same he could not but resent his present servitude. Even Pugh, who was fundamentally decent, treated the dogs essentially as chattels. When they happened to be in the way they were just booted out of it; always with that ingrained rough friendliness of Pugh's, but still it was exasperating. Then there were the village people. Many of them showed an unaccountable spite, kicking him or hitting him for no reason whatever, when Pugh was not looking. At first he thought they must be Pugh's enemies, or Thomas's; but no, they were just letting off some secret pent-up vindictiveness against a living thing that could not hit back. Most dogs had been thoroughly trained to take these cuffs and kicks meekly, but Sirius often surprised his assailants by vigorous retaliation.

One cause of Sirius's incipient contempt for human beings was the fact that since they thought he was "only an animal," they often gave themselves away badly in his presence. When they were observed by others of their kind, they maintained the accepted standard of conduct, and were indignant if they caught anyone falling short of that standard; but when they thought they were not being watched, they would commit the very same offences themselves. It was, of course, to be expected that in his presence they should pick their noses (how he chortled at their unconscious grimaces) or break wind, and so on. What roused his contempt was their proneness to insincerity. Mrs. Pugh, for instance, whom he had once seen licking a spoon instead of washing it, indignantly scolded her daughter for doing the very same thing. And the hired man, Rhys, who was a great chapel-goer, and very righteous about sex, would often, when he was alone, with only Sirius present, do unprintable things to relieve himself of sexual pressure. Not that Sirius saw anything wrong in such behaviour, but the insincerity of the man disgusted him.

This insincerity of the dominant species, he decided, was *one* of the main causes of those sudden uprushings of rage and physical repugnance which sometimes possessed him. At these times the human odour became an intolerable stench. He came to recognize this revulsion as a sign that his "wolf nature," as he called it, was waking. In this mood all the acquired meanings of smells seemed to evaporate, and their natural qualities smote him with exquisite delight or horror. If he was at home he would go out from the oppressive stench of the house to clean his nose with deep sniffs of the fragrant moorland air. A great loathing of man would seize him. He would perhaps plunge into a stream to wash away the pollution, or roll in sweet cow dung. Then he would go hunting, carefully avoiding every human being, irrationally feeling that the hand of man was everywhere against him. Most often his quarry was a mere rabbit; but with sufficient luck and intelligence he might take a mountain hare. The snap of his jaws on the spine, the yielding flesh, the rich blood welling into his mouth, went to his head like alcohol. He felt his spirit washed by the blood of the quarry, washed clean of humanity with all its itching money-inquisitiveness, all its restless monkeying with material things and living things and living minds. To hell with wisdom and love and all cultural dope. The way of life was to hunt, to overtake, to snatch, to hear the sharp scream, to wolf the crushed flesh and bones. Then a drink and a rest in the moorland sunshine, alone, at peace.

During his last month with Pugh, Sirius suffered a distressing alternation of moods. Sometimes he was wholly wrapped up in care of the sheep, sometimes he longed for the life of the mind, sometimes he felt the strange uprush of the wolf's nature in him.

One day, after attending to some sheep that had been badly struck by fly, he was haunted by the stinging smell of the lotions that he had applied. They turned him savage. Why should he be the menial of these

dunder-headed ruminants? Gradually the wolf-mood took complete possession of him. It was a free afternoon for him, and he should have gone
home to read. Instead he cantered off among the hills till he reached a
certain distant "foreign" sheep-run beyond Arenig Fach, a miniature Table
Mountain far to the east. There he sniffed the wind and cast about with
nose to earth till he found the trail he wanted. He had not followed it
long before the quarry stood before him, a great ram with royal head and
a neck heavy with muscle. Sirius checked, and stood looking at the beast,
which also stood, sniffing the wind, pawing the ground. Suddenly the dog
felt the human, the humane, in him coming uppermost again. Why murder
this fine creature? But it was man's creature, and it epitomized all the
tyranny of the sheep-dog's servitude. He rushed at the ram, who met his
onslaught with lowered head and flung him off. There followed a long
battle. Sirius was gashed in the shoulder. He persevered, however, running
in again and again till at last he was given a chance to seize the ram by
the throat. Desperately it tried to throw him off, crashing about among
the heather and rocks; but Sirius hung on, remembering his battle with
Diawl Du. The ram's struggles became feebler, as Diawl Du's had done.
At last they ceased. Sirius let go. His tail tucked itself between his legs. He
looked about to see if any human being was in sight. Then he looked at
the dead ram. Human pity, horror, disgust, welled up in him. But he
fought them down, remembering that he was hungry. He began tearing
off great shreds of the hide, bracing his feet against the ground. Then he
dragged at the warm flesh, and gorged himself. At last he slunk away.

It was sheer luck that Sirius was never charged with this crime. It
so happened that another sheep-dog from a farm near by had run amok
and killed several sheep; so the ram was attributed to him. But Sirius,
when his wolf-mood had passed and he realized the full significance of
his deed, lived in terror of detection. There was the tell-tale wound on his
shoulder. But after all this might have been made by an old nail on a fence.

During the rest of his time with Pugh, Sirius devoted himself conscientiously to the sheep, treating them with new solicitation and tenderness. When at last Thomas came to fetch him away and Pugh made his
final report, the old man said, "Yes, indeed, Mr. Trelone, it is a wonderful
dog he is, and I don't know how I shall do without him. This summer
he is like a mother to the sheep, so loving he is in his ways with them.
And they are all in great health because he has watched over them so
closely, and tended any that would be poorly before it ever showed any
sadness for itself. If only he were a man, Mr. Trelone, I would have my
daughter marry him for the sheep's sake. But she has set her heart on a
two-legged animal, a draper's assistant that has not half the brain of this
dog, though he is no fool in his own business. So now I must look round
and take some other young man into partnership, since Mr. Bran insists
on going." He looked at Sirius with a rueful and affectionate grimace,

then continued, "But surely to goodness, Mr. Trelone, when you make another dog like this one you will not again forget that hands are as needful as a brain. I have often broken my heart for Bran when I have watched him trying to use his mouth to do the things I do so easily with these great clumsy paws of mine. Yes, you must give the next one hands, isn't it, Mr. Trelone."

Unexpectedly, when Sirius was once more at home, the wolf-mood became more insistent than ever. With Pugh he was generally absorbed in some bit of practical work, and had little time to brood; but at home during that summer holiday his future was all uncertain and had to be discussed; and Plaxy was present, with her familiar spell and her increasing remoteness.

Right at the outset, on the walk home from Caer Blai, Sirius had broached the subject of his future. "Well," said Thomas with a guarded voice, "first you need a good holiday at home. Then I thought we might do a walking tour with my young colleague, McBane, in the Lake District, where you would see a different style of sheep-farming. Then you might enter for some of the Cumberland sheep-dog trials, just to surprise the local people a bit. Then it will be time for you to come into residence at the laboratory, so that we can begin a whole lot of fine experimental work on you, physiological and psychological. You'll find it all very interesting, and of course your active co-operation will be needed throughout. You will learn a lot that way. Little by little, we shall train you to be a research worker in animal psychology. If you turn out well we may be glad to publish some of your stuff. Then, of course, scientists of all sorts passing through Cambridge will want to see you. So you will have a very interesting life, and you will be the cynosure of every scientific eye. I hope to God it doesn't turn your head and make you an insufferable prig." Sirius remained silent. Presently Thomas continued, "Oh, yes, and when we can spare you I think you might put in a few weeks now and then on sheep again, either at Pugh's or elsewhere. In time we shall probably have done all the research we need of you, and then—well, you will probably come on to our staff as a permanent member."

"I see," said Sirius, and said no more. He thought about it all the way home. He thought about it by day and by night, and about other matters that were disturbing him.

One of these matters was of course his relationship with Plaxy. Shortly after she came home she learned that she had won a scholarship for one of the Cambridge colleges. Her subject, by the way, was English literature. It had been Thomas's wish that she should become a doctor, but she had steadily veered away from science towards the arts, thus (according to my theory) asserting her independence against the father whom she secretly admired. The study of literature at Cambridge is scientific in temper, and in working for her scholarship Plaxy, I suggest, had both asserted her independence and been true to her father's moral code. She had worked hard for her scholarship, and now for a time she put the life of the mind behind her. Sirius, on the other hand, after his hard labour with Pugh, proposed to spend all his spare time on the life of the mind. He had been hoping for her collaboration. Plaxy, however, was unusually silent and remote. Superficially she was as friendly as ever, and would often go for walks with him. But they were silent walks; and the silence, though apparently she did not notice it, oppressed him. She did not seem really interested in his problems. Even the great problem of his future, though she often encouraged him to speak of it, did not *really* interest her. And she spoke less and less of her school life, because it took so much explaining. Thus nearly all their talk centred round family or local affairs and the natural phenomena of a Welsh summer. This was easy and happy, but Sirius felt that it did not get them anywhere.

One day in mental agony he said, "Plaxy, why have you gone dead on me? I do so want us to be happy together!" She answered, "Oh, I know I'm sometimes a pig to you. The trouble is I'm terribly worried just now, and I can't think of anything else." "Tell me about it," he said; but she replied, "I *can't*. It's too complicated. You wouldn't understand. How could you? There's nothing in your life to help you to begin to understand. No, I'm sorry, but somehow I *can't* tell you. It's—it's just a *human* thing."

It was not the words that offended him so much as the faint tone of superiority in the voice. The wolf-mood, which had been brewing in him ever since his conversation with Thomas, came violently into action. The smell of this human female beside him suddenly lost all its loveliness and became a repugnant stink. Sidelong he looked at her. Instead of seeing the dearest face in the world, he saw the uncouth hairless features of a super-ape, in fact of that species which so long ago had broken in his ancestors to be their slaves in body and soul.

"Sorry," he said. "I didn't want to butt in." He was startled at the snarl in his own voice, and surprised (and oddly resentful) that she did not notice it. All the way home they walked in silence. At the gate she touched his head with her hand, and said, "I'm sorry." He answered, "That's all right, I wish I could help." The snarl was still in his voice, hidden under gentleness. She did not hear it. Her touch sent conflicting tremors down his back, for it was at once the touch of his darling and the touch of the super-simian tyrant.

At the doorway the human smell of the house raised his gorge. She entered. Longing to restore community with her, he actually licked her hand as she passed in; and while he did so, he felt to his horror his lips curl themselves back, baring his teeth for action. She vanished into the house. He turned away, sniffing the fresh air.

He cantered ruthlessly across a flower-bed, leapt the garden wall, and swung easily up the hillside with his tail streaming out behind him.

That night he failed to return home. There was nothing unusual in this, and no one was anxious. On the following night also he was absent. Thomas was disturbed, but concealed his anxiety under annoyance, for he had planned a long walk with Sirius for the next day. On the third night also there was no Sirius. Pugh had not seen him, nor had he put in an appearance at any of the neighbouring farms, nor in the village. Thomas was now alarmed; and Plaxy, thinking of their last meeting, felt remorse for her coldness.

The whole household was organized as a search party, with Idwal and another super-sheep-dog, who were borrowed for the occasion and made to smell Sirius's sleeping-basket before setting out on the search. Since there was no news of him in the cultivated regions, it seemed probable that he had taken to the moor. The searchers spread out fanwise in allotted directions.

It was Plaxy who found Sirius, late in the afternoon. Coming round a buttress, she saw him standing over the carcass of a little moorland pony. She had approached up wind, and Sirius had not seen her. He began tugging savagely at the hide of the mangled neck, tearing it away from the flesh. His legs were driven deep into the bog in the effort to get a solid purchase. His tail curved under his belly. His jaws and shoulders were smeared with blood, and peaty mud was splashed all over him. A great pool of blood and mire spread from the pony's throat. There had evidently been a wild struggle, for the pony's flanks were torn and the bracken and grass were trampled.

Only for a second did Plaxy watch, unobserved and horror-stricken. Then she gasped out, "Sirius!" He let go and faced her, licking his crimson lips and muzzle. The two gazed at each other, she into the eyes of a wolf, he into the white, nude, super-simian face of his ancestral tyrant. His back bristled. A snarl twisted his lips. A low growl was all his greeting.

She was thoroughly frightened and nauseated, but also she realized that some desperate art was needed to save him from ruin. And in that moment (she afterwards said) she realized for the first time the strength of the bond between them. She advanced towards him. "Sirius, *darling,*" she cried, surprising herself no less than him, "what ever will become of us now?" Miserably she approached him, with the bog squelching over her shoe-tops. His growl became more threatening, for the beast in him was jealous for its quarry. His ears lay back. His teeth were more crimson than white. She felt a weakening at the knees, but plodded towards him, and stretched out a hand to touch the savage head. As she did so, she caught a nearer view of the carcass, and suddenly she vomited. When the paroxysm was over, she sobbed out, "*Why* did you have to do it? I don't understand. Oh, they'll want to kill you for it." She sat down on a damp tussock and gazed at Sirius, and he at her. Presently he turned on the carcass and tore at the flesh. Plaxy screamed, leapt up and tried to drag him off by the collar. With a roar he turned on her, and she was flung back on to the boggy ground with the great beast standing over her, and the cold boggy water oozing about her shoulders. Their eyes were close together. His breath smelt of blood.

Some people in desperate moments have a knack of doing the right thing. Plaxy is one of them. "My dear," she said, "you are *not* a wild beast, you're Sirius. And you don't really want to hurt me. You love me, you know you do. I'm your Plaxy." His lips crept back over his teeth. His growl died out. Presently, with a little whimper he delicately kissed her cheek. Stroking his throat, she said, "Oh, my poor darling, you must have been mad"; then, as she rose to her feet, "Come, let me clean you up a bit."

She took him to the edge of the boggy pond, and with a bit of moss for a sponge she wiped the blood from his muzzle and his neck and shoulders. While she was doing so she said, *"Why* did you have to do it? *Why* did you have to leave us? Was I *very* horrid to you that day?" He stood silent, passive to her ministrations, with his tail still tight under him. When he was more or less clean of blood, she kissed his forehead, then straightened herself. She walked over to the carcass. "Poor pony," she said. "He's like our Polly that we used to ride on when Giles and I were little. Do you remember how you used to kiss her nose, nearly getting yourself fallen over?" A sudden tortured whimper was his answer. Then she, still gazing at the pony, said in an altered voice, "If we leave this mess to be found, they won't rest till they have tracked you down, and then? If only we could bury it in the bog! We had better go home and tell Thomas."

On the long walk home she tried to make Sirius tell her all about it, and suddenly she realized that he had never said a word since she had found him. "Tell me, tell me!" she implored. "Oh, do at least say something. What's the matter with you?"

At last he spoke. "You wouldn't understand. There's nothing in your life for you to judge it by. It's just—a canine thing." This echo of her own words startled and pained her. "Oh, I'm terribly sorry," she said, "I *was* horrid." But he said, "It wasn't all your fault. I was going wild before that."

The rest of the search party had arrived home before them. Sirius was given a hearty but anxious welcome. He took it coldly. Refusing his supper, he retired to bed. Plaxy at once told her story to Thomas, who was at first indignant and then increasingly interested, though of course alarmed for Sirius's safety. Next day he traced the owner of the pony and told him the whole story, attributing the murder to "a new, untrained experimental super-sheep-dog of mine." He paid up twice the value of the pony.

The killing of the pony was one of the turning points in Sirius's career. It clarified his relations with Plaxy, and it made Thomas realize that Sirius was being seriously strained, and would have to be treated carefully.

A couple of days later Plaxy and Sirius found themselves talking more freely to one another than had been possible for many months. It began by her telling him about that "human" matter which she had formerly withheld. Consideration for Plaxy forbids me to publish its details, which are anyhow irrelevant to my theme. Let it suffice that Plaxy had allowed herself to become entangled with a young man for whom she felt a strong sexual attraction but no great respect; and that in these circumstances the shameless promiscuity of Sirius's own sex life seemed to her to render him an impossible confidant. But the pony incident had made her realize more clearly how much her intimacy with Sirius mattered to both of them. She felt compelled to do her utmost to restore confidence. Sirius on his side told her of the conflict which was racking him, the alternating moods of respect and loathing for humanity. "You, for instance, are sometimes the dearest of all things in the world, and sometimes just a horrible monkey that has cast a filthy spell on me." She answered at once, "And *you* are sometimes just my father's experimental dog that I have somehow got tangled up with and responsible for, because of *him;* but sometimes you are—*Sirius,* the part of Sirius-Plaxy that I love." A faint change in her fragrance made him realize the warmth of her feeling far better than her words could do, or even the shy frankness of her voice.

Thomas made a point of lecturing Sirius on the folly of killing ponies, but the lecture gradually changed into a discussion about the causes of the wolf-mood in him. At the crisis of this talk Sirius cried, "Unless you help me to be *myself,* you will force me to be—a sham wolf." Thomas countered this with, "And *what* must you be to be 'yourself?'" After a long pause Sirius said, "I don't know, yet. But I must be given a chance to find out. I must be helped to look round at the world. I shall not see much of it if I just alternate between sheep and your laboratory. You see, I feel I have my *own* active contribution to make to—well to human understanding. I can't be just a passive subject for experiments, or at best a tenth-rate research worker. There's something I *must* get clear in my own mind, and when I have got it clear, then I must get it across somehow to mankind." Thomas softly whistled. "Sounds as though you wanted to be a sort of canine messiah to men!" Sirius moved restlessly and said, "No, I'm not as silly as all that. I don't feel superior at all, far from it. But—well, my point of view is so utterly different from man's, and yet at bottom the same. In making me you made something that sees man from clean outside man, and can tell him what he looks like." Thomas was silent, considering this, and Sirius presently added, "There's another point. When I feel I'm not going to be able to be my true self, or not allowed to try to be it, the whole human race turns foul in my nose, and I just go wild. Everything blacks out. I don't know why, but there it is."

Thomas was by now thoroughly aware that his policy for Sirius had been too simple. He undertook to modify it. On the following day he talked it all over with Elizabeth. "What a fool I was," he said, "not to foresee this psychological trouble! I don't think I ever *really* realized that if things went wrong with *this* experiment I couldn't just wash my hands of it all, and start again; any more than a surgeon can wash his hands of an operation that has gone wrong. I feel as God ought to have felt towards Adam when Adam went wrong—morally responsible. The devil of it is that, though moral feelings are mere subjective feelings, you can't ignore them."

After a long discussion Elizabeth and Thomas decided on a new programme for Sirius. He should come to the Laboratory, as planned; but also he should be "shown round a bit" by Elizabeth, so that he could "begin to get the hang of this crazy human world," He would go about simply as her dog, meeting her friends in Cambridge and elsewhere, listening to their talk. She would also help him to do a bit of sight-seeing, if it could be arranged—slums, factories, docks, museums, concerts. This could be done at odd times, from the lab. He could also, with Thomas's aid, make proper use of Cambridge as an educational centre. Thomas would suggest lines of study and get him books from libraries. All this might help him to see more clearly what he could do with his life.

When Thomas explained the new plan to Sirius, he ended with a caution. If Sirius did wander about the country with Elizabeth, he must be very careful not to give the show away. He must behave simply as her dog. No one must suspect him of being able to talk, no one but the people in the know at the laboratory. "But why?" protested Sirius. "Surely it's time I came out into the open. I can't go on pretending for ever." Thomas insisted that the time had not yet come for publicity. "We must have you firmly established in the scientific world before the commercial world can get hold of you. Otherwise some unscrupulous tough, out on the make, will try to kidnap you and run you into some foreign country to show you off for money. Then you really would be a slave for the rest of your life." Sirius snorted. "Let 'em try, that's all." Thomas pointed out that a choloroform cloth would put him out of action very effectively, till they got him away. "Don't think it's just my fancy," Thomas added. "There are some guys on your track already, and it's time I warned you. Only yesterday two townee people called here to inquire about buying a super-sheep-dog. I put them off because I didn't like the look of them. Told them I had no animal ready. They said they had seen one in Trawsfynydd posting a lettter, you in fact. Wouldn't I sell you? They offered £30, £40, and gradually raised it to £250. This was fantastic for a super-sheep-dog, so I began to be suspicious. Well, those fellows have been hanging about here since then, so look out. And remember, chloroform."

Some weeks later, when Sirius had almost forgotten about this story, an attempt was actually made to kidnap him. He had been out hunting, and was returning by his usual route, which passed over a stile in a wall about a hundred yards or so above the house. He was on the point of climbing over the stile when he caught a whiff of something strange. It was sickly-sweet and pungent. He remembered chloroform, and checked. Now unfortunately for his assailants his meditations on the way home from the chase had been sombre. He had been brooding on his subjection to the human race, and so he was in a mood for retaliation. He leapt the stile and crashed into two men, who were waiting for him. They had not expected him to come over like a shell from a gun, exploding on impact. Both men were knocked flying, and in the struggle which followed Sirius got his teeth in the throat of one of the men before the other could apply the chloroform cloth. The choking smell forced him to let go and attack his other assailant. Number one, however, was temporarily out of action, so Sirius had to deal only with number two and the chloroform. The taste, or rather the idea, of human blood had roused the wolf-mood in Sirius. He became just an animal fighting its natural enemy-species. The man did his best with the chloroform, but though Sirius had a few strong whiffs he managed to avoid its full power. Meanwhile the noise of battle had roused Thomas, who was down below in the garden at Garth. He pounded up the hill shouting. The damaged man had risen to his feet to help his colleague, but when he saw Thomas he made off. The other had succeeded in doping Sirius enough to make him no longer dangerous; but he too, when he heard Thomas, clambered to his feet, with blood streaming from his face, and took to his heels, leaving the dog already three parts doped and quite unable to give chase. Both men reached the cart track where they had left their car, and drove off as fast as the bumps would permit. Thomas made no attempt to follow them. Instead, he went to Sirius and gripped his collar, lest the dog should recover in time to pursue his enemies.

Shortly after this incident Thomas took Sirius by car to the Lake District for the projected walking tour with his young colleague, McBane. His main object was to familiarize McBane with Sirius, and particularly to give him an opportunity of learning to understand the dog's speech before undertaking work on him at the Laboratory. Incidentally Sirius was also given an opportunity to see the north country sheep-dogs at work. The party also attended an important sheep-dog trial. Thomas had been persuaded by McBane to enter Sirius as a competitor. Sirius had on several occasions acquitted himself brilliantly at trials in Wales, under Pugh; but Thomas knew nothing of the technique. It very soon became obvious to judges and spectators that the master was no shepherd, while the dog was more brilliant than any dog ought to have been. It did not matter how ineptly Thomas gave his orders; Sirius ignored them and carried out the desired operation with every refinement of skill. Finally it was discovered that Thomas was the famous producer of super-sheep-dogs. He received many offers to purchase Sirius, but laughingly refused. The would-be purchasers had to be content to have their names entered on the waiting list for future dogs.

CHAPTER VIII

SIRIUS AT CAMBRIDGE

WHEN the holiday was over, Thomas took Sirius to Cambridge. A private bed-sitting-room had been prepared for the wonder-dog within the precincts of the Laboratory, near a room which Thomas occupied himself. The senior members of the staff were introduced to Sirius as "man to man," on the understanding that they must keep the secret and behave in public as though this dog were only a rather specially bright super-sheep-dog.

Sirius was at first very happy at Cambridge. The bustle of city and university, though rather bewildering, was stimulating. During the first few days he spent much time in wandering about the streets watching the people, and the dogs. The abundance of the canine population surprised him, and so did the extraordinary diversity of breeds. It seemed to him incredible that the dominant species should keep so many of the dominated species alive in complete idleness, for not one of these pampered animals had any function but to be the living toy of some man or woman. Physically they were nearly all in good condition, save for a common tendency to corpulence, which in some cases reached a disgusting fulfilment. Mentally they were unwholesome. How could it be otherwise? They had nothing to do but wait for their meals, sink from boredom into sleep, attend their masters or mistresses on gentle walks, savour one another's odours, and take part in the simple ritual of the lamp-post and the gate-post. Sexually they were all starved, for bitches were few, and jealously guarded by their human owners. Had not the canine race been of sub-human intelligence, they must one and all have been neurotics, but their stupidity saved them.

Sirius himself had often to act the part of these sub-human creatures. When Elizabeth took him out to visit her friends he allowed himself to be petted and laughed at, or praised for the "marvellous intelligence" that he showed in "shaking hands" or shutting the door. Then the company would forget him completely, while he lay stretched out on the floor in seeming boredom, but in fact listening to every word, and trying to get the hang of some conversation on books or painting; even furtively stealing a glance at drawings or bits of sculpture that were circulated for inspection.

Elizabeth did her best to give Sirius a fair sample of life in a university city. It became a sort of game with her to contrive means to insinuate him into meetings and concerts. After the simple subsistence life of the sheep-country, Cambridge filled him with respect for the surplus energies of the human species. All these great and ornate buildings had been put up stone by stone, century by century, with the cunning of human hands. All these articles in shop-windows had been made by human machinery and transported in human trains, cars and ships from the many lands of human occupation. Perhaps most impressive of all to his innocent mind was the interior of a great library, where, by patient intrigue, Elizabeth managed to effect an entry for him. The thousands of books lining the walls brought home to him as nothing else had done the vast bulk and incredible detail of human intellectual tradition. He stood speechless before it all, his tail drooping with awe. As yet he was far too simple-minded to realize that the majority of the volumes that faced him, shoulder to shoulder, were of little importance. He supposed all to be mightily pregnant. And the naïve belief that he could never attain wisdom until his poor eyes had travelled along most of those millions of lines of print filled him with despair.

Thomas had decided that the time had come to let out the secret of Sirius's powers to a carefully selected public. A number of his scientific and academic friends must be allowed to make the dog's acquaintance and form their own opinions of his ability, on the understanding that the truth must not yet be published. His policy was still to keep the greater public from sharing the secret, lest the forces of commercial stunt-manufacture should be brought to bear on his work, and possibly wreck it.

He arranged for Sirius to meet a few eminent persons in the University, mostly zoologists, biochemists, biologists of one sort or another, but also psychologists, philosophers, and philologists, who would be interested in his speech, and a few stray surgeons, painters, sculptors and writers who happened to be among Thomas's personal friends. These meetings generally took place after a lunch in Thomas's rooms. Over the meal Thomas would tell the party something about his experiments and the success of the super-sheep-dogs. Then he would lead on to his more daring research, and describe Sirius as "probably quite as bright as most university students." When lunch was over, the small company would settle in easy chairs with their pipes, and Thomas, looking at his watch, would say, "I told him we should be ready for him at two o'clock. He'll be along in a minute." Presently the door would open and the great beast would stalk into the room. He did not lack presence. Tall and lean as a tiger, but with a faint suggestion of the lion's mane, he would stand for a moment looking at the company. Thomas would rise to his feet and solemnly introduce his guests one by one to Sirius. "Professor Stone, anthropologist, Dr. James Crawford, President of——College," and so on. The guests generally felt extremely ill at ease, not knowing how to behave, and often suspecting that Thomas was playing a trick on them. Sometimes they remained stolidly seated, sometimes they rather sheepishly rose to their feet, as though Sirius were a distinguished human newcomer. Sirius looked steadily into the eyes of each guest as he was introduced, acknowledging him with a languid movement of his great flag of a tail. He would then take up his position in the centre of the company, generally squatting down on the hearth-rug. "Well," Thomas would say, "first of all you want to know, of course, that Sirius really can understand English, so will someone ask him to do something?" Often the whole company was so paralysed by the oddity of the situation that it took a full half-minute for anyone to think of an appropriate task. At last the dog would be asked to fetch a cushion or a book, which of course he straightway did. Presently Thomas would carry on a conversation with Sirius, the guests listening intently to the strange canine speech, and failing to understand a word of it. Then Sirius would say a few simple words very slowly, Thomas translating. This would lead on to a general conversation in which the guests would often question the dog and receive the answer through Thomas. Not infrequently Sirius himself would question the visitors, and sometimes his questions were such that Thomas was obviously reluctant to pass on. In this way the guests received a clear impression of a strong and independent personality.

And in this way Sirius himself gradually reached certain conclusions about these distinguished specimens of the dominant species. One characteristic about them perplexed him greatly. It was such a deep-seated thing that they themselves did not seem to be aware of it. One and all, they undervalued or misvalued their hands. Many of them, in fact all but the surgeons, sculptors, painters, and research workers, were wretchedly clumsy with their hands, and by no means ashamed of it. Even those whose work involved manual skill, the surgeons, sculptors and so on, though they were so skilled in their own specialized technique, had often lost that general handiness, that manual versatility, by which their species had triumphed. On the whole they were helpless creatures. Hands were for them highly specialized instruments, like the bird's wing or the seal's flipper, excellent for some one action, but not versatile. Those that came on bicycles never mended their punctures themselves. They could not sew on their buttons or mend their socks. Moreover even these specialized geniuses of the hand had to some extent been infected by the general contempt for "manual toil," which the privileged class had invented to excuse their laziness. As for the writers, academics, lawyers, politicians, their unhandiness and their contempt for mere manual dexterity were amazing. The writers couldn't even write properly. They fell back on the cruder activity of pressing typewriter keys. Or they simply dictated. Sirius had heard that in Old China the scholar class let their finger-nails grow fantastically long so that their incapacity for manual work should be obvious. Think of the millions of cunning hands thus wasted! How he despised these regressive human types for the neglect and atrophy of the most glorious human organ, the very instrument of creation; and for infecting with their contempt for manual skill even the manual workers themselves, on whose practical dexterity the whole structure of civilization was founded! Artizans actually wanted their sons to "rise" into the class of "black-coated" workers. What would not

Sirius himself have achieved if he had been given even the clumsy hands of an ape, let alone the least apt of all these neglected human organs! The first few weeks at Cambridge were indeed delightful for Sirius. Every morning some bit of research was done upon him at the Laboratory, with his interested co-operation. Sometimes it was a case of studying his motor or sensory reactions, sometimes his glandular responses to emotional stimuli, sometimes his intelligence, and so on. X-ray photographs had to be made of his skull, gramophone records of his speech. With the co-operation of a psychologist he himself planned to write a monograph on his olfactory experiences, and another on his power of detecting human character and emotional changes by scent and tone of voice. Psychologists and musicians studied his musical powers. His sex life had also to be recorded.

In addition to all this strictly scientific work, in which Sirius collaborated with his human observers, he planned to undertake two popular books entirely on his own. One was to be called *The Lamp-post, A Study of the Social Life of the Domestic Dog*. The opening passage is interesting for the light which it throws on Sirius's temperament. "In man, social intercourse has centred mainly on the process of absorbing fluid into the organism, but in the domestic dog and to a lesser extent among all wild canine species, the act charged with most social significance is the excretion of fluid. For man the pub, the estaminet, the Biergarten, but for the dog the tree-trunk, the lintel of door or gate, and above all the lamp-post, form the focal points of community life. For a man the flavours of alcoholic drinks, for a dog the infinitely variegated smells of urine are the most potent stimuli for the gregarious impulse." The other projected book, *Beyond the Lamp-post*, he kept a dead secret. It was to be autobiographical, and would express his philosophy of life. These works were never completed; the second was scarcely even begun, but I have found the random notes for it extremely useful in writing Sirius's biography. They reveal a mind which combined laughable naïvety in some directions with remarkable shrewdness in others, a mind moreover which seemed to oscillate between a heavy, self-pitying seriousness and a humorous detachment and self-criticism.

It was flattering to Sirius to be the centre of so much interest; and it was very unwholesome. Inevitably he began to feel that his mission was after all simply to be his unique self, and to allow the human race respectfully to study him. Far from retaining the humility that had oppressed him on his visit to the library, he now swung away towards self-complacency. As his presence became more widely known, more people sought his acquaintance. Thomas received innumerable invitations from outside the chosen circle, persons who had evidently heard vague rumours of the human dog and were eager to verify them. When Sirius was out in the streets people often stared at him and whispered. Thomas strongly disapproved of his going out by himself, lest attempts should be made to kidnap him. The anxious physiologist even went so far as to hint that unless his precious charge agreed never to go out without a human escort he would have to be confined to the Laboratory. This threat, however, infuriated Sirius; and Thomas recognized that, if it were carried out, all friendly co-operation would cease. The best he could do was to engage a detective to follow the dog on a bicycle whenever he went out of doors. Sirius conceived a humorous dislike of this individual. "He's rather like a tin can tied to my tail, he and his clattery old bike," said Sirius; and henceforth always referred to him as "Old Tin Can." The game of giving Old Tin Can the slip or leading him into awkward situations became Sirius's main outdoor amusement.

Contrary to his original intention Sirius spent the whole of that autumn term at Cambridge. Though he was often very homesick for the country, and nearly always had a headache and often felt seedy, he found Cambridge life far too fascinating to surrender. Several times he did, indeed, suggest to Thomas that he ought to be moving on; but Thomas was reluctant to break off the research, and Sirius himself was too comfortable to find energy to press the matter.

Very soon the Christmas vacation was upon him, and he went back to Wales with Thomas, Elizabeth, and Plaxy. Once more on the hills, he discovered that he was in a sorry state of physical decay, and he spent much of his time trying to restore himself by long hunting expeditions.

During the spring term Sirius was less happy. The glamour of Cambridge had begun to fade, and he was increasingly restless about his future; the more so because Cambridge was like a habit-forming drug. By now he obtained only a mild satisfaction from it, yet it had got into his blood and he could not bring himself to do without it. He had arrived in Cambridge, an anatomical study of bone and muscle. A soft, inactive life, which included far too many delicacies received in the houses of admiring acquaintances, had already blurred his contours with a layer of fat, and filled out his waist. Once when he met Plaxy in the street, she exclaimed, "Gosh! You're going fat and prosperous, and you waddle like a Pekinese." This remark had greatly distressed him.

Along with physical decay went a less obvious mental decay, a tendency to sink into being a sort of super-lap-dog-cum-super-laboratory-animal. His disposition became increasingly peevish and self-centred. There came a day when a serious difference occurred between Sirius and McBane. Thomas's lieutenant had prepared a piece of apparatus for a more minute research into Sirius's olfactory powers. Sirius protested that he was not in the mood for such an exacting bit of work to-day; his nose was in a hypersensitive state and must not be put to any strain. McBane pointed out that, if Sirius refused, hours of preparation would be wasted. Sirius flew into a whimpering tantrum, crying that his nose was more important than a few hours of McBane's time. "Good God!" cried McBane, "you might be a prima donna."

Thomas had been surprised and pleased at the way in which Sirius had settled down to his new life. It seemed as though the dog had outgrown his romantic cravings, and was reconciled to becoming a permanent property at the Lab. But in his second term, though Sirius was still superficially able to enjoy his work, on a deeper level of his mind he was becoming increasingly perturbed and rebellious. This life of ease and self-gratulation was not at all what he was "meant for." The mere shortage of physical exercise made him miserable. Sometimes he cantered a few miles along the tow-path, but this was very boring; and he was always oppressed by the knowledge that the faithful detective was following on a bicycle. He could not force himself to run every day. Consequently he was generally constipated and disgruntled. He felt a growing nostalgia for the moors, the mists, the rich smell of the sheep, with all its associations of hard work and simple triumphs. He remembered Pugh with affection, and thought how much more real he seemed than these dons and their wives.

He was vaguely aware too of his own moral decay. It was increasingly difficult for him to do anything that he did not want to do. Not that he was incapable of all mental effort, for he still generally carried out his intellectual work with conscientious thoroughness. But then, he happened to like that. What he was failing to do was to control his ordinary selfish impulses in relation to his human neighbours. He was also growing less capable even of prudential self-regard.

For instance there was the matter of bitches. Of the few bitches that he encountered in the Cambridge streets, most were anyhow too small for him, and many had been treated with a preparation which disguised the animal's intoxicating natural odour, and made potential lovers regard her as a filthy-smelling hag. He insisted to Thomas that, since in Cambridge there was practically no scope at all for love-making, bitches must be provided for him. It was not to be expected that a vigorous young dog should be able to do without them and yet maintain his mental balance. So a succession of attractive females was procured for him. These creatures were brought in turn and at appropriate times to his rooms in the Laboratory; and the whole matter was treated as part of the prolonged and complicated scientific study in which he was co-operating. The Laboratory, by the way, had analysed the chemistry of the odours which were sexually stimulating to Sirius, and could choose seductive animals for him with considerable success. But, his appetite instead of being assuaged, increased. Almost daily they brought a young bitch to his room, yet he was never satisfied. Indeed he became more and more lascivious and difficult to please. Thomas urged him to take himself in hand, otherwise his mental vitality would be sapped. Sirius agreed to do this, but failed to carry out his promise. And now a note of sadism crept into his love-making. Once there was a terrible commotion because in the very act of love he dug his teeth into the bitch's neck.

This incident seems to have frightened Sirius himself, for a change now came over him. Dreading the dark power that seemed to rise up within him and control his behaviour, he made a desperate effort to pull himself together. He also determined to leave Cambridge at once and go back to Wales for a spell with the sheep. Thomas reluctantly agreed that he had better go, but pointed out that he was in no condition to undertake sheep work again without some weeks of severe physical training. This was all too true. The best that could be done was that Thomas should arrange with Pugh to take him for a month not as a sheep-dog but as a paying guest. This plan was much discussed, but somehow Sirius could not bring himself to such an ignominious course. In default of a better policy he simply stayed on at Cambridge till the end of the term. There followed an Easter Vacation in Wales, given over wholly to physical training in preparation for a spell of sheep-tending in Cumberland. But as no satisfactory arrangement could be made for him, the lure of Cambridge proved in the end too strong, and he returned with Thomas for the summer term.

In the familiar environment the old way of life proved fatally easy. Laboratory work, meetings with Thomas's scientific or academic friends, a great deal of desultory biological and other scientific reading, a certain amount of philosophy, the writing of his monographs and notes for *The Lamp-post* and *Beyond the Lamp-post,* select parties at which he was lionised by the wives of dons, the perennial shortage of exercise, a succession of bitches, all this told upon his health and loosened his character. He developed more and more the prima donna disposition. He became increasingly self-centred and self-important. Yet all the while, deep in his heart, he felt completely disorientated and futile, spiritually enslaved to the will of man.

At last, when he felt in himself a return of sadistic impulses, he was seized with such a terror of sheer madness that he once more gathered all his moral strength together for a great recovery. He set himself a course of strict self-discipline and asceticism. He would have no more bitches. He would cut down his food by half. Sometimes he would fast; and "pray to whatever gods there be." He would take exercise. He would co-operate conscientiously with the Laboratory staff in their researches on him. He would once more tackle his literary work; for even this, which had for long been his one remaining active interest, had recently been dropped.

For a while he did indeed live a more austere life, punctuated by bouts of wild self-indulgence; but presently his resolution began once more to fail, and he found himself slipping back into the old ways. Terror seized him; and a desperate loneliness in the midst of his social contacts. He felt a violent need for Plaxy, and sent her a note, asking her to come for a good walk with him.

Plaxy gladly made an appointment with him, but the day was not a success. She was naturally very absorbed in her university life; and though Sirius was in a manner a member of the same university, their experiences did not overlap. Lectures, essays, meetings, dances, and above all her new friendships filled her mind with matter that was remote from Sirius. At first they talked happily and freely, but there was no depth of intimacy between them. Several times he was on the verge of blurting out his troubles; but to say, "Oh, Plaxy, help me, I'm going to hell," which was what he wanted to say, seemed somehow preposterous. Moreover, as the day wore on, he began to suspect from a faint change in her odour that she was growing subconsciously hostile to him. He had been talking to her about the bitches. It was then that her scent had begun to take on a slight asperity, though in speech and manner she remained quite friendly. Towards the end of the day a gloomy silence fell upon them both. Each tried to dispel it with light talk, but vainly. When at last they were on the point of parting, and Plaxy had said, "It was nice to be together again," Sirius registered in his own mind the fact that her odour had been growing mellower as the parting approached. "Yes, it's good indeed," he said. But even as he said it the human smell of her, though unchanged in its sensory quality, began to nauseate him.

In order to return to the Laboratory he had to cross the town. He strolled off, without any positive desire to reach his destination, or indeed to do anything else. As he drifted along the streets, he felt stifled by the surrounding herd of the grotesque super-simians who had conquered the earth, moulded the canine species as they trimmed their hedges, and produced his unique self. Feelings of violent hatred surged up in him. A number of significant little memories presented themselves to his embittered mind. Long ago in a field near Ffestiniog he had come upon an angel-faced little boy taking baby thrushes out of a nest and skewering them one by one on a rusty nail. More recently in a Cambridge garden he had watched a well-dressed woman sitting on a seat and fondling a dog's head. Presently she looked about as though to see if she was being observed. There was no one but Sirius, a mere animal. Still stroking the dog with one hand, she reached out with the other and pressed her lighted cigarette end into the creature's groin. This streak of sexual cruelty in human beings horrified Sirius all the more because he himself had indulged in something of the sort with his bitches. But he persuaded himself that this aberration in him was entirely due to some sort of infection from man, due, in fact, to his human conditioning. His own kind, he told himself, were not by nature cruel. Oh, no, they always killed as quickly as possible. Only the inscrutable and devilish cat descended to torture.

It was all due to man's horrible selfishness, he told himself. *Homo sapiens* was an imperfectly socialized species, as its own shrewder specimens, for instance H. G. Wells, had pointed out. Even dogs, of course, were self-centred, but also far more spontaneously social. They might often fight for bones or bitches, and they persecuted one another for the glory of dominance; but when they *were* social they were more wholeheartedly social. They were much more ready to be loyal absolutely, without any secret nosing after self-advantage. So he told himself. They could give absolute, disinterested loyalty; for instance to the human family that claimed their pack-allegiance, or to a single adored master, or to the work that was entrusted to them. The sheep-dog didn't expect to get anything out of his job. He did it for the work's sake alone. He was an artist. No doubt some men were as loyal as any dog, but Cambridge life had taught Sirius to smell out self-regard under every bit of loyalty. Even Plaxy's affection for him seemed in his present mood merely a sort of living up to a pattern for her precious self, not real self-oblivious love. Or take McBane. Was it science or the budding great scientist, Hugh McBane, that really stirred him? Sirius had noticed that he smelt most excited and eager whenever some little personal triumph was at stake. Then there were all those prominent people that he had met at Thomas's lunch parties—biologists, physicists, psychologists, doctors, surgeons, academics, writers, painters, sculptors and God-knows-what-all. They were so very distinguished, and all so seeming modest and so seeming friendly; and yet every one of them, every bloody one of them, if he could trust his nose and his sensitive ears, was itching for personal success, for the limelight, or (worse) scheming to push someone else out of the limelight, or make someone in it look foolish or ugly. No doubt dogs would be just as bad, really, except when their glorious loyalty was upon them. That was the point! Loyalty with dogs could be absolute and pure. With men it was always queered by their inveterate self-love. God! They must be insensitive really; drunk with self, and insensitive to all else. There was something reptilian about them, snakish.

Long ago he had idealized humanity. His silly uncritical, canine loyalty had made him do so. But now his practised nose had found out the truth about the species. They were cunning brutes, of course, devilishly cunning. But they were not nearly so consistently intelligent as he had thought. They were always flopping back into sub-human dullness, just as he was himself. And they didn't *know* themselves even as well as he knew himself, and not half as well as he knew them. How he knew them! He had been brought up in a rather superior family, but even the Trelones were often stupid and insensitive. Even Plaxy knew very little about herself. She was so absorbed in herself that she couldn't see herself, couldn't see the wood for the trees. How often she was unreasonable and self-righteous because of some miserable little self-regard that she herself didn't spot. But *he* spotted it all right, oh yes! And she could be cruel. She could make him feel an outcast and a worm, just for spite.

What enraged him most of all about human beings, and particularly the superior ones that he met in Cambridge, was their self-deception.

Every one of them was quite different really from the mask that he or she presented to the world. McBane, for instance. Of course he really *was* devoted to science, up to a point, but more so to himself; and he daren't admit it, even to himself. Why couldn't he just say, "Oh, I know I'm a selfish brute at heart, but I try not to be"? Instead, he pretended to have a real sheep-dog loyalty to science. But he didn't really *use himself up* for science. Perhaps he might some day, just as Thomas did. Some day he might be ready to die for science even. But if he did, he would really be dying not absolutely for science, but for his own reputation as a devoted scientist.

Oh God! What a species to rule a planet! And so obtuse about everything that wasn't human! So incapable of realizing imaginatively any *other* kind of spirit than the human! (Had not even Plaxy failed him?) And cruel, spiteful! (Had not even Plaxy had her claws in him?) And complacent! (Did not even Plaxy really, in her secret heart, regard him as "just a dog"?)

But what a universe, anyhow! No use blaming human beings for what they were. Everything was made so that it had to torture something else. Sirius himself no exception, of course. Made that way! Nothing was *responsible* for being by nature predatory on other things, dog on rabbit and Argentine beef, man on nearly everything, bugs and microbes on man, and of course man himself on man. (Nothing but man was really cruel, vindictive, except perhaps the loathly cat.) Everything desperately struggling to keep its nose above water for a few breaths before its strength inevitably failed and down it went, pressed under by something else. And beyond, those brainless, handless idiotic stars, blazing away so importantly for nothing. Here and there some speck of a planet dominated by some half-awake intelligence like humanity. And here and there on such planets, one or two poor little spirits waking up and wondering what in hell everything was for, and what it was all about, what they could make of themselves; and glimpsing in a muddled way what their potentiality was, and feebly trying to express it, but always failing, always missing fire, and very often feeling themselves breaking up, as he himself was doing. Just now and then they might find the real thing, in some creative work, or in sweet community with another little spirit, or with others. Just now and then they seemed somehow to create or to be gathered up into something lovelier than their individual selves, something which demanded their selves' sacrifice and yet gave their selves new life. But how precariously, torturingly; and only just for a flicker of time! Their whole life-time would only be a flicker in the whole of titanic time. Even when all the worlds have frozen or exploded, and all the suns gone dead and cold, there'll still be time. Oh, God, what for?

CHAPTER IX

SIRIUS AND RELIGION

AS Sirius walked home to the Laboratory after his day with Plaxy, brooding on the shortcomings of man, and his own loneliness, and the indifference of the universe, he began to slip into the wolf-mood. Frustration always tended to have this effect on him, and he was feeling desperately frustrated. He longed for self-expression, and could find no means of attaining it. When he was a puppy he had decided that he would be a general, deploying his human troops with super-human skill, charging with them to superhuman victory. Ludicrous, impossible dream! Later he had determined to be an explorer of the Siberian Tundra or prairies (a country that he thought suited to his powers); but how could a dog take the necessary gear with him without causing excitement among the human inhabitants? Or perhaps Australian sheep-farming would suit him, or some kind of hunting career in the north of Canada. No, by now it was all too clear that nothing would suit him, nothing was possible but to be a super-lap-dog-cum-super-laboratory-animal.

Yet always there was a strange nagging "something" within him which said, "Get on with it! You have unique powers. There is only one of you, and you exist to make your contribution to the world. Find your calling. It is difficult for you, no doubt, but you must find it or be damned." Sometimes the voice said, "For you, humanity is the pack. You are not one of them, but they made you and you are *for* them. And because you are different you can give them a vision which they can never win for themselves." Could he, after all, fulfil his task, perhaps, through music? Grandiose fantasies assailed him. "Sirius, the unique canine composer, not only changed the whole character of human music, importing into it something of the dog's finer auditory sensibility; he also, in his own incomparable creations, expressed the fundamental identity-in-diversity of all spirits, of whatever species, canine, human or super-human."

But no! It could not be. Man would never listen to him. And what reason had he to suppose that he had the genius to strike his music into the deep incomprehensible heart of man?

On the way back to the Laboratory Sirius heard the familiar nagging voice, calling him to express the "spirit" in him. He greeted it with an inward snarl. What could he possibly do about it? Nothing. He was a misfit, a mistake. He ought never to have occurred.

He felt an increasing impulse to run amok in the street. Life was no good to him. Why not throw it away, why not kill as many as he could of these ridiculously bedecked, swelled-headed apes, until they managed to destroy him? "I won't, I won't," he kept saying to himself. "Even if they *are* apes, or forked worms, they are the same stuff really as I am." Fleeing from himself, he broke into a trot, a canter, a real gallop, needing the seclusion of his own room. There, he paced up and down for many hours, far into the night. These hours form a crucial point in his life, so I shall quote from the account which he himself wrote down on the following day; turgid stuff, but significant of his unwholesome state.

"I walked and walked, rubbing my shoulder painfully against the wall every time I turned, snapping at the curtain as I passed it. This was affectation; I was dramatizing myself as a caged beast. The colleges and churches chimed, quarter by quarter. The noise of passing cars died down as the night advanced. I kept remembering with fury the smell of Plaxy, dear and loathsome; and the scent of my last bitch, so sweet, but false, promising a lovely spirit that did not exist. Then the sudden presence of Idwal's friendly smell, and of a flock of sheep, drenched with mist. The smell of Pugh, sweaty and excited. Of frost, of a summer day, of wind from the sea, of the change of wind from west to east. Trails of rabbit and hare. The infuriating stink of cat. Fox, rich and subtle. The menagerie. Chloroform, and the two toughs that had attacked me. The faint, throat-tightening smell of suffering which sometimes seems to come from the part of the Lab where I have never been.

"Below all this flood of smells there was an undercurrent of sounds; tones of human voices, and dog voices; bleating of sheep and lambs; the wind, whimpering or furious; snatches of human music, and themes of my own singing.

"My whole life seemed to crowd in on me in smell and sound; and touch also, for I felt Plaxy's hand on my neck, and the cracking of bones between my teeth, and the soft flanks of a young setter that I had loved long ago in Ffestiniog.

"Visual shapes came too, but dimly, unsteadily. Sometimes I glimpsed Thomas with pursed lips, considering me; sometimes Plaxy smiling.

"While these memories presented themselves to me, thoughts also kept racing and jostling one another through my mind, chiefly terrified and resentful thoughts about man's power over me, and my own failure to be master of my fate. How could I ever save myself from the breakdown that had already begun in me? What help was there anywhere for me? Thomas did not really understand the creature he had made. Elizabeth was always ready to hear my troubles and comfort me; but somehow she turned them all into child's troubles. And Plaxy was now so far away. It was 'the spirit,' we had said, that mattered. It was 'in the spirit' that we were eternally together. But now? Had we meant anything real at all by 'the spirit'? I wondered. After all we were just animals, with some degree of intelligence;

animals of different species, doomed never really to be at one with each
other, always in discord, and now drifting inevitably apart.

"Why, why was everything so sweet in promise and yet always in
realization bitter?

"But presently, as I paced up and down the little room, a queer thing
happened. It was as though my wandering imagination came upon a new
quality, different from all that I had ever known; yet one which was also
more familiar and intimate than the smell of Plaxy in the mood of love,
more piercing sweet than bitches, more hunt-worthy than the trail of a fox.

"No, I must not romanticize. This is a scientific report. No new sensory quality really came to me. But something happened in my mind which
I can't describe in any other way. If it was a fragrance at all, it was the
fragrance of love and wisdom and creating, of these for their own sake,
whether crowned with success and happiness or not. It was this fragrance,
which somehow came to me with such a fresh poignancy that it was something entirely new to me. It was this fragrance, trailed across the universe,
winding in and out of all its chasms and interstices, that had so often enticed me; but now in my excited state it presented itself to me so vividly
that I had to dramatize it to myself as a new quality, neither odour nor
sound nor visible form, but most like an odour to be pursued.

"And I did pursue it. I stopped pacing, and lay down with my fore-
legs stretched before me; and I laid my chin along them. Ignoring all the
other remembered scents, I pursued this strange new trail, with the flying
feet of inner attention. And as I followed, the trail became stronger, clearer,
more exquisite. Sometimes it escaped me, but casting back I recovered it.
Sometimes my strength failed, and as I flagged the trail grew fainter. But
I gathered myself together again for the chase, and as I pursued, lessening
the distance between myself and the quarry, the scent grew clearer and
more compelling.

"At last a terrible thing happened. As I drew nearer, the quality of
the heavenly quarry seemed to change. Though its exquisite sweetness remained, drawing me on, a new, pungent tang, a stinging, choking, bitter,
exquisite and terrifying perfume, was mixed with it. There was something
in it that made my mind reel, as the chloroform had done; and something
fierce, like the mighty smells of tiger and lion, but with a grimness that
no earthly smell ever had. I could not give up the chase. With staggering
mind I still clung to the trail. The thing that I was hunting must surely
be the source of all fragrance in the universe, and all horror also. And
I was famished for the thing. I must, must reach it; though in the end
surely not *I* should devour *it*, but *it* would devour *me*. Surely the thing that
I was crazily hunting must be the very thing that men called God, the dear
and beautiful and dread.

"At last it was as though the quarry turned at bay and overwhelmed
me. Remembering, I cannot recapture that moment of agony and bliss, the

agony of my slaughtered self, the bliss of the freed spirit in me. It was as though—how can I put it?—as though the trail which had first promised the most succulent prey, and then the most formidable but spell-binding enemy, had led after all not to the universal Tiger but to the universal Master, the superhuman master whom my super-canine nature so desperately needed to take possession of me and steady me with his claim for absolute loyalty and service.

"That supreme moment passed. I can remember only that when it passed I found peace such as I had not known before and shall never, I believe, quite lose. The whole universe now presented itself with a new quality, as though my monochrome vision had suddenly gained the glory of colour. But the colours that I saw were not of sensation. They were the colours that are seen by the eye of the spirit. All the things and people that I had seen hitherto in the plain greys of ordinary life were now enriched with a great diversity of the new quality which I am calling colour, so that they gained a new meaning, much as sounds gain a new meaning in speech or music. I saw them all in their own true colours and suffused with the music of the whole. And even now, on the day after my glorious moment, which is lost save for its afterglow in my mind, I still see everything coloured by the light of the spirit."

There followed a postscript.

"All this was written on the day after my vision, if vision it was. And now another day has passed. I have read it over, and I see that it does not describe at all the thing that happened to me. It is sentimental verbiage. It does not recapture the experience for me, it blurs it. But I am certain that something big really did happen to me. And the proof shall be shown in my life. I will take charge of my life. I will drift no more. I will still be true to science, but I will be true to my new light also. I will be a sceptic about everything but one thing, which does not admit of scepticism (once one has clearly seen it), namely that it does indeed matter to be as quickened a spirit as possible, and to live for the quickening of the spirit everywhere. In fact I am going to be the hound of the spirit. Me? Lazy, excuse-finding me? That's a good joke, isn't it! Looking at the matter with scientific detachment, I am sure I shall be adrift again before the week is out. Well, even if I *am*, the thing that happened the night before last will make a difference. And looking at it all in the light of the thing—no, by God! I shall never be adrift again! Not fundamentally."

With much misgiving Sirius dutifully offered this document to Thomas. Would he be amused, or annoyed? Or would he take it with all his aloof scientific detachment as a psychological datum? Sirius never discovered what Thomas really felt about it. The great physiologist was respectful, almost diffident; and hoped Sirius did not object to having the document typed in triplicate, "for the Laboratory records, and to show to a few of my friends, if you don't mind."

This seemingly mystical experience awakened in Sirius a new interest in religion. Through one of Thomas's guests he stumbled on the literature of mysticism, and was soon devoting a great deal of his time to St. Catherine of Siena, St. John of the Cross, Jacob Boehme, the Vedanta, and so on. It was Thomas who had to procure these works for him; and the task made Thomas smell acrid and disapproving, even though in word and deed he remained sympathetic.

Sirius now conceived a great desire to discuss religion with some sincere and orthodox religious person. No such person, it seemed, was among Thomas's circle of trusted friends who might be admitted into the secret of Sirius's intelligence. They were all either strictly scientific in the narrow sense or inclined to say "One feels in one's bones that there must be *something* in religion, but God knows what." Contact with these people merely increased Sirius's desire to pursue the matter, without helping him.

Sometimes he would hang about the doors of chapels and churches, to watch the congregation enter or leave the building, or to strain his hypersensitive ears to catch reverberations of the music, the prayers, the lessons and the sermon. The fact that as a mere dog he was not allowed into the sacred building increased his sense of exile and inferiority, and his readiness to belive that in spite of the critics it was within those walls that man attained his highest range of experience.

On one occasion his hunger for the truth was so great that he could not restrain himself from a very foolish act. It was summer time, and there was a heat wave. He had been watching the worshippers entering a little Methodist Chapel. Contrary to custom, the doors were not shut before the service began. Emotional prayer and vigorous singing flooded out upon him. To his refined sensibility the music was crude and the execution vulgar, but these very imperfections increased for him the feeling that music was here only a hastily executed symbol of some ulterior experience. A poem might be sincere no matter how hastily it had been scribbled. Jarred by the barbaric sound, yet fascinated, Sirius drifted step by step into the porch and across the inner threshold. He had entered during a prayer. The minister's eyes were reverently closed. His tone of voice was unctuous and complacently servile. With the conventional intonation of penitence and worship, but without any inner experience of them, he affirmed the sinfulness of the whole human race, and confidently, flatteringly, asked his God for forgiveness and eternal bliss for himself and his flock. The backs of the bowed congregation appeared above the pews like the backs of sheep in a pen. But their smell on that hot day was all too human.

When the prayer was ended the minister opened his eyes. He saw the great dog standing in the aisle. Pointing dramatically at Sirius, he exclaimed, "Who has brought that animal into God's House? Put it out!" Several black coats and striped trousers moved towards Sirius. They expected him to retire before them, but he stood his ground, his head and tail erect, his back bristling. A faint growl, rather like distant thunder, made the assailants hesitate. Sirius looked round the building. All eyes were turned on him, some outraged, some amused. He turned slowly to retrace his steps. The ejectors cautiously advanced. One of them said, "Good dog! Go home!" but another began to chivvy him with an umbrella, and rashly tapped his haunch. Sirius leapt round with a bark that echoed through the bare chapel, and his pursuers retreated a pace. He stood looking at them for a few moments, amused at his easy triumph. The hair on his spine subsided. He vaguely waved his tail, and turned towards the door. Then a mischievous idea took possession of him. At the door he once more faced the congregation, and in a clear, accurate, though wordless, voice he sang the refrain of the hymn that had been sung before he entered. As he turned to leave the building a woman screamed. The minister in a rather strained voice said, "Friends, I think we had better join once more in prayer."

On another occasion he marched beside the drums of the Salvation Army, sometimes forgetting himself so far as to add his voice to the trumpets. The open air service gave him, he told Thomas, an irrational sense of salvation. What appealed to him most was one of the hymns, sung with immense gusto. "Washed in the blood of the Lamb," was its theme. He could not resist joining in the singing, though softly. He could not see how the imagery of the hymn agreed with the religion of love, but somehow it had a strange power over him. He vaguely and quite irrationally felt it as unifying all the tenderness of his life with all the wolf in him. He scented again the seductive reek of his killed ram and his killed pony. Somehow the haunting conflict between pity and blood-lust seemed to be resolved. His guilt was washed away. There was no sound reason for this; he just felt it. He and these human animals somehow unloaded their sins upon the Lamb, and found a crude ecstasy of community one with another, and all together. They abased themselves into the personified spirit of the group. The intoxicated minds gave up all attempt to think clearly and feel precisely, and yielded to the common mentality; which somehow seemed to be universal, cosmical, the personified "togetherness" of all individual spirits in all the worlds. Thus he felt, as the barbaric tune soaked through his brain. Yet to another part of his mind the blasting of the trumpets, the thundering of the drums and the lusty human singing seemed as remote as the howling of an alien species in the jungle. Not in this way, said the protesting part of his mind, not in the remission of clear thought and feeling for the sake of the mere warmth of togetherness, could one find the essential spirit, identical in himself and in these humans. Only in the most articulate, precise self- and other-consciousness was the thing to be found; for instance on those rare occasions of spiritual accord with Plaxy, when through their very difference and distinctness they discovered their underlying identity. Yes, and in another manner he had sometimes found that thing, with Thomas, when their two intellects had moved together up the steep path of some argument, Thomas always leading, till they had reached together some pinnacle from which, it seemed, they could view the whole universe.

CHAPTER X

EXPERIENCES IN LONDON

ONE day Sirius demanded very urgently that Thomas should arrange for him to meet a few of the outstanding religious people of Cambridge. "But I don't know any," said Thomas. "They're not my line. And anyhow I wouldn't trust them not to blab." Sirius was not to be put off; and finally it was agreed that Elizabeth should help him to satisfy his curiosity about religion, and at the same time show him London. She had a cousin who was a parson in the East End. He could be taken into their confidence, and the two of them could perhaps visit him.

The Rev. Geoffrey Adams, now well advanced in middle age, was one of those clerics who had cared more for his parishioners than for self-advancement. Long ago he had undertaken a slum parish, and he had stayed there ever since. His life had been spent in comforting the sick and the dying with assurances of peace hereafter, in fighting local authorities on behalf of hard cases, and in agitating for playgrounds, free milk for mothers and children, and decent treatment for the unemployed. Throughout the country he had something of a reputation as a fighting parson, for on several occasions his indiscreet championship of the oppressed had brought him up against the state or his ecclesiastical superiors. Nearly all his parishioners admired him, some loved him, very few attended his services.

Elizabeth wrote to Geoffrey, telling him about Sirius, and asking if she might visit him, with the wonder-dog. He replied that he was desperately busy, that religion was not a thing to be got merely by talking about it, but that if they came to the East End he would show them round, and they might see a little of it in action.

Elizabeth took Sirius by train to King's Cross, a tiresome journey for the dog, as he had to travel in the luggage van. They spent the afternoon walking about the more prosperous end of the metropolis, for Sirius's edification. Oxford Street, Regent Street, Piccadilly and the parks gave Sirius a new impression of the multitude and power of the human race. What an amazing species it was, with its great buildings, its endless streams of cars, its shop-window displays, its swarming foot-passengers, with their trousered or silken legs! He could always detect the familiar sheep smell in the tweed; and in the fur coats there were still odours of the menagerie. Sirius had many questions to ask Elizabeth, but of course they dared not talk, for fear of rousing curiosity.

After a while Elizabeth was tired with all the walking, and wanted her tea. It was difficult to find a café where the great dog was acceptable, but after a while they settled beside a little table. Sirius, of course, lay on the floor, and was much in the way of the waitresses. Elizabeth gave him a bun and a slop-basin full of sweet tea. While she smoked, he watched the company. Someone was overheard to say, "That dog's expression is almost human."

After they had refreshed themselves they went eastwards by tube, and emerged in an entirely different world, the down-and-out world that Plaxy had often described to him. He was amazed by the contrast of *Homo sapiens* in affluence and *Homo sapiens* in penury. Young men hung about aimlessly at pub-corners. Dirty-faced children and shabby curs played in the gutters. Both the smell and the voices of the passers-by gave Sirius an unmistakable impression of defeat and resentment. He walked beside Elizabeth with alert and anxious eyes and heavy tail. This line of country threatened to be too much for him. The only familiar and comforting thing about it was the variety of odours left by his own kind at the foot of each lamp-post. The rest was overwhelming, not only because of the oppressive stink of man, but because it was a stink of man in abject anxiety. The western crowd had smelt mainly of cosmetics, perfume, soap, fresh tweed, tobacco smoke, moth balls and the slaughtered beasts whose furs they had stolen. There was also, of course, a strong undertone of human sweat, mostly female, and of all the other physical odours, including now and then an unmistakable whiff of sexual excitement. But in the eastern crowd the smell of crude human bodies dominated everything else; and it was on the average different in quality from the smell of the western bodies. In the prosperous region the odour was mainly of wholesome physique, but in the poorer region there was a faint but definite and very widespread smell of ill-health, rising sometimes (for his keen nose) to one or other of the repellent stenches of disease. There was another difference, too. Even in the west there was a tell-tale smell of peevish discontent; but in the east, where frustration was far more poignant, the same smell of discontent was stronger, and often accompanied by the acrid stink of chronic but suppressed rage.

Sirius, of course, had come across sordid town areas before, but never before had he imaginatively realized the extent of man's degradation in Britain. So this, he kept saying to himself, is what man has done to man, this is the average condition of the proud tyrant species. Its fundamentally self-regarding intelligence and its inadequate feeling for community has led it to this. The West End cared not a damn for the East End, and both, in their several ways, were frustrated.

The Rev. Geoffrey Adams received his visitors with some embarrassment. He had no idea how to treat Sirius, and even ordinary dogs he felt to be rather remote and incomprehensible. However, he soon learned that this great beast must be treated more or less as a human being; and he showed a surprising quickness in recognizing that Sirius's strange noises were an attempt at the English language. He accounted for his aptitude by saying, "I come across so many queer lingos at the docks." Then, realizing that this remark might seem disrespectful, he looked anxiously at Sirius, who moved his tail slightly in sign of friendliness.

Elizabeth had intended that they should spend a couple of nights with Geoffrey and then return to Cambridge, but Sirius was determined to stay on by himself, if Geoffrey would have him. For here was an aspect of mankind about which he knew nothing, and he could not begin to understand it in a couple of days. Geoffrey had been at first rather sceptical and even offhand about Sirius's search for religion, but some of the dog's remarks during their first interview, interpreted by Elizabeth, had roused his interest, particularly his statement that the heart of religion was love, and nothing else mattered. Here was a truth that called for elaboration and qualification. Geoffrey was also much intrigued by Sirius's real capacity for song, for the cleric was musical, and something of a singer himself. This was an added reason for his unexpectedly warm encouragement of Sirius's suggestion that he should remain in the East End for a while.

It was arranged that the dog should stay with Geoffrey for a week. Actually he remained much longer, He masqueraded as Geoffrey's dog, going with him among the parishioners whenever possible. Often, of course, he had to be left behind. Geoffrey could not take him to share death-bed scenes or difficult interviews with town councillors. But on most pastoral visits cleric and dog would set out together, and on the doorstep Geoffrey would ask, "May I bring in my dog? He's quite friendly." Sirius's amiable expression and waving tail would nearly always gain him a welcome.

In this manner he saw much of the conditions in which the less fortunate members of the dominant species lived. He also listened to many a conversation on matters practical or spiritual. Sometimes Geoffrey would greatly amuse his friends in the parish by including Sirius in the conversation, and Sirius to their delight would "reply." No one, of course, suspected that these little performances were genuine; but the Rev. Adam's queer dog was well received in all but the most unimaginative families. Children were specially accessible, for Sirius allowed them to ride him and maul him, and often showed "an uncanny understanding" of their talk and games. One boy of twelve insisted that Sirius's own talk was not sham at all, and that he himself could often understand it. Geoffrey affirmed, "Of course it's real," then knowingly smiled at the grown-ups.

Sometimes Geoffrey's duties took him to a canteen or mission-hall in dockland, sometimes to a Men's Club, where, followed by the observant Sirius, he would pass from room to room exchanging greetings with the members. Sometimes the parson took a turn at darts or billiards, or watched a boxing match. Once, with Sirius carelessly stretched out on the floor, he gave a talk on "Housing."

It did not take long for Sirius to discover that there were many different reactions to Geoffrey in this club. A few members regarded him with resentment and suspicion; and expressed their spleen by furtive persecution of his dog. Others, while respecting Geoffrey's kindliness and sincerity, regarded him and his religion as survivals from a prehistoric world. A few curried favour by professing conventional piety. One or two, for whom Geoffrey showed a special bantering affection, were for ever trying to convert him to atheism. The arguments, on both sides, rather shook Sirius's faith in the intellectual honesty of the dominant species, for on both sides the calibre of the reasoning was sometimes laughably poor. It was as though neither side really cared about mere logical cogency, because both had already made up their minds. Of all the club members, not one, it seemed to Sirius, was a sincere Christian in Geoffrey's sense of the term; though many were deeply influenced by Geoffrey's personality.

Sometimes Geoffrey took Sirius into the actual land of docks. The strange odours of foreign merchandise greatly interested him. They afforded him, he said, not only information about the goods themselves but something of the atmosphere of the lands from which they came. They enabled him to "travel by nose." He was greatly intrigued also by the new varieties of human odour associated with coloured people. Negroes, Lascars, Chinese, each had their distinctive racial scent, and in contrast with these the smell characteristic of Europeans distinguished itself in his mind.

On one occasion Geoffrey and Sirius came upon a minor riot. The dockers were on strike on account of the sacking of one of their number for political reasons. Blackleg labour was introduced, and the local men attacked the interlopers. Geoffrey and Sirius arrived at the height of the trouble. A large crowd of men was preventing a smaller crowd from going to work. Stones and bottles were thrown. A blackleg was knocked unconscious, and lay in the mud with a bleeding forehead. Geoffrey hastened to him, with Sirius at his heels, the wolf-mood rising. As Geoffrey bent over the stricken man, some of the dockers reviled him for helping their enemy. Someone even threw a stone, and Sirius took up a position between Geoffrey and the crowd, with bared teeth and a terrifying growl. Geoffrey did not take the men's hostile action meekly. In fact, for the first time Sirius saw him lose his temper. "Fools!" cried the parson. "I'm on your side, but this man is as precious to God as any of us." At this point God's damaged treasure recovered consciousness and rose to his feet, using most ungodly language. Then the police arrived in considerable force, drew their truncheons, and charged the dockers, most of whom fled. A few put up a fight and were arrested; two were picked up unconscious.

Before going to bed that night, Geoffrey and Sirius, as was their custom, talked over the affairs of the day. This time Sirius was deeply interested. He had long ago discovered that the human species was not at one with itself, and that authority was not always sympathetic with the common people, but the scene at the dock entrance had brought this home to him. According to Geoffrey the aim of the strike was to make a stand against gross victimization; and yet the police, though their action had been legally correct, had shown unnecessary brutality.

The world that Sirius now lived in was bewilderingly different from both his two other worlds, North Wales and Cambridge. The three worlds were inhabited by such diverse creatures that he could almost believe them three different species. Country people, intellectuals, dockers! Mentally they were far more alien to one another than dogs, cats and horses. Yet, of course, the difference was really all imposed by environment. Well, for the present he was wholly occupied in studying his third world; the others faded imperceptibly into dreamlands. For some weeks he was far too interested in the East End to look back on those other worlds; but at last there came times, chiefly when Geoffrey was busy on committee work, when he found himself hankering after open country and the smell of the sheep. For at these times there was nothing for him to do but wander about the streets watching the rather shabby crowds, listening to their monkey chatter, smelling their slightly unhealthy and frustrated odour, and feeling himself utterly alien to them. Then he would begin to worry about his future. What was to become of him? In Wales he was just a sheep-dog and a chattel; in Cambridge, a curiosity. In London? Well, at least, he was a student of the human species. But what could he ever *do*? It was his nature to *give* himself absolutely to some work; but to what work? To mere sheep-tending? To science? Why, of course, to the spirit. But how? His despondency was largely due to constipation. Do what he would, he could not get enough physical exercise in a town, and he could not help eating far too much for an inactive life. Worse, his soul was constipated. He was always taking in mental food and never doing anything with it.

One day as he was strolling past the entrance to a railway station, he noticed a display of large framed photographs advertising holiday resorts. One of them was a magnificent picture of moorland with mist driving over it. There was a little llyn, and one or two sheep. Waves splashed seductively on the stony shore. In the background the mountain rose darkly into the cloud. The immediate foreground was all tussocks of grass and heather, inviting his legs to action. He stood for a long time looking at this picture, letting the feel of the moors soak into him again, getting the smell of them. He caught himself actually working his nostrils to take the sheep's scent. Were they Pugh's or a neighbour's? It was all so real. And yet so far away and dreamlike. He could scarcely believe that he would ever be there again. Sudden panic seized him.

Then Sirius came to a firm resolution about his future. Science or no science, spirit or no spirit, he would spend his life in that sort of country, not in slums, nor in universities. That alone was his line of country. That was the only world he could ever really live in. Somehow in that world he must express whatever potency it was that was always straining in him to find exercise. But how?

On Sundays Geoffrey was always very busy, and Sirius was of course excluded from his sacred duties. The dog generally took the opportunity of securing a bit of much-needed exercise, cantering off into Epping Forest. On Sunday evenings Geoffrey often seemed dejected and old. Sirius had observed that few people entered the church for any of the services. Unfortunately Geoffrey, though respected and loved by so many, could not attract a large congregation. This incapacity he regarded as a failure in his religious duty. He did not realize, but Sirius did, that the influence of his personality reached far beyond the range of his official ministrations, and that he had given to thousands the essence of religion, though they could not accept from him the ritual and doctrine which, though symbolically true for a past age, was quite out of keeping with the spirit of our times. Some of Geoffrey's warmest admirers were persons who never attended his church or even counted themselves Christians. Of those who did attend, a few were of course sincere believers in the Christian myth as "gospel truth." Others came because they vaguely felt the need of some kind of religious life. They recognized in Geoffrey a truly religious spirit, and he assured them that they ought to join in communal worship. But the living example which he gave them in his life of practical love was somehow not clarified or strengthened by his church services. Geoffrey had no power to infuse the services with the ardent religious passion which he himself felt; and this failure it was which filled him with a gnawing doubt of his own sincerity.

These conclusions Sirius boldly announced to Geoffrey in their many talks over meals or late in the evenings. The ageing priest was saddened by them. He could not for a moment contemplate the possibility that his rituals and doctrines had only symbolical truth, though he could and did doubt his own sincerity as a servant of God. He was saddened that men should be so blind as to doubt the literal truth of Christian doctrine, and specially sad that his friend Sirius should be so blind. For between priest and dog there had rapidly developed a deep mutual respect and affection. They had told one another much of their personal lives, and in particular of their religious searchings. To Geoffrey it seemed that Sirius's vague yearnings and rigorous agnosticism formed only an utterly inadequate shadow of religion. To Sirius it seemed, of course, that Geoffrey's religion was an incongruous tissue of true value-intuitions and false or meaningless intellectual propositions. Sirius had spoken of his love for Plaxy as "at heart a religious love for the universal spirit." He had also told of his strange vision in Cambridge. On one occasion he had said, "I see, indeed I *know*, that in *some* sense God is love, and God is wisdom, and God is creative action, yes and God is beauty; but what God actually *is*, whether the maker of all things, or the fragrance of all things, or just a dream in our own hearts, I have not the art to know. Neither have you, I believe; nor any man, nor any spirit of our humble stature." Geoffrey merely smiled sadly and said, "May God in His time show you the truth that His Son died to manifest."

On another occasion Sirius challenged Geoffrey about immortality. They had been discussing for some while when Sirius said, "Now take me! Have *I* an immortal soul?" Geoffrey replied at once, "I have often wondered about you. I *feel*, indeed, that you are an immortal spirit, and I earnestly prayed that God should grant you salvation. But if you are, and if He does, it is a miracle which I cannot interpret."

Sirius had come to Geoffrey in the hope of finding the true religion. At Cambridge, in spite of all the free and fearless intelligence, there had obviously been something lacking, something that he greatly needed, though Cambridge regarded it as something almost indecent. He had thought it must be simply "religion," and he had come to London to find it. And in Geoffrey he had, indeed, found it. There could be no doubt that Geoffrey had a firm hold on the thing that Cambridge lacked, that Geoffrey was the very embodiment of "religion" in action. But—but—one couldn't have Geoffrey's religion without violating all that one had learnt at Cambridge, all the constant loyalty to intelligence that was the best thing in Cambridge. In a way it was easy to cling to faith and betray intelligence, though Geoffrey's active faith was no easy-going affair. It was easy, too, to cling to intelligence and abandon faith, like McBane, for instance. But was there no way of being equally loyal to both? Vaguely it began to appear to Sirius that there was, but that it involved both keener intelligence and more sensitive religious feeling than either of the other courses. Passion for "the spirit," the awakened way of living, whatever its fortune in the universe, passion for the spirit, stripped of all belief and comfort save the joy of that passion itself—this, expressed in a life of devoted action, like Geoffrey's, this was the only, the true religion. But poor Sirius felt dismally that this was beyond him. He just hadn't the guts. He hadn't either the intelligence or the passion. If only the spirit itself would seize him and set fire to him! But then—he was not prepared. He was not really inflammable. There was too much damp fog drenching all his tissues.

The friendship of the parson and his dog was the source of much comment in the district; the more so when it became known that the Rev. Adams was sometimes to be heard talking to the great animal as though to a human being. The dear old man, they said, was growing more eccentric than ever. Some declared simply that he was crazy. But presently rumour had it that real conversations did take place between man and dog, and that there actually was something mysterious about Sirius. The devout said he was either possessed by the Devil or was an angel in disguise. The scientific wiseheads said it was all quite simple, the dog was a biological sport.

The climax came when Sirius made a dramatic appearance in church. He had for long been secretly planning to gain Geoffrey's consent to this, partly because he wanted to witness one of Geoffrey's services, partly because it rankled to be shut out from the most solemn activity of the human species, and treated as an inferior animal. Geoffrey, of course, felt that he ought not to permit a brute to enter the holy place. His curate would have been outraged, and so would the congregation. But he had been much impressed by Sirius's superb singing voice, and Sirius had subtly induced him to toy with the idea of allowing his canine friend to sing a wordless anthem from behind the vestry door. When they were at home together, Sirius made a point of practising some of Geoffrey's favourite "sacred" music.

With much misgiving, and a sense not of sin but of naughtiness, Geoffrey finally agreed to allow Sirius to sing at a Sunday morning service, unseen, from behind the vestry door. The great day arrived, Dog and man walked to the church, the priest explaining to the canine singer the point in the service at which the anthem should occur. "Keep well behind the door," he said. "This is a bold step for me, Sirius. If they find out there will be trouble."

When the couple reached the gate of the little church, Sirius paused for a moment, looked up at Geoffrey rather anxiously, and then deposited a few drops of golden fluid on the gatepost. With a rather nervous laugh Geoffrey said, "You might have relieved yourself somewhere else." "No," answered Sirius. "It was a religious act. I have poured my libation in honour of your God. And I have relieved my spirit of impurity. I am lightened for the chase, the pursuit of the divine quarry by song."

When the service was about to begin, the verger noticed that the parson had left the vestry door open. He stepped over to shut it, but Geoffrey waved him away with his hand.

At the appropriate point in the service Geoffrey announced, "You will now hear a wordless anthem sung by a dear friend of mine who will remain unnamed and unseen." Sirius's strong pure voice, unaccompanied, then filled the church. Geoffrey listened with delight at its power and delicacy of expression. It seemed to him that in this music lay the truth that he himself had striven all his life long to express in word and deed. And now a dog, interpreting a great human composer (it was Bach) was saying it unmistakably, though without words. Many of the congregation also were deeply moved. The few musical members were impressed and mystified, for the execution was accurate, and it expressed with severe restraint a deep and subtle passion. But what perplexed them was the curiously non-human quality of the voice. Was it perhaps some cunning instrumental imitation of a man's voice, or of a woman's? The range, they said, was too great for either. If it was indeed a singer, why did he or she not appear? Throughout the following week rumour was busy. A great singer, it was said, had consented to do this thing for Mr. Adams on condition that his identity was not revealed. The pious secretly believed that the great singer was not a man but an angel from heaven. Such was the decay of faith, however, that fear of ridicule prevented all but a few simple souls from openly proclaiming this belief.

Next Sunday there were far more people than usual at the morning service, though not enough to make the church look full. The newcomers obviously had come out of mere curiosity. In his sermon Geoffrey scolded them for it. There was no anthem.

Not till the following Sunday, which was to be Sirius's last before returning to Cambridge, did he sing again. His earlier success had made him long for another opportunity, and he wished to face the congregation. This was to be the beginning of his message to the human species. He would sing them something of his own composition. It must be something intelligible to human ears, and indeed to a good proportion of this simple congregation. It must be something which would help them to feel again the essential truth in their own religion, and the unimportance of its mythology.

Geoffrey was reluctant to let Sirius perform again, because too much of a "sensation" had already been caused. But he longed to hear that great voice filling his church once more. And his natural sincerity inclined him to let the singer be seen as well as heard. Moreover, though he knew there would be trouble with the bishop and some of the congregation, he felt that he was under an obligation to welcome his canine friend in God's house. Further, he secretly relished the prospect of shocking his earnest young curate.

Sirius spent several mornings out in Epping Forest, trying over many of his compositions. Though he kept out of view, as far as possible, his strange voice caused several people to seek him out. Whenever anyone discovered him, he let his song turn imperceptibly into a normal canine baying, so that the intruder supposed that the musical quality had been an illusion.

At the morning service Sirius sang from behind the vestry door. But the music was very different from that of his previous performance. All the meaningful intonations of the human voice and all canine ululations seemed to enter into this alien yet intelligibly musical, this sweet yet rather frightening, sound. It ranged from a thundering growl to a high clear piping, almost as of singing birds.

I am not myself sufficiently sensitive musically to judge whether "interpretation" of music is legitimate. In Geoffrey's view, though he was intensely interested in music for its own sake, the supreme function of this art, as of all other arts, was as a medium of religious expression. Hence his eagerness to have Sirius sing in his church, and his intention to interpret the song to his congregation. Sirius, too, held that interpretation was legitimate, though in the hands of the imperfectly musical it often became ludicrous. I have heard him insist that, in so far as music ever had a "meaning" beyond the immediate and exquisite value of the sound-pattern itself, its "meaning" must be simply an emotional attitude. It could never speak directly about the objective world, or "the nature of existence"; but it might create a complex emotional attitude which might be appropriate to some feature of the objective world, or to the universe as a whole. It might therefore create religious feelings. Its "interpretation" in words would then involve describing those features of the universe which should evoke those feelings.

In this sense the strange music that Sirius put forth in Geoffrey's church spoke of bodily delight and pain, and of the intercourse of spirits. It expressed through the medium of sound, and transformed into universal symbols, the particular spirits of Thomas, Elizabeth, Plaxy and Geoffrey himself. It spoke of love and death, of the hunger for the spirit, and of Sirius's own wolf-mood. It spoke of the East End and the West End, of the docker's strike and the starry heaven.

All this it did at least for Sirius himself. To most of the congregation it was an inconsequent mixture of music and noise, and moreover a mixture of the recognizably, comfortably pious and the diabolical.

Geoffrey in his sermon tried to tell the congregation what the strange song had meant to him. "The singer," he said, "must have known love in his own experience and recognized it as good absolutely. He must also have known the presence of Satan, in the world and in his own heart."

In the evening service, when Geoffrey had announced the anthem, he added, "This time the singer will appear in the church. Do not be outraged. Do not think that a trick is being played on you. The singer is my dear friend, and it is good that you should know that God can still work miracles."

Out of the vestry strode the great beast, black and frosty-fawn. Head and tail were proudly erect. Grey eyes keenly watched the congregation. There was an audible gasp of surprise and protest, then dead silence. It was as though the power of "the eye," which the Border Collie used so successfully on sheep, was now being used by Sirius upon a whole human flock. He had made his entry with very solemn feelings; but the spectacle of these spellbound human sheep greatly tickled him, and he could not resist turning his head towards Geoffrey and giving him a very human wink with the eye that was hidden from the congregation. After this lapse, which shocked Geoffrey, Sirius pulled himself together. His mouth opened, displaying the white fangs that had recently killed ram and pony, and gripped the throat of a ˙man. The church was then flooded with Sirius's music. Geoffrey seemed to hear in it echoes of Bach and Beethoven, of

Holst, Vaughan Williams, Stravinsky and Bliss, but also it was pure Sirius. Most of the congregation, on a far lower musical level than their pastor, and a far lower human level also, were merely intrigued by its novelty. Some were sufficiently sensitive to be disturbed and revolted by it. A few conscious musical modernists probably decided that it was a bad imitation of the real thing. One or two, perhaps, were stirred more or less in the manner that Sirius intended. The performance lasted quite a long time, but the audience remained throughout still and attentive. When it was finished Sirius looked for a moment at Geoffrey, who returned his questioning gaze with a smile of admiration and affection. Sirius crouched down, muzzle on paws, tail stretched out along the ground. The service proceeded.

Geoffrey began his sermon by trying to interpret the music, warning his congregation that it might legitimately mean different things to different people, and that to the composer-singer his interpretation might seem very wrong. The congregation were startled. Were they expected to believe that the animal that had produced the music had also composed it, that what they had witnessed was not simply the result of brilliant circus-training but actually a miracle?

Geoffrey affirmed, rightly or wrongly, "The song gave me a view of humanity from outside humanity, from the point of view of another of God's creatures, and one that both admires and despises us, one that has fed from our hands and has also suffered at our hands. By means of echoes of the great human composers mingled with themes reminiscent of the wolf's baying and the dog's barking and howling, the singer conjured up his vision of humanity. And what a humanity it was! With God and Satan, love and hate together in its heart; with cunning surpassing all the beasts, and wisdom too, but also utter folly; with fabulous power, turned as often as not to Satan's will!" Geoffrey spoke of the luxury of the rich and the misery of the workers all over the world, of strikes and revolutions, of the ever-increasing threat of a war more terrible even than the last war. "And yet in our personal lives love is not unknown. In the song, as in my own knowledge, I seem to hear it said that love and wisdom must triumph in the end, because Love is God."

He looked down at Sirius, who was showing signs of protest. Geoffrey continued, "My friend does not agree with that part of my interpretation. But that is indeed how the climax of his song affected me."

He paused, then ended his sermon with these words: "I am growing old before my time. I shall not be able to carry on much longer. When I have gone, remember me by this Sunday. Remember that I once, by God's grace, was able to let you witness a very lovely miracle."

Not many of the congregation imagined even in that summer of 1939 that in a few months not only the ageing priest but many of the congregation themselves would be lying crushed under the East End buildings, or that the little church would become a blazing beacon for enemy planes.

At the end of the service Sirius walked out behind Geoffrey, and before the congregation had begun to leave the church he hurried off in the direction of Geoffrey's home. Soon after the parson had returned, Elizabeth arrived (according to plan) to take Thomas's canine masterpiece back to Cambridge.

During the following weeks Sirius received letters from Geoffrey talking of the excitement in the neighbourhood. Journalists had pestered him, but he had refused absolutely to give them any information. The church was filled on the following Sunday, but Geoffrey surmised that only a small minority had come for religion. Indeed he very soon realized that a daring act which he had undertaken with innocent motives was appearing to the public as no better than a piece of gross self-advertisement. His ecclesiastical superiors reprimanded him, and might well have deprived him of his office, had it not been for the passionate loyalty of his supporters in the parish.

When Thomas was told of the incident, he was at first annoyed, but the humour of it won him over to forgive Sirius for his escapade.

CHAPTER XI

MAN AS TYRANT

IN the summer of 1939 the clouds of war were already gathering over Europe. Everyone was living in dread of the future or hoping against hope that by some miracle the storm would after all not break. Sirius had never taken much interest in the international situation, but now, like so many others, he was forced to be interested. Thomas also was merely bored at the prospect of war. He wanted to carry on his work unhindered, and he feared that war would make this impossible. Of course, if the clash came, we should have to do our damnedest to win; but if only the fool politicians had been more intelligent and honest there would never have been any trouble. This was roughly Sirius's attitude also, except that in addition he felt a rising fury against the dominant species, which had been given such power and such opportunity, and yet was making such a sorry mess of its affairs.

During the summer vac the Trelone family spent only a few weeks in Wales. It was a clouded holiday, for there was no escape from the international situation. Thomas was embittered, and Elizabeth desperately saddened. Tamsy, who had been married some months earlier, spent her week in Wales brooding over the newspapers and the wireless set. Maurice, now a don at Cambridge, argued a great deal with Tamsy about Hitler's chances.

Giles was very quiet, adjusting himself to the idea that he would soon have to fight. Plaxy ignored the war-clouds completely, and went out of the room whenever the subject was raised. Sirius concentrated on recovering physical fitness after Cambridge and London.

When war broke out Sirius was on a Cumberland sheep farm learning the ways of the Lakeland shepherds. Sirius's Cumberland experiences were valuable, but painful. Thwaites, who was by no means typical of the fine Lakeland type, turned out to be a harsh and unreasonable master. He showed Sirius an aspect of humanity with which he had never before had personal contact to any appreciable extent. Sirius suspected Thwaites at the outset because his own dog, Roy, a Border Collie, avoided him whenever possible, and cringed when spoken to. In Thwaites's relations with Sirius some quite irrelevant and probably forgotten conflict seems to have found expression. He conceived an uncontrollable dislike for the dog, perhaps because of a strong suspicion that Sirius was no ordinary super-sheepdog, and was privately judging his character very ruthlessly. Whatever the cause, Thwaites soon began to treat Sirius with crude harshness. I find it difficult to excuse Thomas for his gross carelessness in choosing him as Sirius's instructor. Thomas was always surprisingly insensitive about the psychological aspect of his great experiment; or perhaps not insensitive but unimaginative. But on this occasion his failure to secure decent conditions for Sirius was so flagrant that I am inclined to attribute it to deliberate purpose. Had he determined to afford the dog some first-hand experience of the more brutal aspect of humanity? If so, his purpose was only too well fulfilled.

Anyhow, Thwaites constantly indulged his spite against Sirius, ordering him to carry heavy loads in his mouth, forcing on him all sorts of tasks which only a human hand could perform efficiently, overworking him with awkward jobs that were obviously unnecessary, and laughing bitterly at him in conversation with his neighbours.

At first Sirius was rather pleased to have the experience of contact with a human being of brutal temper. Hitherto his immediate human environment had been on the whole too amiable to be a fair sample. He needed to know what man was like in his harsher modes. There was soon trouble, because Sirius did not cringe when Thwaites gave orders. Instead, he carried out his task with calm efficiency. This provoked the man to curse him on the flimsiest pretext; and when he did so, Sirius would gaze at him with cold and ostentatious surprise. This, of course, made matters worse. In time, Thwaites's harsh voice and the whole atmosphere of the place began to get on Sirius's nerves. The milder human contacts in Wales, Cambridge and London began to fade out of his consciousness, and he found himself feeling that Thwaites was the typical man. Obscurely he dramatized himself as the champion of his own kind against the tyrant race. Thwaites's great cruel hands symbolized for him the process by which the ruthless species had mastered all the living creatures of the planet. Irrationally Sirius, though a hunter who had again and again inflicted agony and death, felt a self-righteous indignation against the sheer cruelty of man. Compassion for the weak, which had been inculcated in him by his own human friends, now turned him against humanity itself.

Thwaites had several times threatened Sirius with his stick, but had always thought better of it, sobered by the dog's great size and a dangerous look in his eye. As time passed, the man's irrational spite against the dog increased. But the incident which caused the final catastrophe was an attack not on Sirius but on Roy. A few days before Thomas was due to come and fetch Sirius away there was some difficulty with a bunch of sheep that Roy had brought into the yard. Thwaites caught the collie a sharp blow on the haunch. Sirius turned on Thwaites in fury and knocked him down; then, remembering himself, he withdrew and watched the man pick himself up. Roy promptly disappeared from the scene. It was a fixed principle with Thwaites that when dogs were rebellious one must thrash them into subjection, which meant in his view thrashing them almost to death. He called to his hired man, "Anderson, the brute's gone savage, come and help me teach him." There was no answer. Anderson was far afield. Thwaites was no coward, but he did not relish attacking the great cunning beast single-handed. However, insubordination must be crushed, at all costs. Besides, such a dangerous animal might do incalculable harm. Better destroy it at once. He could tell Trelone that the dog had gone mad and had to be shot. He went into the house. Sirius guessed that he would emerge with his gun. He therefore rushed to the house door and crouched at one side of it. Thwaites stepped over the threshold, looking round the yard. Sirius leapt at him, knocked him over again, and seized the gun with his teeth. Both antagonists rolled over and over. Thwaites struggled to his feet, and tried to turn the muzzle of the gun against the dog's body. One barrel went off harmlessly, then the other. Sirius let go the gun and sprang away. Thwaites put his hand in his pocket and brought out a couple of cartridges. Sirius leapt at him, knocked him over again and seized his throat, gripping his windpipe with the full power of his strong jaws. The flavour of warm human blood and the sound of the man's stifled gurgle filled him with an exultant, careless fury. In this symbolic act he would kill not only Thwaites but the whole tyrant race. Henceforth all beasts and birds should live naturally, and the planet's natural order should never again be disturbed by the machinations of this upstart species. These thoughts flashed through his mind even as the couple floundered and crashed about, gripping each other's throats.

Presently the man's struggles slackened, his grip weakened. Then a change began to come over Sirius's mind. Fury gave place to a more detached observation of the situation. After all, this creature was only expressing the nature that the universe had bred in him. And so was the

whole human race. Why this silly hate? The human stink suddenly reminded him of Plaxy's fragrance. The blood-taste nauseated him. The
crushed windpipe between his teeth filled him with horror. He let go,
moved away, and stood watching the feeble movements of his non-canine
brother, whom he, Cain, had murdered.

Practical considerations presented themselves to him. The hand of
man would now indeed be relentlessly turned against him. The hand of
two thousand million human beings; all the race, save his own few friends.
A panic of loneliness suddenly seized him. A solitary airman, flying over
hostile territory, with nothing but enemies below and nothing but stars
above, may sometimes feel desperately lonely; but that loneliness is nothing
to the loneliness which now oppressed Sirius, with the whole human race
against him, and his own species unable to comprehend him, and no pack
anywhere to comfort him and accept his service.

He went over to the trough in the yard, drank, and licked his lips
clean. Once more he stood watching Thwaites, who now lay still, with a
torn and bloody neck. His own neck was stiff after Thwaites's desperate
effort. Imagining the pain that his teeth must have inflicted, he cringed.
He returned to the body and sniffed the neck. Already there was a very
faint odour of death. No need, then, to risk his own life fetching a doctor
to save this human being. Obeying a sudden freakish impulse, he fleetingly
touched the forehead of his slaughtered brother with his tongue.

Distant footsteps! He took to his heels in sudden panic, leapt the yard
gate and raced away for the fells. Lest they should come after him with
bloodhounds, he used every fox-trick to mislead them. He doubled on his
track, he took to streams, and so on. That night he slept under the bracken
in a remote ghyll. Next day hunger forced him to go hunting. He managed to secure a rabbit, and took it to his lair, where he wolfed it. He
spent the rest of the day hidden, and haunted by his crime; haunted, yet
strangely exultant. Though it was indeed a crime, it was a positive act of
self-assertion which had emancipated him for ever from the spell of the
master race. Henceforth he would fear no man simply as a man. Two more
nights and the intervening day he spent in hiding. Then he set off to in-
tercept Thomas, who was due at the farm in the afternoon. With great
caution he worked his way back over the hills till he was looking down
on the road to Thwaites's farm. He went to a point on the road where
there was good cover and a hairpin bend. Here the car would have to
slow down almost to walking pace. He hid himself in the undergrowth of
a little wood, and waited. An occasional foot-passenger passed, and an
occasional car. At last there was the unmistakable sound of Thomas's
Morris Ten. Cautiously Sirius crept from his hiding, looking to see if any
other human being was visible. There was no one. He stepped out into
the road. Thomas stopped the car and got out with a cheery "Hello!" Sirius, with tucked-in tail, simply said, "I've killed Thwaites." Thomas ex-

claimed, "God!" then gaped at him in silence. The dog's keen ears heard distant footsteps, so they retired into the wood to discuss the situation. It was decided that Thomas should go up to the farm as though he knew nothing of the tragedy, while Sirius kept in hiding.

There is no need to record in detail how Thomas dealt with the problem. Naturally he did not tell the police that he had met Sirius. He strongly denied that his super-sheep-dogs were dangerous, and he produced evidence to that effect. He insisted that Thwaites must have treated Sirius very badly; and the man (it appeared) was known to be of a sadistic temper. Clearly he had attacked the animal with his gun, and had probably wounded it. In self-defence the dog had killed him. And where was the dog now? The valuable creature had probably died of wounds somewhere on the moors.

This much of the truth Thomas told Sirius, but not till long afterwards did the murderer learn the rest. Things had not in fact gone as well as Thomas had reported. The officers of the law remained suspicious, and ordered that if the dog was found it must be destroyed. Thomas therefore decided that in order to protect his unique canine masterpiece he must resort to trickery. After a suitable interval he would notify the authorities that the man-killing beast had at last found its way home, and that it had been duly destroyed. He would sacrifice a certain large Alsatian super-sheep-dog, and palm off his corpse as Sirius's.

It was not until late on the day of the inquest that Thomas picked up Sirius at the hairpin bend. In spite of the black-out, they drove home through the night, helped by a full moon.

CHAPTER XII

FARMER SIRIUS

IT was not till dawn on the following day that Thomas and Sirius in the Morris Ten drove up the familiar Welsh lane, and came to a stand in the yard of Garth. Elizabeth and Plaxy were still asleep. When they woke, they were very surprised to find that man and dog had returned already. They were surprised also at the wretched condition of Sirius. He was filthy, his coat lacked its customary gloss, he was painfully thin, and he was silent and dejected.

Plaxy, fresh from a busy and happy term at Cambridge, was in the mood for a happy holiday. Moreover she was aware that in recent meetings with Sirius she had somehow proved inadequate, and she was anxious to make amends. She therefore set about being "sweet" to Sirius. It was she who gave him a thorough wash and carefully groomed his coat. She also took a thorn out of one of his feet, and dressed a bad cut in another. He surrendered himself to the firm and gentle touch of her hands and the subtle odour that was for him her most poignant feature. She pressed him to tell her all about his doings in Cumberland, and he told her—everything but the main thing. It was obvious that he was holding something back, so she pressed him no further, though suspecting that he really wanted to tell her. He did indeed long to confess to her. The memory of the crime was a constant source of turmoil in his mind. He had committed a murder. This was the stark fact that had to be faced. It was useless to pretend that he had been forced to kill Thwaites in self-defence, for he had hung on to him much longer than was necessary to put him out of action. No, it was murder, and sooner or later Thomas's ruse would probably be found out. Even if Sirius remained uncaught he would have this thing hanging over him for ever; not just the fear of retribution, but the deadly remorse for the destruction of a creature who, though biologically alien to him, was none the less his fellow in the spirit. He longed for Plaxy's sympathy, but feared her horror. And anyhow, Thomas had insisted that no one should be told.

During that Christmas holiday Sirius and Plaxy spent many an hour talking about themselves and their friends; about art, particularly Sirius's music; about philosophy and religion, particularly his experiences with Geoffrey; about the war, for though both of them felt it to be utterly unreal and remote, and "not their fault anyhow," it could not be ignored. Several of Plaxy's friends were already in it.

But though at first they had much to say to one another, later they often fell into silence, and as time advanced these silences became longer and more frequent. He brooded over his prospects, she retired into her memories. She was beginning to yearn once more for human companionship. His nose told him that it was one of those phases when she was fully ripe for the love of her own kind. Her behaviour towards him alternated between exaggerated tenderness and aloofness. She seemed to want to maintain contact with him, but at these times the gulf between the human and the canine was generally too great. But not always. Sometimes the intensification of animal sex-feeling in the young human female linked up with her deep affection for the dog, so that she treated him with an altogether novel shyness, which somehow stimulated a similar sexually toned warmth of feeling in him. He would then, if she permitted, caress her with a new tenderness and ardour. But these passages were rare, and often they were followed on Plaxy's side by a frightened aloofness. It seemed to her, so she told me long afterwards, that in those strange, sweet moments she was taking the first step towards some very far-reaching alienation from her own kind. Yet while they lasted they seemed entirely innocent and indeed beautiful.

Once Sirius said to Plaxy, "The music of our two lives is a duet of variations upon three themes. There is the difference between our biological natures, yours human and mine canine, and all the differences of experience that follow from that. Then there is the love that has grown up between us, alien as we are. It has gathered us together and made us one fundamentally, in spite of all our differences. It feeds on differences. And there is sex, which alternates between tearing us apart because of our biological remoteness and welding us together because of our love." They silently gazed at one another. He added, "There is a fourth theme in our music, or perhaps it is the unity of the other three. There is our journey along the way of the spirit, together and yet poles apart." Plaxy replied with sudden warmth, "Oh, my darling, I do, I do love you. We are never really poles apart, not in the spirit, I mean. But—oh, it's all strange and frightening. And you see, don't you, that I must be properly human. Besides— men can mean so much more to me than bitches can mean to you." "Of course," he answered. "You have your life and I have mine. And sometimes we meet, and sometimes clash. But always, yes, always, we are one in the spirit."

He wondered whether, if she knew about Thwaites, it would make any difference; and he realized that it wouldn't. She would be horrified, of course, but not revolted against him. Suddenly he realized that ever since the killing he had been anxiously condemning himself on behalf of Plaxy, and so nursing a sore resentment against her. But so deeply had he nursed it that he never till this moment recognized its existence. And now somehow he knew that she would not condemn him, and so the resentment became conscious and at the same time vanished.

Later in the vacation Plaxy busied herself with her studies. She was all behind-hand, she said. And when at last the day came for departure, she was as usual both sad and pleased. At the station she found an excuse to stray with Sirius to a less crowded stretch of the platform. "We have drifted apart again lately," she said, "but *whatever* happens I never forget that I am the human part of Sirius-Plaxy." He touched her hand and said, "We have a treasure in common, a bright gem of community."

During the vacation Sirius had been anxiously concerned with other things besides that treasure. He had been carrying on an urgent discussion about his future with Thomas and Elizabeth, with Plaxy as a disinterested critic. Sirius was determined not to go back to the subtly enervating life of Cambridge. The time had come, he said, when he really must strike out on his own. He was ready to agree that at least for a while he might be able to find self-expression through his skill with sheep, but he could do so only in a responsible position, not as a mere sheep-dog. What did Thomas propose to do about it?

In the end a bold plan was adopted. Owing to the scarcity of labour, Pugh, whose health was failing, had found great difficulty in carrying on

his farm. Thomas decided to tell him the whole truth about Sirius's powers, and to propose that Sirius should join him not as a sheep-dog but as a
prospective partner. Or rather, the Laboratory would legally be his partner,
contributing capital to the farm. Elizabeth would be the Laboratory's resident representative, and would lend a hand with the work. Sirius, being
only a dog, could sign no contract and hold no property. But he would
in effect be in the partnership relation to Pugh, who would initiate him
into the whole management of the farm, and the business of marketing
sheep and wool. An important side-line would be the training of super-
sheep-dogs for sale.

There were several long discussions with Pugh. This was perhaps an
advantage, as it gave him an opportunity of learning to understand Sirius's
speech with Thomas and Elizabeth present to help him. The old man was
very ready to enter into the spirit of the game; but he was cautious, and he
thought of many difficulties, each of which had to be patiently smoothed
out. Mrs. Pugh regarded the arrangement with misgiving. She secretly
feared that Satan, not God, was the worker of this miracle of the man-dog.
That Thomas himself was responsible she never seriously supposed. The
only other person who might have been concerned in the new arrangement
was Pugh's daughter, but she was by now married and settled in Dolgelly.

It was not long before Sirius was established at Caer Blai in his new
capacity. It was arranged that normally he should sleep at home at Garth,
since he could cover the distance between the two houses in a few minutes;
but at Caer Blai the room formerly occupied by the daughter of the house
was allotted to him for emergencies. To the new quarters Thomas transferred the dog's accumulation of books on sheep and sheep-farming, also
a spare writing glove and other writing materials. In addition Sirius kept
at the farm several of the girths and panniers that had been made for him
from time to time to enable him to carry things while keeping his mouth
free. In early days the apparatus had to be fastened on him by human
hands, but by now, owing to his increased "manual" skill and an ingenious
fastener, he could saddle or unsaddle himself in a few seconds.

Pugh could not teach Sirius anything about the actual care of sheep.
The dog had a closer practical experience of them, and a far more scientific
knowledge. He was eager to improve the breed on the farm and to develop the pasture. But on the side of farm management he had everything
to learn. Not only had he to understand prices and the whole book-keeping
problem; there was also the small but important agricultural side of the
farm. Before the war this had been entirely subordinate to sheep, producing only hay and roots and a very small amount of grain. But in war-time
every possible acre had to be ploughed up to produce food, and by now
Pugh had a good deal of land under oats, rye and potatoes. The handless
Sirius could never do much on this side of the work, but he was determined
to understand it and learn to direct it. The necessity of employing hired

human labour raised the whole question of Sirius's contact with the outside world. Thomas, with his phobia of publicity, was very reluctant to let the countryside know just how developed a creature Sirius was, but clearly it would not be possible for him in his new life to masquerade as a dumb animal. However, said Thomas, let people discover the truth gradually. In this way it would be less of a shock to them. Pugh could begin by holding simple conversations with Sirius in public places. Gradually he could let it be realized that he respected the dog's judgment in all matters connected with sheep. In this manner Sirius would little by little become a congenial figure in the neighbourhood.

For some time Sirius was too busy learning his new responsibilities to undertake the training of super-sheep-dogs. Old Idwal and another of these animals, Mifanwy, a young bitch, were on the farm already, and able to do far more intelligent work than the brightest normal animal. Juno, who had been one of the most intelligent of super-sheep-dogs, had developed some obscure kind of brain trouble, so that Pugh had been forced to destroy her.

After a while Sirius wrote to Thomas saying that he now felt ready for the new venture, and Thomas sent him three puppies of the right age for training. Sirius privately believed that with sympathetic education by one of their own species (though superior to them in intelligence) these animals could be made into something far more capable than Idwal and Mifanwy, or even Juno. He had also secret hopes that one of them, or one of some future batch, might turn out to be a creature of his own mental rank; but this, he had to admit, was very unlikely, for presumably Thomas would have detected any such animal long before it was old enough for training. Many attempts had, as a matter of fact, been made to produce another Sirius, but without success. Sirius himself seemed to have been something of a fluke. The effort to repeat his type had produced at best large-brained and highly intelligent animals that were too frail to reach maturity, and more often mental defectives of one sort or another. It seemed that, if the cerebral hemispheres were increased beyond a certain size, the discrepancy between them and the normal canine organization was too great for reliable viability. Even in man, whose brain and body had developed in step with one another for millions of years, the large cerebrum seems to put a strain on the system, and to be in fact something of a morbid growth, leading all too often to mental disorder. In the case of the dog, when it is suddenly given an enlarged brain, the stress is far more serious.

Not only Sirius but Elizabeth also had to be trained for work on the farm. Though normally she now spent more time in Cambridge than in the country, it was arranged that for some months she should live at Garth. She was now a middle-aged but sturdy woman, and during the last war she had been a land-girl. Pugh at first found it almost impossible to treat her otherwise than as a lady visitor, but the two of them gradually evolved a relationship which fitted his humour perfectly. She posed as the lazy and grumbling servant, he as the exacting master. He greatly enjoyed disparaging the results of all her labour, scolding her for idling, and threatening that he would report her to Sirius and have her sacked if she couldn't keep a civil tongue in her head. She, for her part, treated him with mock servility and affectionate insolence. It took Mrs. Pugh a long time to realize that the constant wrangling was all friendly. She was confirmed in her anxiety by the fact that Sirius, entering into the spirit of the game, sometimes acted the part of the faithful dog defending his beloved mistress against threatened attack. One day when Mrs. Pugh earnestly tried to curb her husband's tongue, Pugh shook a finger at her, winking at Elizabeth, and said, "Ah, but you don't know, my dear, how Mrs. Trelone and I behave together when you are not watching. Yes indeed, for all you know it is then we are the love-birds, isn't it, Mrs. Trelone?"

Both Sirius and Elizabeth were very busy during the Lent Term. Thomas contrived to spend several weeks in Wales to see how the venture was proceeding. On one occasion he brought two scientific friends to meet Sirius. On another, as Sirius was much interested in improving the local moorland pasture, dog and man went off for a couple of days to Aberystwyth to visit the Plant-Breeding Station. Sirius returned full of daring ideas to put before the sympathetic but cautious Pugh.

In a way this was probably the happiest time of Sirius's life, for at last he felt that he was using his super-canine powers adequately, and he had attained a degree of independence that he had never known before. The work was often worrying, since he was in many respects a novice, and he made many mistakes; but it was varied, concrete, and (as he put it) spiritually sound. There was little time to think deep thoughts, and less to write; but now that he was doing responsible work he did not feel the same urge for intellectual activity. And anyhow he promised himself that later, when he was more at home with the work, he would take up once more the threads of his former literary and musical activities.

His only recreation was music. In the evenings, with Elizabeth yawning in an easy chair after the day of fresh air and exercise, he would listen to broadcast concerts, or try records on the radio-gram. Sometimes, when he was out on the moors with his young pupils, he would sing his own songs, some of which, the less humanized ones, had a strong emotional appeal for the super-sheep-dogs.

Then there was the bright young bitch, Mifanwy. She was an attractive creature, mainly collie but with a dash of setter. She was slim as a leopard, and had a luxurious silken coat. Sirius had intended to refrain from all sexual relations with his underlings. Moreover he regarded Mifanwy as Idwal's preserve. But Idwal was growing old. Merely a super-sheep-dog, he was bound to sink far more rapidly into senescence than

Sirius, who was still in early maturity. When Mifanwy was in heat she refused her former lover and did her best to seduce Sirius. For a while he took no notice, but one day he indulged in dalliance with this sweet sub-human though super-canine charmer. Of course there was protest from Idwal; but the heavier and biologically far younger dog could, if necessary, easily have shown his senior that protest was futile. In fact, however, Idwal was so overawed by, and faithful to, his canine master, that his protest never developed beyond a conflict-expressing whimper and an occasional rebellious growl.

In due season Mifanwy had a litter of five puppies. Their heads, of course, were of normal size, but most of them bore on their foreheads the large fawn patches which distinguished Sirius, and his mother before him. In a few weeks the Alsatian strain in them was obvious to all the world. It was obvious too that if Sirius was not their father he must at least be their grandfather. He was the original source of the Alsatian characters which were now fairly common among the dogs of the neighbourhood. There had been a time when the local farmers had perversely hoped (without official encouragement) that in allowing the man-dog to have intercourse with their bitches they would acquire super-canine puppies. Inevitably this hope was disappointed, though a dash of Alsatian had proved a useful stiffening to the local sheep-dog strain. Even when both parents were super-canine, the offspring were of course normal. As for Sirius, he took no interest in his numerous moron progeny. His three sons and two daughters by Mifanwy were treated as mere chattels. One of each sex was promptly drowned. The other three were allowed to remain with their mother considerably longer than was usual, in fact until her super-canine but sub-human maternal feelings had waned sufficiently to make it possible to deprive her of her offspring without causing her distress. Sirius then sold his two remaining sons and his daughter.

Meanwhile super-canine puppies continued to arrive from Cambridge for Sirius to train. Mostly they were turned into super-sheep-dogs, but owing to the war a new profession seemed to open up for Thomas's bright animals.

The need for war economy was seriously interfering with the work of the Laboratory. Thomas foresaw the time when the whole organization would have to close down or turn over to some kind of war research. It was at this time, in the spring of 1940, that the war changed from its "phony" to its violent phase. The collapse of Holland, Belgium and finally France made the British feel that they really had to fight for their lives. Thomas had always regarded the war as a gigantic irrelevance. It was beneath the notice of minds that were given wholly to the advancement of science. But at last he was forced to recognize that this gigantic irrelevance must not be ignored or it would destroy the very possibility of science. He began to puzzle over two problems. How far, if at all, could his present work be made useful for winning the war? If it was quite useless, what kind of war-work could the Laboratory undertake? He saw that his super-sheep-dogs, if they could be produced in large enough numbers, might have an important function in war. The Government was already training normal dogs for running messages in the battle area, and clearly the super-sheep-dog mentality would be far more useful. He therefore set about the task of discovering a simplified technique for the mass-production of these animals. He also told Sirius to give some of his brightest pupils special training in running messages.

The time came when Thomas was ready to display three of his animals to the brass-hats, and after much importuning he secured an interview with a high military authority. The performance of the animals was brilliant. Thomas was assured that the War Office would undoubtedly make use of his super-canine messengers. He then waited impatiently for many weeks, wrote many respectful letters, and was repeatedly assured that the necessary machinery was now in action for adopting his suggestion. But somehow nothing happened. Every official whom he interviewed was at least sympathetic, and often eager to take any amount of trouble to help the great scientist. Yet nothing resulted. The vast and venerable institution remained unresponsive. Meanwhile the whole energy of the Laboratory had been turned over to the mass-production of "missing-link" dogs for war. The more interesting but less useful task of producing creatures of the calibre of Sirius had been abandoned; and Thomas's dearest dream, the stimulation of a human foetus to super-normal brain growth, now faded into mere fantasy.

Sirius, no less than Thomas, now realized that the war had to be won, otherwise all that was best in the tyrant species would be destroyed. But he lived in the depth of the country, and he was wholly absorbed in his new work; which, moreover, seemed to him a piece of worthy national, or rather human, service. Consequently he did not realize the war emotionally as fully as Thomas. Moreover, though one side of his nature was wholly identified with this glorious human species, another side was secretly and irrationally gratified by the tyrant's plight. Intellectually he knew that his future depended on the future of Britain, but emotionally he was as detached from the struggle as, at a later stage, the threatened millions of India were to be emotionally aloof from the menace of Japan.

When Plaxy came home, she found the Caer Blai atmosphere rather unreal. Of course she could not help being impressed by Sirius's success. He really did seem to have come into his own, even from the point of view of war. But she was rather shocked at his aloofness from the agony of the human race, and perhaps also a little jealous of his new-found peace of mind. For she herself was painfully torn between revulsion from the whole crazy disgusting mess and the urge to play her part in the desperate crisis of her species. In Cambridge she always made a point of maintaining her accustomed detachment, for so many of her friends seemed to her obsessed by the war; but in Wales she found herself warning Sirius that he was living in a fool's paradise, and that at any moment all familiar and precious things might be swept away in a tide of German invasion. She herself, she said, was feeling uncomfortable about her own work, a teaching post which she was to take up at the end of the summer. Perhaps she ought to do something more directly useful.

Sirius was impressed by all this talk, but emotionally he remained as unenthusiastic as ever. Perhaps he ought to go and be an Army messenger dog. (Anyhow he was training messenger dogs.) But to hell with the whole war! He had found his job, for the present, producing wool and food for the dominant species; which was probably destroying itself, anyhow. And good riddance, too! Good riddance? No, he didn't really mean that. But damn it, anyhow it wasn't his fault, and man was not his responsibility.

At this time Plaxy had become very much concerned with politics. For a short spell she had been a member of the Communist Party, but she had resigned, "because, though they are energetic and devoted, they're also intolerably cocksure and unfair." Nevertheless she remained very much under the influence of Marxism, though she was hard put to it to find room in Marxism for her faith in "the spirit," which was playing an ever deeper part in her life. "The spirit," she said, "must be the highest of all dialectical levels, the supreme synthesis." While she was at home she talked much to Sirius about "equality of opportunity," "the class war," "the dictatorship of the proletariat," and so on. And she insisted that if Communism was not, after all, the whole truth, then nothing short of a great *new* idea, based on Communism, could win the war and found a tolerable social order. Sirius had always been sympathetic with the desire for revolutionary social change. His spell in the East End had shown him how necessary it was. He had heartily agreed with the plea for common ownership of the means of production, and for creative social planning. But now that he had property to look after he found himself, much to his own surprise, looking at the whole matter from a different angle. "That's all quite true," he would say, "but I'm a bit anxious about your new order. Are you going to merge all the farms into great collective farms? It all smells a bit dangerous. It's too theoretical. And what about eccentric creative enterprises like Thomas's? And what on earth would become of oddities like me, if I ever existed at all? The point is, *who* is to do the social planning? It's all very well to say the people will do it, but God save us from the people. Anyhow they can't *really* do it at all. Some minority will do it, either mere demagogues or bosses. Somehow we have to get the *wide-awake* people to do it. It's always the wide-awake people who do everything worth while, really. The rest are just sheep." "But surely," said Plaxy, "it's *ordinary* people that all the planning is *for;* and so its the ordinary people that must settle the aims of all the planning, and control it. The wide-

awakes are servants of the community. The sheep-dogs serve the sheep."
"Rot," said Sirius, "sheer tripe! The dogs serve a master, who *uses* the
sheep, and the dogs." Plaxy protested, "But the people, if they are a free
people, have no master but themselves. The people as a whole are the
master." "No, no!" cried Sirius. "You might as well say the sheep as a
whole are the master. I, at any rate, acknowledge only one master, not
forty-five million two-legged sheep, or two thousand million, but simply
and absolutely the spirit." The answer came promptly, "But who is to say
what the spirit demands? Who is to interpret the spirit?" "Why, the spirit
itself, of course," he replied, "working in the minds of its servants, its
sheep-dogs, the wide-awake people." "But, Sirius, dear, dangerous, ridiculous darling, that's the way straight to Fascism. There's a leader who
knows, and the rest do what they're told. And there's a Party of faithful
sheep-dogs who make them do it." Sirius protested, "But a Fascist Party
is *not* made up of wide-awake people. Its members don't really know at all
what the spirit is. They don't know the smell of it. They can't hear its
voice. All they can ever be, even at their best is just sheep-dogs run amok,
wild sheep-dogs, wolves under a wolf leader." "But, Sirius, my own, don't
you see, that's just what they would say about *us*. Who is to judge between
us?" He had his answer ready. "Who judged between Christ and the High
Priest? Not the people. They said 'Crucify him.' The real judge was Christ's
master, the spirit, speaking in Christ's own mind; *and* in the High Priest's,
if only he would listen. The point is, if you serve the spirit you can't serve
any other master. But what the spirit demands always is love and intelligence and strong creative action in its service, love of the sheep as individuals to be made the most of, not *merely* as mutton or as coral insects in a
lovely coral pattern, but as individual vessels of the spirit. *That* spirit—
love, intelligence and creating—is precisely what 'the spirit' is." Plaxy's
reply was merely ribald. "The Reverend Sirius preached one of his most
profound and helpful sermons."

They were sitting together on the lawn at Garth, and he playfully
attacked her, pushing her over and making for her throat. Accustomed
from childhood to such battles, she gripped his ears and tugged hard. Before
his teeth had softly seized her, or his tongue had begun its tickling caresses,
he squealed for mercy. They smiled into each other's eyes. "Sadistic little
bitch!" he said. "Sweet cruel bitch!" With one hand she seized his lower
jaw and pressed it backwards and downwards into his neck. The sierras
of ivory closed gently on the back of her hand. Dog and girl struggled
playfully for a while, till she let go, exhausted. Wiping her hand on his
coat, she protested, "Slobbery old thing!" They lay quietly on the grass.

Suddenly Plaxy said, "I expect you have great fun with Mifanwy,
don't you?" He heard a faint tension in her voice. There was a pause before
he answered, "She's lovely. And though she's so deadly stupid, she really
has the rudiments of a soul." Plaxy pulled a piece of grass and chewed it,

looking at the distant Rhinogs. "*I* have a lover, too," she said. "He wants me to marry him, but that would be so binding. He has just joined the R.A.F. He wants me to have babies, lots of them, as quickly as possible. But it's too soon. I'm much too young to pledge myself for ever to anyone." There was a long pause. Then Sirius asked, "Does he know about me?" "No." "Will he make any difference to—us?" Promptly she answered, "*I* don't *feel* any different. But perhaps I don't really care enough about him. I love him terribly as a human animal, just as you love Mifanwy, I suppose, as a canine animal. And I love him very much as a friend too. But I don't know whether that's enough for marriage. And it must be marriage, for the children's sake, because they need a permanent father. They ought to grow up in the community of their parents." Another long pause came between them. She threw him a quick sidelong glance. He was staring at her, his head very slightly tilted to one side, his brows puckered, like any puzzled terrier. "Well," he said at last, "marry him, and have your litter, if you must. And of course you must. But all this is much more serious than bitches. Oh, Plaxy, fundamentally it's you and I that are married, for ever. Will he spoil that? Will he put up with it?" She pulled nervously at the turf, and said, "I know, I know we're somehow married in the spirit. But if that makes me ever unable to love a man whole-heartedly enough to want to be his wife and have babies with him, oh, I'll *hate* the hold you have on me." Before he could reply she looked squarely at him and continued, "I didn't mean that. I *can't* hate the hold you have on me. But—oh, God, what a mess!" Tears were in her eyes. He stretched forward to touch her hand, but thought better of it. Then he said, "If I am spoiling your life, it would have been better if Thomas had never made me." She put a hand on his shoulder, and said, "If you had never been you, then I should never have been I, and there would have been no difficult, lovely 'us.' And even if I do hate you sometimes, I love you much more, always. Even while I am hating you, I know (and the best of me knows gladly) that I am not just Plaxy but the human part of Sirius-Plaxy." He answered quickly, "But to be that properly you must be as much Plaxy as possible, and so you must somehow live your human life fully. Oh, yes, I understand. Being human, and a girl, and in England, and middle class, you can't *merely* have lovers and an illegitimate litter. You must have a husband." To himself he added, "And I perhaps, must sometimes kill your kind." But the memory of Thwaites murdered suddenly came upon him, and revolted him with its contrast to the present happy situation. It was as though, running on the moor in bright weather, he had suddenly been swallowed by a bog. And somehow it seemed that only Plaxy could pull him out. On a sudden impulse he told her the whole story.

CHAPTER XIII

THE EFFECTS OF WAR

BY the autumn of 1940 Sirius was well established at Caer Blai, was planning great improvements for the pasture, the breed and the arable land, and was known in the neighbourhood as "Pugh's man-dog." Precisely what his mental stature was, no one could decide. Pugh, by telling the whole truth about him, had put them off the scent. It was known that the man-dog had a marvellous facility with sheep, and was managing them on the latest scientific principles. But all this was vaguely thought to be less a matter of intelligence than of a sort of super-instinct mysteriously implanted in him by science. It was known too that he could understand a good deal of speech, and was actually able to use words himself to those who had the key to his queer pronunciation. He was learning a bit of Welsh; and the fact that his Welsh was so rudimentary, and that this was the language which alone was familiar in the district, disguised from everyone his true linguistic gifts and his fully human mentality.

Even so, had it not been war-time, the newspapers would certainly have publicized him, and with far more success than befell the stunt of the talking mongoose at an earlier date.

Sirius made himself thoroughly popular with most of the surrounding farmers and villagers, but there were a few who stubbornly regarded him with suspicion. Devout chapel-goers affirmed that the man-dog's real master was not Pugh but Satan, and that Pugh had sold his soul to the Devil to help him out of the labour-shortage. Some of the sexually obsessed, aware of the great affection that held between the man-dog and the scientist's younger daughter, whispered that it was Thomas, in the first instance, who had sold his soul, in order to gain scientific fame, and that Satan, incarnate in the dog, habitually gratified himself in perverse sexual intercourse with Thomas's daughter. And she, they said, for all her charm, was little better than a witch. Anyone could see that there was something queer and inhuman about her. Rumours of a different type were spread by the cruder sort of patriots. They declared that Thomas was in the pay of the Nazis, who had found in his man-dog the ideal kind of spy. It was no accident that the animal was established in the neighbourhood of a big artillery camp.

Most people were too sensible to take these rumours seriously. Pugh was popular, and so was Sirius; for he was certainly a genius with sheep, and he lent distinction to the district. Thomas, though an Englishman, had won a place in local esteem; and his daughter, in spite of her new-fangled ways, was an attractive girl. Not till the pressure of war had been much prolonged, driving simple folk to look for scape-goats, was public opinion to become hostile.

When the great air attacks on London began, Elizabeth received a long letter from Geoffrey describing conditions in his parish, and urging her to take in some of his refugee children, and plant out others in suitable homes in her district. Geoffrey was one of those who believed in personal responsibility. He suspected all Government organization; consequently he was anxious to avoid as far as possible merely handing over his charges to the official evacuation authorities.

Geoffrey's account of the devastation, heroism, muddle, callousness, and human kindness in the great blitzes had a deep effect on Sirius. He remembered vividly the smell of Geoffrey's home, and of the bare little church and all the stuffy houses that he had visited. And these olfactory images called up in his mind a rich picture of human beings struggling against a hostile environment and their own inadequacy. He remembered many of the people whom Geoffrey reported as casualties, and many of the children for whom hospitality was required. He had a generous impulse to rush off to London at once with his panniers filled with first-aid equipment. But it was a foolish impulse. He would only be in the way. Besides, it was one thing to enjoy a generous impulse and quite another to put it in action. He suspected that he would be a thorough coward in an air raid; and anyhow, fundamentally he felt aloof from the whole war. If the human race was fool enough to torture itself in this crazy manner, what had *he* to do with it? Nevertheless he could not help being deeply moved by Geoffrey's story, and by affection for Geoffrey himself. The plight of London became even more vivid to him and to the local population when, by one of those flukes which seem common in war, a single bomb, dropped at random by a stray raider, fell neatly on a lonely cottage in the neighbourhood, killing or wounding all its occupants.

Elizabeth undertook to take three London children into her house, and Mrs. Pugh, with much misgiving, agreed to accommodate two more. Sirius gave up his room at Caer Blai. Most of the local wives had already either taken on evacuees from blitzed towns in the north-west, or had refused to do so; but Elizabeth, after paying many calls, was able to tell Geoffrey that she had accommodation for fifteen more children and two mothers. It so happened that the neighbourhood had been rather lucky so far with its little immigrants. Though there had been a good deal of grumbling on the part of some hostesses, on the whole the scheme had worked. But the twenty little Londoners were a different kettle of fish. They were smelly, lousy, unruly little brats, and it was said in the district that no decent housewife would have had them across her doorstep if she had known what they were like. They made horrid messes in the house, broke the furniture, ruined the garden, lied, stole, bit one another and their hostesses, tormented the cat, and used dreadful language.

Some of the hostesses had the wit to realize that these children were simply the product of circumstances. It was shocking, they said, that society should allow its more unfortunate members to grow up in such degradation. The less imaginative housewives, however, indulged in orgies of self-righteous indignation against the children themselves and their parents. Some took the line that the immigrants were English, and that was what the English were like. As for Elizabeth, her popularity suffered somewhat. She alone was responsible for this recent affliction. It was remembered in some quarters not only that she was English, but that her husband had sold his soul to the Devil. Matters were made worse by the fact that her own evacuees turned out quite well. She was one of those who had a natural gift for treating children as human persons and expecting to be treated decently in return. There were troubles enough at first. But in a few weeks the little girl and her two small brothers were proudly helping with the house and the garden.

One day Elizabeth had news from Geoffrey that his church had been destroyed, but that he was continuing to devote his whole time to the care of his parishioners. He was elated that after long agitation he and others had secured great improvements in the public shelters in the district. A few days later she received a letter in an unknown hand saying that her cousin had been killed.

The news of Geoffrey's death seemed to bring the war strangely near to Sirius. For the first time someone whom he knew and loved had vanished. This somehow put the whole thing into a new perspective. It should not have done so. He thought he had imagined the personal impact of war pretty well, but evidently he had not. Geoffrey had simply ceased to be, like a match flame when it is blown out. So simple, and yet somehow so incredible! For in a queer way Geoffrey now seemed more real than before, and nearer to him. For days he caught himself quietly talking to Geoffrey and getting perfectly good answers from him in his own mind. Queer! Just a trick of imagination, no doubt. But somehow he couldn't really in his heart believe that Geoffrey had simply been snuffed out. Or rather, part of him believed it confidently and another part just couldn't. He had a fantastic dream. Geoffrey sought out Thwaites in Hell, and found him with Sirius's soul in his pocket. Somehow Geoffrey brought Thwaites up to Heaven, and his reward was the freeing of Sirius.

The war was soon to come even nearer to Sirius. In May Thomas took him by car to visit a farm near Shap, where several super-sheep-dogs were being successfully used to do practically the whole routine work on the sheep. The route back to North Wales passed through Liverpool. There had been a good deal of raiding on Merseyside from time to time, and Thomas judged it wise to be well across the river before dark. Unfortunately they were late in starting, and did not arrive in Liverpool till dusk. Somewhere in the outskirts of the town they developed engine trouble, and by the time an overworked garage hand had put matters right it was dark. They set out once more, but were much delayed by the condition of the town. There had been a bad raid on the previous night, and the streets had not yet been properly cleared. The result was that, before they could reach the entrance of the famous tunnel under the Mersey, a raid began. It was not far to the tunnel, so Thomas decided to hurry on. Sirius was terrified. Probably the noise was even more trying to his sensitive ears than to the duller human organ. Anyhow he had always been a coward, save in the wolf-mood. The moaning of planes, the prodigious smack and racket of anti-aircraft guns, the tearing rush of bombs (like a raucous and vastly amplified whisper, he thought), followed by such a crash as he had not believed possible, and then the clatter of falling masonry, the roaring and crackling of fires, the scurrying of human feet, the screams of casualties demanding help as the car passed a wrecked shelter, all this had a shattering effect on his morale. Sitting there in the back of the car he had nothing to do but be terrified. Then there were the smells, the stinging smells of gases from explosives, the dusty smell of shattered masonry, the pungent smell of burning woodwork, and occasionally the stench of mangled human bodies.

It seemed madness to go on any farther, so Thomas drew the car into the side of the road, and they dashed for the nearest shelter. The blast from a bomb pushed the side of a house across the street at them. Thomas was pinned under it; Sirius, though bruised and cut, was free. The lower part of Thomas's body was covered with masonry. With great difficulty and in great pain he gasped out, "Save yourself. By the tunnel. Down the street. Then to Wales. Save yourself, for my sake. Please go, please!" Sirius tried frantically to shift the debris with his paws and teeth, but could not. "I'll get help," he said. "No, save yourself," Thomas gasped. "I'm—done—anyhow. Good luck." But Sirius hurried off, and presently was tugging at a man's coat, and whimpering. It was obvious that he wanted help for someone, so a party came back with him. But when they reached the place where Thomas had been, they found only a fresh crater. The men returned to their former task, leaving Sirius blankly gazing. He sniffed about for a long while, whimpering miserably. Then his terror, which had been blotted out by action, welled up again. But his head was clear. He must find the tunnel entrance, which Thomas had said was quite near. He hurried along by the light of fires reflected from the clouds. At one point the road was completely blocked by fallen masonry, and he had to clamber over it. At last he reached the tunnel and managed to sneak in unobserved. He cantered along the footpath; and though a stream of cars was travelling towards Birkenhead, making a terrifying noise in the confined space of the tunnel, no one took much notice of him. At the Birkenhead entrance he made a dash for liberty, and found himself once more in the threatening racket of war and under the firelit sky. But the bombs were falling mostly on the Liverpool side of the Mersey.

Sirius gave me a very full account of his long trek from Birkenhead to Trawsfynydd, but there is no need to report it here in detail. Tired and mentally shattered, he made his way westward through the town and out across the Wirral towards Thurstastone Common. As he cantered through the night his mind kept reverting to the complete disappearance of Thomas, the being who had made him, whom he had at first adored with uncritical canine devotion, and more recently had strongly criticized, while always retaining a deep affection for him, and a deep respect for his powers. Intellectually he had little doubt that Thomas had simply ceased to exist; yet, as with Geoffrey's death, he could not really believe it. Lobbing along a stretch of road, he found himself arguing with Thomas on the subject. The dead man insisted that there was now nothing anywhere in the universe which could reasonably be called Thomas Trelone, no mind continuous with that mind's thoughts, desires, feelings. "Well, you ought to know," said Sirius; and then came to a sudden halt, wondering if he was going mad.

From Thurstastone he travelled along the shore of the Dee Estuary and over the salt marshes to Queensferry, then by road and field and moorland, always in a south-westerly direction. Often he wondered how much he was guided by the sub-human mammal's proverbial "homing faculty," how far by vague memory of Thomas's maps. The long stretches of road he found very tiring. The motor traffic was a constant worry, for the drivers gave him little consideration. He imagined the tyrant species as a composite creature made up of man and machine. How he hated its harsh voice and brutal ways! Yet only yesterday he himself, sitting in Thomas's open tourer, had exulted in the speed and the wind as they streamed across the Lancashire plain. His present plight made him realize more clearly than ever how contemptuous and heartless men were towards "dumb animals" that did not happen to be their own pets.

Whenever he passed through a populous area he was careful to attract as little attention as possible. He slowed down and strayed about the road, sniffing at lamp-posts, like any local dog. When anyone made inquisitive or friendly advances, which was fairly often, for he was a striking animal, he replied with a nonchalant tail-wag, but never stopped. After crossing the Clwydian Range and the wide Vale of Clwyd, he made his way up into ample moors, and went badly astray in mist; but at last he dropped down into lower country near Pentrevoelas, and soon he was heading for the high wild hills of Migneint. Toiling up a steep grassy spur he entered heavy cloud, and it began to rain. Tired as he was, and with a painful task awaiting him, he exulted in the cold wet wind, the scents of the bog and turf and sheep. Once he caught the unmistakable odour of

fox, that rare, intoxicating smell of the most illusive quarry. God! How
the qualities of sensation seemed to hint at exquisite hidden things, always
to be pursued, never found. Even sight could do it. The driving mist, the
half-seen rocks, appearing and vanishing, and all the little grass-plumes
jewelled with mist-drops, how they stabbed him with sweet familiarity
and with a never-comprehended lure! No doubt it was all electrons and
wave-trains and the tickling of nerve-endings, but oh how sweet and mysterious and frightening with uncomprehended truth! Somehow the beauty
of it all was intensified to the point of agony by the horrors that he had so
recently witnessed.

On and on he climbed, surprised at the height. Then suddenly the mist
cleared for a moment, and he found himself almost at the top of a considerable mountain, which he soon identified as Carnedd Filast. Long ago,
before he had taken to sheep, he used to hunt on these moors from Garth,
but it was not often that he came quite so far afield.

Now that he was once more on the high hills, a change of mood came
over him. Why should he go back to the tyrant species at all? Why give
himself the pain of telling Elizabeth that her husband would not return?
Why not live wild on the moor, free, spurning all mankind, feeding on
rabbits and perhaps an occasional sheep, till at last a man did him to death?
Why not? He had lived wild for a time after killing Thwaites, but that
had been spoilt by conscience. This time it would be different. It was clear
by now that life had little to offer him. True, he had found a niche of sorts,
but only by man's aid and tolerance. And it was a cramping niche. He
could not extend his powers thoroughly. Strangely, on this occasion, it was
the thought not of Thomas but of his sheep unshepherded that turned his
attention from these gloomy meditations.

The mist now closed down heavily on the mountains, and it was already twilight; but he had taken his bearings, and was able to grope his
way down towards a high boggy valley, and then up round a shoulder of
Arenig Fach. Soon he was on little Carnedd Iago, then stumbling down
in darkness towards the road, which he crossed near the head of Cwm
Prysor. Leaving the wild moorland valley on his left, he came into home
pastures. Now, even in darkness, every crag, every hummock, every pool,
almost every tussock of heather or grass was familiar, and redolent with
associations. Here he had found a dead sheep and half-born lamb. Here
he had sat with Thomas, eating sandwiches on one of those long walks
that would never be repeated. Here he had killed a hare. But though every
step was familiar, increasing darkness and the heavy mist greatly delayed
him. It was almost midnight when he reached Garth. I calculate that, since
leaving Thurstastone Common in the early morning, he must have covered
altogether, including all his lengthy aberrations from the direct route, well
over eighty miles. Much of the journey was on hard roads or through difficult, hedged agricultural country.

At the door of the darkened house he gave his special summoning bark. Elizabeth promptly let him into the blinding light and the familiar smells of home. Before he had said a word, she had closed the door, knelt down, and put her arms round him, saying "Thank God one of you is safe." "Only me," he said. She gave one small moan, and clung to him in silence. Held in a rather awkward position, tired out after the strain of the last few days, and oppressed by the indoor atmosphere, he suddenly went deadly faint, and wilted in her arms. She laid his head low on the floor and went to fetch some brandy. But in a moment he recovered, staggered on to his feet, dutifully but feebly wiped them on the door-mat, and walked unsteadily into the sitting-room. Then he realized that his under surface was covered with the wet black mud of the bog. When Elizabeth returned, he was standing with trembling legs and hanging head, wondering what to do. "Lie down, precious," she said. "The mess is nothing." Presently she had him lapping up sweet tea, and then eating bread and milk.

CHAPTER XIV

TAN-Y-VOEL

THOMAS'S death affected the female members of the Trelone family very deeply. The two boys were away at the war, but Tamsy and Plaxy both came home to spend a week or so with their mother. Sirius at a later date told me that Tamsy was superficially more distressed than Plaxy. She wept a good deal, and by her too demonstrative sympathy she increased rather than assuaged the emotional strain that inevitably fell upon Elizabeth. Plaxy, on the other hand, was strangely cold and awkward. With a pale face, and an almost sullen expression, she occupied herself mainly with housework, leaving her mother and sister to dwell upon the past. One day Tamsy unearthed from Thomas's chest of drawers a dilapidated handker-chief-case which Plaxy as a child had made and given to her father on his birthday. With swimming eyes Tamsy brought this relic to her sister, ob-viously expecting it to be a stimulus to sweet sorrow. Plaxy turned away, muttering, "Oh, for God's sake, don't!" Then, unaccountably, and with a look almost of fury, she rushed at Sirius and gave him so brusque a hug that he wondered whether it was meant as a caress or as the opening of a wrestling bout. I mention this incident because it suggests that Plaxy's re-lations with her father were in fact rather complex and emotional.

As for Sirius himself, his very real grief, he told me, was mingled with a new deep sense of independence. His canine nature lamented the loss of his master, and he was haunted by memories of Thomas's affectionate guidance; yet his human intelligence now breathed more freely. At last he was his own master, not literally perhaps, but emotionally. At last he would be master of his fate and captain of his soul. Sometimes the thought frightened him; for he had grown up in complete emotional dependence on Thomas's ultimate authority over him. Even when he stood out for his own will, he did so always in the hope of persuading Thomas to agree with him, never with any depth of intention to resist the will of his revered creator. And so, now that Thomas was gone, his creature was torn between anxious self-distrust and a strange new decisiveness.

But though Sirius was now emotionally freed from Thomas, he was destined to be for a while bound more closely than ever to his foster-mother.

Though Thomas's death was a heavy blow to Elizabeth, she would not let it crush her. She carried on with her normal life, looking after the three little evacuees, digging and planting in the garden, helping Sirius with the sheep; for Pugh had grown very rheumatic and found the outlying pastures almost inaccessible. Plaxy had offered to give up teaching and settle down at home, but Elizabeth would not hear of it. "The child must live her own life," she said.

Inevitably Elizabeth became more and more devoted to Sirius, who was the supreme achievement of Thomas's creative power, and also her own adopted child. Indeed Sirius now seemed more to her than her own children, who were independent, and in no further need of her help. But Sirius constantly needed her more than ever. Once when she found him struggling to repair a wire fence with his teeth, he had cried out, "Oh for hands! At night I dream of hands." She answered, "My hands belong to you till I die." Between the dog and the middle-aged woman a very close, affectionate, but not entirely happy relationship developed. Elizabeth had always maintained towards her children a friendly detachment towards which they had readily responded. Sirius also she had formerly treated in the same way. But now, her devotion to her husband combined with maternal hunger to fix her attention obsessively upon Sirius. Helping him became her constant passion. Now that Pugh was partially incapacitated, and skilled labour was so hard to obtain, her help was valuable. But Sirius came to find it rather tiresome. She was *too* anxious to help, and *too* full of suggestions, which he tended to reject if he could find any plausible excuse for doing so. It was strange and tragic, and entirely unexpected, that a woman formerly so quiet-hearted and so unpossessive should in middle age have become so clinging. I cannot account for the change. It is easy to point to influences in her life making for neurosis, but why should they have taken effect so late, and so extravagantly as they were destined to do? How frail a thing is the human spirit, even at its best!

Elizabeth showed an unwelcome inclination to take part in the actual management of the farm, and particularly all contacts with the outside world. Sirius strongly disliked this, not only because she had insufficient experience and sometimes made bad mistakes, but also because he was anxious to accustom the local population to dealing with him direct, and it was his ambition to play an active part in the common life of the district. Already he had earned respect. Not only the local papers but the great national dailies had referred to "the brilliant man-dog of North Wales." Only the paper shortage and the over-mastering interest of warfare had prevented them from using him for a stunt. Consequently he had been able to make himself known in the neighbourhood by personal contact without attracting too much attention from the rest of the country. Intellectuals of one sort or another did visit him now and then with introductions from the Laboratory; and these visits he greatly enjoyed, because they enabled him to keep in touch with movements of contemporary cultural life. He never gave up his intention of playing a part in that life as soon as the farm had been fully developed and regularized.

To return to Elizabeth. Perhaps out of loyalty to Thomas, who had always been extravagantly fearful of publicity, she did her utmost to keep Sirius from the public eye, and indeed from all social contacts. When at last she sent away her three little evacuee children in order to devote all her time to the farm, Sirius was torn between satisfaction at the prospect of having more help and fear of increased interference; and between affection and an exasperation which kindness forbade him to express. Why was it that one who had always been so tactful and detached in her relations had suddenly turned so difficult? He put it down to overwork and the emotional strain of losing her husband. No doubt advancing age had also something to do with it. Only when one or other of her own children was at home did she return almost to her normal self. Then Sirius would feel with relief that he was no longer the apple of her eye, and would be able to devote himself to his own affairs without having to consider her.

It was in the autumn of 1941 that Elizabeth fell ill. Her heart was tired, but Dr. Huw Williams told her that there was nothing seriously wrong with it. She had merely overstrained it, and must take things easy for a few weeks. Sirius saw the doctor to his car, and asked him whether he had told the truth or merely said what would comfort the patient. After Sirius had repeated the question several times, the doctor understood, and assured him that he had spoken the truth, and emphasized the need for a long rest. In a week Elizabeth refused to stay in bed any longer, and insisted on taking up light jobs on the farm. This led to another collapse, and the whole cycle was repeated several times in spite of Sirius's strong protest. It was obvious that Elizabeth would work herself to death. She seemed to be impelled by some obscure passion for self-expression through self-destruction in service of Sirius. The perplexed dog could not keep a constant watch over her unless he gave up his work entirely. In despair he wrote to Tamsy, but she had just had her second baby; she could find no one to look after her family and free her to nurse her mother. Sirius and Mrs. Pugh took turns with the invalid; but when at last Elizabeth was taken more seriously ill, and the doctor's optimism had given way to exasperation and despair, it was suggested to Elizabeth that she had better have a real rest in a nursing home. She rejected the idea with scorn. Very reluctantly Sirius now summoned Plaxy.

For several weeks Sirius and Plaxy and Mrs. Pugh kept a close watch on Elizabeth. The common task drew the girl and the dog closer to one another than they had ever been before. They were often together, but seldom alone together. This frequent compresence and infrequent intimacy generated in each a great longing for unrestrained talk, and an increasing sensibility towards each other's slightest changes of mood. Both, of course, were mainly and anxiously concerned with the patient. Some exasperation was inevitable, but was tempered and indeed almost wholly silenced by the strong affection which both had felt for her since their infancy. Both were put to strain by the necessity of sacrificing their own urgent activities, perhaps for a very long time. Each knew that the other was strained, and the two were drawn closer by that knowledge.

Under Plaxy's firm and loving treatment Elizabeth made good progress; but as her health improved she became increasingly restless. One day she insisted on dressing and going downstairs. It so happened that on the table there was an unopened newspaper. She picked it up and opened it. "BRITISH CRUISER SUNK," said the main headline. It was the ship on which Maurice was serving. Owing to the fact that the Germans were the first to announce the sinking, the Admiralty had been forced to break their rule and publish the information *before* the next of kin had been told of the casualties. The shock of the news, and the suspense that followed it, killed Elizabeth before word came through that her son was among the survivors.

Plaxy, though "scarcely human," though cat-like and fay, was human enough to have deep feelings for her mother, who had always shown special affection for her youngest child, and yet had built up with her an even freer, happier relationship than with the elder children; for she had learnt by her own past mistakes with them. Elizabeth's death therefore hit Plaxy hard. Sirius too was greatly distressed, on his own account, and still more on hers. For himself, he was again strangely perplexed by this business of death. The dead Elizabeth kept talking to him. And it was not the Elizabeth that had just died, the over-strained and difficult Elizabeth; it was Elizabeth as she was in her prime. Again and again, with variations, she made or seemed to make a very intelligent contribution to his thoughts. She said, "Don't puzzle your old head about it so! Minds like ours just aren't clever enough to understand, and whichever way you decide you're sure to be wrong. Don't *believe* I still exist, for that would be false to your intellect; but don't refuse the *feeling* of my presence in the universe, for that would be blind."

Shared grief and common responsibility tended to bring Plaxy and Sirius into an ever closer intimacy. They now sank exhausted into mutual dependence. And there was much work to do together. With the aid of the family solicitor and a representative of the Laboratory, they had to wind up the Trelone affairs. Obviously the house must be sold. But the decision to surrender the home in which they had been brought up together was momentous both to girl and dog, for it meant severing the remaining tangible link between them. They spent many hours of many days sorting out the contents of the house. All the furniture had to go, save the few pieces that Tamsy wanted for her own house, and the fewer that were to be given to Sirius, who must now be re-established at Caer Blai. Books, crockery, kitchen utensils, clothes, all the multifarious possessions of the dead parents, had to be sorted out. The property of the absent children must be separated from the rest, and packed up and dispatched. Plaxy's own and Sirius's own things must be collected and sorted. A great bonfire of sheer rubbish was made every morning, and carefully extinguished at night, because of the black-out. Photographs of the parents themselves, of *their* parents and relatives, of the four children and Sirius at all ages, of super-sheep-dogs, of holiday expeditions, of Sirius at work with sheep, all had to be looked at by dog and girl together, squatting on the floor of the dismantled sitting-room. All had to be talked over, laughed over, sighed over, and finally assigned either to the rubbish pile or to the collection of things too good to destroy.

When the labour was over, when the furniture was all gone, when there was nothing in the house but a few packing cases not yet dispatched and the few crocks and scraps which the two had been using for their meals; when the floors were bare board and the house was the mere shell of a home, Plaxy prepared a final meal for the two of them. It was lunch. She was to leave by train early in the afternoon, and he was to begin at once to catch up with arrears of work at the farm. They sat together on the floor of the empty sitting-room, and ate almost in silence. They had as a matter of course settled down in the spot by the fireplace where they had so often sat together during the past two decades. The old soft hearth-rug had gone. They sat on Plaxy's mackintosh, spread on the floor boards. She leaned against a packing case instead of the vanished couch. The solemn little picnic was soon finished. Sirius had licked out the last drop of his last bowl of tea. Plaxy had stubbed her cigarette-end in her saucer. Both sat silent.

Suddenly Plaxy said, "I have been thinking hard," And he, "So it seems, oh wise woman." "I've been thinking about us," she continued. "Mother was useful on the farm, wasn't she?" He agreed, and wondered how they would manage without her. "The new land girl," he added, "is not a patch on the last. She tries to keep her hands soft." "Suppose," said Plaxy, looking hard at her toe, "well—would you like it if I stayed to help you?" Sirius was licking a cut on his paw. He stopped to say, "Wouldn't I just! But that's impossible." He went on licking. "Well," said Plaxy, "why *shouldn't* I, if I want to? And I have decided that I do want to, very much. I *don't* want to go, I want to stay, if you'll let me." He stopped licking, and looked up at her. "You *can't* stay. It's all arranged. And you don't *really* want to stay. But it's nice of you to think you do." "But, Sirius, sweet, I do really want to, not for always, but for the present. I have thought it all out, right here. We'll rent Tan-y-Voel." This was the labourer's cottage on Pugh's land, where later I was to discover them. "It'll be fine," she cried brightly; then with sudden shyness, for he was gazing at her sadly, she added, "Or *wouldn't* you like it?" He reached out and nuzzled into her neck. "You needn't ask," he said, "but you have a life of your own to lead. You can't give it all up for a dog." "But," she answered, "I am sick of teaching, or rather trying to. I suppose I'm not really interested enough in the little brats. Perhaps I'm too interested in *me*. Anyhow, I want to live." "Then what about Robert," he said, "and being a mother, and all that?" She looked away and was silent for a while, then sighed. "He's a dear. But—oh, I don't know. Anyhow, we have agreed that I must be myself, and being myself just now means staying with you."

In the end she had her way. They went straight off to tell the Pughs of the change, and announce that they intended to seize the empty cottage at once. Pugh was of course overjoyed, and with innocent mirth he remarked, "I congratulate you, Mr. Sirius, on your bride." Plaxy coloured, and did not respond well to this sally; so that Pugh had to smooth matters over by saying, "Just an old farmer's joke, Miss Plaxy. No offence, indeed." Mrs. Pugh scolded him, "For shame, Llewelyn! You are a horrid old man, and you have a nasty mind like a bubbling black bog." They all laughed.

Before the lorry came to transport the last load from Garth, Plaxy had opened one of the cases and taken out some bedding, towels and so on. She dumped the remaining crocks and pans into the one empty case. Together they made a list of essential furniture which must be fetched back from the store and sent to Tan-y-Voel. When the furniture removers returned, they were mildly annoyed at the change and the confusion, but Plaxy used all her charm, and they duly delivered the goods at the cottage.

Even a two-roomed cottage takes some settling into, and Plaxy spent most of the following day arranging their new life. She brushed out the two rooms, scrubbed the stone floors, cleaned the grate, improvised blackout curtains for the little windows, and bought such stores as were possible in war-time. In the evening Sirius returned from his work to find a smiling home and a smiling though rather exhausted Plaxy. The table was laid for her supper, and on the carpet beside her chair was Sirius's customary "table-cloth" and bowl. Sirius had two distinct styles of feeding. In the wild he fed wild, on rabbits and hares and so on; in the house he was given porridge, soup, bread-and-milk, bones, crusts of bread, cake and a good deal of tea. At one time it had been very difficult to buy enough to feed him adequately, because of the rationing system; but Thomas had pulled wires and secured a special ration for him as a valuable experimental animal.

After the meal, when Plaxy had washed up, they sat together on the couch that had been rescued from the old home. They had been gay, but now a sadness settled on them. Sirius said, "This is not real. It is a very lovely dream. Presently I shall wake up." And she, "Perhaps it will not last long, but it is real while it lasts. And there is a rightness in it. It had to be, to make us one in spirit for ever, whatever else may come. We shall be happy, never fear." He kissed her cheek.

They were both tired after the day's work, and very soon they were yawning. Plaxy lit a candle and put out the lamp. In the next room her familiar bed was awaiting her, and on the floor was Sirius's old sleeping basket, a vast pan of wicker containing a circular mattress. Strange! They had been brought up together, child and puppy, sharing the same room; and even when they were grown up she had been thoroughly used to undressing before him without any self-consciousness; yet now, unexpectedly, she was shy.

At this point I cannot resist pausing to ask the reader a question. Does not Plaxy's momentous decision to give up her career and live with Sirius need some explanation? Here was a young woman of outstanding charm, with many admirers, and one of them her accepted lover. She had taken up a teaching post which she filled with distinction, and in which she was finding a good opening for self-expression. Suddenly she gave up her work and practically broke off relations with her lover in order to join her life with the strange being who was her father's most brilliant creation. Does it not seem probable that the underlying motive of this decision was the identification of Sirius with her father? Plaxy herself, now my wife, scorns this explanation, holding that it does not do justice to the power of Sirius's own personality over her. Well, there is my theory, for what it is worth.

On the morning after the occupation of Tan-y-Voel, Plaxy began her apprenticeship on the farm. She cleaned out a pigsty, harnessed the horse, loaded muck into the cart and unloaded it on the manure heap. She also helped Sirius to attend to a sick sheep on the moor. Towards the end of the day she put in some hard work on the wilderness that was meant to be the cottage garden. In such style, with variations, the days passed. Her face took on the healthy glow that delighted me when in due season I discovered her. With mingled distress and pride she watched her hands go blistered, grime-ingrained, scratched, cut and hard. Mrs. Pugh taught her to milk. Pugh himself taught her to broadcast a field with oats, while the instrument which she insisted on calling the "sowing machine" was out of order. Always there were countless nameless jobs to do about the farm. Her main function, she said, was to save Sirius's teeth, which were beginning to wear down with too much gripping of wood and iron. So far as possible he confined his attention to the sheep and the super-sheep-dogs, but there was no end to the number of small unexpected tasks which really called for hands but could most easily be disposed of at once by his own clumsy jaws. On the farm premises he was always, in spite of his painfully acquired skill with those unsuitable instruments, too pitifully handless. But on the moors he was in his element. Plaxy greatly enjoyed the expeditions into the hills with Sirius and his canine pupils. Bounding through the bracken, he was a storm-tossed but seaworthy boat. Trotting around, giving orders to his pupils, he was a general and his charger all in one. When a sheep broke away and had to be retrieved, he would streak after it, belly to earth, like a torpedo.

In this new life there was almost no leisure, no time for reading, music, writing. Contact with the world beyond the hills was at a minimum. Expeditions to sheep sales were rare excitements. On these occasions both Sirius and Plaxy would accompany Pugh, she as Pugh's unofficial land-girl. The bustle, the babble of Welsh voices, the clamour of sheep, the variety of human and canine types, the social atmosphere of the pubs, and of course the young men's unconcealed admiration of this bright and humorously self-important, this forthcoming but rather queer land-girl (not in uniform)—all this Plaxy vastly enjoyed as a change from the seclusion of the farm.

Apart from these infrequent excursions, social intercourse was to be had only on expeditions to the village, and on visits to neighbouring farms to borrow or lend tools, or simply for friendly intercourse. Often Plaxy would tidy herself up and revert as far as possible to the gay young lady; and it was with deep peace of mind that she walked through the fields with the great sinewy beast at her side. With a careless, queenly self-confidence she accepted the inevitable admiration of the young farmers and shepherds, and sensed their puzzlement over her indefinable oddity.

After she had been with Sirius for several months, however, something happened which spoiled these social occasions for her. She was made to realize that, though she was so popular with many of the local people, there were some who were outraged by her living alone with the man-dog. Increasingly it was made difficult for her to be unselfconscious with Sirius in public. And her observed shyness with him fomented the salacious rumours.

The trouble began with a visit from a local nonconformist minister. This earnest young man took it upon himself to save Plaxy from damnation. He was simple enough to be impressed by the notion that Sirius was inspired by Satan, and he listened to the rumours of perverse relations between the dog and the girl. As the cottage lay within his sphere of responsibility, he felt it his duty to intervene. He timed his visit well. Plaxy had returned from the farm to prepare supper, and Sirius was still at work. Plaxy foresaw a late meal, but she treated the Reverend Mr. Owen Lloyd-

Thomas with friendly ease. Indeed she made a point of being sweet to him, knowing that his good opinion counted. After beating about the bush for some time, he suddenly said, "Miss Trelone, it is my difficult duty as a minister of the Lord to speak to you on a very delicate matter. It is believed by simple people in the neighbourhood that your dog, or Mr. Pugh's dog, is not merely an extraordinary animal but a spirit clothed in a dog's flesh. And simple people, you know, sometimes go nearer to the truth than clever people. In spite of all the wonders of science, it may really be *less false* to say that the dog is possessed by a spirit than that it is just the work of man's scientific skill. And if it is indeed possessed, then perhaps the spirit in the dog is of God, but perhaps it is of Satan. By their fruits ye shall know them." He fell silent, cast a self-conscious glance at Plaxy, and fell to twisting the brim of his soft black hat. At last he continued, "It is felt by the neighbours, Miss Trelone, that for you to live alone with the animal is unseemly. It is believed that Satan has already snared you through the man-dog into sin. I do not know what the truth is. But I believe you are in danger. And as a minister I offer you advice. Change your way of living, even if only because it is an offence to the neighbours."

According to the reverend young man's reading of womanly nature, Plaxy should have blushed, either with innocent modesty or with guilty shame. If indeed she was guilty, then she might be expected either to confess with tears of penitence or to deny with self-righteous and unconvincing indignation. Her actual behaviour disconcerted him. For some time she just sat looking at him; then she rose and silently moved off into the minute larder. She came back with some potatoes, and sat down to peel them, saying, "Excuse me, won't you, I must get the supper ready. We can talk while I do this. You see, I love Sirius. And to leave him alone now would be unkind. And it would hurt our love, because it would be a running away. Mr. Lloyd-Thomas, your religion is love. You must surely see that I can't leave him."

At that moment Sirius appeared in the doorway. He stood with his nostrils moving, to catch the smell of the visitor. Plaxy stretched out her arm to welcome him to her, and said. "Mr. Lloyd-Thomas thinks we ought not to live together, because you may be Satan dressed up as a dog, and perhaps you have taught me to live in sin." She laughed. This was not a very tactful beginning, but tact had never been Plaxy's strong suit. It is possible that if she had not made this remark their whole future would have been different. Lloyd-Thomas flushed, and said, "It is not good to jest about sin. I do not know whether you have done this thing, but I know now that your spirit is frivolous." Sirius moved over to her, and she laid a hand on his back. He was still analysing the visitor's smell. She felt the hair on his back rise against her hand. A very faint growl made her fear lest he should go wild. He advanced half a pace towards the cleric, but she clasped him round the neck with both arms. "Sirius!" she cried, "don't be silly!" Lloyd-Thomas rose with careful dignity, saying, "This is not a good time for us to talk. Think over what I have said." In the garden he turned, and saw through the open door Plaxy still holding Sirius. Girl and dog were staring at him. She bowed her head to the dog's head, and laid her cheek to it.

When he had gone, Sirius said to Plaxy, "He smells as if he were in love with you. He smells a decent sort, really; but probaby he would sooner see you dead than living in sin with me; just as McBane, I suspect, would rather see me dead than fail to squeeze every drop of information out of my body and mind. Morality and truth! The two most relentless divinities! I'm afraid we're for it with Lloyd-Thomas sooner or later."

Lloyd-Thomas's sermons began to have obvious references to Plaxy and Sirius. He prayed for those who had been snared into unnatural vice. Some of his congregation were very receptive to the new minatory trend of his services. Little by little, among those who had no personal contact with Plaxy, there grew up a considerable movement of censure and indignation; and also anxiety, for would not the Lord punish the whole neighbourhood for harbouring the wicked couple? Fresh rumours seemed to sprout every day. Someone claimed that he had seen Plaxy swimming naked in a lonely llyn with the man-dog. This harmless story developed into unpublishable accounts of dalliance on the turf while they were basking in the sun before the bathe. A boy also reported that one Sunday he had peered through the hedge at Tan-y-Voel and seen Plaxy lying naked on the grass ("black as a nigger, she was, with the sun"), while the dog licked her from head to foot. The patriots and spy-hunters were also roused. It was affirmed that Sirius's panniers contained a radio-set with which he signalled to enemy planes.

Sirius's friends ridiculed these stories, or indignantly reprimanded those who spread them. Plaxy was still able to do her shopping in an atmosphere of friendly attentiveness. There were, however, a few unpleasant incidents. A village girl who worked for Mrs. Pugh on the farm was forbidden by her mother ever to enter Tan-y-Voel; and after a while she ceased to come to Caer Blai at all. Sometimes, when Plaxy entered a shop, conversation between shopkeeper and customers would suddenly cease. Some young hooligans, apparently in the hope of collecting evidence for scandal, haunted the spur of the moor overlooking the cottage. One evening, just before black-out time, a bold lad crept up to the window and peered into the lamp-lit room. Sirius with ferocious clamour chased him out of the garden and half-way to the main road.

These little incidents were of no great moment in themselves, but they were significant of a spreading movement of hostility. Plaxy began to be reluctant to go to the village. Both she and Sirius grew suspicious of callers. And between them there developed a rather tense emotional relationship, which alternated between reserve and tenderness.

Hitherto they had lived very happily. Their days were spent in hard work on the farm or away on the moors, often in co-operation upon the same task. Plaxy found a good deal to do in the cottage itself, cleaning and cooking, and there was always work in the little vegetable garden. The evenings they sometimes spent with the Pughs or at one or other of the neighbouring farms, where music often formed the medium of social intercourse. The musical Welsh were at first hostile to Sirius's own unconventional creations, but his singing of human music won their applause. And in a few houses the more sensitive were becoming interested in his distinctively canine modes. But under the influence of scandal these social occasions were reduced. Far more often Plaxy and Sirius spent their evenings at home upon household chores, or singing in private the strange duets and solos that Sirius still occasionally conceived. Sometimes they would spend their evening with books. Sirius still took a deep delight in listening to prose and poetry read aloud by a good human voice. Often he would persuade Plaxy to read to him. And not infrequently he would suggest subtle modifications of tone or emphasis; for though his own reading was inevitably grotesque, his sensitive ear had detected many emotional cadences and changes of timbre, which human beings were apt to overlook until their attention was drawn to them.

As Plaxy and Sirius became more aware of the hostility and suspicion round about them, their relationship began to change. It became more passionate and less happy. Isolation, combined with contempt for the critics, drew girl and dog into closer intimacy, in fact into a manner of life which some readers may more easily condemn than understand. Plaxy herself, in spite of her fundamental joy in her love for Sirius, was increasingly troubled by a fear that she might irrevocably be losing touch with her own species, even that in this strange symbiosis with an alien creature she might be losing her very humanity itself. Sometimes, so she tells me, she would look at her own face in the little square mirror over the dressing-table, and feel a bewildering sense that it was not *her* face at all, but the face of the tyrant species that she had outraged. Then she would find herself in the same breath hating her unalterably human physiognomy and yet being half surprised and wholly thankful that it had not suffered a canine change.

This fear of ceasing to be human occasionally induced in her a dumb antagonism towards Sirius, which sprang not from any real sense of sin or even of indecorousness, for she was convinced that her behaviour was a fitting symbol of their deep spiritual union. No, the source of her infrequent fits of gloom was simply her consciousness of alienation from the world of normal human beings. The call of her kind was still strong in her, and she was tormented by her outlawry. The solemn taboos of humanity still dominated her through her unconscious nature, though consciously she had long since declared her independence of them. Once she said to Sirius, "I must indeed have become a bitch in a girl's body, and so humanity has turned against me." "No, no!" he answered. "You are always fully human, but just because you are also more than merely human, and I am more than merely canine, just because we are both in essence intelligent and sensitive beings, we can rise far above our differences, to reach across the gulf that separates us, and be together in this exquisite union of opposites." Thus, in the rather naïvely formal diction that he was apt to use when he was speaking most earnestly, he tried to console her. In his mind there was no conflict over their intimacy. His love of her combined a dog's devotion with human parity in comradeship, and blended the wolf's over-mastering hunger with the respect of spirit for spirit.

At a later date both Plaxy and Sirius told me much about their life together at this time; but though after our marriage she urged me to publish all the facts for the light they throw on Sirius, consideration for her feelings and respect for the conventions of contemporary society force me to be reticent.

It was at such times that she would write those tortured letters to me, and by all sorts of devices contrived to have them posted far from home, lest I should track her down. For while she longed increasingly for human intimacy and human love, while she yearned to take up once more the threads of her life as a normal English girl, she clung with passion to the strange life and the strange love that fate had given her. It was clear from her letters that in the same breath she longed for me to take her away, and yet also dreaded the disruption of her life with Sirius.

CHAPTER XV

STRANGE TRIANGLE

I HAVE already told how I found Plaxy with Sirius at Tan-y-Voel, and how clear it was to me that any attempt to persuade her to leave him would have alienated her from me. It was not till some days after our first meeting, and after many talks with Plaxy, that I realized how intimate her relations with the dog had become. The discovery was a shock to me, but I took pains not to betray my revulsion; for Plaxy, finding me sympathetic, soon poured out in a flood of confession the whole story of her emotional relations with Sirius. When she had many times dwelt upon this theme I found myself putting aside the conventional feelings of the outraged lover. I could not but realize that the passion which united these two dissimilar creatures was deep and generous. But this made me all the more fearful lest I should never win my strange darling back again. And I was deeply convinced that for her own sake, no less than for mine, she must in the end be won back to human ways.

During the few remaining days of my leave I spent much time at Tan-y-Voel, sometimes with Plaxy alone, sometimes with the two of them. Sirius was busy all day, but Plaxy allowed herself a good deal of time off duty to be with me. We used to work together in the garden. Indoors I helped her to clean and cook, and so on. I also constructed a number of labour-saving gadgets for her. I have always been fairly apt with my hands, and I thoroughly enjoyed putting up shelves and curtain rods, and improving the arrangements for washing up. Sirius's sleeping-basket needed repairing, but it seemed better not to put this right until much later, when I had established friendly relations with him. While I was occupied with all these little manual tasks we would talk, sometimes seriously, sometimes with the old familiar banter. Sometimes I even ventured to tease her about her "canine husband"; but on one of these occasions (she was washing up and I was drying) she broke into tears. After that I was more tactful.

It was my fixed intention, of course, to wean Plaxy from her present life, though not to tear her from Sirius. I made no suggestion that she should come away with me. Indeed it was part of my plan to persuade her and Sirius that I fully accepted the continuance of their intimacy and of their present régime. My improvements in the house were calculated to strengthen this impression. They also accidentally served another purpose. They allowed me to take a rather mean advantage over Sirius, who could not himself help in this way. I could see that my handiness galled him; and, seeing it, I was ashamed of hurting him. Yet whenever an opportunity offered I failed to resist the temptation of triumphing over him and delighting my darling. After all, I told myself, all is fair in love and war. But I was ashamed; the more so because Sirius with inhuman generosity encouraged me to help Plaxy whenever possible. Perhaps it was in the long run a good thing that I indulged myself in this manner, for Sirius's magnanimity forced me to realize quickly how fine a spirit he was, and compelled me to treat him with warm respect, not merely for being loved by Plaxy, but for his own sake.

Relations with Sirius were at first very awkward, and I feared at one time that our presence in the same house would prove intolerable to both of us. He made no attempt to get rid of me. He treated me with friendly politeness. But I could see that he hated to leave Plaxy with me. Obviously he feared that she might at any moment vanish out of his life. One source of strain between us was that I had at first very great difficulty in understanding his speech. Though in the end I learned to follow his uncouth English fairly easily, during that first visit to Wales I was often entirely at a loss, even when he spoke word by word and with many repetitions. In these circumstances it was almost impossible for us to come to terms at all. However, before we parted I succeeded at least in dispelling the initial chill by showing him that I had no intention of acting as the jealous rival, and that I did not condemn Plaxy for her relations with him. I went so far as to assure him that I did not want to come between them. To this he replied with a little speech which I laboriously made out to be, "But you *do* want to come between us. I don't blame you. You want her to live with you, always. And obviously she *must* live with you, or some man. I cannot give her all that she needs. This life is only temporary for her. As soon as she wants to, she must go." There was dignity and sanity in this statement, and I felt rebuked for my lack of candour.

By judicious wangling I was able to secure an extension of leave, so that I could spend some ten days with Plaxy and Sirius, conscientiously returning to my hotel every night. Sirius suggested that I should sleep at the cottage, but I pointed out that if I did there would be an added scandal. It seemed strangely tantalizing to me, who had been, and in a manner still was, Plaxy's acknowledged lover, to kiss her good night at the garden gate while Sirius tactfully remained indoors. A revulsion little short of horror (which I was at pains to dissemble) would sometimes seize me at the thought of leaving her with the non-human being whom she strangely loved. On one of these occasions I must have somehow infected her with my own distress, for she suddenly clung to me with passion. A surge of joy and hunger swept over me, and I lost my presence of mind so far as to say, "Darling, come away with me. This life is all wrong for you." But she disengaged herself, "No, dear Robert, you don't understand. Humanly I do love you very much, but—how can I say it?—super-humanly, in the spirit, but therefore in the flesh also, I love my other dear, my strange darling. And for him there can never possibly be anyone but me." I protested, "But he can't give you what you really need. He said so, himself." "Of course not," she answered, "he can't give me what as a girl I need most. But I am not just a girl. I am different from all other girls. I am Plaxy. And Plaxy is half of Sirius-Plaxy, needing the other half. And the other half needs me." She paused, but before I had thought of an answer she said, "I must go. He may be thinking I shall never come back." She kissed me hastily and hurried to the cottage door.

The next day was Sunday, which the Welsh keep with dreadful strictness. No work could be done on the farm, beyond feeding the beasts, so Sirius was free. I went round to Tan-y-Voel after breakfast and found Plaxy working in the garden, alone and rather self-conscious. Sirius, she said, had gone off for the day, and would not be back till after sunset. I was surprised, and in answer to my questions she explained, "The wild mood is on him, he says. It takes him and then leaves him. He has gone over the Rhinogs by the Roman Steps to a farm near Dyffryn to his crazy-making Gwen, a beautiful super-sheep-dog bitch. She should be ripe for him just now." I showed signs of disgust and sympathy; but she promptly said, "I don't mind. I did mind once, before I understood. But now it seems quite natural and right. Besides——" I pressed her to continue, but she went on digging in silence. I forcibly stopped the digging. She looked me in the eyes, laughing, and said nothing. I kissed her warm sunned cheek.

There was human love-making in the cottage that day, and a great deal of talk. But though my darling responded to my caresses with ardour, I knew that she was all the while withholding her inmost self. Sometimes I found myself imagining with horror how a beast had awkwardly mauled the sweet human form that I now so fittingly embraced. Sometimes, on the other hand, it seemed to me that, after all, the lithe creature in my arms, though humanly, divinely shaped, was inwardly not human at all but some exquisite fawn-like beast, or perhaps a fox or dainty cat transformed temporarily into the likeness of a woman. Even the human form was not quite human; so spare and supple and delicately muscular was it that she did indeed seem more fawn than girl. Once she said, "Oh lovely, lovely to be human again, even for a little while! How we fit, my dear!" But when I urged, "This, Plaxy darling, is what you are meant for," she answered: "This is what my body was meant for, but in spirit I cannot ever be wholly yours." How I hated the brute Sirius in that moment! And she, sensing my hate, burst into tears, and struggled in my arms like a captive animal till she had freed herself. But the quarrel was soon made up. We spent the rest of that day as lovers do, wandering on the hill, sitting about in the garden, preparing and eating meals.

When the sun was low in the west I prepared to leave her, but she said, "Wait for Sirius. I do so want you to be friends." Not till late in the evening, when we were sitting talking in the little kitchen, did we hear the garden gate. Presently Sirius opened the door and stood blinking in the lamp-light, his nostrils taking the scent of us. She held out both arms towards him, and when he reached her she drew his great head to her cheek. "Be friends, you two," she said, taking my hand. Sirius looked at me steadily for a moment, and I smiled. He slowly waved his tail.

During my last few days I saw more of the dog than I had done before. We no longer avoided one another; and by now I could understand his speech rather better. One morning, while Plaxy was helping Mrs. Pugh in the dairy, I went out with Sirius and his pupils to the high pastures. It was wonderful to watch him controlling these bright but sub-human creatures with barks and singing cries that were to me quite unintelligible. It was wonderful, too, to see them at his bidding capture a particular sheep and hold it down on the ground while their master examined its feet or mouth, sometimes treating it from the panniers, which, by the way, were carried by one of the pupils. Between whiles we talked of Plaxy and of her future, and of the war, and of the prospects of the human species. Conversation was difficult, because he had so often to repeat himself, but gradually we established a genuine friendship. On the way home he said,

"Come often to see us while Plaxy is still here. It is good for Plaxy. And it is good for me too to have your friendship. Some day, perhaps, it will be my turn to visit you two, if you will have me." I felt a sudden warmth towards him, and I said, "If she and I have ever a home, it must certainly be your home too."

CHAPTER XVI

PLAXY CONSCRIPTED

DURING the next few months I spent frequent week-ends at Tan-y-Voel. The more I saw of Sirius, the more I was drawn towards him. Always, of course, there was a latent but an acknowledged conflict over Plaxy. All three of us, however, were determined to work out a tolerable relationship, and between Sirius and me the strain was eased by a genuine mutual affection. Sometimes, of course, the latent conflict became overt, and only by heroic tact and restraint on one side or the other could friendliness be maintained. But little by little the identical spirit in each of us, as Sirius himself said, triumphed over the diversity of our natures and our private interests. Had I not actually experienced this close-knit triple relationship I should not have believed it possible. Nor should I, perhaps, have been able to sustain my part in it, had not my love for Plaxy been from the onset unpossessive; owing to the fact that I myself, like Sirius in his canine style, had sometimes loved elsewhere.

The three of us were drawn more closely together by the hostility of a small but active section of the local people. The Rev. Owen Lloyd-Thomas had on several occasions issued veiled warnings from his pulpit. A few other ministers, realizing, perhaps subconsciously, that the theme of the "unnatural vice" of a girl and dog was likely to increase their congregations, could not resist the temptation to use it for that end. The result was that a small but increasing number of persons who were in one way or another emotionally frustrated and in need of an object for persecution were using Plaxy and Sirius for the same sort of purpose as the Nazis had used the Jews. The neighbours were mostly far too friendly to be accessible to this disease of self-righteous hate; but farther afield, in fact throughout North Wales, rumours were spreading both about the vice and the supposed treasonable activities of the couple in the lonely cottage in Merioneth. Plaxy received anonymous letters which caused her much distress. Messages for "Satan's Hound" were pinned on the door at night, including several threats that unless he released the spell-bound girl he would be shot. Pugh's sheep were sometimes found maimed. One was slaughtered and laid at the cottage door. Obscene drawings of a girl and dog were scrawled on blank walls. A local paper published a leading article calling the population to action. A battle occurred on the moors between the canine inhabitants of Caer Blai and a number of youths and dogs who had come out to do Sirius to death. Fortunately they had no firearms, and they were routed.

Meanwhile events of another type were threatening to change the fortunes of all three of us. I was expecting to be sent abroad very soon. The prospect caused Plaxy to treat me with increased tenderness. And if Sirius's grief was feigned, the imitation was very convincing. But worse than the prospect of my departure was the official order that Plaxy herself must take up some form of approved national service. We had hoped that she might be allowed to remain in peace as a farm worker, but her position was anomalous. The authorities could not see why a girl with a university training, living alone with a dog in the depths of the country, should be let off merely because she voluntarily helped on a neighbouring farm. The officials, however, were at first friendly, and anxious to interpret the regulations in a human manner. But just when it seemed most probable that Plaxy would be allowed to remain with Sirius, there was a marked and unaccountable change of tone. I suspect that some local enemy of Sirius had been telling tales of the scandalous and reputedly treasonous actions of the strange couple. Anyhow, whatever the cause, Plaxy was told that her appeal was rejected. Pugh put in a strong plea for her retention, but it was pointed out that he could easily find a land-girl to take her place. She could then be used for national service more suited to her capacity. Pugh offered to take on Plaxy herself as a land-girl, paying her the official wage. This was too obviously a put-up job. Authority became increasingly suspicious and uncompromising. Plaxy must either join one of the military organizations for women or take a temporary post in the civil service. She chose the latter, hoping to get herself attached to one of the great government offices evacuated into Lancashire or North Wales.

Plaxy was greatly distressed at the prospect of leaving. "This is my life," she said to Sirius. "*You* are my life, for the present, anyhow. The war matters terribly, I know; but I can't *feel* that it matters. It *feels* an irrelevance. At least, I can't feel that it makes any difference to the war whether I stay or go. Surely I'm doing more useful work here, really, even for the war. It's as though the hand of man were turning more and more against us. And oh, my dear, my sweet, what will you do without me to brush you and wash you and take thorns out of your feet, to say nothing of helping you with the sheep?" "I shall manage," he said. "And you, though part of you hates to go, another part will be glad of it, wanting to be entirely human again. And you will be freed from all this silly persecution." She replied, "Oh, yes, part of me wants to go. But that part of me isn't really *me*. The real I, the whole real Plaxy, desperately wants to carry on. The bit of me that wants to go is just a dream self. The only consolation is that perhaps when I am gone the persecutors will leave you alone."

At last the day came for Plaxy to go. Sirius would henceforth live with the Pughs, but Tan-y-Voel was to be kept ready to receive them whenever Plaxy had her leave. On the last morning Sirius did his best to help her with her final preparations, his tail (when he could remember it) kept bravely up. Before the village car was due to take her to the station she made tea for the two of them. They sat together on the hearth-rug, drinking it almost in silence. "How glad I am," she said, "that I decided as I did on that last morning at Garth!" "And I," he answered, "if it has not drawn you away, too far from your kind." They heard the taxi hoot as it turned out of the main road. It roared up the hill in bottom gear. Plaxy sighed deeply and said, "My species has come to take me from you." Then with sudden passion she clung to him and buried her face in the stubborn mane on his neck. Twisting himself round in her embrace, he snuggled to her breast. "Whatever happens now," he said, "we have had these months together. Nothing can destroy that."

The taxi stopped at the garden gate and hooted again. They kissed. Then she stood up, tossed back her hair, seized some luggage and met the taxi-man at the door. Seated in the car, she leaned out of the window to touch Sirius, saying only "Good-bye, good luck!" It had been arranged that this should be their parting. He would not go with her to the station.

CHAPTER XVII

OUTLAW

PLAXY had hoped to be stationed in North Wales, but she was sent to a much more remote part of the country, and would only be able to visit Sirius for a fortnight in the year. Meanwhile he was having a difficult time. Pugh had engaged an extra land-girl, Mary Griffith, to take Plaxy's place. She had not been long on the farm before she began to be frightened of Sirius. She could not reconcile herself to the fact that the dog could talk and was in authority over her. Presently she began to hear of the scandal connected with him. She was terrified, and fascinated. Badly equipped by nature as a charmer of the male of her own species, she had never suffered the flattery of persecution. Though her moral sense was outraged by the possibility that the great brute would make love to her, something in her whispered, "Better a dog for a lover than no lover at all." Spell-bound, she awaited pursuit. Sirius gave no sign. She did her best to understand his speech, hoping that his instructions might include endearments. Sirius's conduct remained coldly correct. She herself began to make clumsy attempts to entice him. His failure to give any sign that he had ever noticed these signals roused a perverse hunger in her, and the thought that even a dog rejected her was too repugnant to be admitted to her consciousness. She protected herself against it by illusions that, as a matter of fact, it was he that had made unseemly advances, and she that had refused. She began to invent incidents, and allowed them to be transformed in her mind from fiction to false memory. She recounted her stories to her acquaintances in the village, and began to gain a welcome notoriety. Once, when she had vainly done her utmost to excite Sirius, she stayed out in the fields for half the night. Next day she declared that the animal had driven her with snarls and bites to the lonely cottage to rape her. Rents in her clothes and marks on her arm were said to be due to his teeth.

This improbable story was welcomed by Sirius's enemies. They did not trouble to inquire why the girl did not complain to the Land Army authorities and get herself transferred to another post. They merely redoubled their activities against Sirius. A deputation called on Pugh to persuade him to destroy the lascivious brute. Pugh laughed at their stories and dismissed them with a quip. "You might as well ask me to destroy the nose of my face because you don't like the way it dribbles. No! It's worse than that, because my poor old nose does dribble, but the man-dog does none of the foul things you say he does. And if you try to do any harm to him, I'll put the police on you. If you hurt him there'll be gaol for you, and thousands of pounds damages to pay to the great Laboratory at Cambridge." He sacked the Griffith girl, but found to his horror that no substitute was to be had. Rumour had been busy, and no girl would risk her reputation by working at Caer Blai.

Sirius's enemies were not to be intimidated. Whenever he went to the village, a stone was sure to be thrown at him, and when he whisked round to spot the culprit no one looked guilty. Once, indeed, he did detect the assailant, a young labourer. Sirius approached him threateningly, but immediately a swarm of dogs and men set on him. Fortunately two of his friends, the local doctor and the village policeman, were able to quell the brawl.

Meanwhile Pugh and his wife were sharing the unpopularity of Sirius. Cows and sheep were damaged, crops trampled. The police force had been so depleted by the war that the miscreants were seldom caught.

Matters were brought to a head by a serious incident. This I recount on the evidence of Pugh, who had the story from Sirius himself. The man-dog was out on the hills with one of his canine pupils. Suddenly a shot was fired, and Sirius's companion leapt into the air, then staggered about yelping. The charge, no doubt, was meant for Sirius; it winged the other dog. Sirius at once turned wolf. Getting wind of the man, he charged in his direction. The second barrel of the shot-gun was fired, but the assailant had lost his nerve; he missed again, and then he dropped his gun and ran to some steep rocks. Before he could climb out of reach, Sirius had him by the ankle. There followed a tug of war, with the human leg as rope. Sirius had not secured a good grip, and presently his teeth slipped on the ankle bone, coming away with a good deal of flesh. The dog rolled backwards down the slope, and the man, though in great pain, clambered out of reach. Sirius's rage was now somewhat cooled. He wisely sought out the shot-gun and sank it in a bog. His companion had vanished. Sirius overtook him limping homewards.

When the wounded man, whose name was Owen Parry, had dragged himself back to the village, he told a story of gratuitous attack by the man-dog. He said he had found Sirius squatting on a hillside overlooking the camp, counting ammunition cases that were being unloaded from lorries. When the brute saw him it attacked. The more gullible villagers believed the whole story. They urged Parry to prosecute Pugh for damages, and to tell the military of the canine spy. Parry, of course, took no action.

Some weeks later Plaxy received a telegram from Pugh saying "S.O.S. Sirius wild." As she had a good record with her superiors she was able to secure a spell of "compassionate leave." A couple of days after Pugh had telegraphed she arrived at Caer Blai, tired and anxious.

Pugh told her a distressing story. After the incident with Parry a change seemed to come over Sirius. He carried on his work as usual, but after work hours he avoided all human contacts, retiring to the moors, and often staying out all night. He turned morose and touchy towards all human beings except the Pughs. Then one day he told Pugh he had decided to leave the farm so that the flock and the crops should be safe from violence. "He was very gentle in his speaking," said the farmer, "but there was a look of the wild beast in his eye. His coat was out of condition, not all glossy as it used to be when you were here to look after him, Miss Plaxy, dear. And there was a little wound on his belly, festering with the mud that was always being splashed on it. I was frightened for him. He made his wildness so gentle for us that my eyes dribbled like my nose. I said he must stay, and not be beaten by a bunch of dirty-tongued hooligans. Together we would teach them. But he would not stay. When I asked him what he would do if he left, he looked very strange. It gave me the creeps, yes indeed, Miss Plaxy. As though it was a wild beast I was speaking to, with no sense and no human kindness. Then he seemed to make an effort, for he licked my hand ever so gently. But when I put my other hand on his head he jumped like a shot thing, and stood away from me, looking at me with his head cocked over, as though he was torn between friendliness and fear, and didn't know what to do. His tail was miserable under his belly. 'Bran,' I said, 'Sirius, my old friend! Don't go off till I have fetched Miss Plaxy.' Then he wagged his old tail under his belly, and he cried softly. But when I put out a hand to him he sprang away again, and then he ran off up the lane. When he was beside Tan-y-Voel he stopped for a moment, but soon he lolloped away up the moel."

After Sirius's disappearance several days passed without incident in the neighbourhood. No one saw anything of the fugitive. Pugh was so busy with farm work, and trying to find help to replace Sirius, that he could not make up his mind whether or not to tell Plaxy of the dog's disappearance. Then one day he came upon Sirius outside Tany-y-Voel and hailed him, but in vain. At this stage Pugh telegraphed to Plaxy. Then a farmer in the Ffestiniog district found one of his sheep killed and partly eaten. Nearer home a dog that had been one of Sirius's opponents in the battle was found dead with its throat torn. The police then organized a party of armed men and dogs to search the moors for the dangerous beast. The party, said Pugh, had just returned. They had drawn the whole district round the slaughtered sheep, arguing that Sirius would return to the carcass to feed, but they had seen nothing of him. To-morrow a larger party would search the whole moorland area between Ffestiniog, Bala and Dolgelly.

While Pugh was telling the story Plaxy listened in silence. "She stared at me," he afterwards said, "as if she was a frightened hare, and me a stoat." When Pugh had finished she insisted that she must sleep at Tan-y-Voel. "In the morning," she said, "I will go out and look for him. I *know* I shall find him." Mrs. Pugh urged her to stay at Caer Blai, but she shook her head, moving towards the door. Then she checked, and said piteously, "But if I bring him home they will take him from me. Oh, what am I to do?" The Pughs could give no helpful answer.

Plaxy groped her way over to Tan-y-Voel in the dark, lit the kitchen fire, and changed into her old working clothes. She made herself tea, ate a large number of biscuits, and stoked up the fire, so that there might be smoke visible in the morning. Then she went out again into the dark. She made her way over the moors by a familiar route, until after several hours she reached the place where long ago she had found Sirius with the dead pony. The eastern sky was already light. She called his name, or chanted it with the accustomed lilt that she had used ever since childhood. Again and again she called, but there was no answer; nothing but the sad bleating of a sheep and the far-off rippling pipe of a curlew. She wandered about till the sun rose from behind Arenig Fawr. Then she searched carefully round the bog where the pony had lain, until at last she found a large dog's footprint. Bending down she scrutinized it eagerly, and others. One of them, the print of a left hind paw, gave her what she wanted. The mark of the outer toe was very slightly irregular, recording a little wound that Sirius had received when he was a puppy. Plaxy surprised herself by weeping. After standing for a while mopping her eyes, she unbuttoned her coat and dragged out from her waist a corner of the old blue and white check shirt, well known to Sirius. With her clasp knife, often used in the past for paring the hooves of sheep, she cut the hem, and tore out a little square of the material. This she laid beside the footmark. Sirius's monochrome vision would miss the colour, but he might pick up the bold pattern from afar, and when he came near he would recognize it. Moreover, since the shirt had been next her body, it would hold the smell of her for a long time. He would know that she had seen the footprints and would return.

Then she wandered about the moor again for some time, frequently using a little monocular field-glass that I had recently given her for use with the sheep. (In the choice of a gift I had perhaps unconsciously emphasized the pleasure of human eyesight, which was so much more precise than any dog's.) At last fatigue and hunger forced her to return to Tan-y-Voel. There she made herself tea, ate the rest of the biscuits, changed into smarter clothes and went straight into the village. People stared at her. Some greeted her warmly for old time's sake. Others looked away. Most of the hostile ones were sufficiently impressed by her elegant appearance to treat her with respect, but a bunch of lads shouted at her in Welsh, and laughed.

She went to the police station, where the search party was already collecting. Her old friend the village constable took her into a private room and listened with distress to her earnest appeal for mercy. "I shall find him," she said, "and take him away from Wales. His madness won't last." The constable shook his head, and said, "If *they* find him they'll kill him. They want blood." "But it would be murder," she cried. "He's not just an animal." "No, he's far more than an animal, Miss Plaxy, I know; but in the eyes of the law that's just what he is, an animal. And the law says that dangerous animals must be destroyed. I have done my best to delay matters, but I can't do more." In desperation Plaxy said. "Tell them he's worth thousands of pounds and must be taken alive. 'Phone the Laboratory at Cambridge, and they will confirm this and put it in writing." He fetched the inspector, who had come over from H.Q. to take charge of the search. After some discussion the inspector allowed Plaxy to call up the Laboratory. She summoned McBane and told him, incidentally, to come with his car as soon as possible to take Sirius away if she could recover him. The inspector then spoke to McBane and was sufficiently impressed to alter his plans. The search party would do their utmost to bring the animal back alive. With some reluctance he even agreed that the search should be called off for a day to give Miss Trelone a chance to capture her dog undisturbed.

When she left the police station she was almost light-hearted. And though she was shocked by the cold reception given her at the grocer's, where she laid in a store of food, the baker was kindly and hopeful, and the warm-hearted lame tobacconist, whose meagre stock was sold out, produced a packet of cigarettes from his own pocket and thrust it upon her, "because you will need them, Miss Plaxy, and for old time's sake." She toiled up the lane to Tan-y-Voel, with a reeling head, made herself a good meal, changed into working clothes, called to tell the Pughs how things stood, and went straight out on to the moor. All morning she searched in vain. Then after eating her lunch she lay down in the sun, and sleep overcame her. Some hours later she woke, sprang to her feet, and renewed her search. At the pony-bog the bit of shirt remained as she had left it. She hurried away in the afternoon light to explore a remoter region, and in particular a certain rocky cleft in the wildest part of the moor, which in the past they had sometimes used as a lair. Near this she found a dog's excrement, not recently dropped; but there was no other sign. Once more she left a piece of her shirt as a token. Then with weary limbs and a heavy heart she groped her way back in the dusk, and arrived in pitch darkness at the pony-pool. At a loss to know what to do next, she finally decided to wait there till dawn. She found a sheltered spot among the rocks and heather overlooking the bog, and made herself as comfortable as possible. In spite of the cold, she fell asleep. Not till the sun had risen did she wake, chilled and aching. Once more there was no sign of Sirius. After some desultory searching and calling she set off for home.

At the cottage she made herself breakfast, changed her clothes, attended to her haggard face, and returned to the police station. There she learned with horror that on the previous day a man had been killed and partly eaten. It had happened on the eastern shoulder of Filast, far beyond Arenig. He was a local sheep-farmer. Hearing that Sirius had been seen in the neighbourhood, he announced that he would hunt the brute down and destroy it, no matter what its value to the godless scientists. He went out with an old army rifle and a dog. In the evening the dog returned in great distress without his master. A search party had found the man's body, and near it the rifle, with an empty magazine.

After this incident the police determined to bring about the destruction of Sirius as quickly as possible. Parties of Home Guards were being sent out to comb all the moorland areas of North Wales.

In great distress Plaxy hurried away to the moors again. At the pony-bog the bit of shirt was missing, and there were fresh canine footprints; but whether they were Sirius's or not she could not determine. She put down another bit of shirt, then set off towards the lair, searching every hillside and valley with her field-glass. Once she saw on the distant skyline two men with rifles on their shoulders, but there was no other sign of the searchers. It was a bright day, with the wind in the north-west; no day at all for avoiding detection. But the moors were vast, and the searchers few.

As she was approaching the lair, she saw Sirius, his tail between his legs, his head low, like a tired horse. She was coming up wind, and behind him, so that he was unconscious of her presence till she called his name. He leapt at the sound, and whisked round, facing her, with a growl. In his mouth was the bit of shirt. She advanced, repeating his name. Seeing her, he stood still with his head cocked over and his brows puckered; but when she was within a few paces he backed, growling, away from her. At a loss, she stood still, with outstretched hand, saying, "Sirius, dear darling, it's Plaxy." His tail under his belly trembled with recognition and love, but his teeth were still bared. He whimpered with the stress of conflict in his bewildered mind. Every time she advanced, he backed and growled. After Plaxy had tried many times to win his confidence, her spirit broke. She covered her face with her hands and threw herself on the ground sobbing. The sight of her impotent distress evidently worked the miracle which her advances had frustrated; for Sirius crept forward, crying with the strife of fear and love, till at last he reached out and kissed the back of her neck. The intimate smell of her body woke his mind to full clarity. While she continued to lie still, fearing that any movement might scare him away, he nuzzled under her face. She turned over and let his warm tongue caress her cheeks and lips. Though his breath was foul as a wild beast's and the thought of his recent human killing revolted her, she made no resistance. At last he spoke. "Plaxy! Plaxy! Plaxy!" He nosed into the open neck of her shirt. Then she dared to put her arms round him.

"Come to the lair," she said. "We must hide till after dark, then we'll go down to Tan-y-Voel and wait till McBane comes with his car to take us away. I told him to hurry."

The lair was as good a retreat as they could expect. At the foot of the cliff was a tangle of heather and broken rocks. A huge slab had split from the side of the cliff and moved away, leaving a gap. This formed the lair. Its floor was below the surrounding wreckage and heather clumps. The buttress above was inaccessible, so no one could look down on them. Inside lay the remains of the heather which Plaxy herself had gathered to form a couch long ago. She now added a fresh supply. They nestled close together, and little by little, by talk about their common past, she weaned his mind away from madness. For some hours they remained talking with increasing ease and happiness. Plaxy often spoke about their future, but whenever she led his attention forward a dark cloud seemed to settle on his mind. Once she said, "We will leave this district and start a flock somewhere in Scotland, as soon as we can find a place." He answered, "There is no place for me in man's world, and there is no other world for me. There is no place for me anywhere in the universe." She answered quickly, "But wherever I am there is always a place for you. I'm your home, your footing in the world. And I'm—your wife, your dear constant bitch." He caressed her hand, and said, "In the last few days, whenever I was not raging mad against your whole species, I was longing for you; but you—must not be tied to me. And anyhow you cannot make a world for me. Of course, any world that I could live in must have you in it for its loveliest scent, drawing me along the trail; but you can't make a whole world for me. Indeed, it's not *possible* for me to have a world at all, because my own nature doesn't make sense. The spirit in me needs the world of men, and the wolf in me needs the wild. I could only be at home in a sort of Alice-in-Wonderland world, where I could have my cake and eat it."

A distant voice set both their hearts racing. She clung to him, and they waited in silence, thankful for the deep shadow of the lair, for it was already almost sunset. They heard quite near at hand the scrape of a nailed boot on rock. Sirius began to move in her arms, and growl. "Idiot! Be quiet," she whispered. She tried to hold his mouth shut with one hand while she desperately gripped him with the other. Footsteps moved past the entrance of the lair, then faded into the distance. After some minutes she could hold on no longer. Cautiously she let go, saying, "Now, for God's sake keep quiet."

For a long time they sat together waiting and occasionally talking. Twilight was now far advanced, and Plaxy began to feel that the worst of their ordeal was over. "Soon it will be dark enough to go home," she said, "home to Tan-y-Voel, my dog, and a great big meal. I'm hungry as hell. Are you?" He said nothing for a moment; then, "Yesterday I ate part of a man." He must have felt her shudder. "Oh," he said, "I was savage. And I shall be again, unless you hold me tight with your love." She hugged him, and a surge of joy made her softly laugh. Her imagination leapt forward to the time when they would be safely on the way to Cambridge.

Presently she rose, and went cautiously out to look round. The sunset colour had almost gone. There was no sign of the enemy. She moved round a projecting rock, and still there seemed to be no danger. After straying about for a few moments, searching the landscape, she felt the need to relieve herself. She crouched down in the heather, and sang softly the little tune which since childhood had been associated in both their minds with this homely operation. He should have responded with one or other of the appropriate antistrophes, but he was silent. She repeated her phrase several times, but there was no answer. Suddenly alarmed, she hurried round the intervening rock and saw Sirius standing outside the lair sniffing the wind. His tail was erect, his back bristling. At that moment another dog came into sight, and Sirius, rousing the echoes with his uproar, charged the intruder, who turned tail, with Sirius on his heels. Both dogs vanished round the shoulder of the hill. There was a savage sound of dog-fight, then human voices, and a shot, followed by a canine scream. Plaxy stood fixed in horror. After a moment's silence a man's voice cried, "Blast! I've hit the wrong one. The devil's got away." Two more shots were fired. Another voice said, "No bloody good. Too dark." Plaxy from behind a rock peered at the men. They strode over to inspect the dead dog; then moved off down the valley. When they were out of sight, she wandered about looking for Sirius. After a while she returned to the lair, hoping to find him there. It was still empty. Anxiously she strayed about in the dark, sometimes softly calling his name. For hours she wandered. Some time in the middle of the night she heard the sirens wailing far off in the villages. Searchlights fingered the clouds. After a while the wavering drone of a plane passed overhead towards the north-east; then another, and many others. There was distant firing, and one larger thud. Dead tired, Plaxy still strayed farther and farther over the dark moor, sometimes calling.

At last, almost at her feet she heard a little sound. She stepped aside and found him stretched out on the grass. The end of his tail beat feebly on the ground for greeting. She knelt beside him. Passing her hand along his body, she found that his flank was wet and sticky. One of the Home Guards' last shots had taken effect, though in the failing light he had seen only that the dog had not been immediately stopped. The badly damaged animal had staggered off towards the mountains, but shock and loss of blood had at last brought him down. With the first-aid outfit that she had carried on all her searches she put a pad on the wound and contrived to pass a bandage round his body to hold it, though he trembled with the added pain. Then she said, "I must go and get help and a stretcher." He protested, with feeble earnestness; and when she rose to go, he cried piteously for her to come down to him again. In despair she sank beside him, and lay down to put her face to his cheek. "But, my darling," she said, "we *must* get you home before daylight, else they'll find you." He feebly cried again, and seemed to say, "Dying—stay—Plaxy—dear." Presently he said "Dying—is very—cold." She took off her coat and laid it over him, then tried to lie closer to him to warm him. He said something which she guessed to be, "I don't fit you. Robert does." Stabbed with love and compassion, she said, "But dearest darling, our spirits fit." His last words were "Plaxy-Sirius—worth while." Some minutes later she saw his mouth fall open a little, revealing the white teeth in the faint light of dawn. His tongue slipped out. She buried her face in the strong fur of his neck, silently weeping.

For a long while she lay, till discomfort forced her to move. Then a shuddering sigh heaved her body, a sigh of bitter grief, but also of exhaustion; of love and compassion, but also of relief. Presently she realized that she was deadly cold and shivering. She sat up and rubbed her bare arms. Gently she took away the coat from dead Sirius, and put it on herself once more. The act seemed callous, and she wept again; then stooped once more to give the great head a kiss. For a while she sat by Sirius with a hand in the side pocket of her coat. She found that her fingers had closed upon the little field-glass that I had given her. Even this seemed a disloyalty to the dead; but she reminded herself that Sirius had accepted me.

Presently the sirens sounded, far down in the villages, steady, sad and thankful. A sheep called mournfully. Very far away a dog barked. Behind Arenig Fawr the dawn was already like the glow of a great fire. "What must I do now?" she wondered. She remembered how, a few hours earlier, with happiness too soon in her heart, she had sung for him to answer, but in vain. The memory overpowered her with a sense of the gulf that now divided them. He that had been so near seemed now as remote as their common mammalian ancestor. Not again would he sing to her.

But now at last she thought of a fitting thing to do. She would sing his requiem. Returning to her dead darling, she stood erect beside him, facing the dawn. Then in as firm and full a voice as she could muster, she began singing a strange thing that he himself had made for her in his most individual style. The wordless phrases symbolized for her the canine and the human that had vied in him all his life long. The hounds' baying blended with human voices. There was a warm and brilliant theme which he said was Plaxy, and a perplexed one which was himself. It began in playfulness and zest, but developed in a tragic vein against which she had often protested. Now, looking down on him she realized that his tragedy was inevitable. And under the power of his music she saw that Sirius, in spite of his uniqueness, epitomized in his whole life and in his death something universal, something that is common to all awakening spirits on earth, and in the farthest galaxies. For the music's darkness was lit up by a brilliance which Sirius had called "colour," the glory that he himself, he said, had never seen. But this, surely, was the glory that no spirits, canine or human, had ever clearly seen, the light that never was on land or sea, and yet is glimpsed by the quickened mind everywhere.

As she sang, red dawn filled the eastern sky, and soon the sun's bright finger set fire to Sirius.

A CATALOG OF SELECTED
DOVER BOOKS
IN ALL FIELDS OF INTEREST

A CATALOG OF SELECTED DOVER
BOOKS IN ALL FIELDS OF INTEREST

CONCERNING THE SPIRITUAL IN ART, Wassily Kandinsky. Pioneering work by father of abstract art. Thoughts on color theory, nature of art. Analysis of earlier masters. 12 illustrations. 80pp. of text. 5⅜ x 8½.   0-486-23411-8

CELTIC ART: The Methods of Construction, George Bain. Simple geometric techniques for making Celtic interlacements, spirals, Kells-type initials, animals, humans, etc. Over 500 illustrations. 160pp. 9 x 12. (Available in U.S. only.)   0-486-22923-8

AN ATLAS OF ANATOMY FOR ARTISTS, Fritz Schider. Most thorough reference work on art anatomy in the world. Hundreds of illustrations, including selections from works by Vesalius, Leonardo, Goya, Ingres, Michelangelo, others. 593 illustrations. 192pp. 7⅛ x 10¼.   0-486-20241-0

CELTIC HAND STROKE-BY-STROKE (Irish Half-Uncial from "The Book of Kells"): An Arthur Baker Calligraphy Manual, Arthur Baker. Complete guide to creating each letter of the alphabet in distinctive Celtic manner. Covers hand position, strokes, pens, inks, paper, more. Illustrated. 48pp. 8¼ x 11.   0-486-24336-2

EASY ORIGAMI, John Montroll. Charming collection of 32 projects (hat, cup, pelican, piano, swan, many more) specially designed for the novice origami hobbyist. Clearly illustrated easy-to-follow instructions insure that even beginning papercrafters will achieve successful results. 48pp. 8¼ x 11.   0-486-27298-2

BLOOMINGDALE'S ILLUSTRATED 1886 CATALOG: Fashions, Dry Goods and Housewares, Bloomingdale Brothers. Famed merchants' extremely rare catalog depicting about 1,700 products: clothing, housewares, firearms, dry goods, jewelry, more. Invaluable for dating, identifying vintage items. Also, copyright-free graphics for artists, designers. Co-published with Henry Ford Museum & Greenfield Village. 160pp. 8¼ x 11.   0-486-25780-0

THE ART OF WORLDLY WISDOM, Baltasar Gracian. "Think with the few and speak with the many," "Friends are a second existence," and "Be able to forget" are among this 1637 volume's 300 pithy maxims. A perfect source of mental and spiritual refreshment, it can be opened at random and appreciated either in brief or at length. 128pp. 5⅜ x 8½.   0-486-44034-6

JOHNSON'S DICTIONARY: A Modern Selection, Samuel Johnson (E. L. McAdam and George Milne, eds.). This modern version reduces the original 1755 edition's 2,300 pages of definitions and literary examples to a more manageable length, retaining the verbal pleasure and historical curiosity of the original. 480pp. 5³⁄₁₆ x 8¼.   0-486-44089-3

ADVENTURES OF HUCKLEBERRY FINN, Mark Twain, Illustrated by E. W. Kemble. A work of eternal richness and complexity, a source of ongoing critical debate, and a literary landmark, Twain's 1885 masterpiece about a barefoot boy's journey of self-discovery has enthralled readers around the world. This handsome clothbound reproduction of the first edition features all 174 of the original black-and-white illustrations. 368pp. 5⅜ x 8½.   0-486-44322-1

LIGHT AND SHADE: A Classic Approach to Three-Dimensional Drawing, Mrs. Mary P. Merrifield. Handy reference clearly demonstrates principles of light and shade by revealing effects of common daylight, sunshine, and candle or artificial light on geometrical solids. 13 plates. 64pp. 5⅜ x 8½.　　　　　　　　　0-486-44143-1

ASTROLOGY AND ASTRONOMY: A Pictorial Archive of Signs and Symbols, Ernst and Johanna Lehner. Treasure trove of stories, lore, and myth, accompanied by more than 300 rare illustrations of planets, the Milky Way, signs of the zodiac, comets, meteors, and other astronomical phenomena. 192pp. 8⅜ x 11.

0-486-43981-X

JEWELRY MAKING: Techniques for Metal, Tim McCreight. Easy-to-follow instructions and carefully executed illustrations describe tools and techniques, use of gems and enamels, wire inlay, casting, and other topics. 72 line illustrations and diagrams. 176pp. 8¼ x 10⅞.　　　　　　　　　0-486-44043-5

MAKING BIRDHOUSES: Easy and Advanced Projects, Gladstone Califf. Easy-to-follow instructions include diagrams for everything from a one-room house for bluebirds to a forty-two-room structure for purple martins. 56 plates; 4 figures. 80pp. 8¾ x 6⅜.　　　　　　　　　0-486-44183-0

LITTLE BOOK OF LOG CABINS: How to Build and Furnish Them, William S. Wicks. Handy how-to manual, with instructions and illustrations for building cabins in the Adirondack style, fireplaces, stairways, furniture, beamed ceilings, and more. 102 line drawings. 96pp. 8¾ x 6⅜.　　　　　　　　　0-486-44259-4

THE SEASONS OF AMERICA PAST, Eric Sloane. From "sugaring time" and strawberry picking to Indian summer and fall harvest, a whole year's activities described in charming prose and enhanced with 79 of the author's own illustrations. 160pp. 8¼ x 11.　　　　　　　　　0-486-44220-9

THE METROPOLIS OF TOMORROW, Hugh Ferriss. Generous, prophetic vision of the metropolis of the future, as perceived in 1929. Powerful illustrations of towering structures, wide avenues, and rooftop parks—all features in many of today's modern cities. 59 illustrations. 144pp. 8¼ x 11.　　　　　　　　　0-486-43727-2

THE PATH TO ROME, Hilaire Belloc. This 1902 memoir abounds in lively vignettes from a vanished time, recounting a pilgrimage on foot across the Alps and Apennines in order to "see all Europe which the Christian Faith has saved." 77 of the author's original line drawings complement his sparkling prose. 272pp. 5⅜ x 8½.

0-486-44001-X

THE HISTORY OF RASSELAS: Prince of Abissinia, Samuel Johnson. Distinguished English writer attacks eighteenth-century optimism and man's unrealistic estimates of what life has to offer. 112pp. 5⅜ x 8½.　　　　　　　　　0-486-44094-X

A VOYAGE TO ARCTURUS, David Lindsay. A brilliant flight of pure fancy, where wild creatures crowd the fantastic landscape and demented torturers dominate victims with their bizarre mental powers. 272pp. 5⅜ x 8½.　　　　　　0-486-44198-9